CRADLE

Other fiction by James Jackson:

James JACKSON

CRADLE

ZAFFRE

First published in Great Britain in 2017

This paperback edition published in 2018 by

ZAFFRE PUBLISHING
80–81 Wimpole St, London W1G 9RE
www.zaffrebooks.co.uk

A CIP catalogue record for this book is
available from the British Library.

ISBN: 978-1-78576-119-5

also available as an ebook

1 3 5 7 9 10 8 6 4 2

Typeset by IDSUK (Data Connection) Ltd
Printed and bound in Great Britain by Clays Ltd, Elcograf S.p.A.

Zaffre Publishing is an imprint of Bonnier Zaffre,
part of Bonnier Books UK
www.bonnierzaffre.co.uk
www.bonnierbooks.co.uk

*For Freddie Forsyth – his thrillers inspired me and
his support encouraged*

Hell is empty, and all the devils are here

The Tempest, William Shakespeare

In May 1607, some thirteen years before the legendary *Mayflower* and her Pilgrim Fathers made landfall in America, three ships deposited one hundred English settlers in the wilds of Virginia. There they erected a rudimentary wood fort and named it Jamestown. It would come to symbolise the frontier of the New World, and mark the bloody and harrowing genesis of the nation we now know as America

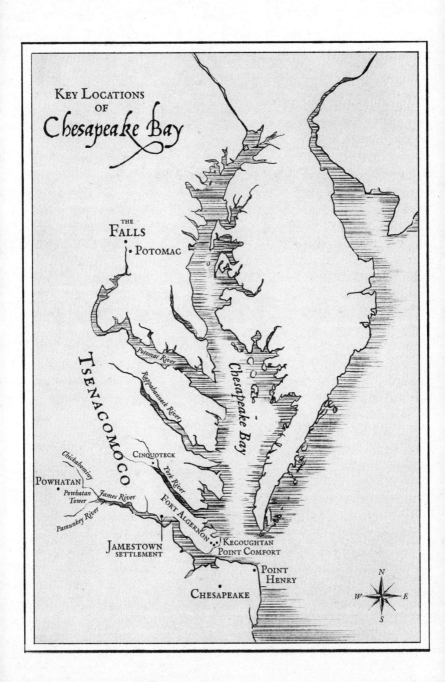

BEGINNING

Autumn 1607, Virginia

The priests danced and death was close. It was the worst of times to be a prisoner of the natives. They had brought him to the fire, bound, hunched and weeping, his naked skin pale in the dancing light and his English mutterings strange to his audience's ears. It would soon be over.

'My master will give you gold and precious stones. I mean you no offence.'

Yet offence had been taken and punishment was due. He had been unwise to venture with others from the palisaded settlement. The touching belief that their fire sticks and lead shot would counter any foe was gone. Now rattles shook and drums beat and howling chants pierced the cold night air. As the frenzy built, the sacrificial captive trembled at its centre, recoiling from the painted demons edging near.

Again, the pleading voice. 'Spare me, I beg you. For the love of Christ, have mercy.'

They preferred to play. After all, he was weak and cowardly and no match in a fight; scarcely worth slaughtering to the warrior god Okeus. A priest swayed before him, hissing contempt, his head adorned with deer antlers and his body daubed red and black, his bone necklaces and festooned skins of snake and weasel shivering with the exertion. Always the feet beat time.

So much for a Promised Land! Only that April the colonists had arrived in the territory they called Virginia, a hundred or so of them stumbling ashore to stake their claim, and found an outpost for England. Almost instantly they had been attacked, the feathered flights of Indian arrows raking them from every quarter. Men fell and were buried; the first blood had been shed.

So the newcomers erected earthworks and a stockade of split logs, building their swamp-encircled enclave on a small promontory jutting into the river. But although a foothold had been gained, they had suffered for it. The fort was a triangle, its boundary patrolled and its angles protected by culverin guns mounted high on platforms. Enclosed within was what passed for a settlement, a single acre scattered with tents and rudimentary shelters with a sailcloth church in its midst. Welcome to Genesis, to disease and starvation and sudden death; welcome to America. The name Jamestown sat bitter in the mouth.

Near delirious with fright, the Englishman knew nothing could save him now. Perhaps his comrades were already dead, either victim of the fever and bloody flux that had come upon the settlement, or butchered and scalped by the marauding savages. As they brought him to the camp, he had seen a wooden pole set between trees, heavy with human trophies. He sobbed another incoherent prayer.

Opechancanough watched. How unimpressive these outsiders were; how foolhardy to trespass in his domain. These wearers of leg coverings were no match for his braves. As military commander of the Powhatan people and defender of their lands, he answered only to his half-brother and ruler of the people, the supreme Mamanatowick, the mighty Chief Powhatan.

Threat lay everywhere. To the north, the raiding canoe parties of the Iroquoian tribes; to the west, the probing attacks of Siouan and their cannibal allies; to the south, other Algonquian fiefdoms like his own, jostling to expand. And now strangers had come across the ocean to establish a meagre colony. He doubted their intention was benign; he suspected their number would grow. Disrespect was a capital offence.

A shaman sprinkled powder onto the fire and the flames leapt in myriad hues. The noise ebbed and, in the quiet, the thin notes of a reed pipe carried clear. Howling now, the prisoner was pegged out on the earth, the archpriest moving and singing around him. Then the priest knelt and, with the sharp edge of a mussel shell, began to joint the body. A shin bone came away and next a thigh, each item deftly removed and raised up to a tumultuous cheer before being cast upon the fire. Expert hands did their careful work, applying the cauterising brand while the reed pipe played.

Shorn of his limbs, the prisoner writhed and screamed as his body parts cooked close by. But the execution was not yet finished. Rolling the torso onto its front, the priest crouched in a slick of blood and made an incision in the back of the neck. As the scalp and face were peeled clean away, the remnants of the man shuddered and perished. Justice had been done.

A second prisoner was brought, cowering and vomiting as Opechancanough approached. Terror has its own stench. The two men stared at each other, two opposing worlds divided by only five paces. The skin of the native was painted red, the right side of his head shaven, his hair hanging long in a knot to his left shoulder. Keen eyes peered through a mask of white. To the Englishman he seemed a demon in a place of hell.

'Let me go,' stuttered the man. 'I will tell all of your mercy and greatness.'

He would indeed. With a gesture, Opechancanough gave the order. The captive was to be returned unharmed to his own people. He would serve the Powhatan cause well by spreading fear and consternation among the settlers. Opechancanough watched the scrabbling man hurl himself out of the camp, and considered his future strategy. Many seasons past, his leader had consulted spirit guides about his visions of invaders journeying on great swans from afar and marauding his lands. Yet there were several ways to interpret such a dream, and Opechancanough would not be cowed. This foreign tribe had its vulnerabilities: it possessed scant food, it could be manipulated and it would be brought to destruction. Corpses would litter the earth, and he would finally inherit the land as saviour and overlord. He turned away.

In far-distant Spain, deep within the monastic gloom of the Escorial palace in the barren hills above Madrid, another encounter between prisoner and authority was in train. A man was dragged from his cell and up flights of stairs, blinking at the candlelight and gulping the fresh air and wondering at his summons. At least he could content himself that while they still noticed him he remained alive, and if he stayed living, it suggested they might need him.

'Here we are, confronted by our sins.'

There was nothing regal in the figure or the voice: only the rich sobriety of his clothes defined him as a monarch. Yet although King Philip III of Spain ruled the greatest empire on earth and owned territories so remote his advisers lacked the requisite maps, there were challenges to his power. Not only did his subjects chafe and agitate, but old enemies also manoeuvred for advantage. He would not forget the names of Queen Elizabeth or Sir Francis Drake, nor the spymaster Sir Francis Walsingham and his intelligencer Christian Hardy. Nor could he ever forgive the perfidious sons of Albion who had provoked his father and ambushed his treasure fleets and harried his Armada to oblivion. Vigilance was essential.

'Beware. Beware. God sees.'

Philip spoke almost to himself. He was standing in front of a painting, *The Seven Deadly Sins* by Hieronymus Bosch. There at the centre was the eye of God, and Jesus ascending triumphant. Judgement, it reminded him, was ever near.

He broke his gaze. 'Are we not all of us prisoners of our frailties?'

'I am also a prisoner of Spain, Majesty.'

'For good reason, Reino.' The King glanced at the man, now bound to a chair. 'We are unforgiving of those who would defy us.'

'All that I do is for our faith and this nation.'

'Yet you have threatened the peace.'

True, the captive silently conceded. As an English renegade and agent of Spain code-named 'Realm', he had devoted his life to waging war upon Protestantism and his former homeland. During the great Armada of 1588, he had landed in England ahead of the invasion to assassinate Queen Elizabeth. The fates had proven unkind. Undaunted, he had been in London again in 1605, aiding Catholic plotters as they sought with gunpowder to alter history and overthrow King James and his heretic brood. Once more he had been thwarted: because of chance, because of Spanish caution, and because his nemesis Christian Hardy had remained one step ahead of him. Now anxious to pursue diplomacy and maintain benign relations with their former adversary, the Spaniards kept him chained and under sentence of death. A wary calm prevailed, and he was an embarrassment. Yet while he breathed, he still had utility.

The King watched him. 'Have I not reason to have you executed? Would the garrotte not erase a source of trouble from our midst?'

'Giving counsel is not my strength, Majesty.'

'Nor is obedience to your King.' Philip squinted at the man.

'Yet you bring me here, Majesty.'

Philip hesitated. 'I am an emperor without rival, ruler of Spain and Portugal and Sicily, Prince of Swabia, Marquis of the Holy Roman Empire, master of the oceans and possessor of dominions scattered wide, from the Philippines to Peru.' He paused. 'Yet there is dissonance and mutiny everywhere.'

Realm nodded. So they really did need him alive. There was always a role for men like him, always a troubled corner of the Spanish Main that required his skills. He sat patiently.

'In every quarter we are assailed: taunted by the Ottoman and pricked by corsairs, challenged in the New World by the traders and merchant fleets of others.'

'Thieves are always drawn by the lure of riches, Majesty.'

'And we must safeguard what is ours.' Philip let his gaze wander. 'My treasure fleets from the Indies each year bring me some thirty million pesos in gold and silver. Yet I am in default to my lenders and my exchequer totters at the brink.'

'A vexing thing, Majesty.'

'Made more so by the English.'

Realm felt his interest sharpen and his heartbeat climb.

'In the place they call Virginia, they have built a fort and plan to create a colony.'

'What is their intent, Majesty?'

'One that bodes no good for Spain. One that would plant the noxious weed of Protestantism, and strangle our wealth with piracy.'

'Force would soon uproot them.'

'My Council of State and my Council for War in the Indies do indeed favour that course.'

'You look to another method, Majesty?'

'I do not need war with England.' The dark eyes gave nothing away. 'I would prefer to engage more subtle and devious practices, the blacker arts in which you are well versed.'

'You honour me, Majesty.'

'I do not. But I do spare your life. In exchange, you will give me loyalty and you will bring this infant colony to its grave.'

'Consider it gone, Majesty.'

'And you shall consider yourself reprieved.'

CHAPTER 1

They meant to kill him. He saw it in their watchfulness, their movement within the crowd, in that contrived sense of ease that turns to sudden violence. Christian Hardy drank from his pot of beer and checked the windows and doorways. He was no stranger to unprovoked attack, and had faced worse odds than three hired and clumsy street toughs who believed they held the advantage. Still, it was an inconvenience. He took another pull on his drink, rehearsing scenarios and readying to depart. Better to carry the fight outside and lessen the chance of a random blade.

He should have anticipated that his coming voyage to Jamestown would reopen wounds and bring his enemies flocking. It might be the Spanish, or even his former employer, the spymaster Robert Cecil, who had arranged for his murder. Gratitude was short-lived in the world of espionage, and favours were rarely returned.

Around him, the conversation surged as the tallow candles guttered and tobacco smoke cast its haze. Memories slid in of other nights and previous dangers: of the gunpowder plotters he had chased to their doom; of the traitor Realm who had walked a bloody trail through his life. The past always returned.

Out in the street, the night air was chill and smelt of sea coal. The occasional lantern glimmered. Hardy kept a steady pace on the Strand and loosened the leather strap of the Katzbalger at his side. The cat-gutter was his weapon of choice, a short sword designed for the close-quarter savagery of a street fight. From somewhere behind he heard footsteps. He calculated the distance, aware of how close he was to the Duck and Drake tavern in which Catesby and Guido Fawkes had vowed to annihilate the King; conscious of other figures positioning themselves ahead of him. Someone truly had a grudge.

A shout skittered after him. 'Did you think you would go ignored? Did you not trust such a moment would come?'

He failed to answer, and ducked instead into a narrow passage leading to a courtyard. They would follow, believing they had laid a trap. Whoever sent them possessed a touching faith in numerical superiority and brute force. Hardy drew his sword and felt the spike of energy in his gut. These were the moments he relished.

There was a pause, as time and his breathing slowed and his body adapted itself from passive wait to active kill. It had been the same when he had steered a fireship for Drake towards the Spanish fleet at anchor in the Calais Roads; when he'd stood with Sir Richard Grenville on the deck of the *Revenge* and headed straight into the maw of sixty Spanish galleons lying in ambush off the Azores. An enemy's misjudgement could always be exploited.

Funnelled by the alleyway they had clattered through, they were blind and unchecked in their eagerness. The Katzbalger thrust deep. It summoned a scream and the panic of surprise as the first attacker collapsed on the cobbles with a groin wound. Rage could throw an adversary even further. More men rushed in, determined to finish their business. As they raised their lamps to chase off the shadows, Christian Hardy appeared before them.

'There is some mistake, gentlemen. I reserve my displays of fencing for the south bank.'

'Reserve your tongue as well.' A ringleader wielding a cudgel stepped forward. 'We have our orders – to see you dead. You have no chance.'

Hardy removed the dagger from his belt and held it point down, shifting the weight on his feet. 'Who will be the first to take me?' Perhaps they had been promised gold coins for their effort, or only a miserly few pennies. It made little difference.

A large man raised a knife and charged, then fell clutching his stomach as Hardy struck out and then danced back. Two more came on and died in a flurry of blows.

Hardy stooped and wiped his blade on a corpse. 'The contest is unequal.'

'We will yet down you!'

'At what cost?' Hardy peered at the strangers. 'Go to your beds and your women and rise to greet another dawn. There are nightwatchmen afoot and constables to hunt you.'

'They will sleep soundly through this dispute,' said the ringleader, preparing to leap forward.

Sometimes the absence of the law provided Hardy with a certain freedom. Yet this, he thought, hinted at a deeper conspiracy, and at those who would stop at little to prevent him from joining his ship. At Gravesend, the *John and Francis* and the *Phoenix* were waiting to take resupply to Jamestown.

Fortunately, it seemed, someone still intended him to sail. From high above the jettied courtyard, a salvo of ash quarrels flew down to find their mark. Hunting crossbows were deadly at close quarters, and his would-be assassins tumbled to the ground around him. As the survivors fled the carnage, Hardy looked about him.

'Show yourselves, and grant me proof of friendship,' he called. He had yet to sheathe his sword.

'Is there not proof enough?' a measured voice replied.

A shuttered lantern flared in an open window as though the murderous incident was nothing more than a piece of theatre to entertain the gallery.

'Did enough players die?' Hardy stared up into the shadows. 'Was the comedy to your liking?'

'We are only part way through the night. A saddled horse awaits you, with a mounted troop attending.'

'I do not need anyone to guard me.'

'Really?' Above him, the shadowy figure pointed to the litter of bodies. 'Prince Henry commands you to make haste to his side.'

Hardy bowed. 'Then it would be churlish to delay.'

There were few to whom Hardy was prepared to swear fealty or bend his knee; few for whom he would shed his blood. Yet his protector and royal patron was sufficiently astute to keep a personal operative close. Prince Henry, eldest son of King James, deserved both public and private approbation and loyalty unto death.

'You have escaped murder again, Mr Hardy.'

Though only thirteen, there was a gravitas and self-possession that belied the youthful years of the Prince of Wales, heir apparent, the new

Hal, the future of the nation. While the father was a drooling sybarite, mistrustful of all and scared of his own shadow, the son had the touch of a leader. Dressed in black, a sword at his side and a single pearl and lace ornamental collar at his throat, he looked to be both a warrior and a novice priest with his blond hair close-cropped and brown, heavy-lidded eyes.

Prince Henry dismissed his attendants and beckoned Hardy forward. 'So you are unscratched from your endeavour? I am glad you are not harmed.'

'I am pleased to serve Your Grace.'

'There is no one else I would call on.' Henry spoke earnestly. 'Was it not you who saved the life of our Queen Elizabeth? Was it not you who tracked and foiled the conspirators of the great Powder Treason?'

Hardy bowed his head in acknowledgement.

'Yet it has earned you both repute and a surfeit of enemies.' Concern flickered in the prince's eyes. 'I am unsure if they dwell more at the Escorial in Spain, or lurk in the court of my father.'

In a world of rivalry and intrigue, jealousies multiplied and secret agendas were rife. The King resented the popularity of his son; his son in turn had established a separate camp. In place of corruption and dissipation and the squandering of treasure, Prince Henry's world, at the palace of St James, was one of prayer and thought and learned discussion. To enter it was to swear a new allegiance and forsake the values of the old.

Henry rested his palm on the pommel of his sword. 'I know my father, Mr Hardy. He will not allow a colony in Virginia to thrive and provoke a war with Spain.'

'Even though Jamestown bears his name?'

'Such flattery makes no difference. The King is content to see it perish along with those who would support it.'

'And you, Your Grace?'

A smile broke through the solemnity. 'I shall strive to preserve the settlement for England and for posterity. I will do what I can to plant our standard, tame the wilderness and bring the natural savage to our cause.'

'Much lies in our path, Your Grace.'

'Not least that malevolent pygmy Lord Chancellor Robert Cecil.'

Hardy had studied the reports. Jamestown was imperilled. Beset by disease and treachery and under constant attack, it seemed unlikely to outlast a year. That would suit Cecil fine, and accrue him even greater power and plaudits from the King. Upsetting Spain was not conducive to good trade or heavy coffers; a viable colony backed by parliamentarians and City merchants could easily act as a focus for dissent against the Crown. And if the tiny enclave should fail, it would be the ennobled hunchback Cecil who would slit its throat.

The intelligencer prepared to take his leave. 'I will do my duty, Your Grace.'

'Some might wager you will die.'

'They have lost their money before.'

'Be then my senses and my sentinel, Mr Hardy. Defend Jamestown well, and let no one but God destroy it.'

'To arms! To arms!'

Though sick and malnourished, the settlers responded, tumbling once more from their shelters to meet the attack. A bell clanged and the uproar grew, and above it all came the howls of the Indians. The Paspahegh had come in strength. This was their land, their ancestral home, their quarrel. No outsider could settle here and go unharmed; no wood palisade could prevent repeated assault. It helped that the white men were weak and scarcely able to mount a defence. Gradually the Paspahegh would wear down the adversary and restore the land they knew as Tsenacomoco to a world free of foreign trespass. Tonight was another chance to harvest scalps.

'They've breached the stockade!'

'The gate – they are coming through the gate!'

'Stand fast! They shall not prevail if we are strong!'

War cries mingled with oaths and screams and the sporadic report of pistol and musket. *Yea, though I walk in the valley of the shadow of death, I will fear no evil.* Kneeling in the midst of the carnage, arms outstretched and his words bellowed loud, the chaplain sought to comfort and encourage. His prayers went unheeded, yet his flock was fighting hard, battling to retake ground and move to the offensive. A bronze culverin disgorged a canister of shot, its muzzle belching flame and the light dazzling for an instant. No quarter would be given.

Framed in the interior was a running scene of mayhem. Here, President John Ratcliffe discharging a pistol in the face of a native; there, the aristocrat George Percy coolly fencing with another and sweeping aside a sword fashioned from bone to plunge his rapier deep; there, too, the gunner Robert Tyndall improvising with a cannon rod to crush the skull of his opponent. The Indians were losing their advantage.

'Satan is loosed and the savages infest us!'

A stocky, bearded figure strode untroubled through the chaos. He was not about to yield to fear or permit death to take him. An Indian had the misfortune to confront him and was quickly dispatched with a shovel; a second reached to fit an arrow to his bow and was similarly cut down. Captain John Smith trudged on. In his almost thirty years he had sailed the seas and fought Spaniard and Ottoman alike, encountering all manner of heathens and pirates. Indeed, he had once been enslaved by Tartars, and only escaped after employing a threshing bat to beat out the brains of his master. Experience was rarely wasted.

'To me, boys. We have them!' Smith drew and fired a pistol and then reversed it to club a native to the ground. They had to learn, these red-painted warriors who considered the settlers their enemy and had no notion that their wilderness was already named Virginia. If Spain or France or the Dutch had not seized it, England surely would; if territory existed ripe for the taking, an armed merchant from Europe was bound to investigate.

A boy called out. 'They falter, Mr Smith!'

'I'm not taking victory for granted.' The adventurer dodged an arrow. 'Keep behind, for the savages may yet bite.'

'What do they gain by this?'

'It is a mark of intent and a test of their courage. They are probing our defence.'

'Their losses are high,' the boy pointed out.

'Yet they pierce us to the core.' Smith reloaded his pistol and blew excess powder from the pan. 'Some here have no fight, and others embrace invasion by the savage.' There was a gruff disdain in the Lincolnshire voice, a belligerence that suffered neither fools nor authority. What Sir Walter Raleigh had once claimed for England, Smith had pledged the Virginia Company to help explore and settle and sow. The bloodshed was hardly a surprise.

Sighing softly, the boy pitched forward, an arrow protruding from his chest. Smith knelt briefly at his side and cradled the lolling head. It was a dungheap of a place in which to die, but at least it had been quick. Better a turkey spur or sharpened iron crystal to the heart than the slow agonies of dysentery or the fever. He laid the body down and returned to the fray.

At dawn, to the muffled beat of a drum, the mourners gathered to bury their dead. The night had taken its toll. Four were slain, including the boy. The colonists committed by their brethren to the earth might be considered fortunate to have had an early release from their travails. Out in the woods the savages still taunted. Yet within the confines of the palisade, the haggard band of survivors bent their heads, muttered their prayers and clung on. Ashes to ashes.

'We shall endure, my brothers.' As soil was heaped on the cadavers, the chaplain addressed his congregation. 'We will overcome all privation to walk with the Lord in this land.'

'We will?' A gaunt-faced labourer jabbed an accusing finger.

'Be certain of it, brother. For God is with us and will bring us to salvation.'

'He brings us no food.'

'Reward lies in heaven.'

'And death here.'

It was a verdict delivered with a ball of phlegm spat into the earth. Others joined in, their voices loud and their objections coarse. The grim conditions and ceaseless threat had done little to foster unity. Dispute was common and would rapidly spark to violence. The gentlemen despised the labourers and the labourers detested all; and religious divide pitted one side against another. Papism was there, and so too were the Puritans. Condemned men were a fractious breed.

'We believed this was a colony. Instead it has proved to be our prison, and it will be our grave.' The first labourer spoke angrily.

The chaplain raised his hand. 'Repent of your sins and you shall be saved.'

'Speaks a charlatan and fool.'

'One that seems well fed.' A mutinous growl rose in the hungry ranks. 'One that deems himself better than the rest.'

'Let us see if he swings better from a tree.'

The mood darkened. Small wonder Edward Wingfield, the previous incumbent as president, had lasted only weeks in office. He was now under arrest.

A musket blast silenced the noise. From behind the smoke John Smith emerged.

'What curs are we to chase our tails and turn upon each other? Why should I risk my life to find you provisions while you waste your effort on this?'

'You are not our master.'

'Yet I speak the truth.' The adventurer cradled his gun and stared pugnaciously at the sullen faces. 'United we may survive a while, but divided we are damned.'

'Are we not already so? God has forsaken us, and even the redskin savage has abandoned this pestilential site.'

'We shall find new places. We will grow and spread and prosper.'

'A quaint notion, should you care to peer about.' But the heat had gone from the confrontation and in its aftermath stood a patchwork of dispirited and hollow-eyed men. Relief would not come from England for months. Who knew if any of them would live long enough to see it?

'I must applaud your steadfastness, Captain.' Insincerity seeped from the lips of President Ratcliffe. 'I would never have thought you would be the saviour of the hour.'

Smith bridled. 'I do as I must, Ratcliffe.'

'You will know to address me as your president.'

'I see you as you are, Ratcliffe, and I discern only a viperous snake.'

Ratcliffe and Smith eyed each other. As always, the lawyer Gabriel Archer stood at the president's shoulder, whispering his sly counsel. They were a dangerous combination. Smith stood his ground.

'Over what do you preside, Ratcliffe? A stinkhole that decays within your grasp?'

'Accusation will bring you only harm, Captain. Sedition and mutiny are punishable by death.'

'I have no fear for myself.' Smith indicated the crude fortifications. 'What vexes me is the ease with which the natives invaded our position. Are they blessed with friends within these walls?'

'Once more you are too free with your thoughts and tongue.'

'I will be freer with my knife should I discover a base traitor.'

'Be of more use to us, Captain.' It was more a command than a suggestion. 'Take the shallop and crew to raid upriver and bring us bushels of grain.'

Smith shouldered his weapon and strode off with his entourage. He would rather face the challenge beyond the fort than the stalemate inside it.

He noticed the youngster hunched on an empty bran barrel with his head clutched in his hands. 'Why are you weeping, boy?'

'It is my friend Jack Ashley you have buried.' The whisper was hoarse and the eyes bruised by tears.

'There is little comfort save that God now tends him.'

'Jack wished to live and make his mark.'

'Though he rests in a grave, he has accomplished much. For he is a founder, an English soul who laid down his life for our future. Be not downcast.' Smith reached out a hand to lift the chin of the boy. 'Your name?'

'Edward Battle, sir.'

'So be true to it and to the memory of your friend. Battle is a finer thing than whimpering surrender.'

'I will remember it, sir.'

Smith bent down to speak low in the boy's ear. 'Remember, too, that you must stay alert and breathing. Our trials are just begun.'

He strode off to the waterfront. There were stores to load and gunpowder to collect and men to be mustered. It was time to prove the settlement was not finished; to bring justice down upon the natives and seize their harvest.

In the distance he could hear the faint chant of the deserters carrying above the ramparts.

'Guard your backs and watch your front. We have come to avenge and to take.'

As his men spread out in a fighting line, Smith scanned the deserted village, waiting for the ambush. He relished the simplicity of his task. He had no need to contend with John Ratcliffe or Gabriel Archer here; no need to police the insidious squabbling and gnawing hunger, or the attempts to besmirch his name or reputation. There was an honesty in wearing a wool coat, in holding a musket and smelling the woodsmoke. Captain John Smith would show the Indian that the English were not done.

'If they come, it will be from the thicket over there.' Smith nodded to his right.

Scattered about were native homes, their frames constructed from bent saplings and their shelter provided by animal skins. Fields had been cleared in the woods and fishing runs set along the river. European eyes stared with envy. Should the local tribes refuse to yield, it was likely to prove their funeral.

Behind the dense thickets of oak and sassafras, the arrayed might of the Powhatan empire might be hidden. The settlers had learnt enough to know of the supreme leader; had heard from returning and traumatised captives about the barbarities heaped upon their fellow countrymen. The savages intended to terrorise. Smith could also play such games.

'They are close, boys. I smell it.'

He was right. The Indians emerged now, chanting, their bows and clubs raised. Against the autumn trees, their painted skins were a ribbon of moving colour. A dozen Englishmen faced them, muskets loaded with cartridges of pistol shot to decimate the enemy when the skirmish came.

A soldier inched his finger for the trigger. 'They dance prettily enough.'

A second soldier made a final check of his wheel lock. 'Let us see how well they fight.'

'Steady, boys.' Smith kept his voice low. 'They will soon take us at a rush.'

'It will be a shame to spoil their plumage.'

'A greater one if we are trounced. Use every trick and give no quarter.'

Their ritual complete, the natives charged. In the vanguard was a priest emitting piercing cries and shaking a small effigy of a deity before him.

The doll would blunt the aggression of the strangers, would protect the village and ensure the arrows of the warriors sped true.

It did not work. The face of the priest blew apart and his cohorts dropped among the plumes of smoke and shot. Now it was the turn of the English to advance. They had drawn their swords and pistols and worked the field, swiftly and systematically dispatching the wounded and chasing down the stragglers and the brave.

There remained the grain store to pillage and further dwellings to explore. One of the Englishmen paused at the entrance to a hide, his attention caught by a native girl hiding inside. He had never seen such beauty, such perfect limbs, such full breasts. To a European starved of the sight of a woman, she was a vision. He reached in to touch her. It earned him a bone knife thrust to his throat and he fell to his knees choking on blood.

Reinforcements crashed through, eager to avenge. They could do nothing for their comrade twitching on the rush-strewn floor. But the girl was different. She sat mute with defiance in her eyes, the evidence of her crime in her hand. It would be a waste not to seek some form of revenge.

'You murderous siren.' A settler began to unfasten his britches. 'I will show you the best kind of swordplay.'

'First you take from us, and now we take from you.'

The transaction seemed fair to them. She tried to rise and was clubbed with a sword hilt. One of the men clambered to bind her arms behind her as his companion sought to spread her legs.

'She tries to bite,' the first man said. There was a vicious laugh. 'I welcome spirit in a hellcat.'

A forearm pressed into the girl's throat. 'Do you ask for Sodom or Gomorrah, whore?'

She could not answer. They would break her. Hands explored her skin, breath feverish, accompanied by grunts and oaths.

A new voice interrupted. 'Call yourself a Christian?' Smith pushed the muzzle of his pistol hard into the neck of his sprawled subordinate. There was real anger in his tone. He would not tolerate his men descending to the level of beasts. The pressure did not ease. 'You would bring shame upon our kind?'

'She is nothing to you.'

'Yet I would kill to guard her honour.'

'What honour is this?' Contempt was spewed through clenched teeth. 'The savage is scarce human.'

'Then why prey on her so?'

'Our brother is slain by her hand.'

'Violating the girl will not bring him back.' Smith kicked the man aside. 'To your tasks, before my font of mercy dries.'

Out in the open, the butchery had ceased and the men busied themselves ferrying baskets of grain to empty into the waiting hogsheads on their craft. They moved urgently, watchful in case of an enemy counter-attack. Perhaps in future they would learn to trade with beads and copper instead of lead.

Stooping to retrieve the discarded effigy of the native god, Smith placed it against the trunk of a black maple and pierced it through with a nail. The redskin people would understand the message and remember the visit. They would be wise to choose peace over conflict.

Incarceration had done little to diminish the questing mind and restless energy of the prisoner. In the past, he had been a courtier and favourite of Queen Elizabeth; a seafarer and a privateer. Now he was landlocked and held in the Bloody Tower. It was how many a glittering career finished for the political rivals of Robert Cecil, but Sir Walter Raleigh would not allow it to destroy him. He would smoke and write and dream of better times, and count in the new inmates condemned to the Tower of London for their imagined treason. To breathe, it seemed, was almost as great a crime as plotting against the King.

Christian Hardy watched as Raleigh inserted a folded note inside the collar of a small greyhound and sent the dog on its way to the prison lodgings of the Earl of Northumberland. The nobleman had been caught in the trawl for suspects in the aftermath of the Powder Treason. His distant cousin Thomas Percy had been a key conspirator, and with all the plotters dead, the vengeance of the state had fallen on prominent figures left behind. It suited Cecil to tie up loose ends.

'Permit me my petty diversions, Christian.' Raleigh straightened and smiled. Outwitting his gaolers was one of the few pleasures remaining for the ageing adventurer. There was still the intellect, the joy of risk, the contempt for those who would impose their rules.

'Had I the power, I would permit you a ladder.'

Raleigh laughed. 'No one would countenance a ghost like me treading the streets of London once more.'

'I would pay in gold to witness the face of Cecil at such an event.'

'How does our little pygmy?'

'As eager as ever to please the King, and amass power for himself.'

'Take care, Christian.' Raleigh gave him a warning glance. 'Cross him and you will suffer.'

'I suspect he has already tried to kill me.'

'He will try again. What he wants is peace with Spain, and Jamestown does not help this.'

'My ship lies ready at Gravesend.'

'Cecil will perceive it as a further slight that you take the shilling of Prince Henry and snub his own patronage and the kindness of the King.'

'I am to guard the settlement against danger.'

'You would do well to remember the threat that is here too.' Raleigh unstoppered a hip flask and took a nip of firewater before offering it to his friend. 'Eau de vie from my private still, the best in all of England.'

'I shall miss it when I make landfall in Virginia.'

'Perhaps you are safer there.' Raleigh took back the bottle. 'The Earl of Northumberland has sent out his younger brother to ensure one of the line survives.'

'It is said George Percy is a frail weakling, a wastrel runt of the litter given to fits and convulsions.'

'Virginia will make him a man.'

Virginia was Raleigh's touchstone, his discovery; the territory he had named after his beloved Virgin Queen, a concession stolen and then ignored by Robert Cecil. Here at last was a venture to exploit what he had found, a chance to return it to the centre of things. Grey stone walls could not imprison hope or ambition.

'I swear to you, Christian. Though I write the history of England, there will be no greater or more lasting moment than Jamestown and the birth of an English colony.'

'Others are less confident.'

'Leave them to their doubts and petty spite. There will be gold in the Appalachia, an inner sea, a passage through to the Pacific and the riches of the Orient.'

'How can you know this? We do not even have a map.'

'Its steps may be faltering, but the child will grow.'

Outside Raleigh's quarters a lion roared, its anger hanging distant in the air as it paced the confines of its pen. The royal menagerie held many exotic beasts at the Tower. At least, Hardy thought, the animals would never face the ritual gutting and hanging on the scaffold; at least their severed heads would not be placed on spikes for the delight of the spectating masses.

Raleigh embraced his old friend. 'Triumph in Virginia might win me freedom, Christian.' He pulled a small leather pouch from a purse and tossed it to the younger man. 'Take this with you. Seeds of Spanish tobacco. What I steal from King Philip, I gift to England.'

Hardy left the prisoner to his thoughts and dwelt instead on his own. He had once believed he might emerge from the shadowlands of espionage, but too much blood had been shed and too many secrets absorbed ever to let that happen. He could never again be an ordinary citizen of England.

As he acknowledged the guards and retrieved his sword, passing beneath the raised portcullis, he considered how few men escaped the consequences of political machination and religious divide. It was simply a matter of degree and the level of injury suffered. He crossed the bridge spanning the moat and stepped to the world outside.

The English renegade known as Realm stood on the ramparts of the Castle of St George and stared out over the city of Lisbon. Once, an Armada had gathered on the Tagus River below, setting out with invasion in its heart and holy crosses emblazoned on its sails. How long ago it seemed. In this very fortress he had trained the sharpshooters tasked with the assassination of Queen Elizabeth, watched as they picked off captured English crewmen stumbling panicked through the courtyards. Too bad such effort was squandered. But he was not given to regret. There was always another day, another operation; and now there was the news to digest that Christian Hardy was preparing to depart for Jamestown. Soon he too would embark for the place his enemies called Virginia. The eternal game continued.

CHAPTER 2

'I know what you bring, Hardy. It is trouble and not luck.'

His reputation had preceded him. The intelligencer stood with the doughty admiral on the poop deck of the *John and Francis* and watched as his pair of oak chests was brought aboard. So many expeditions had started this way. The creak of the blocks and rigging, the shrill call of the bosun whistle, the grunts and shouts of men putting their shoulder to the capstan. All were familiar and redolent with memory. Once it had been Sir Francis Drake beside him, bracing as his *Revenge* took the weather gauge and heeled to attack the Armada; then it had been Sir Richard Grenville, mortally wounded and propped against a toppled cannon, having plunged his ship into the heart of the enemy. Today he prepared to depart with a different seafarer. Captain Christopher Newport was himself a veteran, a commander trusted by his crew and respected by the King, a survivor of combat with a missing right arm as testament to his courage.

In his azure-blue eyes and handsome features traced by the scars of conflict, Newport detected in Hardy a soldier or spy set apart from ordinary concerns. His orders were to transport and protect the man and not to ponder why. Peace with Spain meant a surfeit of cashiered officers seeking new lands and opportunity.

He glanced at the intelligencer. 'How light you travel.'

'My needs are few and indulgences less.'

'Thus speaks a true soldier.' There was a nod of approval. 'If it is harsh challenge you desire, you will find sufficient in Virginia.'

'I am told you were reluctant to return.'

'Reluctant?' A snort of near mirth. 'Look at your fellow travellers, Hardy. Tell me if they fill you with hope.'

'From poor beginnings may come improvement.'

'Not at Jamestown. It is waste ground, a latrine into which we tip our most quarrelsome and absurd.'

'Some would wish it survive.'

'Others that it would not.'

Hardy surveyed the final preparations of the crew. 'What then persuades you to keep it resupplied?'

'I live in hope there will be gold and minerals, and I may take my share.'

'It is as noble as any motive, Captain.'

'What then is yours?'

'Perhaps hatred, or remorse, or love of the fray.' Hardy rarely delved too deep. He did not like to revisit in his mind the scene at his home off Fetter Lane, the image of his wife, Emma, butchered by Realm. There were other memories, too; the vignettes that threaded together to make the whole. Fra Roberto, his childhood mentor, the belligerent priest who had fought the Turk during the siege of Malta with a crucifix in one hand and a sword in the other, later hanged from a tree by the Inquisition; his own mother, whose hand he had touched in a Lisbon dungeon, burned at the stake for some imagined heresy; his toiling as a slave in the silver mines beneath the great mountain of Potisí. All his loathing led to Spain.

Newport bellowed an order and returned to Hardy. 'Where we go is hell.'

'I have visited worse.'

'Never a place so replete with rogues and scoundrels. Among our company here are tailors. I vouch it is shrouds they will be asked to make.'

'Each to his own task.'

A quizzical look. 'I received a sealed note from Prince Henry. He demands I take great care of you.'

'His Grace is kind.'

'His kindness adds a further burden to my duties.' There was a hint of complaint. 'My mission is the resupply of Jamestown and the safety of my ships.'

'It is not my intent to hinder it, sir.'

'You are the kind of man for whom repercussions are not foreseen.'

'At least I may promise adventure.'

Newport grunted, part intrigued and mostly vexed by the passenger he carried. He cast a glance towards the *Phoenix* and noted the longboats clustering at her bow, readying to edge her from the wharf for the estuary. It might be the last time either vessel glimpsed the other. Still, the challenge of the open sea made it worth the hazard. The breeze was steady and the tide running and everything was stowed. It was the morning of 8 October 1607. Departure was imminent.

Beside him, Hardy put his fingers to his mouth and directed a loud whistle to the shore. A final crew member had been summoned. Racing up the gangplank, a brown, athletic dog leapt to join his master and to introduce himself to all. Buckler was aboard.

The captain watched the proceedings with an air of resignation. 'We have yet to put to sea, and already we have been boarded by a pirate.'

'An Irish one at that.' Hardy stooped to welcome his companion. 'As sentinel or ratter, you will find none better.'

'There will be rats aplenty for us all.'

The moment had come and the order was given, and with pennants flying and to the dip and pull of longboat oars, the two ships swung towards the sea.

One observer witnessed the event with particular interest. He sat awhile in the saddle, his gaze fixed on the diminishing specks until they vanished from view. This was no chance sighting. His eyes had recorded the details and committed them to memory, and his mount would now carry him to his rendezvous. He pulled on the reins and wheeled the animal round, encouraging it to a canter.

He made swift progress, heading west across the marshland for Kent Street and the approaches to the flow and bustle of London Bridge. There was always traffic, the carters and drovers and merchants thronging to enter the City. He was just one more anonymous figure on an errand. Navigating his way across, the messenger threaded up to St Paul's and crossed the Fleet Ditch at Ludgate. Then a northward track past Newgate and the tenements and scrub fields beyond. It was a route often taken by the condemned, by those conveyed by tumbril for their last drink beside the church of St Giles and their appointment with the gallows at Tyburn. Everyone had their stations of the cross.

Dismounting in a tavern courtyard, the rider entered the building and climbed the stairs. Sufficient eyes watched to ensure there was no unwarranted interruption. He knocked at a door and entered.

'They sail, my lord. The *John and Francis* and the *Phoenix* together.'

'A stirring sight, I am certain.'

His audience might have intended to mock, but deciphering the words was hard. The small hunchback with the inscrutable gaze was not given to revealing secrets. As spymaster and Lord Chancellor and the power behind the throne of England, Robert Cecil liked to be informed. Where there was a hidden priest, his roving pursuivants would sniff the papist out; where there was conspiracy, his agents would report it. A year before, Guido Fawkes and the surviving gunpowder plotters had been butchered on the scaffold. It was Cecil who had orchestrated this; Cecil who had gained reward and had his status reinforced. He would stay watchful, for it paid to be guardian of the King.

The messenger was dismissed. Gesturing to a plate of sweetmeats and raising a glass of claret to his lips, Cecil addressed another man richly garbed and seated opposite.

'You hear it for yourself, Don Pedro. Supply is now sent to Jamestown.'

'It is news that scarcely pleases.' The Spaniard reached for a sugared almond. 'Some might regard it an aggressive act, and in violation of our treaty.'

'No violation occurs and no aggression is intended.'

'Yet one hundred more settlers head across the ocean.'

Cecil paused. 'I have scant powers over the Virginia Company, Don Pedro.'

'A legal ruse and a convenient excuse.' Scepticism was etched upon the features of the Spanish ambassador. Don Pedro de Zúñiga had learnt to mistrust the protestations of the English. They were emollient enough, speaking soothing words and seeking diplomatic resolution. Even King James had recently played the charming host in an audience at Hampton Court. Denial could not alter the truth.

Cecil leant forward. 'We must not allow a local dispute to mar our friendship, Don Pedro.'

'Global ambition begets wider conflict, my lord.'

'Then it is fortunate that Jamestown has no value.' The Lord Chancellor drank more wine. 'Be assured, we shall not intervene should you direct force against the settlement.'

Zúñiga smiled. 'You are casual in delivering a sentence of death.'

'Consider me well practised.'

Jamestown would perish, for that was ordained. The nascent colony was little more than a hobby of Prince Henry and a pipe dream for romantics, an ill-dreamt-of conceit that might fester and become a sore.

No one could know for sure if that small wooden stockade in Virginia would grow into a centre of religious and political dissent. This was why King James hated it so, and his servant Cecil had leaked the details of its paltry defences to Madrid.

The ambassador studied the diminutive Englishman. 'Christian Hardy still lives.'

'An inconvenience and an oversight.'

'Was he not one of yours? Your most prized intelligencer and feted guardian of the kingdom?'

'We dwell in different times.'

'There is ever a need for such men, my lord.'

'Some are privy to too many secrets.'

'Thus you discard him and he finds fresh employ.' Zúñiga allowed himself another sweet. 'Perchance he will be as dangerous abroad as he proved to be in England.'

'Accidents may happen, and a blade strike when least expected.'

'He has shown himself resilient.'

'It is rare I lose a battle.' There was a pledge implicit in the statement. Cecil raised his glass. He and the Spaniard had an understanding and several common interests; a desire to resolve outstanding issues without recourse to war. Neither the English nor the Spanish monarch enjoyed frittering their wealth on hostilities and shot. This was where diplomacy had its merits.

Reassured, Zúñiga took his leave. As his unadorned carriage rumbled north towards his Highgate residence, he sat alone in its dark interior and considered their discussion. Robert Cecil, Earl of Salisbury, was no easier to read than usual. The little pygmy was forever an enigma, a master of falsehood and bluff. Yet the ambassador too could trade in deception. For even as he swayed here with the progress of his vehicle, out at sea the renegade Realm was bound for the eastern coast of the Americas. In matters of espionage and international rivalry, contingency planning was essential.

Early evening, and an escape attempt was in train. It had been a mistake to confine the troublemaker to the pinnace, to hold a prisoner aboard a vessel newly rigged to sail up the James River. Yet prison facilities in the settlement were lacking, and keeping malcontents offshore provided an easy solution. It was November 1607. A man named George Kendall was arranging a breakout.

'Are you with me, brother?' He spoke in an urgent whisper.

'It is either the sea or the savages.' Assent came with a grip of the hand. 'You have the wheel and my support.'

'Then we move quick, for tide and time are pressing.'

They had little to lose but their lives. The sentence for such a misdemeanour would be a flogging or a rope about the neck. Survival was a similarly dismal prospect, for there would be a long winter and the committal of more bodies to the earth. England did not care and would not miss them; England was to blame. Desperate now, Kendall and his skeleton crew would commandeer the pinnace and set course for Spain.

'What happens here?' a voice called from the shadows.

The challenge was followed by a scuffle that turned in an instant into a full-throated affray. The prison guards would not go quietly. Somehow the anchor was raised and sails unfurled and the boat tacked to move downriver. But now a longboat was in pursuit. A cannon fired and a heavy round skimmed close. With a shudder, the pinnace grounded itself on a sandbar.

To furious shouts and residual violence, the mutiny was quelled and the exodus halted. There would be no transatlantic voyage this night. A bruised and bloodied Kendall was taken ashore and dragged inside the fort, a crowd materialising to vent their rage.

'Hang him now!'

'I have a rope. Let us string him from a tree.'

'First he should be scourged and branded and forced to make a confession!'

But formalities would be observed. In the flickering light of a brazier, the chief accused stood before his judge, President Ratcliffe.

'At whom do you stare?' Kendall snarled at the other settlers. He would not be cowed by the starving and baying company about him. 'Had you the balls or backbone, you would do as I.'

Ratcliffe cocked his head. 'Run away?'

'Yes, run. Flee this pestilential sty and slough off every vestige of its memory.'

'In law that is deemed mutiny.'

'While in Jamestown it is sense.'

'You stand condemned by deed and word.'

'Who is not in these parts, Ratcliffe?' Kendall looked about him. 'Who is pure of heart and motive? Who is as he seems?'

'So tell us, Kendall. Where would you flee to?'

The man glared defiantly. 'Spain. I would reveal everything to them, to the last barrel of powder and ounce of shot.'

'Your charge grows from mutiny to treason.'

'I know you, Ratcliffe. You are no better than I.'

'Take care how you speak.'

'Or I may die?' Kendall sneered. 'It is you who must be careful, *Catholic*.'

There was momentary bewilderment in the crowd, then a weary resignation. So many here had secrets and agendas and even assumed names. Most in Jamestown had left something behind. Ratcliffe turned to his henchman, the lawyer Gabriel Archer. 'I hear no defence from the prisoner.'

'Nor any grounds for clemency.'

'Our case, then, is closed.' Ratcliffe looked to the senior echelons. 'We cannot brook such treasonous acts. We are tasked to make an example.'

Kendall protested. 'On whose authority?'

'That of the Virginia Company and letters patent, and the council here that elected me. You will be taken beyond these walls and shot dead for your offences.'

In the ensuing commotion, the babble of voices rose to cheer or vent their spleen. Due process was an affectation, a luxury reserved for those with full bellies back in England. Virginia had its own kind of justice.

As the noise of the mob abated, a gap opened in its ranks to reveal the figure of John Smith. Attended by his shallop crew and dressed in his weather-stained coat, the adventurer held a dead turkey in each hand.

'Each time I return, I bring provisions. Each time I return, I find a settlement at the brink.'

Ratcliffe offered no welcome. 'Order is restored, Captain.'

'At what cost?' Smith dropped the birds and turned to walk away. Already the ravenous had switched their attention from the prospect of an execution to the imminence of a feast.

The ground was hard and the air chill on the morning George Kendall was marched out and tied to a stake. The settlement was witnessing its first act of capital punishment. A show of sorts was required. After all, the man was a troublemaker and deserved his fate. So the drum beat loudly, the firing squad paraded and the curious jostled for the clearest view.

'Do you confess to your crimes and repent of all sin?' The chaplain spoke in a sonorous tone. 'Do you stand before God and ask His forgiveness?'

'I do.'

'Are you ready for His judgement?'

'I am.'

'Then go in peace and may the mercy of the Almighty be with you.'

At five paces, the executioners could not miss. Four muskets discharged, the sound abrupt and the smoke heavy, the wooden post shattering on impact. In the ringing silence, the eyes of the gathered were wide, directed towards the grim remnants of a human through the haze. For a time, discipline had been restored.

Over the next two weeks, the atmosphere in the camp became calm and the men went back to their duties. It allowed Smith once more to consider a return to exploration. Gathering together his crew and provisions, he set off to discover the Chickahominy, a tributary of the James River.

Forty miles upstream, he was ambushed. Wanderlust and recklessness found him bound helpless to a tree.

The adventurer gazed now at the natives arrayed against him, their bows drawn. He would not aggravate the situation. That he was still alive was something of a miracle. Sprawled beside the shallop were the corpses of the crew he had posted as guards, their firearms scant protection against the blizzard of arrows.

The bows lowered as Opechancanough appeared. He had stepped into the clearing accompanied by his personal retinue of forty warriors. These were his hunting lands. For a while he studied the intruder whose progress he had tracked. The English were not so impressive when denied their loud weapons and held fast with twine.

'You are John Smith?' He spoke slowly in the Algonquian tongue and saw that the captive understood.

'I am he.' The soldier was careful in his reply. 'I come in friendship and to trade.'

'Yet you bring us fire and death, from the mouth of the river to the falls.'

'I will pay with precious things.'

'Though you prefer to steal.'

Smith would brazen it out. 'Take me to your emperor, Powhatan. We shall be as brothers and fight our common foes.'

'It is you that is the enemy.'

'Would you spurn the chance of riches? Turn your back on the wealth and power I may bring?'

His words deserved consideration. A flurry of snow speckled the head of the Indian.

Smith waited, sweat pooling at the base of his spine and blood seeping from the flesh wound to his thigh. He would not show fear, yet he felt the intensity of the Indian's eyes and the sharpness behind them, the raw authority vested in this imposing figure. Decisions over life and death were as commonplace as skinning a deer.

Without a word, Smith's ropes were cut. It signalled the start of a progress in which the Englishman was marched, either as prisoner or prize. He went along without complaint. There were miles to cover, the landscape wild and desolate, the swamps frozen and the trees stiff with frost. The adventurer had intended to explore, and now he was taken to a place far beyond those he had ever known.

'See what is become of invaders.'

Others had plainly pre-empted him. As Opechancanough pointed, Smith stared. He had not expected such a dramatic reacquaintance with a fellow colonist, to find the scalp and skinned face hanging on display. It was a salutary reminder that he was not among friends. Yet the savages had come in force to greet him, were dancing and howling before a central fire and forcing him to sit. Maybe he was an honoured guest; or maybe with the bread and venison they proffered on wooden platters they meant to fatten him for the pot.

Opechancanough crouched beside him and passed across the ivory compass taken when Smith was seized.

'Tell me of this.'

'It is what we call a compass.'

'A thing of magic? A summoner of spirits and Manitu?'

The soldier held the device flat in his outstretched palm. 'Like an eye, it directs me where to journey and finds me when I am lost.'

'I cannot touch what moves within it.'

'It is sheltered by glass.' Smith tapped the cover. 'There are many things I and my people will explain.'

'Show then the direction in which your settlement lies.'

Smith was happy to oblige. Standing to take his bearings, he squinted at the compass and jabbed his finger towards a clump of mulberry. 'Follow a straight path and you will reach my camp.'

'And your canoe?'

A further pointing of the finger. 'You may return to it there.'

The native commander appeared satisfied and the demonstration ended. Smith had other tricks in hand. He wished to show himself useful. Certainly he had attacked villages and inflicted casualties with sword and musket. They respected a fighter. But parley had its place and understanding could be created. He asked for the other objects taken from him, and raised the pen and notebook in his hand.

'With these I may summon things from my people.'

'For what do you ask?'

'A cloak and cap and coloured beads.' Smith proceeded to write. 'Accord between us must go rewarded.'

'You make marks and they will conjure gifts?' Suspicion slid into Opechancanough's eyes.

Smith tore out a page. 'If you fetch messengers and bid them hasten to Jamestown, upon their return they will carry each thing I have demanded.'

'You will die if they do not.'

Worse deals existed. Arrangements were made and the runners set out, heading across the frozen wastes. Smith marvelled at their hardiness. Had the natives possessed guns or steel blades, Jamestown would already be razed and its inhabitants cut to pieces.

But Opechancanough was not finished. He desired to learn more, to gauge the strengths and weaknesses of the strangers. They covered their legs and bodies and yet shivered in the cold. He allowed the bearded and pale-skinned man his pistol and stepped back to join his braves. Should John Smith pose a threat, he would bring a storm of arrows on himself.

A target was selected. Smith would not be hurried. He applied powder, rodded home the ball and then cocked the firing mechanism. Hitting a tree at ten paces was no insurmountable test.

The gun malfunctioned with a snap, the wheel lock failing to strike the pan or create a spark. The Indian commander stayed motionless. Then the arrows flew and the same tree was raked in a choreographed display of force.

Smith was seized and a new trek began. He called over his shoulder, 'Where do we head? Where do you take me?'

There was no answer.

Standing in the fighting tops at the zenith of the mast, Hardy scanned the scene below: the vistas of rainforest stretching to the mountain peaks; crewmen toiling to heap bananas and pineapples on the white sands; a longboat splashing to ferry the commander of the *Phoenix* ashore for conference with Captain Newport. A man could lose his focus in the warm embrace of Dominica and the Caribbean. Jamestown would afford less comfort.

His dog Buckler was on the beach engaged in chasing a ball with sailors, his barking faint and enthusiasm infectious. The Irish terrier had befriended all and acquired new tricks on the voyage. Even Newport had coursed him from beak to stern and delighted in the ease with which he took the obstacles. It left Hardy to other things: to rumination on the objectives of his mission.

He slipped the sealed letter from the pocket of his canvas jerkin, glancing at the wax cipher of Prince Henry before breaking it to study the pages folded within. They contained his orders, and gave a warning of what he might encounter. Names were included. The intelligencer committed them to memory and then let his gaze wander back towards the shore. Buckler was still wheeling in frantic play. It was better to dwell in ignorance, safer to be a canine than an officer on a secret task.

Realm too thought of his mission. Yet he was distracted, drawn by the gruesome spectacle of an African slave master beating a negro to death. It took a while for the victim to succumb. After the screams and moans, the man made futile attempts to ward off the blows before eventually his quivering limbs became still. It was ritual slaughter. Killing was so easy.

Here in Havana, no one would wonder at such things. Casual brutality was the norm. Many of the weak or sick taken in raids and then thrown into the holds of ships along the west coast had already been dumped overboard in passage across the ocean. Slavery was a business that allowed for a certain attrition. Once arrived, the surviving human merchandise would be penned and sold and branded for onward march to the interior, or for voyage to further islands. Demand from the plantations of sugar and tobacco was insatiable. Cuba was the key, the rampart of the West Indies and gateway to the New World, a heavily armed sentinel to protect the territorial interests of the King of Spain. That king must be nervous. Outside the town, additional defences were being built and within it the wood houses were proliferating.

'They are known as Imbangala.' A senior lieutenant from the caravel had joined Realm and now indicated the black slave master. 'Woe betide any they hate.'

'Who are they?'

'Some claim they are the spawn of the fallen angel; others that they are demons expelled from hell by Satan himself for the level of their savagery.'

'We appear to have found a use for them.'

'Without them we would have few slaves. They are African marauders, the warriors that raid villages and collect the natives.' His laugh was harsh. 'I have seen one scoop out eyeballs with his thumbs and another cut free a heart to eat raw.'

'Then I will speak to them.'

A restraining hand gripped his shoulder. 'Keep your distance, Reino. You cannot count on their response.'

'Nor they on mine.'

Realm approached the African and paused, his stare brazen and unflinching. If the black slaver perceived it as a challenge, the man remained silent. He turned slowly, the corpse prone and bloodied at his feet. The Imbangala nodded. It was a meeting of minds.

CHAPTER 3

'Halt, or we shall fire!'

They had appeared like wraiths, grainy in the half-light of dawn against the crusted backdrop of ice and snow. The natives kept at a distance, clad in little and apparently immune to the cold: a war party or emissaries, watchful and unhurried. It was 2 January 1608, and the sentries at Jamestown had sound reason to be nervous. Winter and the Indians had not proved kind to their enclave.

Again a challenge, the shout deadened in the frozen air. 'State your purpose, for our patience wears thin!'

A familiar voice called back. 'This is not the welcome I expected from my countrymen.'

'Captain Smith?'

The adventurer trudged into view, a knapsack on his back and warriors at his side. A man in rude health, confident and returned from the dead.

He waved. 'Did you think me gone forever? Skinned alive? Buried in the fastness?'

'We ceased to suppose on your fate,' one of the guards said sourly.

'Yet I sent warning you should stay alert and wrote of my circumstance and wishes.'

He entered with his escort, settlers emerging now to gather round and shake off their sleep, frowning in disbelief.

'Fetch a millstone for our friends,' Smith said. 'I have promised one to them as a reward.'

A stone was duly found and presented, and the Indians tried to carry it. Their attempts failed, earning laughter and applause. Arms folded and his beard jutting, Smith orchestrated the event, both showman and prodigal hero.

'So we provide the means for bread. Now let us show them the further merits of peace.' He summoned the settlers back through the gate and signalled to the gunners.

A cannon fired and stone ordnance flew, branches and icicles falling. It caused the Indians to scatter and vanish into the woods. The homecoming of Smith was complete. He shook hands and embraced his fellows. Soon their questions came, loud and constant.

'All shall be told.' He beamed and raised his hands. 'Let me rest and warm myself, for I need my strength to regale you.'

'What did you encounter?'

'Diverse things, amazing to the eye. There was savagery and beauty, warriors and priests, comely and lascivious maidens generous in their love.'

'You consorted with native girls?' There was yearning in the guard's voice.

Smith laughed. 'I defy any man to shrug off the honeyed charms of the female naturals. They bewitch, they entice, they seduce.'

'Yet you return to us.'

'It was always my intent. It was my abiding duty to escape.' He looked about him. 'I am not one to shirk my task or our destiny to build an empire.'

'What of the king named Powhatan? What of his tribes that threaten us?'

'They will, I am certain, agree to peace. I met Powhatan and calmed his wrath. I conversed with him as with a brother.'

'A brother?' Men who had endured attack and countless sleepless nights as sentries murmured in hope and incredulity.

'As a brother, I say. As an emperor with whom we may trade and conduct our daily business.'

Not everyone was swayed by his words. President Ratcliffe and his entourage stood silent, hostile and aloof. They were not inclined to cede the limelight or the initiative to John Smith.

Smith was unconcerned. 'You do not greet me, Ratcliffe?'

'I reserve generosity for sights that please me.' Ratcliffe took a step forward. 'While you caroused with the savage, we fought him. While you lost men in your vainglorious quest, we sent others to find you.'

'Did I not send word to arm yourselves and strengthen the watch?'

'It is a poor return for the cost.'

Smith shook his head. 'Would you prefer I cower here, like you? Engage in petty squabbles and debate rather than go out and find food?'

'I gave you no authority to range so far, or to put the shallop and crew at risk.'

'I had no choice.'

'It was mutiny.' The president waved his hand at the guards. 'Bind him.'

'On what grounds?'

'Sedition and treachery and wilful disobedience of the council.'

'The council has no such right.'

Ratcliffe motioned to Gabriel Archer at his side. 'The vote is cast. Archer has been appointed and we find against you.'

'Is this what our land is to be built on? The word of liars and lawyers?'

As the guards descended on him Smith fought hard, kicking and cursing and throwing punches, attempting to cast off his adversaries until he sank beneath their weight. He lay in the snow and glowered at his captor.

'You would do this to me, Ratcliffe? Devour the hand that feeds you? Turn Jamestown into nothing but a prison?'

'A prison, no.' The president gazed down on him. 'You are to face execution.'

'Yours is the greater villainy.'

'I hear no one speak in your defence.'

The boy Edward Battle pushed his way through from the back of the crowd. 'Captain Smith has shown me kindness, sir. And I know no other who serves our settlement so well.'

'Impudence will see you flogged.'

The boy was trembling but determined. 'I will take a beating rather than stay silent.'

'Those that protest are in league with the condemned.'

Enraged, Smith struggled to his feet. 'Is this how low you stoop? Threatening boys? Stifling every vestige of our freedom?'

'My task is to govern.'

'You will end up ruling dust.'

The guards dragged the adventurer away.

The verdict was a foregone conclusion. By the end of the day, the body of John Smith would hang from a tree.

Smith took a gulp of brandy wine. There was nowhere he could run or hide, and no one present to fight his cause. He would bow to the inevitable. The cowards and ingrates who accused him would rue this day when their own lives were at stake. How he would laugh from the beyond. Justice was bound to come eventually, and Ratcliffe and his cohorts would suffer the full consequences.

He scanned the assembled settlers. 'Mark my words, gentlemen. When you starve or the redskin arrows fly, you will wish I were here. I met the emperor Powhatan. We had a chance to discourse openly with the natives.'

Archer smirked. 'It is discord and not discourse; that is your way.'

'My way?' Smith stared at the prosecutor. 'My way is to reach beyond this flimsy palisade and set down more than just our headstones on this soil.'

'I doubt we shall mark *your* grave.'

'It matters not. Jamestown will be as fleeting and abandoned as Roanoke, should you and your kind prevail.'

Roanoke, the colony founded by Sir Walter Raleigh some twenty years before, whose settlers had simply vanished. A foothold in the New World could be precarious and short-lived. Smith saw the name strike home.

He gestured with his flask. 'I tried to bring life to this sick estate, and yet you have decreed my death.' The adventurer looked round at the settlers and their squalid surroundings. 'I wish you well in your endeavour.'

Archer shrugged. 'There is first your execution. The rope is ready.'

'I deserve an end more fitting for a soldier.'

'A musket ball?' President Ratcliffe interjected. 'We cannot spare our precious lead on a common miscreant.'

'You serpent, Ratcliffe! You whore of Satan. You filth from the deepest sewers of hell.'

The guards closed in to pacify the prisoner. Smith had proved to be an awkward defendant, neither begging for clemency nor confessing to his crimes. The noose would soon choke off his defiance. But a new sound juddered faint in the air, its shock waves travelling from a distance. The settlers stirred, their puzzlement dissolving to disbelief, then rapture. Salvation and resupply were at hand.

'It is a ship! A ship from England!'

'Admiral Newport is come!'

'We are saved! Rejoice, for God is with us!'

Smith watched the receding pack and gave silent thanks for his reprieve. He might have guessed that Indian scouts would have spied any vessel nosing into Chesapeake Bay and followed it up the James. So the emperor Powhatan had timed his release for the arrival. Smith smiled. He had claimed Admiral Newport to be King of all the Oceans and told him that he, Smith, was the favourite son. The ploy had worked. Ratcliffe would be incandescent.

'So the wayward dog survives.'

They regarded each other before embracing, Christian Hardy lowering the rifle carried on his shoulder before striding to greet his friend. The intelligencer and the adventurer were old acquaintances. Smith stepped back to grip Hardy's arms and better view the newcomer.

'Tell me you are no ghost, Christian.'

'As I live and breathe, I am the same.'

'No one could be more glad than I.' Smith cuffed him in approval. 'It is no paradise to which you venture.'

'I should worry if it was. An intelligencer is made for darker places.'

There was both happiness and foreboding in the reunion, an unspoken appreciation of the events that had summoned Hardy. Jamestown was at risk, and now the former protégé of the late and legendary spymaster Sir Francis Walsingham had landed on its shores. He and Smith were different in many ways: one the denizen of intrigue and a master with the sword, and the other a younger man, bluff and belligerent in his manner. Yet each in his way was an outsider, and most at ease when confronted by overwhelming odds. With his Katzbalger stabbing-sword sheathed at his side and his armoured brigantine jacket, Hardy surveyed the scene. His skills would be needed.

They feasted as they had not done since they first established the colony. With the food came cheer and a new purpose. Men talked and sang, and a few danced too. Green parrots brought from Dominica stared enquiringly from their perches. Around the fire, it seemed the future at last might brighten. Already the crew of the *John and Francis* were erecting a store, a warm room and additional shelters and constructing a permanent church; already confidence replaced the bitter misery of the previous months. For sure the *Phoenix* had gone missing, lost to fog in the approaches to the Chesapeake, but through the grace of the Almighty it would arrive. People spoke of home and loved ones and the native redskin. Always the redskin. The savages were out beyond the palisade now, and hidden by the swirling snow.

With the arrival of the ships, the balance of power within the settlement had shifted again. No longer the condemned prisoner, Smith had an audience. It was his moment, his chance to regale his countrymen with tales of adventure and the encounter with the mighty chief Powhatan. Their attention was assured.

'It is no lie, brothers. He is the greatest of chiefs, the ruler of a dozen tribes, the emperor whose kingdom crosses three vast rivers.'

'Does he intend peace or war?' Hardy asked.

'A question too hard to answer.' Smith scratched his beard. 'Of all the beasts, the savage is the most changeable and strange.'

'Powhatan released you.'

'Yet he was ready to beat out my brains. It was his young daughter Pocahontas who interceded, laying her cheek upon mine and entreating her father to spare my life.'

'He heeded her?' There was incredulity.

'In an instant we were as friends, as though there never was enmity between us.'

'Can we trust those who once would break our bones to break bread?'

Smith patted his sword. 'Show strength and they will parley. Reveal our weakness and they will come to kill.'

Newport listened. The admiral was glad peace reigned for a while. Jamestown was a dismal place, rent by division and hatred. It would take stern intervention to bring a semblance of order and the prospect of future riches to sustain the hope of the colonists. He was not here for charity. The Virginia Company had agreed his terms and granted him a share of the bounty.

He spoke up. 'Where does this Powhatan reside, Captain Smith?'

'At his town of Werowocomoco on the bank of the Pamunkey, sir.'

'Should I not take an embassy to meet him? Am I not the King of all the Oceans of whom he has heard?'

'He would expect such favour and honour.'

'Is there gold about his head and neck?'

'None that I observed.' Smith had a practised eye. 'He wears strings of beads and pearls, but I saw no precious metal.'

'A native without knowledge of the value of things is one with whom we may trade.'

'They are no fools, sir. They watch and learn and may yet plan to vanquish us.'

'Yet my orders are to nurture them and create good relations.' Newport was decided. 'Let us make our journey to pay our respects and see the wonders you have spied.'

Later, when the chill of the night had descended and talk gave way to sleep, Smith and Hardy walked the bounds. Ahead, Buckler prowled and foraged, ever close to his master. The two men kept their voices low.

'He is a fine sentinel, Christian.'

'I have never known one better. And he is a constant friend.'

'Cherish it, for it is rare enough in this hell pit.' Smith rubbed his neck. 'Had the *John and Francis* not arrived, my carcass would now be frozen on a tree.'

'I think you more useful to us, John.'

'Tell that to Ratcliffe and his devil lackey, Archer. There are those hidden in our midst who conspire against us.'

'You have suspects?'

'They are too many to name and too careful to give me any proof. Trust no one in Jamestown, Christian.'

'Was the traitor Kendall not captured?'

'There are others besides. Brownists and schismatics who desire to break from England; Puritans that seek rebellion and upheaval; Newgaters and malcontents freed of late from prison; secret Catholics loyal to Spain and wreckers in the pay of Robert Cecil.'

'It seems that I am needed.'

'Do not jest, brother.' Smith rested a hand on his shoulder. 'Beneath every rock here lies a snake that plans to bite.'

They paused and heard the call of the night watch. Beneath the light of the moon the waterside beacon dissipated to grey within the fort interior. There the men still shivered in tents and fields were left unsown; natives lurked outside with bow and arrow and would prey on any weakness.

'Christian, there is something else.'

'More gloom and dire warning?'

'The last time the savages attacked, I found the gate had been unlocked and the neck of the sentry on the rampart broken.'

'Another serpent had crawled from beneath its stone?'

'An arrow had been thrust into his chest, but I saw the bruising at his collar.'

'You are sure?'

'I swear it, Christian. And I have told no one but you.'

'Break your silence, and I doubt you will reach the age of thirty or I much beyond these forty years.'

A shout broke into their thoughts. 'Fire! There is fire! In the name of God, there is fire!'

The warning was irrelevant. Already the flames had leapt from the storeroom to the other shacks and raced along the palisade, feeding on pine pitch and tar and travelling at speed. A keg of gunpowder detonated, adding to the conflagration. Through the choking smoke, figures dashed to save themselves and their scant possessions as officers shouted orders. Hemmed in by burning timbers, the men were helpless and the chaos multiplied as the scorching fury rose. Another blast and burst of flame, and the logs collapsed into incineration.

Smith and Hardy were among the throng fighting the flames long into the night. With determination and luck something might be salvaged from the catastrophe, but the inferno had taken hold and the two friends understood the battle might be lost.

As they feared, it was a blackened dawn, smudged with soot and acrid with vapour and ash. Jamestown had lost much. The supplies brought ashore from the *John and Francis* were gone, the defences were ruined and the confidence ignited by the new arrivals had been extinguished. Bewildered, the settlers gathered. Whether this was an act of God or sabotage, ordained or simply an accident, they had starved and fought, suffered and born hardship: for this.

A man spoke. 'The Lord despises us and visits on us His punishment. He does not wish us here.'

Another agreed. 'We are sinners in the wilderness; strayers from the truth.'

'Or this is sorcery and witchcraft.' The settler stared dejected at a pile of embers. 'Someone has placed a curse upon our enterprise.'

Random voices and conflicting views came from every quarter. Yet they all realised that the fates did not smile on their venture. Men who had once sought new lives now hankered for the certainties of the old. This was no place to colonise or tame.

Admiral Newport clambered up and stood on a hogshead cask. His empty coat sleeve pinned to his chest and his only hand clutching a sword, he surveyed the dispirited throng.

'Hear what I say and doubt not my words.' His gruff authority snapped the settlers from their thoughts. 'You live, and that suffices. You have hands to build anew. You may perish, forgotten, or create a colony worthy of your memory.'

A dissenter called out. 'We have lost too much.'

'Not everything is burned. Henceforth we look to the morrow and the future. We will clear tracts and cut down trees; we will dig the soil for gold.'

'Your *John and Francis* brought us and has room to carry us home,' cried one man. Others muttered in agreement.

'I shall do as you propose. Yet for the crime of your desertion, I will hang each one of you from the yardarm within sight of England.'

'I meant no presumption or offence.' The man spoke hastily.

'None is taken, for we are brothers in arms.'

'What shall you do while we hew and toil?' Disgruntlement flared elsewhere. 'How will you and the gentlemen fritter the hours away, as we bleed and sweat in the snow?'

'I shall meet the emperor Powhatan to gauge his strength and intent; to offer friendship, to ensure peace and cohabitation between our nations.'

Hardy watched the faces of the men and saw hope – or was it disenchantment? – flicker in their eyes. Among the cindered ruins, it was hard to believe in a future. Perhaps some good might come from rapprochement with the natives, but it could just as easily invite further attack. It could all be in vain; might end with weeds and wilderness reclaiming this frozen ground.

As the crowd began to disperse, grumbling, Hardy noticed a settler at the back. The man had discovered the remains of a Dominican parrot baked by the inferno and was chewing on it hungrily.

Newport stepped ashore to the sound of a trumpet and with his own honour guard of twenty soldiers formed up on either side. The English would not stint on the pomp. They would show Powhatan the might of their kingdom and the majesty of their ways, would announce the arrival of the King of the Oceans with a grandeur befitting his title. Smith had already spent the night in the company of the Indians, preparing the way for the main event. Gifts had been given and kind words exchanged, and a message sent to the pinnace. Now the white Weroance had come, a chief among chiefs, a grizzled and wounded veteran of many battles. He deserved respect.

Warriors danced and women sang and priests howled and whirled and shook their rattles. Then, silence. The ranks opened and Powhatan stood before his guests, his officers and counsellors resplendent at his side. John Smith, too, attended.

Newport doffed his hat and bowed his head a fraction. 'We come in peace, and seek to be as brothers.'

'Had you offered battle, by now you would be dead.' Powhatan spoke as Smith translated. 'Why do you settle on our lands?'

'To trade, and nothing more; to find refuge from the storms and from our enemies at sea.'

'What do you bring me?'

'Beads and fine cloth and precious things; a white greyhound and here, a boy to raise as your very kin.'

Each item was presented and the youngster pushed forward, shivering in his fright. Diplomacy required such a sacrifice. Powhatan received the tribute without comment or expression, an ageing ruler accustomed to deference and adept in negotiation. This was his domain, his Tsenacomoco.

He gazed at the admiral. 'You say you wish to be as brothers?'

'On my honour, it is true. For your foes will be ours, and any who draw your blood will suffer at our hands.'

'We have enemies beyond the falls.'

'I know of them from Captain Smith. They are the hated Monacan that forever raid your lands, and the Pocoughtronack, those feared devourers of human flesh, that scavenge and feed on your people.'

'They shall not defeat us.'

'Yet united we may conquer them.'

The native chief considered the words. Plainly the wearers of leg coverings intended to convince. He lowered his hand in a gesture to his guests. 'Lay down your weapons so that we may talk further.'

'No friend would ask it of us.'

'As no brother would come armed into our homes.'

It provoked hesitation in the English, the men exchanging glances. Instinct cautioned against such folly. Yet refusal might jeopardise the mission. Newport did not move.

A girl ran to stand between Powhatan and Smith, taking and holding their hands in her own. She smiled at the foreigners, and they understood. Her name was Pocahontas, the child princess of whom the adventurer had spoken, the luminous beauty who could pacify with a word the native king.

Newport murmured to Hardy stationed behind. 'You have counsel for me?'

'Do as Powhatan bids you. Pocahontas intervenes and fortune may favour us.'

'Should you be wrong?'

'There will be a massacre and all shall judge you a fool.'

'I would wish to be remembered for greater things.'

'We do not choose our eulogies.' Hardy shifted his gaze to the waiting Indians. 'There are weapons hidden on me and a saker cannon with canister and solid shot ready on the pinnace.'

'It brings me little comfort.'

'Are you not lord of all the waters, a demigod arrived by ship? Are you not the man in whom the Virginia Company has placed its trust to ease relations with the natives?'

The admiral sighed. 'I said you would vex me and give me trouble, Mr Hardy.'

He drew his sword and surrendered it to a minion, commanding his immediate entourage to do the same. Arrows might fly and cudgels fall at any moment. Yet the dancing started and the tension ebbed, and women and warriors clustered round in welcome. Newport strode forward. Should he survive and negotiations succeed, his embassy would continue up the Pamunkey to meet the military commander Opechancanough at his capital, Cinquoteck. Bravery or madness, the English were committed.

'Regard them, Christian. They are fevered with the thought of gold.' Smith did nothing to hide his disgust. About him, the settlers rolled barrels of soil to and from the assay tent and through the gateway to the waterfront. No precious metal had been found. Yet still they toiled, sifting dirt and panning streams in search of hidden riches. Spring had arrived, and Newport was eager to depart, and the London merchants would expect something in return for their support. For the while, the clearing of land was postponed and the sowing of crops could wait. Everything was directed to a single aim. 'They speak gold, dream gold, would eat gold if they could,' the adventurer continued his complaint. 'Yet they will be quick to whine when we have no harvest or provisions for the table.'

Hardy was stropping a knife. 'Let them to their madness, John.'

'Insanity it is. There are lands to explore, and here we mine dirt. Is this the greed and illusion on which a nation is founded?'

'Colonies have been forged from less.'

'I would have rather more vision.'

They heard laughter nearby as Pocahontas ran and played with Buckler. She had come with a delegation to trade with the English, and was a symbol of warming relations. Powhatan, it seemed, would keep his word and restrain his warlike tribes. After all, peace was of benefit to everyone. So the natives brought corn and beans and venison, and received in turn cloth and trinkets and glass beads. A fair exchange.

Some Indians had even joined the settlers to live among them and aid them in their daily tasks. It did not mean an end to the patrols though, or a lessening of the night watch.

Hardy whistled and, to the delight of the girl, Buckler dropped to crawl on his belly.

'He is more obedient than most in this place.'

'Quicker too to fetch a stick.' Smith scanned the scene. 'You trust the savages, Christian?'

'They are as murderous and deceiving as any settler.' He smiled. 'It may gladden you to hear that I have convinced the admiral to carry home the lawyer Archer.'

'I concede that is one fewer problem to address. Yet Ratcliffe remains.'

But the intelligencer was distracted, his attention veering to another young native woman standing quiet and apart from the industry about. She had accompanied Pocahontas, and served as an indulgent chaperone and companion; Smith thought she was perhaps a concubine of Powhatan. Hers was a position of status and trust. There was a sweetness to her, a warmth and dignity that must have transmitted to her younger charge. Their fondness was plain. Yet it was Hardy whose stare did not waver.

Smith nodded. 'She notices you, Christian. Her name is Awae.'

'An elder sister to the princess?'

'Some relation of sorts, or a hostage from another tribe. She and Pocahontas are close. Be careful,' he added, 'for the naturals bewitch us. She is a beauty, but is owned by Powhatan.'

'He has proved to be understanding.'

'Yet would be less generous should you trifle with his property.'

'We shall see where my appetites lead.'

Suddenly they heard the sound of a sharp detonation. On the far side of the camp, men ran towards a figure crouched in pain. As Smith and Hardy moved a little closer to the scene, they saw there had been an accident: the discharge of a pistol for the entertainment of the natives had led to an explosion and a shattered hand. President Ratcliffe was the victim.

Smith betrayed no concern. 'It seems the president lives.'

'He will be permanently maimed, I am sure.'

'May it remind him that we all of us are formed of flesh and blood.'

Hardy studied his friend. 'Is it crime or circumstance which conjures this event?'

'Let us call it judgement. Let us give thanks, too, that Ratcliffe is diverted for a time.'

'You make for a vicious enemy, John.'

'I believe I am also a sound friend.' The adventurer indicated the scene. 'Our wounded president governs with false motive and masked identity. I hear a rumour he was once a priest and was persuaded to our side.'

There were many such men, and Hardy had captured his share. Something resonated deep within his memory. He tried to reach for it, but for now the secret remained hidden.

On 10 April 1608 Newport's ship, laden with samples of earth, departed for home, the captain's resupply mission completed.

CHAPTER 4

'To arms! It is the Spaniard!'

Their greatest fear, it seemed, was realised. Settlers snatched up their weapons or raced to man the guns, straining to catch a glimpse of the encroaching threat. They had few illusions as to how events would unfold. Broadsides would splinter the palisade in seconds, and then the infantry would surge through, their swords drawn, their breastplates and morion helmets bright, hunting down and slaughtering all. It had happened before, when a surprise Spanish attack expunged a French colony from the face of Florida. The barbarism had been extensive and prolonged. Now the hated foe was here. Men waited, held slow matches, readying their muskets and their cannon, muttering prayers beneath their breath. Battle would soon begin.

'She is the *Phoenix*!'

Relief and disbelief mingled before despondency was transformed to joy. It was true. Less than a fortnight since the *John and Francis* had headed downriver for the Chesapeake and for home, her long-lost consort was arrived. Her cannon sounded and her pennants flew, and settlers lined the banks to cheer. She deserved her welcome.

His shattered hand bandaged and held in a sling, President Ratcliffe stood at the jetty as the longboat pulled in.

'Greetings to you, Captain.'

The captain raised a hand. 'Your colony survives, and that is to the good.' He climbed from the craft and peered about him. 'So it is I, set foot on the soil of America.'

'Our men give thanks.'

'As do we, though the weather conspired against us. For three months we were forced to winter in the Indies.'

'There are worse places to be.'

The captain glanced at the palisade. 'I can scarce imagine.'

They toured the encampment of tents and hovels and the rebuilt sections of the fort. It was not a sight to lift the spirits. Yet already the new settlers were streaming ashore and provisions were being offloaded. These latecomers seemed perplexed. After a year of existence, the colony appeared little more than a temporary slum.

Once the excitement of the *Phoenix*'s arrival had died down, Smith and Hardy and the boy Edward Battle returned to their game of cards.

'I vouch the captain will be eager to depart by the time he completes his circuit.' The adventurer shuffled and dealt. 'Ratcliffe sucks the life from all.'

'He clings with tenacity to his own.'

'In spite of my best efforts. Now he diverts men from their principal task and directs them to build him a palace.'

'It gives them purpose.'

'Or creates pure mischief.' Smith slapped a card on the trestle's surface. 'Are we not ordered to clear and to plant? To explore? To push into the lands west beyond the falls?'

'I have little doubt it shall occur.'

'As I have none that the president will deploy mischief and excuse to sabotage our mission.'

Hardy nodded his head to the boy and to Buckler at his side. 'He does not count on other weapons in our arsenal.'

'They will hardly cover us against what Ratcliffe plans.'

'Let us not predict the outcome.' Hardy drew a card.

'Trust no one, Christian. Not even the natives who come among us with trade and smiles.'

'I will keep my guard.'

'What of the female savage, Awae?'

The intelligencer took and discarded another card. 'A man is permitted his frailties.'

'Not if it should endanger him.' Smith stared at his friend. 'Reveal your hand, Christian.'

'It is not my nature.'

Despite the appearance of the *Phoenix*, the fears of the colonists were well founded. Some thirty miles north-west of the mouth of the James, another ship from Europe had sailed into Chesapeake Bay and dropped anchor. She was a caravel, a transport that had made leisurely passage from Havana, and would refrain from announcing her arrival with the same bombast as the English. Her captain was well briefed. En route, he had presented gifts to tribal chiefs, spreading goodwill and learning much too. The chiefs liked to talk, and spoke of the strangers dwelling in their land. Tsenaco-moco was defiled. Yet the supreme leader and Mamanatowick, the mighty Powhatan himself, seemed to vacillate and ponder. It was thus to his military commander, Opechancanough, that the Spaniards would turn.

Realm congratulated himself on his perseverance with the Indians. He might die, bludgeoned by scores of cudgels or pierced by a dozen arrows in an instant, but the opportunities outweighed the risks. Besides, his three black Imbangala bodyguards carried spears and swords and would acquit themselves well. The braves of Opechancanough had no concept of the ferocity that might be unleashed.

Now the military chief eyed him, his warriors falling back at an unspoken command. There was something fearless in his manner; a complete understanding of life and death and whatever came beyond. His curiosity alone kept the English renegade alive.

Opechancanough began to circle the Imbangala, pausing to study, reaching to touch a cheek. Dark skin or paint, the colours did not run. Satisfied, the Indian faced the renegade once more.

'You speak our tongue?'

Realm nodded.

'Are you Weroance? A chief?'

'I have no tribe and need no village.'

'Then you possess no power.' Opechancanough searched for a hint of trepidation. 'Do you not fear us?'

'It is not I whose lands are invaded, whose authority will wane as the pale men multiply and spread out from their fort.'

'They will starve and perish.'

'And if they should not?' Realm remained as impassive as the native. 'If their number should grow, and their forces march to seize your territory?'

'We will outfight them in the forest.'

'For how long? How will you hold them when your warriors fall and your villages burn, when your women and children are taken?'

'I tell you again, the pale men will submit.'

'Already they name your land Virginia and scheme to have it for themselves,' the renegade continued.

'What of you? What is it that you scheme?' Opechancanough's eyes glittered with danger.

'To become a counsellor and friend to you.'

'Without an army of warriors? Without strong magic or spirits or the wealth of a nation?'

'My gods will smile on us.'

Realm felt the cold heat of the commander's gaze and refused to waver beneath it. Plead for mercy, and they would show none; display the slightest weakness and they would have his skin hanging from a tree. He preferred to engage Opechancanough as an equal.

His scrutiny continued.

'Powhatan received the King of all the Oceans, the one who is called Newport.'

'Such a chief cannot be trusted.'

'He offered tribute and gave solemn pledge of accord.'

'Yet he does not tear down the fort or bear his people home.' Realm leant forward a fraction. 'He will not keep his promises. His friendship is a ruse.'

'You too state that you are my friend.'

'I build no camp and make no claim to land.'

'Something draws you.'

'Hatred for our common foe. I desire, as do you, the destruction of these settlers. I will show you how they may be overcome.' In the hold of the caravel were steel blades to empower an Indian nation reliant on bone and flint.

'They speak of their enemy the Spaniard, and train their weapons upon the river.'

'Now the Spaniard is come.'

'You forget the pale-skins are well armed.'

'A thing of little consequence, for their fort will prove to be a grave.' The Englishman regarded the military chief. 'Defeat them, and your renown and greatness are secure. Fail and you will forever be despised.'

'I could kill you, stranger.'

'And I would die as easily as any other. But grant me life, and you shall be all-conquering and a worthy successor to the mighty Powhatan.'

He had made his offer. Seconds elapsed, counted in breaths, as the implications were considered. He had seen a flash of jealousy in Opechancanough's eyes at the mention of his overlord. The renegade had chosen well.

'You have a name, pale-skin?'

'I am known as Realm.'

'Leave me.'

Zúñiga was curt in his instruction. The Spanish ambassador was accustomed to obedience from those around him, and the deference of his staff in particular. Besides, he intended to work late on his papers and file a dispatch, to provide his monarch with the latest intelligence.

Matters were too threatening to be left. Every day there were fresh concerns and new information, the drip feed of gossip and chatter from the court and royal council. Jamestown was set to grow like a cancer on the flanks of the Spanish Main. It would corrupt and kill the flow of treasure to Spain. Such things deserved his attention.

In the ambient glow of the oil lamp, he started to write urgently, the tip of his quill scratching against the page. King Philip could depend on him to unearth the truth. Again he exhorted his master to intervene, calling on Madrid to gird itself and send an expedition. For all the soothing words and protestations of Robert Cecil, events could overtake them. Better to be prepared, better to excise the English settlement, avoid a war.

He glanced up at the timepiece and saw its hand had moved on another hour. Cocooned in his study, surrounded by tapestries and other trappings of wealth associated with his position, he could forget the reality of dwelling within a Protestant realm. There on the wall was an image of the Blessed Virgin, and opposite, her crucified son. For the glory of God and Spain he would persevere in his endeavours.

Rising from his desk, he poured claret into a goblet and then unlatched an oak door to reach his private terrace. No one would disturb him here; he was free to clear his head, to breathe the cool Highgate air. It suited him to reside apart from the coal-fogged streets of London; it was better to observe from afar. A high wall and prowling guards ensured the uninvited and unwelcome never got close. He sipped from his glass.

'Do not turn, Don Pedro. If you wish to live.' The voice was low and commanding.

'Speak your business.'

'A wheel lock pistol loaded with three balls and an extra charge is aimed at your back.'

'You are more coward than gentleman.'

'And more murderous than kind.'

Zúñiga swallowed. Caution was advisable and diplomacy essential if he were to avoid being blown apart. He would make no sudden moves.

'Kneel,' the man ordered.

'This is an affront!' Zúñiga cried.

'Do as I say or perish.'

'You will be captured.' Zúñiga lowered himself to the ground. 'It is Spanish territory on which you trespass. It is an insult to the King of Spain.'

'I delight in such a thing.'

Trembling with indignation, Zúñiga croaked, 'Who are you?'

'One who sees you plainly. One who kills the agents of death you send against Christian Hardy.'

There was silence, a pause for reflection. Zúñiga understood that he was dealing with more than a criminal hireling. His tactics had been countered and his security compromised.

'Prince Henry is your master?'

The intruder was not in a convivial mood. 'Open your ears and not your mouth.' He pressed the gun harder into Zúñiga's back. 'Plot against our realm, subvert our interests overseas and you will leave for Spain in your coffin.'

'I am protected by King James.'

'I do not spy his dribbling countenance here, nor that of his gnome, the Earl of Salisbury.'

'Cecil will hear of this.'

A foot toppled Zúñiga onto his front. 'Call off your dogs, or I shall return.'

The intruder slipped away. His message had been delivered. Still Zúñiga lay motionless, his heart beating erratically. It was not the evening he had expected. Yet if the intruder believed he would betray his principles and abandon his actions, he was mistaken.

Martial sounds echoed in the fort as the men honed their drills and their skill at arms. It was Smith who lambasted and encouraged, his shouts loud and exhortations strong, his presence everywhere among the ranks. Their survival and the success of future expeditions might depend on what they remembered here.

'You laggards! You slugs!' the adventurer bellowed at a stumbling squad of settlers. 'You want the savages to pepper you with arrows? You wish the cannibal Pocoughtronack to feast on you beyond the falls?'

Always the falls, the clifftops and cascades upstream that acted as a barrier to the hinterland. To reach the mountains and the promise of an inner sea, the settlers would require nerve and resourcefulness and the ability to fight. Smith was unrelenting.

He tripped a soldier over and wrenched free his musket. 'You deem it some trifle? A toy to be dropped or fumbled with?'

'I will not disappoint you, Captain.'

'A redskin warrior will be less kind than I.' He pulled the man upright and raised the musket high. 'Listen to me, all. In the woods, you carry your gun close. You will use it in combat as firearm, club and shield.'

Across the compound, Christian Hardy too provided instruction. He would leave Smith to the basic soldiering. Here, his students were gentlemen, officers eager to sharpen their fencing skills and acquire the rudiments of Destreza. It was the martial art that had saved him in countless skirmishes, the controlled action and precise movement of blade or tool to annihilate the enemy. The intelligencer was an acknowledged master.

He dodged the thrust of a blunted rapier, brought a stick down hard upon the wrist and a small buckler shield up into the face. His opponent was disarmed.

'Had I struck with force, you would own neither teeth nor face.' He prodded the belly of his rival. 'This mere stick could disembowel you too.'

'I will remember it.'

'Attack from off the line and judge your distance and angle.'

Another pupil had been dispatched and the audience left wondering at Hardy's prowess. A replacement volunteer stepped up, George Percy, a dandy with sickly features and a thin moustache and yet dressed in beribboned finery. Hardy had met many such genteel fops. They were more at home in the long galleries of their English manors than beneath the begrimed canvas of Jamestown.

The intelligencer viewed him. 'I am flattered by your custom.'

'Are you not the best?' Percy gave a courtly bow. 'No text is substitute for practice and experience.'

'Nor will our play now do justice to the feel of a sword tip piercing through ribs into a heart.'

Percy toyed with the pommel of his rapier. 'I believe you are a friend of Sir Walter Raleigh.'

'We shared in many adventures, and I visited him in the Tower.'

'And how fares my brother Henry? I think you know him too.'

'His lordship is in sound humour and keeps his spirits high.'

The news seemed to satisfy the younger sibling of the Earl of Northumberland. While the head of the noble family languished at the pleasure of King James and his servant Robert Cecil, another victim of the aftermath of the great Powder Treason, George sat in self-imposed exile across the ocean.

'I would rather take my chances here than suffer the vagaries of English law,' he said, studying the face of the intelligencer.

'A wise choice.'

'I hope you are right, Mr Hardy. I trust too that I am not disabused when enemy action befalls me.'

'Watch the man and not the weapon; the instinct in his eye and the impulse in his shoulder. Then strike with aggression and not anger.'

'En garde.' Percy raised his blade.

A cry intruded, and the men's attention slid to a confusion of figures running for the gate. Trouble had ignited with the natives present in the camp.

'They steal!'

'I see the thief! Flight proves his guilt!'

'Seize him!'

'There are others. Restrain them all!'

In the rush of bodies, a native slipped from a store shed and attempted his escape. He was hampered by the bundle on his back and his sloping progress between cover. Hardy spied him, but it was Buckler that gave chase, the dog responding to a single command and then speeding to cover the ground. With snarling ferocity he leapt at the Indian, his teeth sinking deep and his weight pitching his prey forward.

Hardy called out. 'Hold him, Buckler.'

The dog needed little encouragement. He prowled about the cowering form, guarding his prize, waiting for his master. Scattered around were the items stolen by the man, the hatchets and tools prized by the natives. There were also weapons.

Hardy stooped to retrieve and unwrap a package bound in cloth. 'A bow? A shooting glove? A skin of arrows?'

The native shook his head, shying from Buckler's growling jaws. 'We are your brothers.'

'No brother would arm himself in secret or take what is not his.'

'I mean no wrong.'

'Yet you go against our laws. We hang men for less.'

'My Weroance will pay you ransom.'

'Your life has little worth.' Hardy frowned, taking in the other skirmishes happening around them. 'It seems you do not act alone.'

'Have we not laboured for your people? We fell trees and clear the land and toil to plant your corn.'

'Corn will scarce feed us if we are dead by your hand.'

'That hand is one of friendship.'

'While the other seeks to plant a blade in our backs.' The intelligencer kicked the native onto his front and knelt to bind his wrists. 'We will show your chiefs that there is reward for good relations and a cost to any treachery.'

John Smith had come to watch the scene. He had also found concealed weapons and now turned a feathered arrow contemplatively in his hands.

'Should we admire their nerve, Christian? Or condemn them for their deceit?'

'They do as they are ordered.'

'So we must delve into their plot.'

Hardy regarded his prisoner. 'Would that more of us were made of such mettle.'

Remote atop the barbican platform, President Ratcliffe surveyed the events below. The Virginia Company had decreed its colony should strive for an understanding with the natives, for that was the key to longevity and wealth. It mattered not. He had long ago decided Jamestown was doomed.

'Bring the first savage to the deck.'

Aboard the pinnace moored close to the fort, the interrogation was about to commence. There were seven captives in all, the vanguard of what might have proved to be a bloody assault. It would be down to Smith to extract a confession and ensure the plans of the enemy were laid bare. Powhatan had expressed a desire for peace, and yet his warriors had infiltrated with foul intent.

Struggling against his captors, an Indian was roped and fastened in position at the mainmast. His interrogator would not be hurried. He appraised the man, letting the minutes lapse and anticipation feed his terror. It took finesse to break these naturals.

He peered close. 'Who sends you? Who bids you do us harm?'

'I shall not give reply.'

'Is it Powhatan? Is it Opechancanough? Is it the chief of your Paspahegh tribe?'

'You seize and settle our land.'

'With a mere few hundred men?' Smith gestured like a lawyer in full cry. 'Is our camp here not a hundred paces wide?'

'It is a trespass and affront.'

'Have we not been kind? Have we not offered goods and trade and a fraternal bond of peace?'

'None may enter Tsenacomoco.'

'Is that so?'

Smith stood back as muskets were raised and levelled towards the captive. At such range, flesh and bone would disintegrate. The native understood. He might already have witnessed the effects of lead shot on the human body in previous raids. Yet his defiance radiated still.

The captain stared. 'Reveal your conspiracy and I shall set you free.'

'I obey no pale-skin.'

'Would you endanger the lives of your brothers?' Smith let the implication hang.

Still there was resistance. Further prisoners were hauled and paraded on deck. Smith had use for them. Each was presented and then taken away, a shot ringing out over the water. A splash followed and then the next victim was called. Blindfold now, and tied at his post, the native was reconsidering.

'We steal hatchets and metal tools for our Weroance,' he said finally.

'Why do you need to become equipped for war?'

'It was commanded.'

'By whom? Who decreed such treachery?'

A pause. 'Powhatan.'

Confession earned the prisoner a reprieve. Only when Smith cut his bindings was the captain's deception revealed and the native confronted by the sight of his companions, who lived and breathed as he did. The adventurer placed an arm about the Indian's shoulders and walked him to the stern.

'We are not brutes or butchers, yet we will slay our foes.' He halted before the heavy frame of a rack and rested a hand on a lever. 'Be thankful I spared you the agonies of this thing.'

'What is it?' The man was curious.

'An instrument of torture, a device so cruel it will break your body and have you screaming for death.'

The native turned his head. 'I will not see it.'

'Take a look.' Smith was insistent. 'We shall civilise and settle with either treaty or force.'

The Indian bolted, leaping overboard and floundering in the water, his head and arms submerging and reappearing in a frantic fight to survive.

'I think he cannot swim.' Hardy appeared alongside Smith. 'Yet I commend his effort.' He shook his head and then dived into the water, letting the man sink before pulling him back to safety. The task was not easy, yet eventually the pair returned, coughing, and sprawled on the deck, the native near unconscious.

'You risk your life, Christian,' Smith observed.

'It is when I am happiest.'

'Maybe you are saved for a higher purpose.' The adventurer pointed to the silver cross on a chain that was revealed around his friend's throat. 'And maybe you should not flaunt a symbol of papist superstition.'

'My father wore it before me and I wear it now.'

Smith shrugged. 'As you wish. Yet it will not win you favour.'

Hardy was unconcerned. The talisman was part of him, as vital as Buckler or his Katzbalger blade. Throughout the Great Siege of Malta his father had worn the crucifix when he manned the ramparts and faced the Ottoman horde; throughout the Armada, the son had done the same when he paced with Drake the deck of the *Revenge*. He would not surrender his past or tremble at his future.

Punitive raids had been mounted and native settlements torched higher up the James River. The English could not afford to show weakness. Yet neither could they survive a full war with the Indians. They needed to tread with care. At least they held captive several hostages. It provided a means to bargain and extract concessions from the adversary and gave respite from harassment and attack. Now a delegation from Powhatan had arrived, and finally there was talk of peace.

At the head of this group was Rawhunt, the wizened Indian elder, a man whose deformity was matched only by his cunning. With him too came beauty: Pocahontas and her companion Awae and a retinue of maidens bearing gifts. Even the military commander Opechancanough sent an archery glove and other tokens of goodwill. Rival tribes could ever reach an understanding.

The boy Edward Battle whittled a stick and viewed the arrival of the old man. 'An ugly sight, is he not? What think you of him, Christian?'

'I perceive a form as twisted as Robert Cecil and a mind just as sharp.'

'I do not know his lordship.'

'Then you are most fortunate.' The intelligencer flipped a dry rusk into the waiting jaws of his dog.

'You have met him?'

'On occasion I have served him.' Hardy kept his gaze on the Indians. 'He is as cold and ruthless as his enemies claim.'

'Yet he guards the King.'

'His first loyalty is to himself. No good will come to any who dare cross or anger him.'

The youth studied him. 'Do you cross him?'

'As much as I am able.'

Hardy nodded to the boy and saw him smile. He was glad of their alliance, yet he had no wish to imperil or ensnare him in a dangerous plot, so he would say nothing more. He moved away, Buckler trailing after him, making for the gate and the woods and small fields beyond. Out here he could breathe; out here he could escape the rivalries and hatred that festered within the settlement. A simple life had much to offer. Ahead Buckler paused, pricked his ears and whimpered.

Awae stood before him, emerging from a habitat of which she seemed to be a part. There was both challenge and coyness in her eye; a shy modesty that was overcome by the deeper instinct to meet. For a moment, the intelligencer did not speak. He appraised her, drinking in this vision of smooth skin and sinuous limbs, her warm and watchful gaze.

'You followed me?'

'Should it anger you, I will go.' She spoke softly.

'Stay, and we may speak.' He kept Buckler at his side. 'Are you not a consort of Powhatan?'

'I am a Kecoughtan, given to him as tribute.'

'Then we must both seek to placate him.'

She smiled. 'You are different from Captain Smith, from Ratcliffe your chieftain, from the other wearers of leg coverings.'

'How so?'

'I know not, yet you stand apart.' She continued to stare. 'You are a warrior?'

'I have fought in many places.'

'Your gods must favour you.'

'Perhaps they have learnt to ignore me. Yet today they bring us together.'

They talked and communed and a connection was made. Then Awae was gone. Hardy remained. He was drawn to the girl, but pitied her the consequences of their meeting. He wanted to protect her, to ward her off, to signal to her the danger. But events had been set in motion.

Late May 1608, and Admiral Newport had steered the *John and Francis* safely back to England. In the hold there was cedar and sassafras aplenty, and barrels full of spoils. Yet there was no gold, no minerals or precious ores to reward the backers of the venture and to silence its critics. The royal council deliberated, the King smiled and the merchants counted their losses. Jamestown was in trouble.

At the home of Robert Cecil in the Strand, a visitor had come calling. He avoided the petitioners and fawning suppliants gathered in the lobby and did not advertise his presence. His audience with the Lord Chancellor was an altogether more discreet affair.

'Do you see what is written?' Cecil pushed a pamphlet across his desk. 'They are the preachings and sermons of Puritans, the opinions of men who would see Jamestown survive.'

Gabriel Archer took and read the paper. As a lawyer, he was accustomed to absorbing detail; as a loyal servant of Cecil returned from Virginia, he was eager to please and to impart his news.

He looked up at his master. 'They are mere words, my lord.'

'Words may sabotage and subvert; may send the highest-born to the scaffold.'

'We have little to fear, my lord. Jamestown teeters at the edge of oblivion and will soon be tipped over by our friend Ratcliffe.'

'He continues our work?'

'With diligence, my lord. Daily he sows discord, fuels dissent and rots the carcass from within.'

'There are those who will resist.'

'John Smith will fall prey to his own bluster and conceit. We near had a noose about his neck, when Admiral Newport spared him.'

'Thus he survives to be a thorn in our flesh.' Cecil took his gaze to the window. 'What of Christian Hardy?'

'Prince Henry will find it hard to guard his back in the woods and fields of Virginia.'

'It would be foolish to dismiss him.'

'I defer to your wisdom, my lord.'

Most did, reflected Cecil. Hope was the enemy, he knew. It could give people false belief and inspire them to endure; encourage them to cling to a position that was hopeless. The longer the notion of Jamestown prevailed, the more it would gather adherents. Protestant evangelicals saw it as a bastion from which to fulfil a sacred duty to civilise the world and rid the savage of his barbarous and pagan ways; parliamentarians viewed the colony as a means to build their power independent of the King. Things could not stand or be left to chance.

He retrieved the pamphlet and placed it with a sheaf of notes. 'We must persist in our endeavour, for I have given a solemn promise this colony will expire.'

'It will run its course, my lord.'

'Pray God it shall be quick.' The Lord Chancellor sat expressionless in his chair for a moment. 'I will spread further rumour of Jamestown dying; persuade settlers and investors to spurn it.'

Cecil turned again to his papers and the interview was done. Outside, hawkers called and carts rolled by. Not so long ago, Guido Fawkes and his fellow plotters had been dragged this way on their journey to the scaffold. He reached for his quill. Neither Prince Henry nor the mercenary Christian Hardy would ever best him.

On 2 June 1608, Captain Francis Nelson took the *Phoenix* to the mouth of the James River and waited on the tide and a fair wind to sail home for England. In attendance, yet on a separate mission, the shallop commanded by John Smith and carrying fifteen men prepared to embark on a voyage across the expanse of Chesapeake Bay. Behind them, Jamestown was once more left to fend for itself.

CHAPTER 5

They swayed and chanted and prayed to their god Okeus that the pale strangers who had settled on their land would perish. Here, at their commander Opechancanough's base in Cinquoteck, there was every reason to have confidence in the deity.

It was the turn of the Imbangala now, the African marauders who acted as Realm's bodyguards. The trio moved slowly and with menace, beating their war clubs on rawhide shields, advancing and retreating to an ancient rhythm. They were masters of pillage and wholesale slaughter. Around them the native Indians watched, transfixed by the sight of the negro bodies and their striking display. That these blackskins were servants of their white master would win Realm grace and time. He would not waste the opportunity.

The Englishman rose and wandered to sit beside a Pamunkey brave chewing on cornbread and observing the dance. Only days before, the warrior had been released from his imprisonment at Jamestown, a consequence of negotiations and ensuing peace. However fragile the accord, it allowed the colonists to cling to hope, and for intelligence to flow back to those that opposed them. Every musket and hogshead of grain within the palisaded compound had been diligently counted.

Realm tore off a hunk of bread for himself. 'I am glad you are freed,' he said.

'Opechancanough commands and I obey.'

'I would expect no other course. Yet the dwellers in the fort have no love or care for your people.'

'They are weak. It is in their eyes and in their grumbling bellies; the graves they are forced to dig, the complaints they raise against their chief.'

'He is not respected?'

'At every moment his men plot and whisper, and every new dawn this Ratcliffe gives them fruitless tasks.'

'They yet have their weapons and their shot.'

'Such things have no use when consternation reigns.'

'Some will fight hard.'

The brave picked at his bread. 'Such things are as nothing against a nation.'

'Is there one among them named Christian Hardy?'

The native paused. 'He has the scars of a warrior and the blue eyes of a demon.'

'A demon he is.'

'It is he who sent his beast to bring me down.'

'You are lucky to live.'

'I know it, for I have seen him instruct many in the art of war.'

'Does he hold rank?'

'I cannot tell.' The brave pondered further. 'He does as he wishes and answers to no one.'

'Then he is indeed as I remember.'

Realm probed for every detail. He wanted to conjure the exact image of Jamestown, to stalk in his mind the figure of Hardy.

Finally satisfied, he left and moved through the village, the stars above him shining bright now and the sounds of pagan ritual pulsing on the warm night air. A man could grow primitive and cruel in such surroundings.

He entered a hut and sensed the scuttling presence of the hostage backing away from his approach. Ensuring obedience was a brutal affair. Yet as the captive had learnt, like his compatriot held in another shelter, pain was the most effective of tutors.

Realm stared into the shadows. 'You were foolish to leave Jamestown, to stray from your own kind.'

'We starved and suffered there.'

'And here?' Realm took a step forward. 'Do you see how you are nothing? Do you grasp the futility of it all?'

'I should never have departed England.'

'You do wrong to trespass in another land.'

'I shall atone, I swear it.' There was trembling in the voice. 'Forgive my sins.'

Realm kept his tone neutral. 'Jamestown rots from within and is destined for oblivion.'

'I fled it for such a reason.'

'Now you will return.'

Stillness prevailed, confusion and fear preying on the prisoner's mind. He could scarcely conceive that a temporary ceasefire between Powhatan and the settlers heralded an exchange of captives.

Realm continued. 'You will go back as commanded, will be embraced once more to Jamestown's breast.'

'Is it not promised to fall?'

'Your aim is to advance such an end.' The renegade let his orders permeate. 'Seek out the man named Christian Hardy and ensure his murder.'

'One death will affect the whole?'

'More than you might hazard. Succeed, and you will earn reward; but fail me and there is only torment.'

It was an argument Realm was happy to drive home. At once he was on the man, beating him hard, hearing his gasping cries. There was an art to inflicting pain. So often he had breathed in the terror of others, savouring the rankness of their sweat, like pigs at the moment of slaughter.

When he was finished, he rose without a word. As he walked out of the hut he thought about what was to happen next. Naturally, Opechancanough preferred Jamestown to endure a while, for it provided a threat that made him indispensable, reinforcing his status. Yet eventually there must be a conclusion. No harm in helping matters along.

Hardy had waited until darkness before slipping from the fort. The truce with the Indians and idleness among the sentries allowed him to clamber undetected down the landward wall. The snores of the gun crew were heavy and the night watch sat smoking their harsh tobacco and speaking quietly of home. Few enjoyed being at the edge of the known world. But there was an element of freedom, too; the chance to prowl in forests unexplored.

He reached the clearing in which the half-completed structure of the presidential quarters lay. It had pretensions to grandeur and no merit as a fortification. Yet it was worthy of inspection. Hardy launched the grapnel and felt the hook catch and the line tauten. Without making a sound, he followed it upward and over the wall. Few guards had either the nerve or stupidity to stay the night here.

The intelligencer landed and crouched low. Instinct had brought him to this place; a curiosity that required feeding. He might discover nothing, or he might find some kind of trove: hidden ledgers or a cache of weapons, evidence of misdeeds.

Entering the shell of the deserted edifice, he took a glowing slow match from a perforated phial and lit the wick of a stub candle. Set within the case of a small pewter lantern, its shrouded beam would cast sufficient light. Exploration could begin. He would not rush. Every loose nail would be examined, every join and corner probed. It had been the same with the great Powder Treason, when his nose and patience carried him to the barrels lodged beneath Parliament. Now, there was once more the hot prickle of expectation.

In an upper chamber he made a discovery, stooping to recover the rosary. Perhaps like his silver crucifix it was nothing; perhaps it was a mere token of things past. He ran the beads through his fingers. People sought comfort in whatever way they could.

'You take what is not yours.' President Ratcliffe spoke from behind the raised barrel of a pistol.

'Did your earlier play not wound you enough?' Hardy indicated the bandaged and disfigured hand.

'I may yet pull the trigger.'

'A move that would betray you.'

'Mistakes arise and accidents occur. The night masks so many things.'

Hardy watched the muscles in the president's face; searched for a flash of decision in the eye. He could not outrun a ball of shot but might yet predict its discharge.

'You are not as you seem, Ratcliffe.'

'Are you?' It was a fair question. 'I suspected we might finish here; trusted you would come.'

'What are you so scared of?' Hardy asked. 'Is it this?' He dangled the rosary.

'Have a care how you speak.'

'Or you will shoot?' The intelligencer exuded calm. 'You will need to slaughter all for the colony to die.' He studied the president. 'Is this your intent? Is this why you stoke indolence and dissent, let the fields go unplanted, waste effort on your palace?'

'You discern conspiracy in everything.' The president squinted along the barrel of his raised gun. 'We reach either impasse or ending, Hardy.'

'It seems you are decided.'

'For my sins, I would concur.'

There was no loud report, no close-range execution. Hardy had moved fast. He parried the weapon and stepped into the arc, disarming and over-powering Ratcliffe in one seamless movement. The president was down. He lay on his stomach, his breathing ragged, his own pistol wrenched hard against his throat. Above him, Hardy pressed a knee between his shoulders and maintained his choking hold.

'A president whose dignity is fled.'

'I cannot breathe,' Ratcliffe mewled.

'Yet you will talk.' Hardy tightened his grip. 'What do you know of me?'

'That Prince Henry pays you.'

'What else besides?'

'You are an intelligencer, a hunter of traitors.'

'Thus you know I may kill.'

'I am president.' The words ended in a strangled hiss.

'You forfeit such honour.' Hardy leant close. 'Who are you?'

'Another who seeks a new life in this place. A man who has pledged to do his duty.'

'To whom?'

'My vow is to serve England.'

'Yet it is Robert Cecil that whispers in your ear.' Hardy brought the pistol butt down onto Ratcliffe's injured hand. 'Isn't it?'

The president screamed and panted. 'We each have our master.'

'Mine is not the devil.'

'It will bring you no good should you kill me.'

'A threat?'

'I know your son is in London, in the employ of the Lord Chancellor.'

'He has no part in our dispute.'

'Word of my demise will soon see him embroiled.'

'Then for the moment I will talk.' The intelligencer pressed harder with his knee. 'Within two months, your presidency is expired. You will not seek to stand again.'

'I take no orders from a villain.'

'Be grateful, for I give you a chance. When Admiral Newport brings resupply, you would be wise to accompany him home.'

'My work is here.'

'Consider it done.'

Hardy thought about his son and the hand of Cecil stretching across the ocean. Small wonder the King relied on him. The intelligencer stood and disarmed the pistol, tucking it into his belt. Below him, the president lay mute. Whether their truce was temporary or permanent, time alone would tell.

'Are we to be cowed? Are we to give up, to abandon our discoveries?'

There had been a storm. To be in a shallop in the midst of a tempest was not for the faint-hearted. They had lost sails and foremast, bailed water for their lives, had huddled without food beneath a tarpaulin and prayed their trials would end. Now Smith stood at the prow and exhorted them to continue.

'Where is your spirit?' He regarded his reluctant crew. 'Where is your desire to strive for glory and claim this land for England?'

'For two weeks we have endured, and this is where it leads.' A soldier pointed to the tattered remnants of sailcloth.

Another intervened. 'He is right. We lost our shirts to patch the canvas; we will lose our lives if we proceed.'

'You are no safer at Jamestown.' Smith braced himself against the coming swell. 'Would you rather die while cowering behind a palisade, or journeying on an adventure?'

'Fifteen men cannot challenge the world.'

'Yet they may acquit themselves with honour. There are rivers to explore and mines to be found and minerals and metals aplenty.'

'We fail to make such discoveries.'

'Do we let things lie? Leave it to the Spaniards? Permit future generations to brand us as fools?'

'What is more foolhardy than tempting fate?'

'Turning our back on chance.'

Pride or greed could overcome much and encourage the weariest onward. Smith nodded. He was certain that the mutinous stirrings were quelled for now and there was every reason to continue. They had crossed the mighty Chesapeake Bay and explored its northern shores; had skirmished and traded, met new tribes and imagined the wilderness tamed. They held the future in their hands.

'The winds rise, Captain.' Anxiety pierced the voice.

Smith peered seaward. 'Shorten sail.'

'We have scant sail.'

The adventurer glanced to the sky and jumped down from his temporary stage. 'Secure yourselves and batten down. A storm approaches fast.'

The men scrambled in their urgency, shouting instructions, aware of the pressing danger. Their voices were already faint below the gusts. The shallop pitched and rolled, useless in the broken peaks, its hull skidding or ploughing without direction. Inlets and shallow waters were its natural home. Now it lay once more before the grinding force of a wider sea.

A wave broached, knocking men from their benches to sprawl on the deck. Above them, the blackened skies erupted and lightning flashed with searing brilliance. Previously the vessel had beached on a tiny islet the men had named Limbo. Here at this moment, they finally encountered hell.

Smith yelled a command that was snatched and carried away. 'Commit yourselves to God! Find peace in the ferment!'

No one could hear his words. The crew were curled despairing on the bare planks, moaning and vomiting and half-immersed by sluicing torrents. Smith crouched among them, a leather pail in hand to bail the stricken craft. He would not abandon hope.

A hand gripped his arm. 'Chance is not, after all, so kind.' There was accusation in the soldier's sickly face.

Smith grunted a response, then bailed and repeated the action without a pause.

The shallop was faring poorly now and in danger of breaking up. Hope and visibility had vanished in the gale. It was Smith alone who persevered, singing psalms or cursing, raging against the weakness of his men. He would not allow them to slip so gently to their graves. Lightning sparked and the storm went on unabated.

At the mouth of the James, the settlers were catching fish. With provisions at the settlement scarce, there was a need for basic sustenance. No one could tell when the next resupply from England would arrive; an increase in numbers at Jamestown meant additional mouths to feed. The harvest had been paltry, and the natives seemed less than obliging in making up the shortfall. They could see the colony was finished.

'Beat the water with oars and drive the fish towards the nets.' Hardy gave the command and the crew obeyed instantly. Even bringing the pinnace downstream had provoked jealousies and suspicion of a planned escape. Ravenous stomachs could poison any mind. Yet the settlers would die without more food, and so the vessel had departed.

Shouldering a crossbow and grasping a rifle and with Buckler at his side, Hardy climbed into the longboat and was ferried ashore. There might be game in the woods he could bring home for the pot.

A shout rang out. 'Christian!'

It was the boy, Edward Battle, scrambling to catch up, abandoning his rod and line on the bank further upstream. Buckler raced to greet him.

'I will accompany you, Christian.' The youth panted for breath. 'It cannot be wise to venture alone.'

'So now you are become my counsellor?'

'I would rather be a friend.'

'That you are, Edward.' Hardy smiled. 'But you need to fish, and I am required to hunt.'

'What if the savages should lie in wait?'

The intelligencer took the boy's arm and gently urged him back. 'I have a musket, a bow, a Katzbalger blade and a watchful hound as sentinel.'

'Be careful, Christian.'

'My luck has held so far.'

He slipped into the woods, leaving the fishing scene and the chatter of his countrymen behind. Within a few paces, the might of England meant nothing. Here, he was the interloper; here, he lived or died at the whim of the native people.

Buckler whined, his ears cocked and nose pointing. He never missed an ambush. Hardy backed against an oak, eased himself around its trunk and peering into the deep shadow cast by the forest canopy. The Indians had been waiting.

He took one down with a rifle shot. The blast momentarily threw the attack, yet the natives soon regrouped. Hardy ran, threading between the trees, hearing the air part and the arrows whistling around him. A stone arrowhead buried itself in the bark to his right. At least his fishing party had fair warning and the chance to get away.

Kneeling, Hardy loaded an ash quarrel into his hunting crossbow and aimed for the torso of a native straining to reach him. The bolt sped and struck, a war club fell and the body dropped. As he drew and fitted a second bolt, Buckler dashed forward to seize an ankle and hold the prey. Hardy took aim. It was an efficient execution. Still the hunting party came.

They had chased him into a clearing, their whooping cries incessant and predicting a kill. Five warriors trained their bows, their strings taut and poised for release. Hardy breathed, calculating the odds, knowing he was out of time. His dog growled, steadfast at his side.

'You surrender to us?'

'I do not.' Hardy felt his skin tighten in anticipation of the death blow. 'A warrior should die in battle.'

'Lay down your weapons, stranger.'

'You have no right to demand it.' The intelligencer stared unblinking at the Indians' spokesman. 'Powhatan decrees we are at peace.'

'We are the Paspahegh, and it is on our land that you settle.'

'You tracked us here?'

'Quarry is less protected when it strays outside its camp.'

Hardy guessed they wanted him alive, to parade as a trophy. He would not oblige. The natives' muscle sinews tensed, waiting for an order, eyes peering from behind the red and white masks of warpaint. They were tiring of conversation.

There was movement, the commotion of more warriors emerging into view. Yet their weapons were levelled not at Hardy, but at the initial group of braves. Awae was at their head.

She gazed scornfully at the Paspahegh. 'What is happening here?'

'He is ours.'

'It is Kecoughtan land on which you tread, a Kecoughtan princess you address.'

'We shall take our prize.'

'You will surrender him, should you wish to live.'

'Our complaint is not with you.'

'Remain and it soon shall be.' She walked to stand beside Hardy. 'You would challenge the authority of Powhatan? Incite conflict between our tribes?'

'We hunt a pale-skin and nothing more.'

'He is under my protection.'

'What is he to you, Awae?' Rage and consternation scarred the voice. 'How will sparing his life bring honour and not shame?'

'Go on your way or face my wrath.'

The stalemate was broken and retreat got under way. As the hunting party melted into the woods, Hardy watched as Awae closed her eyes and shuddered.

'You risked yourself for me,' he said.

'I did as any in my tribe would do.'

'It is deserving of my thanks.' He touched her arm and she turned towards him.

'You bleed,' she said. She reached and examined the flesh wound to his arm.

'A scratch, and nothing more. No chase is complete without some injury.'

'Come, and I will bind it.'

The village was little more than a scattering of shelters, huts formed by branches and draped with reeds and animal skins. Cooking smoke filled the air. Buckler was already befriending every child he met.

In the darkened interior of a home, Hardy and Awae sat. They would not be interrupted. The intelligencer let his fingers glide over her skin, tracing the taut contours and curves and feeling her smoothness and warmth. Reason had no say here, for what mattered was need. They slid together to the rush-strewn floor.

'Aim low, and skim your bullets on the water! Give them rapid volley!'

Obeying the command of Captain Smith, the soldiers on the shallop let fly. The vessel shuddered and the Indians on the shore of the creek dropped their bows and fled.

Smith peered with satisfaction from behind the cover of a cleat. 'I spy blood. Reload and wait for them to parley or attack.'

A soldier replied, 'I doubt we shall see them again.'

'Doubt it not, for they are persistent.'

There were murmurs of agreement, the mutterings of men experienced in the antics of the savage. One river was like any other, and a single tribe liable to vary only in the degree of its hostile intent.

'Onward, boys. We will journey as far as we may.'

The boom swung and the sail tautened as the battered shallop limped unsteadily on its course. On 16 June 1608 it had entered the wide maw of the Potomac, a solitary craft dwarfed by a river mouth seven miles wide. There was every reason to explore. Ahead might lie the inner sea of which the natives spoke and a passage to the Pacific. Find it, and the captain and his fifteen crew would be forever feted.

The miles passed until they glimpsed a gathering of tents, huts and low buildings ahead.

'Potomac town approaches,' a soldier called. 'They send out canoes.'

Keeping their distance, the natives watched from their vessels, a guard of honour of sorts. They would have heard of earlier battles, and perhaps had no wish to become embroiled.

Smith nodded. 'Hold your fire and your nerve. Reason at last informs them.'

'They appear curious.'

'It is the nature of the savage. Yet they will assail us with arrows if we display weakness.'

'Should we not offer a gesture of goodwill?'

'We neither plunder nor kill, and that alone suffices.'

'Perchance peace is what they crave.'

'In due course they shall have it.' The captain applied himself to his notebook. 'Proceed as we planned.'

Marshland and tributaries framed their advance and the course of the river narrowed. Here there were shallow outcrops and rock formations and scree of gleaming white boulders.

'Here endeth our venture.' Smith leapt ashore and clambered up an incline to survey the panorama. 'We must proceed on foot.'

'I believe the natives call this Nacotchtank,' a soldier said.

'One day it shall be something else. Dream, and you will see the vision. Plantations and mansions, streets and statues, a place alive with a parliament and laws.'

'All this you glean from a wilderness, Captain?'

'A wilderness to be tamed, sown and civilised.' He stepped to another rock, certain he had secured for himself and his men a position in the vanguard of history. 'We are unscathed by storm and ambush. Now we seize our destiny.'

Enthusiasm was more scarce behind the Jamestown palisade. Even the delivery of fish from downriver had failed to lift spirits for long, and the return of two hostages from captivity had merely provoked grumbling at the number of bellies to feed. Doubt and hunger stalked the camp. Come the autumn, there would be scant harvest, and the endless wait for resupply from England would challenge both patience and sanity. Survival was precarious.

On a patch of earth beyond the fort, Hardy watched the Spanish tobacco seeds he had planted take root and push up shoots and foliage. Sir Walter Raleigh would delight at such beginnings. It made a change to burying corpses, and proved something could flourish in these hostile lands.

He glanced back at the fort. A thief had been caught stealing supplies and was nailed by his ears to a pillory board. The colony needed to preserve the use of his hands. In a harsh environment, where men struggled and mutiny simmered, cruelty was often the cure. Hardy stayed aloof from the divisions and resentment. His task as watchman demanded a clear and uncluttered view. It would not prevent him meeting Awae, though. She was a link to the interior, to the thoughts and whims of Powhatan and the beating heart of the natives.

CHAPTER 6

'Sound the petard! A vessel approaches.'

As the mortar was fired and the late July evening's lethargy dissolved into frantic action, the battered silhouette of the shallop floated more starkly into view. John Smith had arrived back at Jamestown. There were no rousing cheers or crowding round to question or congratulate. This was a sick colony, a site inhabited by the hungry and diseased and by settlers waiting for salvation. More graves had been dug and filled in Smith's absence. After a journey of almost two months and over five hundred miles, the returning prodigals would not be welcomed with a fatted calf. Whatever their story, they provided little respite.

'I scarce expected Jamestown to survive.' Smith scanned the desolation. 'On consideration,' he added, 'I see it scarce has.'

Hardy stood with him. 'It clings to hope.'

'Yet barely clings to life. Fever, ague, flux; every malady is represented.'

'At least you return, John.'

'That too was sometimes doubtful. At the mouth of the Rappahannock, a stingray struck me with its barb and I thought my agonies a precursor to death.'

'It will take more than a fish to destroy Captain Smith.'

'Other things conspire against us.' The adventurer dropped his voice. 'Ratcliffe?'

'Our president is for the while tamed.'

'I detect your hand in such matters, Christian.'

'Perhaps I persuaded a little.'

'Maintain your guard. I trust neither him nor the aims of his overlord in London.'

'Cecil would kill us both.'

'The more reason to place myself beyond the palisade.'

'You intend another voyage?'

'We cannot civilise without first seeing.'

The friends toured the camp, pausing to speak to the wearied and ill and climbing to inspect the guns. There was nothing here to foster optimism. Outside the cook tent, the thin and enfeebled queued for their evening meal of thin gruel and a piece of rusk.

'Regard them, Christian. I vouch each one regrets setting foot aboard their ship.'

'Sojourn in Virginia never promised to be sweet.'

'Nor was it sold as anything so sour.'

'We endure.'

'For how long?' Smith folded his arms. 'Everywhere there is canker, the rot of disillusionment.'

'Humour may change and dejection vanish.'

'If we do not vanish first. I tell you, Christian: should the Spanish invade or the natives attack again, they will inherit a place of skeletons and ghosts.'

Hardy looked to his dog. 'I confess even Buckler is not himself.'

'And the boy, Edward?'

'I set him to work tending my tobacco.'

'Then we can stuff our pipes, if not our bellies.'

It was news that seemed to cheer the captain. A supply of sweet Spanish leaves would provide a better smoke than the coarse native plants, and add to the crops to spread across the land. Smith possessed the instinct of a colonist and the eye of a planter. He whistled and beckoned to a settler. 'You are one of the pair fresh released from the clutches of the savage?'

'I am, sir.'

'How think you on your new surroundings?'

'My place is here, whatever our condition.'

'A laudable sentiment.' Smith gave him an encouraging smile. 'I thought the same when I too was held captive.'

'You set an example for us all, sir.'

'You have a name?'

'It is Stone.' His eyes flickered to Hardy and back again.

'I shall not keep you, Stone. Yet we share experience, and a fraternal bond that should be cherished.'

'I value it, sir.'

The man went on his way, eager to avoid conversation and to mingle with his kind. Hardy observed the retreating figure. There was an awkwardness to Stone, an unwillingness to engage born from diffidence or fear.

Smith made for the main gate. 'I count on you to keep Ratcliffe at bay, Christian.'

'His tenure expires in under fifty days.'

'He may yet cause trouble.'

'Be sure I will counter it.' Hardy was confident. 'Come the tenth of September, it will be you who is named president.'

'Amen, and a hearty prayer for it. Jamestown must be steered from its decline.' Smith smiled. 'Things will change, Christian. Greater purpose, a strengthened fort, settlers and soldiers more able to fight.'

'Not a moment too soon, John. But what of your journeying?'

'There is no reason to pause and every reason to proceed. A few days hence, I will take the shallop north once more across Chesapeake Bay and see what I may find. I shall return by September.'

'Cultivate the foes of Powhatan, for they might prove their worth.'

'I have in mind the Massawomeck. They are Iroquois, savage raiders that strike by canoe and journey by river from their great northern lakes.'

'Like us, Powhatan is himself encircled.'

'He will thus lash out at the weakest.'

It boded ill for the English.

Smith and Hardy watched as another litter bearing a corpse headed for the graveyard.

Little wonder Smith had gone again so soon after his arrival. Ratcliffe stood at the waterfront and savoured the moment as the shallop caught the breeze and manoeuvred away. Losing a rival was no bad thing. It meant fewer distractions and thirteen absentees who would not interfere in his plans.

'Breathe it deep.' He spoke to the lieutenant beside him, gesturing towards the camp. 'There is nothing quite like the stench of despair.'

'I pity those who suffer.'

'Sentiment is not your task. Nor will it earn you a reward.'

'I cannot help but feel for the wretches in this place.'

'Most were as wretched in England.'

'There they had fuller bellies and no savages to slit their throats.'

'Yet each volunteered for the journey.' Ratcliffe calmly perused the scene. 'I will not weep for the damned.'

They strolled awhile, ignoring the glazed and accusing stares. With the truce with Powhatan holding and local hostilities abated, responsibility for undermining the colony rested with its president.

The lieutenant idly scanned the palisade. 'Do you ask for another blaze? Provocation of the Paspahegh?'

'Both may be required. Then it will take but a nudge to topple Jamestown into the void.'

'Admiral Newport will return soon with fresh recruits.'

'Their fate will be as dismal as for any gathered here.'

'Christian Hardy?'

'Rarely does one man alter destiny. Rarely do my adversaries outwit poison or a blade.'

'He is resourceful.'

'Mortal, nevertheless.' Ratcliffe shaded his eyes against the sun. 'He will not impede my purpose.'

Daily and piece by piece, the foundations and future of the colony decayed. It was the symbol of a proxy war, an unseen battlefront between King James and Robert Cecil and Prince Henry; between the established church and those who would oppose it. Always, too, in the shadows was Spain.

Out on the northern reaches of Chesapeake Bay, Smith and his dozen crew members were engaged in friendly diplomacy with the Tockwogh. There had indeed been an encounter with the Massawomeck, the fearsome marauders appearing in their canoes and then paddling out to inspect the strange craft standing offshore. Yet these shaven-headed warriors had kept their distance, wary of the muskets trained upon them. Soon they had disappeared entirely, and the English could breathe again, dismantling their facade of tarpaulins and guns that had created an illusion of strength.

'The heavens declare the majesty of God, and the skies proclaim the work of His hands.'

Psalms and prayers were part of the campaign. Smith raised his hand and addressed the Tockwogh chiefs. Their people had suffered, and hid in fear now behind their trellis palisades, at the mercy of the Massawomeck tribe. Now their leaders and their Iroquoian-speaking allies, the Sasquesahanock, had come to greet and befriend, to smoke pipes and give praise to the visiting pale-skins. Already an English physician had treated their wounds and tended their sick. Cordiality was assured.

A heap of gifts had been presented at Smith's feet and a prized bearskin draped across his shoulders.

Smith gazed upon his hosts. 'Though we seem few, we are mighty. Your friends will forever be as kin.'

The reply came. 'Protect us from the Massawomeck, for they raid and take at will.' It was a Sasquesahanock elder who responded, his tall, muscular braves standing at his shoulder. His eyes were bright and his tone defiant, his words translated by a Tockwogh into the Powhatan tongue.

'Already we have met them and they shrank from the encounter. See here my sword.' Smith drew his blade and held it aloft. 'No foe is a match for it. No foe may outrun the fire and death we can unleash.'

'We shall serve you as Weroance.'

'I will repay with kindness your loyalty and trust.'

'Will you fight the Massawomeck?'

'When such a time is right.' The captain lowered his sword. 'Tell me of them: of their lands, the place from which they journey.'

'They are of our people and yet not of us. Their desire is to enslave and kill. To this end they travel far, heading south from their great saltwater lakes and bringing hundreds of their warriors by canoe.'

'You resist them with success.'

'Courage and vigilance hold them for the while. Yet they are emboldened, and are driven to attack as their season or mood decree.'

'What else do you know of these lakes? Are they an inner sea, a confluence of rivers that carve a passage to the west?'

The aged native shook his head. 'My tribe busies itself with defence and stays within its own territory. There is rumour, though, of other pale-skins, a host of ships brought by the wind and disgorging men to trade and settle and claim land.'

Other pale-skins? Smith exchanged glances with a senior member of his company. Whether Spanish or French, there could be little doubt that European rivals were sending missions to lay claim to this unexplored continent. All the more reason for the English to stand fast; all the more reason to fear too. Much depended on that tiny stockade built in a Virginian swamp.

Smith regarded his men and spoke quietly to them. 'Thirteen of us and a shallop. And against us, the papist legions of Rome.'

'Did Howard and Drake not shatter the Armada?' the soldier said.

'Our ships were well-armed, our captains close to the homeland they defended.' The adventurer rested his hands on the pommel of his sword. 'Our fight is more isolated and hidden from view.'

The natives again came forward, bowing and clapping and stamping their feet. They had found their guardian and intended to appease him. Smith was stoic in the face of such affection. He allowed their fingers to caress his face and neck and place more beads about his throat. There were advantages to being a deity. Soon he would ask his men to form up, to fire a departing fusillade in salute and then sail for new inlets and rivers. Mapping the landscape and naming its features gave both a sense of purpose and of permanence. Zeal would overcome the travails of Jamestown. Whatever it took.

'You must drink, Edward.'

The boy was burning to the touch, his torso rank with sweat and his eyes unfocused, his breath light as he panted. It was the early hours, and still Hardy sat with him. He would not leave until death came or the fever broke. On occasion he mopped Edward's face and body and whispered soothing words; he held his hand as the boy spasmed or cried out in delirium. A piteous sight. At the foot of the cot, Buckler lay with a watchful eye, his muzzle resting on his paws.

Awae entered the tent and lit another candle. She had brought local herbs and medicines and helped to tend the patient. The boy was a trusty of John Smith, who was in turn revered by her mistress Pocahontas.

A good deed was demanded. Besides, Christian Hardy cared for the suffering youth, and that alone merited her calm and quiet presence.

'You have fight in you yet.' The intelligencer dribbled water from a sponge onto the boy's lips. 'Do not disappoint me.'

'I would not wish it.' The voice was faint.

'I have kept vigil too long to see you submit, and will tend you until you are cured. Slacken in your effort and I will summon Mr Russell.'

Humour glimmered briefly in Edward's eyes. 'Spare me the physician and I promise to obey.'

Hardy stood to let the youngster rest. Experience had taught him that fate betrayed fondness and death was ever perverse. Yet he would do what he could, would guard this boy like a father.

The boy began to choke and he moved back swiftly, cradling him in his arms. 'I am here, Edward.' The struggle seemed unequal. Hardy felt the gossamer breath that signalled a life almost spent.

Between gasps, a trembling plea. 'Do not let me die, Christian.'

'You have my word.' Hardy held the body close. 'As I live, you will too. Speak loud your wish.'

'I want to survive.'

'Again, with gusto.' The intelligencer heard the weakened shout emerge and fade. 'Then it is settled.'

Sleep enveloped the boy once more. Awae would take the next watch. She kissed Hardy as he rose. There was sweetness and compassion there, a fierce desire to nurse the youngster back to health. He was grateful for her presence.

Stepping from the tent, he let the warm night air soak his skin, washing away the sour-sweet stench of camphor and disease. In the darkness beyond, a tobacco pipe glowed and wafted its harsh scent towards his nostrils.

'Another who finds no rest.' Hardy approached and murmured a greeting to the settler, who stood alone, smoking. 'We have all dwelt in finer abodes.'

'And none as sparse as this.'

Hardy sniffed the man's pipe. 'Already King James condemns the noxious weed. He would have scant patience for this.'

'It is fortunate then that he keeps his distance.'

'Yet he has his servants.'

'So long as they let me drink my share of smoke, I cannot complain.'

Hardy was in accord. 'A man must have his comforts.'

'You too favour a native strain.' There was an edge of sarcasm to the voice.

'Our task is to conjure understanding with the locals.'

'A trick you well perform.'

The intelligencer had recognised the man; he was one of the hostages returned from sojourn with the Indians. Perhaps he was embittered at his repatriation, or still grappled with the demons unleashed by his imprisonment. A captive could suffer torment without visible scars.

'You are pleased to be back among us?'

'I give thanks to be alive.'

'Tell me of Opechancanough.'

There was hesitation, the same nervousness Hardy had witnessed before.

He tried again. 'Were there things you saw? Matters affecting the future of Jamestown?'

'You trust we have a future?' The retort was spat out with anger.

'I believe we shall try, will give it our best endeavour.'

'If it should not suffice?'

'We take our chances and pray to God.'

The conversation ended and the settler withdrew to nurse his thoughts and grievances. Tobacco smoke trailed after him. Insomnia affected many in the camp, for their situation scarce promoted peace of mind. Hardy would continue to patrol tonight, watching and listening for discordant rhythms.

Hours later a hand touched his arm. It was Awae, summoning him to the sickbed. He hastened back, quelling his grief, intending to murmur a prayer above the corpse. Loss was nothing unusual here. But the boy was awake, his fever passed and the light restored to his eyes. Hardy nodded. Hope was not vanished from Jamestown.

Sorcery was afoot. Smith crouched low in the deck well of the shallop and peered from behind the cover of the shields lashed along its length. His little floating fortress had never seemed so vulnerable. Here on the

Rappahannock River, the diplomacy and charm that earlier had born such fruit now appeared to count for little. His summer encounter with a stingray barb close to the entrance of this very waterway was plainly some kind of harbinger.

'See, Captain,' a crewman whispered at his side. 'It is the bushes which are full of magic.'

'Or instead are filled with savages.'

The captain maintained his gaze. He had underestimated the animal cunning of the natives, had been wrong to hope that all would give welcome. Not everyone wished to place a ceremonial bearskin about his shoulders. Along white clay banks framed with sedge and reeds, the vegetation was lush and unthreatening. Yet in the boat, the Indian guide had thrown himself flat in expectation of an ambush. Smith knew from whom to take his cue.

He nodded to the prone man. 'He is not alone in discerning treachery and trap.'

'Shall we fire?'

'We keep low and silent.' Smith squinted, trying to penetrate the foliage. 'Any moment it will come.'

'It does no harm to show our mettle.'

'Nor to learn the art of patience.' Smith nudged the cowering guide with his foot. 'Why so shy, Mosco?'

The man spoke face down. 'These people are no friends.'

'Experience teaches me such.'

Only through skill at arms and frantic oarsmanship had they extricated themselves from a violent incident several miles behind. A native hostage had been shot and an English soldier pulled to safety as arrows fell thick around them. Bruising episodes were the norm.

'Captain!'

As the arrows flew, Smith responded. 'You have your targets, so volley now.'

His men obeyed, their barrage opening up in fiery unison and shrouding the vessel in smoke. As the shallop glided on, the warriors emerged by the riverbank in a camouflage of leaves and branches to dance and chant defiance.

'Mr Featherstone is hit, Captain.'

So he was. He lay groaning on his side, a gentleman draining blood and colour, an arrow protruding from his chest. The sucking sound suggested he would not live long.

'Cover him and do as you must.' Smith surveyed the scene. 'Would that these savages presented gifts instead of arrowheads.'

Stopping by an island in the river, they dug a grave and with prayers and a gun salute buried the corpse. Featherstone had been a valiant soul. His resting place was marked with a cross.

Proceeding on, they reached the navigable extreme of their venture, alighting to explore the terrain and collect samples of herbs and rocks.

A shout raised the alarm. 'In the trees! Savages!'

Balancing on branches and leaping unhindered between the trees, a hundred warriors loosed their arrows as the crew fell back to the shallop. Even muskets could not stay the fury of this assault.

'Retire, quick! They will outflank us!'

'We have no time to reload!'

'Take cover where you may!'

Confusion and cursing accompanied the retreat, the English sheltering beneath the covering arrow fire of their guide. He at last had found his moment. Dispatching a projectile, he then drew a second shaft from his quiver as a victim tumbled from a tree.

The battle died down and quiet prevailed once more, interrupted only by the occasional scream and whimper of a wounded Indian captive being beaten. The guide Mosco had his reward.

'You bait him enough, Mosco,' Smith called. 'He is of more use alive than dead.'

'I will play awhile.' The native twisted the arrow jutting from the thigh of the injured man. 'Listen how he sings.'

'I would prefer to hear his wisdom.' The adventurer strode over to address the prisoner. 'Tell me why you attack?'

'Because you come from the world below to steal the world about me.'

Smith laughed. 'Is that so?'

'Our duty is to defend our lands.'

'While mine is to bring order and brotherhood.' Smith looked down at the battered and shivering form. 'No further harm will befall you.'

'Your mercy is kind.'

'My wrath worse when I encounter betrayal. Now let us bear you to the boat and dress your wounds. We will talk a little further.'

At nightfall, the prisoner was released and the shallop cast off to head downstream. Smith had learnt much but had outstayed his time beyond the Jamestown palisade. Strangely, he looked forward to resuming his familiar pattern of existence and encountering again the vexed issues of peace and war with Powhatan. Soon, though, around the vessel came a soft patter as of rain. It was the sound of arrows dropping onto the water.

'You have your orders.'

By the light of a single lantern, President Ratcliffe regarded his loyal band of underlings. All were carefully selected and understood their mission. They were men who chafed at their sorry circumstances in Virginia; men who yearned to return home across the sea. He alone offered a solution.

'A desperate malady requires a desperate and unkind cure.' His tone was low and measured. 'By night's end, Jamestown will have no harvest.'

'Our fellow settlers will not thank us,' one man replied.

'They will scarce suspect. It is the natives they will blame and God against whom they will rail. And you will be rewarded with your own supplies.'

'If we are discovered?'

'Ensure that you are not.' Ratcliffe scanned the shaded faces. 'Neither word nor alarm must reach the camp. You carry blades, so use them if you must.'

'You ask us to murder?'

'I ask you to do whatever it takes.'

Another settler ventured to speak. 'You may depend on us.'

Not a grain of corn would survive their labours. Without bread, Jamestown could never be sustained, while its plight would infect opinion back in London. Investors would run for cover. King James enjoyed his games of chess, and Robert Cecil expected much. It was unwise to disappoint such a man. There was always the threat, the pliers and maiming gauntlets, the rack. Ratcliffe buried such thoughts. For the present he still commanded, and would yet bring catastrophe.

Each element was in place and every sentry vetted. There would be no cry or challenge; a sleeping draught of local herbs had been added to the paltry evening meal. Yet it was hardly needed, for weakness and sickness prevailed and most kept to themselves.

The group divided and sloped in silence from the fort.

Close to the fields, they met again and readied for their task, moving to their stations. With shuttered lamps and scythes they set to their exertions. Even a few ragged strips of planting presented a formidable challenge.

'We have you marked.' It was the voice of Christian Hardy that rang out in the darkness. 'Throw down your tools and weapons. Resist and you will die.'

One man bolted and was brought roughly to the ground. His fellows were more pliant, their blades thudding to the earth. His Katzbalger drawn and a pistol leant against his shoulder, the intelligencer walked among them.

'What a crop we harvest.' He paused before the squad leader. 'I knew such an eve would come.'

'I will not answer to you.'

'Am I too unmannered? Too free with my threats?'

'This is no concern of yours.'

'Sabotage and treachery are ever my concern.' Hardy lowered his pistol and pressed its muzzle to the man's forehead. 'Obstinacy will see a single lead ball shatter your skull to pieces.'

'What do you seek?'

'Give me the name of he who sends you.'

The trembling confession. 'Ratcliffe.'

Hardy had his evidence.

His old adversary had not lost his instincts, Realm mused from the shadows. It was no surprise. Over many years and several encounters, the intelligencer had always proved himself adept. A pity his severed head would one day end up in a bag to be dropped at the feet of Prince Henry. That should teach the young heir to the English throne not to back a lost cause or meddle overseas.

How well conceived the ambush had been. Realm envied Hardy his performance. He stayed under cover, masked by the night and the undergrowth, as the lights flickered and faded and the commotion headed back to camp. What a sad and benighted place Jamestown was! Doubtless some would try to save it; maybe Hardy would enjoy the occasional success. Yet the orders from Madrid were clear. There would be no deviation from the intended outcome.

CHAPTER 7

'I owe you much, Christian.'

President John Smith, the new incumbent, stood with Hardy and surveyed his small domain. September had brought changes. With Ratcliffe imprisoned aboard the pinnace for his mutiny and subversion, hope was in the ascendant. Already the palace in the woods was being dismantled and its timbers redirected into a strengthened palisade; already George Percy was travelling the length of the James in the shallop to trade for bushels of corn.

'Regard them.' Smith almost beamed. 'They have belief and purpose now. It is worth a thousand ships of grain.'

'Your expeditions have inspired them.'

'Nothing I did would have counted had you not ensnared Ratcliffe.'

The newly strengthened fort would be ready within weeks, and would present the most formidable of barriers. Even an armed Spanish flotilla would find it difficult to uproot, confronted by earth berms and ramparts and overlapping arcs of fire dominated by heavy cannon. Attacking waves of natives simply stood no chance.

'Now for the saker.' Smith pointed with relish at the light shrapnel cannon being hoisted onto its mount. 'It has proved an excellent companion.'

'You choose your friends with care, John.'

'Am I not alive because of it?'

From across the compound, the boy Edward Battle waved. He had survived the ordeal of his illness. Others too were convalescing, emerging from their sickbeds to sit dazed in the sunlight, or to shuffle feebly on some errand. It would take a while for the camp to recover fully.

'Our darkness is past, Christian. I feel it.'

'My caution yet remains.'

'I expect it of your kind.' Smith gave an expansive gesture. 'But see how we endure, how we pull back from the brink. Even as we speak, our men train and practise their skills.'

'I will not fault their diligence, nor you your capacity to berate them.'

Smith laughed. 'Better that I am at their backs than a native lodge an arrow between their shoulders.'

'It's good we are at peace.'

'It brings forth much fruit.' Smith indicated Pocahontas and her entourage. 'The Indians return to us, and I do not complain.'

A few of the natives helped to carry planks from the disassembled palace to carpenters working on the storerooms and church. Darting from her group, Pocahontas ran to embrace the president. There was no need for ceremony. She had saved his life by pleading with her father, and was in thrall to the gruff explorer that had strayed into their midst. Powhatan might wax and wane in his opinion of the newcomers, but his young offspring had scant doubt. She hugged Smith and then lay her head against his chest.

He stroked her hair and, looking up, addressed Hardy. 'Rarely are my own fellows so pliant or so obedient.'

'She has not encountered their trials and privations.'

'I pray to God she never does.' The adventurer kissed her forehead lightly. 'Though she is a savage, I would protect her as my own.'

'Beware the vicious parent of that playful cub.'

'I forget neither her father nor the nature of her tribe.'

'They are a mercurial race.'

Pocahontas smiled up at the two men and spoke in her own tongue. 'Of what do you speak?'

Smith pressed her close and switched to the Algonquian language. 'How we delight in the love of your people. I prefer to trade bread than arrows with your father.'

'He also is eager for peace.'

'When my own chief, the Admiral Newport, returns on his mighty ship, he will once again bestow fine things on the great Powhatan.'

'Is your emperor back in England as powerful as my father?'

'Only his god commands more armies.'

'Where does he dwell?'

'In vast palaces and forts of stone. Stand on a mountain and still you will not spy the extent of his lands.'

'Are there many deer?'

'Too numerous to count.' Smith held her at arm's length and looked into her eyes. 'One day, I swear, you shall see it for yourself.'

Her face filled with happiness. 'I will?'

'A princess may go where she chooses, and has the right to meet her kin.'

'I would wish to explore like you.'

'Our nation would give you welcome.'

They watched as Pocahontas raced to share the news, Buckler dancing attendance. Pawn or princess, a diplomatic tool of the natives or of the English, she was a symbol of warming relations. Her companion Awae had a different role. Hardy felt the light touch of her gaze now from the other side of the camp and returned it. Longing needed no words.

He turned to Smith. 'Spirits do revive, John, but some still harbour resentment.'

'At least they lose their champion.'

Summoned by a shout, the president strode for the gates. On the ground beyond the palisade – now dubbed Smithfield in jest – a company of settlers were conducting military drills and stood drawn up for inspection. Hardy stayed behind. He pulled from the pocket of his canvas jerkin a carved and polished stone he had found hidden in his bedding. It was a hex, a thing of witchcraft, a black curse placed upon his head. There had been truth in his words to Smith. Some of the colonists were still bitter; any number might wish him dead.

Salvation had many guises. Hardy stood in his hidden plantation of Spanish tobacco and fingered the dry and yellowing leaves. The plants were ready for harvesting. With just a few seeds he had created future revenue, a crop that could become a staple and transform the future of Virginia. One day, the monopoly of Spain could be shattered; one day, the coffers of King Philip would sound hollow. He bent to inhale the aroma. It was the smell of victory over Madrid.

Through the woods came the fragmented hollers of men labouring to fell trees. The development at Jamestown encouraged an insatiable demand for wood. Besides, there was a ready market in Europe, ever a need for oak and cedar and sassafras. Every colonist who was not sick had a duty to contribute.

The intelligencer approached the group and hefted a piece of lumber on his shoulder. 'Tell me when you tire,' he said. 'I will lend my hand to axe or saw.'

'Would you not rather the company of gentlemen?'

'I find their table a little bare.'

With aching backs and blistered palms they toiled, their rhythm interrupted only by the occasional warning cry and the creak and crash of timber. It permitted them all to begin to believe in the permanence of their home.

Another trunk descended and Hardy moved to dismember it. A woodsman gripped the opposing handle of the blade.

'You have the strength of three of us, sir.'

'Did you think me some courtly gallant? A perfumed fop untrained in any skill?'

'Your sword and scars tell a different tale.'

He positioned the saw and then let it run forward. 'Few of us discard our past.'

'They say you served with Drake.'

'I did. There is scarce a night when I do not dream I still stand with him on the deck of the *Revenge*.'

'Lesser mortals seem to populate these parts.'

'They may yet achieve greatness.'

'Perhaps so.' A shrug. 'If they ever pause in their bickering and spite.'

'Be hopeful.'

'Ignorance is my friend, sir.' The woodsman pushed the steel teeth back through the wood. 'Did you meet Elizabeth, our Virgin Queen?'

'Her teeth were rotten and her breath foul.'

'But how she shielded us from the Spaniard! I know each word of her speech at Tilbury.'

Gloriana had indeed defended them, and summoned her nation to arms. None could compare. In her armour and mounted on a white steed, she had addressed her army as they awaited invasion. Hardy had been present. It was here he had given chase to the lurking assassin, cornering the renegade Realm and then duelling with him through the royal kitchens.

The woodsman wiped his brow. 'You recall the moment, sir?'

'They were heroic times.'

'And these?' The fellow spat in the earth. 'She would not have spurned us or turned her back on our adventure.'

'I grant you, our wood fort is not well beloved by her successor.'

'What would a Scot know of English destiny?'

What would a woodsman comprehend of the forces that conspired against him? Ratcliffe might be detained, yet there would be others labouring to undermine the settlement still. The Lord Chancellor was meticulous in his scheming.

Hardy applied himself to his task. They split logs and stacked, dragged and carried, the sun eventually dipping below the horizon.

Lifting another load, Hardy led a party through the trees. This simple life could be enticing. Reaching the collection site, he set down his burden and paused to catch his breath. There was a loneliness to the place, the feel of a borderland in which an ambush might occur. He listened, and then the stale odour of native tobacco wafted to his nostrils.

Swivelling and manoeuvring to the side, he drew his stabbing sword and lunged. The Katzbalger went in true. As he perished, the expression of his assailant did not change, the intensity of concentration frozen by the sudden impact of the blade.

Hardy lowered the corpse to the ground and patted it down, searching for evidence. Everyone carried their history in the detritus they left, and someone had commanded this deed.

Walking back towards the camp, he noted the settlers' stares as they stopped to view his progress. For certain it was the severed head he dangled at his side that caught their attention. There was method in his violence. He marched on, bearing his trophy, sensing the shock of his approach pulse outward through the fort.

He found the man he was looking for: Stone. 'Meet again your friend,' he said. He placed the head upon a stump. 'He acquired poor habits while in the company of the natives.'

'It is no concern of mine.'

'You quake as though it were.'

'I am not accustomed to such sights.'

'How well acquainted are you with treason?' Hardy rested his hand on top of the bleeding head. 'What strange encounters did you have as hostage of the redskins?'

It provoked the response he had expected, Stone choosing flight over explanation. The attempt was short-lived. Two men tore after him, then, pinning him by the arms, held him before his judge.

'Some would claim your guilt is proven.' Hardy gave no quarter.

'I swear I am innocent of all crime.'

'Yet you try to run.'

'On the holy book, I mean you no harm.'

'There is a darker purpose at work.' The intelligencer pulled the fragment of black glass from the man's pocket and raised it. 'You know what this is?'

'I cannot say.' His eyes betrayed complicity.

'Denial will only beget suffering. Tell me of the renegade, the Englishman you met.'

The settler stared about him. 'You are deceived.'

'Obsidian does not lie.'

Realm had intended to be discovered. The obsidian was his gift, his salutation, his encrypted message. What once had been used by the Aztecs as a fighting edge had become his signature weapon. With obsidian blades he had left his mark, cutting a swathe and killing at will. The man who had voyaged with the Armada to attempt the murder of Queen Elizabeth, who had abetted the regicidal plotters of the great Powder Treason against King James was back. For a moment Hardy let his thoughts drift again to that house off Fetter Lane in which he had discovered the butchered body of his wife. All pain and reckoning led to Realm.

Hardy turned the sliver in his palm. 'I wait.'

In halting words, admission came. 'He was there.' Stone swallowed. 'A creature as cold as death.'

'He bid you kill me?'

'I had no choice but to agree.'

'Such a pact will see you punished.' The intelligencer held the captive in his gaze.

There would be time for further questioning. Whatever Realm planned, he had surely anticipated Hardy would survive his opening move. That was his sport and pleasure. Kings and princes and native chiefs might vie for power and land, but it was a simple contest between two rivals that unfolded now. Hardy was happy to oblige.

'Watch well and heed.'

Realm addressed the natives as his trio of black Imbangala displayed their martial skills. He had furnished each warrior with a buckler shield and steel sword. They would be trained to become the vanguard of his mission.

At his side, Opechancanough looked on. The military chief suffered the presence of the renegade for a reason. He would benefit from a personal bodyguard equipped to wage war against any who might oppose him. Even the all-powerful Powhatan could one day receive a blade across his throat. The pale-skin too might go to his ancestors, should he antagonise or disappoint.

'Few things will stand against such weapons,' the chief said.

'You have seen bone cleaved and antlers shattered. No further proof is needed.'

Opechancanough considered. 'Yet our arrows and bows rain death quicker than any musket.'

Realm studied the impassive face. 'Each tool will have its place. Remember how John Smith voyaged around the bay and confronted warlike tribes with but a handful of men.'

'It is why Powhatan agrees truce with the pale-skins. He fears their wrath and what they might do.'

'And you, Opechancanough?'

'I fear no one.' It was a statement of fact.

'There will come a reckoning, a time when the settlers are betrayed by their conceit and devoured by their own greed.'

'We shall be ready.'

'Scarce will they have breath to call out before they are overrun.' Realm looked back at the drill in progress. 'Today we stand here at your home of Cinquoteck. Tomorrow, even the capital of Powhatan at Werowocomoco will owe you its loyalty.'

'Our god Okeus may choose for me a different fate.'

'Does he not favour the bold?'

'He also rewards the cunning.' Opechancanough turned his gaze to the distance. 'You know their thoughts. Tell me what these settlers intend.'

'To lull and deceive and make false promises. To flatter and pledge their fraternal love.'

'I am not persuaded.'

'Nor should you be, Opechancanough. For in spite of their protestations, conquest is their aim. When the season is right, new ships will bring supply and more fields will be sown. The number of the enemy will grow by the day.'

'Sickness and starvation will take their toll.'

'Sufficient to stem the tide?' Realm shook his head. 'Theirs is a race with cause and greater purpose. It has proved itself resilient.'

'You forget we too have warriors that I may summon from every quarter of Tsenacomoco.'

'I am a servant to them as I am to you.'

The military chief swivelled to peer into Realm's eyes. 'What persuades you to this path?'

'Hatred of an enemy tribe.' Realm could see that he was understood. 'Their king is a thorn to mine. His chiefs and captains battle with us around the world.'

'This is why you chase them here?'

'Let a wound infect, and it will kill the whole.'

Before them, the braves sparred and tumbled to the command of the Africans. The Imbangala were not gentle in their instruction. Occasionally a whip descended or a foot thudded into a ribcage. Those who spent their lives capturing slaves were by nature impatient. Yet their pupils appeared to be learning.

A fracas broke out, a native resisting his punishment and pushing back against the stranger. Within seconds, the Imbangala had unhooked his club and brought it down hard to shatter the native's skull. The beating continued until the corpse was pulped.

Opechancanough spoke. 'He kills one of my braves.'

'Misfortunes do arise.'

'It is dishonour and insult when there is no redress.'

'What do you ask?'

'Blood for blood.'

'Should we not parley and confer?'

'The decision is already made.'

A gesture was demanded. It was of no consequence to Realm. Anything to keep the peace.

Drawing his sword, the renegade stepped among the assembled and walked through the silence towards the lone Imbangala. His imminent demise appeared not to trouble the African. He had already been deserted by his comrades. He stood unblinking, staring at Realm's measured approach.

Realm did not speak. Eulogies were for those who mattered. He studied the man's face for an instant. There was a certain nobility there, a life force hidden deep within. A pity to lose such an asset. He struck hard and felt the trembling on the blade, the body dropping down, soundless. Stooping over, the Englishman cut into the corpse, prized wide the ribs and reached in to cut free the heart. With little ceremony, he cast the organ aside and then turned to rejoin his host.

To the casual eye he was just another horseman, a rider on errand travelling across the meadow and heathland from Highgate and heading into London. Anonymity suited his trade. His master was the Spanish ambassador, and his mission, to bear coded messages to a plethora of espionage contacts and middlemen throughout the realm of England.

Don Pedro was adroit at avoiding the conventional diplomatic channels. In an atmosphere of surveillance and mistrust, tradecraft was ever required. At his side, the courier wore a sword and dagger and, concealed beneath his jacket, a loaded pistol hung. An opponent would not find him easy prey.

He trotted his mount on, veering east towards the squalid tenements of St Giles. It was a place on the margins, a grimed world of taverns and brothels that teemed with criminality. The perfect location for rendezvous.

There was time to kill. Threading his way through the labyrinth, the Spaniard dismounted in a courtyard and flipped a coin to the bored stable hand. He climbed the stairs and stepped inside.

'Welcome again to our house, sir.'

The woman's bad teeth and pocked skin did not diminish the warmth of her greeting. Her clients paid well and often returned. They expected the best of her girls. Even the occasional act of sadistic murder could be forgiven for a fee.

'She is here?' the Spaniard grunted.

'As pleasing as ever, and eager to serve you.' She smiled and gestured towards the staircase. 'I will send wine and dainties to your room.'

'A second girl, too, and then leave us in peace.'

'Whatever you desire, sir.'

No embassy official could discover his pastime. While men were allowed their recreation, Don Pedro de Zúñiga would flay him alive or return him to Madrid in disgrace should this breach of protocol ever become known. Such worries could be dismissed for the present. May his sins be forgiven.

Wine had flowed and clothes were discarded and the revelries had moved from parlour to perfumed bedchamber. The girls were eager, competing and combining, applying themselves with practised gusto. Tongues flickered and hands caressed and pretty mouths whispered of love.

The monasticism of embassy life soon dissolved in low and whimpering moans. His business could wait.

They waited until he slept. The opiates would keep him sedated while a transaction of a different nature was in train. In the adjoining room, expert hands searched his clothing and extracted a message pouch, unfolding the thin pages within. A scribe set to work. In forty minutes he had transcribed the text; in a further forty, a messenger had ferried the coded language for decryption at St James's Palace. By the end of the day, Prince Henry would know the identities of those on the royal council who conspired against the Jamestown settlement and acted as agents for Spain.

Descending the stairs, the leader of the team passed a bag of silver coins to the bewigged madam in the vestibule.

'I thank you, Margaret.' The young man bowed as though to a lady of rank. 'You have never yet failed me.'

'How may I deny one so gallant and handsome?' She smiled. 'Ours is the roughest of games. It seems we need each other.' The purse vanished into the woman's skirts.

In an upstairs room, the Spaniard slept. He would doubtless awake groggy and spent and satisfied by the climax of his outing. Elsewhere, a secret servant of a royal prince whistled a tune as he strode through the streets. His mission was accomplished. It was too easy to thwart the moves of the hated Spanish enemy.

With her sails removed, the pinnace, moored off Jamestown, was in no condition to journey far. Yet as a prison to a former president, the vessel served her purpose well. Ratcliffe still had his supporters. His solitary confinement remote from the fort gave less risk of trouble.

'I tire of my books,' the prisoner complained. Down in the hold, Ratcliffe whiled away the days of his incarceration. He was only rarely brought on deck to take the air and exercise.

'Silence below!' the guard shouted. 'A prisoner may not speak.'

Hands gripped the bars of the hatch. 'Is that so?'

'You know the regulations.'

'I know them to be foolish. I know we must each fill our hours of isolation.'

'You are still the prisoner.'

'Yet both of us, it seems, are sentenced to this pinnace.' Ratcliffe's voice was calm and reasoning. 'No harm is done by discourse.'

'Save it is I that face sanction should we be caught in conversation.'

'Who is near?'

The guard's resistance was eroding. 'I have my orders.'

'From whom? That usurper, John Smith? A knave and misadventurer who sallies forth in a shallop while we face hardship and hunger.'

'He is now president.'

'In name, and not in fact.' Ratcliffe was persistent. 'He scarce has the qualities of a leader.'

'Jamestown has become stronger and the settlers more content.'

'A passing thing.'

'You were arraigned for mutiny, put here as a danger to the peace.'

'It was a charge invented by my enemies.' Regret and resignation carried in the tone of his voice. 'High office forever stirs jealousies and hatred.'

'Such matters are not for me to decide.'

'But you are a good man, who may see the truth. We are all of us trapped in Virginia and endeavouring to survive.'

'That we are.'

'Then we are brothers in arms.'

It was no different from tickling trout, Ratcliffe thought, lulling the unwary and catching the stupid with measures designed to trick. Before long, it might be Smith himself held festering in a cell, or hanged from the nearest tree as originally planned.

He began again. 'I ask no real favour, but crave what is my due.'

'Name it and we shall see.'

'You will find I am a loyal and grateful friend.' Ratcliffe let his words issue upward. 'If I become leader once more, I would not forget a kindness.'

'You seek to perplex me?'

'Solely to reassure. There will be pay.'

'Then I am your man.'

The prisoner's hands gripped tighter on the iron grille. 'Take a message for me and bring soon the reply.'

'Its nature?'

'One of hope to my silent followers.'

Ratcliffe's request was followed by a high-pitched cry as a heavy boot stamped down hard upon his fingers. Ratcliffe fell back into the gloom. Hardy knelt above, peering through the grate.

'You do not lose your base instinct, Ratcliffe.'

'Nor you,' Ratcliffe cried out with a snarl. 'There is not a shadow where you fail to flit or hide. Beware your conceit, Hardy.' The former president nursed his injured hands. 'There is many a turn before the end.'

Hardy pressed nearer to the bars. 'Be advised, Ratcliffe, I will return you to Robert Cecil in London whether you are living or in a box.'

'How unfortunate for your wider family. You should have a care, for their sakes.'

The intelligencer smiled into the dark. 'A pistol once exploded in your hand. Few would grieve should worse arise.'

Hardy stood. For the moment, Ratcliffe's threat was contained and he could instead dwell on the challenges posed by Realm. Too many people desired Jamestown gone. It went beyond Powhatan and his native people, beyond the scheming of an erstwhile president. The truth lay in London and Madrid. If the colony endured, it would be because Cecil, that disfigured and diminutive Lord Chancellor, was outmanoeuvred or coerced.

Climbing to the tender, Hardy gave departing instructions to the prison guard. 'Should you wish to piss, feel free to aim upon the captive.'

The burgeoning peace with the natives had encouraged trade and barter along the James. Still there was wariness; still the English kept their muskets primed. Yet the Indians handed over their corn and received in exchange copper and beads, each Weroance vying with the other to display the riches gained. It was not uncommon for a chief to parade around his village in a jacket or velvet cap, or to sport a brooch from London. The days of daily raids and volleys of arrow and shot appeared to be long past.

'Remember, we are their friends.'

Beribboned and dressed as though ready for the Strand, George Percy stood at the boat's stern with the tillerman and commanded the shallop to the riverbank. There were deals to be struck and influence to be bought. Here, at least, he could escape the tensions of Jamestown.

He nodded respectfully at the receiving party and let a crewman translate. 'We come in peace and with greetings from Jamestown.'

The headman had a painted face and wore a cloak of swan feathers. 'You are welcome,' he said. 'We have grain to trade.'

'It pleases us much. We give thanks to you and to the great Powhatan.'

'He bids us live beside you as brothers.'

'That is how it shall be. Hatred and suspicion are of no use to our people.'

Wares were offloaded and set out for the hosts and dancing and chanting followed. There was always ritual. Dignified and correct, Percy reviewed the proceedings. He was a roving ambassador, representative of a foreign nation feeling its way into the interior. Neither side lay down its arms completely. The natives understood, too, that harmonious relations might be temporary.

Business was good and the hogsheads filled. There could be no easing of the pace or pause in the feeding of the colony. No one at Jamestown could foretell when an English ship might heave into view. Investors might have pulled their funds, or vessels foundered in a storm; opponents of the colony might finally hold sway and force its cruel abandonment. Many things could upset the vaunted goals of the Virginia Company in London.

'Stow the corn and we will soon depart.' It had been an uneventful visit, yet George Percy paled. He appeared to stumble as he turned to mutter into the ear of a companion. His men comprehended.

'Return the master, quick!'

'Be gentle now! It comes upon him.'

'Lay him down and it will pass.'

The convulsions struck and Percy fell, his eyes wide and his mouth foaming. His crewmen mumbled prayers and watched in blank concern. They knew a seizure could signify possession; trembling limbs be proof a demon nested deep within. For all his mannered ways, this scion of an aristocrat was now reduced to the level of a slavering beast. They hurried to make ready and bear their commander away.

In the woods, a foraging soldier heard three shrill blasts of the whistle and prepared to return to the shallop. His role was to reconnoitre as much as to gather food, and he was diligent in his task. Across his shoulder, a canvas bag was almost filled.

A brace of wood pigeon had fluttered upward in sudden panic. 'Who goes there?' The soldier called.

'It is I.' A ligature went tight about the neck. 'You will not know me.'

The soldier did not take long to die. He struggled, of course, his face darkening and his speechless mouth falling agape.

'Accept what befalls you,' Realm murmured behind him. 'There is no point in struggle.'

Realm lowered the corpse, the hands and feet fluttering beyond the final throes. The renegade studied the swollen visage. Back at the shallop it would be assumed the man had deserted, had become another of the disappeared. Jamestown was accustomed to such occurrences. Realm caressed the man's face before leaning to kiss the blackened lips. Death had a singular look and taste.

Through the trees, the calls faded to silence.

In late September 1608, the second supply ship arrived from England in the form of the *Mary Margaret* and her escort, the *Star*. Admiral Newport again commanded, and with him came seventy additional settlers including a married woman and her maid. Also among their company were Dutchmen and Poles, experts in the production of soap ash and pine pitch. Someone had faith in the venture yet.

CHAPTER 8

'You have released Ratcliffe? You have restored him to the council?'

Rage and incredulity creased Smith's features. He glared at Newport. At a stroke, the admiral had countermanded his orders, freeing the former president and placing two newcomers onto the governing council too. The president could no longer do as he wished. Worse, the veteran seafarer brought from London admonishment at every turn, as well as a series of demands. Such intervention was not welcome.

Newport was unmoved. 'This is not your private fiefdom, Mr Smith. You are subject to the code of the Virginia Company, guided by the strictures of the royal council.'

'They meddle and interfere.'

'Yet they are your masters.' The admiral would brook no argument. 'Rail as you please. It changes nothing.'

'What do noblemen and perfumed courtiers know? How may they conceive of all that we endure?'

'Such matters are of scant concern. It is the cost and small return that perplex; the price in terms of blood and treasure.'

'Our investors must be patient.'

Newport was emphatic. 'Month after month, Jamestown drains resources, and month after month her supporters await fair news.'

'We try.'

'You disappoint. Where riches were promised, barrels of worthless spoil are sent.' Newport jabbed with an admonishing forefinger. 'Forget your dreams of plantations and your overweening ambition. We need trade, and little more.'

'Is this what you travel to decree?' Contempt erupted in Smith's voice. The adventurer had mapped the land and fought for grain. He would not be lectured by a servant of those who opposed him. They were the enemies of reason and progress, and of everything for which he had sacrificed so much. He turned to Hardy, standing close by. 'Tell him, Christian. Tell him how we strive, cling on, toil for the sake of England.'

'No one could doubt our endeavour, John.'

'Yet our efforts are dismissed. Speak to this man, for he does not listen to me.'

'I will shoot neither the messenger nor the admiral.'

'Then the task falls to me.' Smith glowered. 'You expect us to wither and die, Newport?'

'I require you to do as you are bid.'

'Is it not I who ranged far to gather corn and feed the colony when it starved? Is it not I who drilled the men and rallied their spirits, who bolstered the defences of the fort?'

'The royal council deems it insufficient.'

'The royal council is an ass.'

'Its authority flows from His Majesty.' Newport delivered his words slowly. 'While I visit, you will prove yourselves and show your worth. You will fill my ships with produce to the value of two thousand pounds.'

A sardonic grunt. 'You make other demands?'

'Indeed, Mr Smith. I am to travel again to meet the ruler Powhatan and, for the sake of peace and trade, will crown him as a king.'

Smith stared, his fists balled. His face first turned ashen and then mottled red. He shook himself and paced for a distance. Hardy watched. Every order from London seemed arbitrary; each intervention designed to sabotage or disrupt. But the movers of England had not counted on the immovable will of a stubborn adventurer.

Smith returned, his anger curbed and his bearded chin jutting defiant. 'You will crown Powhatan?'

'With pomp and ceremony and a circlet of gold, a scarlet cape placed about his shoulders.'

'A dukedom, perhaps, as a vassal of King James. But as a king himself?'

'The scheme has its merits.'

'Its dangers too.' Smith shook his head and then pulled a pitying face. 'He will see us as his subjects, minions to be tamed or crushed as his pleasure takes him.'

'We seek harmony.'

'What you sow is the seed of our annihilation.'

'Such matters are not for you to decide.'

Smith laughed now until his torso shook and he had to lean on his knees for support. There could be little doubt what he thought. Whether through the slavering Scottish goblin King James or his midget Cecil, or the nervous investors of the Virginia Company, madness was presented as policy. If Newport were an undertaker sent to commit Jamestown to the earth, he was to create some display.

The admiral let the reaction subside. 'Your levity surprises me.'

Smith wiped a tear from his eye. 'You take leave of your senses. Am I not for a moment permitted to flee mine?'

'As you wish, Mr Smith.'

'All that I wish for is ignored. Every item of reason and sound judgement goes discarded.'

'Trust in one thing. I do not face the dangers of the ocean merely to bring bad tidings.'

'I see no good in your delivery.'

'Further settlers and a second shallop, the residual hope of some in England.'

'Morsels and crumbs for hungry men.'

'Eke them out, Mr Smith.' Newport had tired of the debate. 'We all make do with what the Lord provides.'

Newport clutched reflexively at the empty sleeve pinned against his chest. Journeying with supplies to and fro and keeping the peace was an unrewarding business. The Virginia Company had offered him a share of the profits, and so far these were scarce. He would not be petitioned by a chancer and upstart like Smith. The conversation was closed.

Hardy found Smith at the riverside. Grim-faced and with his arms folded, he looked on as sailors and settlers bent to empty the holds of the arrived ships. It was a scene both ordered and chaotic, hoists working and men hollering, the contents lifted and swung ashore. Among the objects was a bedstead, finely made and furnished with a mattress deep-filled with down. No expense would be spared for Powhatan. Better to bribe than to subjugate; better to trade than to remain ever on guard against a native attack. Buckler too had seen advantage in the policy. The Irish dog lay sprawled on the mattress, oblivious to all and to the envy and humour of those about. No one had experienced such comforts since landing in Virginia.

Smith nodded. 'At least there is one that warms to the coming of Newport.'

'He makes his peace, as we all must.'

'With folly? With madness? With a plan that will end in catastrophe?'

'Should it be a mistake, we shall discover soon enough.'

'A coronation!' Smith almost spat the words. 'Elevate the natives and they will perceive us as weak.'

'We yet have our ramparts and guns.'

'They will count for nothing if we should starve, Christian. They will be emblems of impotent pride when sickness and misfortune visit again.'

'Do not provoke the admiral.'

'Am I to stand idle as he taunts me? Stay my tongue while he performs theatre with the savages?'

'Let him to his play.' The intelligencer offered his advice in measured tones. 'You are still president of Jamestown.'

'In name, but no longer in practice.'

'There will be a day when Newport sails again, taking the odious Ratcliffe with him. Dwell on it, and not on the slings and arrows you now suffer.'

Smith smiled. 'For a murderous brute, you offer fair counsel.'

'For a pugilist hothead, you listen enough.'

They watched as more luxuries and wooden chests were lowered to the ground. On the gangway, a crewman carried a basin and ewer to add to the gifts for Powhatan. Dress a native as an Englishman, enthral him with new habits and customs and he will join the ranks of the civilised. That was the intention.

Smith exhaled a barely audible sigh. 'Behold the creation of a circus, Christian.'

'Is it not sport to garb a bear in finery and then bait it?'

'Finery will scarce bring it to heel.' The adventurer cast his friend a sceptical look. 'Even if Powhatan is tamed, there are others perhaps more vicious.'

'Opechancanough?'

'He is younger and more vital than his emperor. Meanwhile, I am an officer hobbled and silenced.'

'You shall have your time.'

'Unless Cecil and his servants of darkness reach me first.'

Those servants might be anywhere, secreted among the newcomers or living blamelessly in the fort until opportunity arose. A mind could grow unbalanced attempting to perceive the threat.

On the waterfront a larger shallop was taking shape, its offloaded sections fitting together then pegged and hammered into place. It would ferry Newport and his delegation up the Pamunkey for the crowning of a redskin chief. Hardy frowned. Somewhere out there, Realm stalked the woodlands and meadows. The renegade had plans, and would not cease until the settlement lay ruined and Hardy was destroyed.

'You are diverted, Christian.' Smith regarded Hardy with narrowed eyes.

'A man may pause for thought.' The intelligencer held up the fragment of obsidian. 'What do you see?'

'Volcanic glass.'

'Where is such a volcano sited?'

'Spanish America, I would suppose.' Smith peered at the object awhile. 'Is this a trick or riddle?'

'Rather it is a message, sent by design. I plucked it from the pocket of a settler directed to murder.'

Smith took and inspected the piece. 'I see it did him no good.'

'Nor was it meant to, John. It was intended to be found, placed by a figure I thought consigned to my past.'

'Who, Christian?'

'One that I first met in an alleyway in Lisbon as the Armada prepared to sail. One that came to London to kill Queen Elizabeth, that returned again to abet the gunpowder traitors against King James.'

'He is here?' Smith shook his head. 'What name is given to our mystery foe?'

'The Spaniards call him Reino.'

'Realm.' The president ran his tongue around the word.

'Though he is English, I know few with a greater hatred for our kingdom.'

'And I know no one with greater skill than you to beat him.'

Side by side, the men continued to observe the vessels disgorging their loads. Doggedness had sustained the colony towards another season. Yet nothing was assured. Winter would soon be drawing in and Newport would depart. The isolated settlement would be bound by ice and snow. Perfect conditions for Realm to strike.

They reached the Pamunkey River, a handful of men trekking on foot from Jamestown and heading for Werowocomoco. They brought a message of friendship and the offer of a crown. Though he led the party, Smith still had few illusions and little hope for such meaningless theatre. Yet his task was to deliver news, and no one knew the Indians better. Should all efforts fail, he could hardly take the blame.

'What do you think, Christian?'

'It is as silent as a tomb.'

'An unnatural quiet, to be sure.' Smith crouched beside the intelligencer. 'An ambush?'

'Powhatan would not attempt it with Newport at hand. He would risk annihilation.'

'I trust you are right.'

Much depended on judgement. They kept low, their weapons poised and senses sharp, listening to the night.

Among their company was Namontack, a native sent by Powhatan to England and now returned with Newport with vivid stories of his travels. He could be forgiven for exaggeration, and was expected to provide his master with eyewitness accounts of the majesty and might of the pale-skins. Awe was ever part of diplomacy.

This, however, was the Indian's domain and the English took nothing for granted. They would have been watched all the way. In the moonlight, tucked between the reeds, an empty canoe awaited them. Their arrival was anticipated.

Hardy whispered, 'It is the moment to decide.'

'We go forward.'

As they paddled for the far bank a single light appeared, comforting in the dark. Yet they remained wary. At any moment the arrows might fall: a hundred warriors could be upon them.

A boy held a burning brand aloft and motioned for them to follow. They were being summoned. Glancing left and right and turning on occasion to check the rear, the small group proceeded. It was never comfortable to be separated from their sole means of escape. Smith led and his entourage followed, Hardy marshalling from behind. Should violence ensue, the intelligencer would take Namontack hostage or kill him where he stood. Understanding was built on such things.

A crew member peered with suspicion at the campfire ablaze in the open field. 'What is this?'

'I judge it a welcome.' Smith strode forward and then lowered himself onto a rush mat set before the flames. 'It is churlish to spurn either greeting or custom.'

'Where is Powhatan? Where are his men?'

'All in good time, I am sure,' Smith said.

Their fears somewhat allayed, his crew joined him, hoping for a fine spectacle. After all, they were honoured guests. The savages could be fierce and unpredictable, but they were committed to their rituals. Minutes passed, and the fire hissed and roared.

'To arms!'

In an instant they were on their feet and circling back-to-back, their swords drawn and firearms cocked. Whatever it was they could hear, the sound was hellish. Hardy pressed himself close to Namontack in readiness, his intentions clear. Shrieks and howls emanated from the woods.

Hardy spoke into the ear of the Indian. 'They mean to attack?'

The man shook his head. 'Our women honour you while the Mamanatowick is away.'

'Powhatan is not here?'

'In his absence they chase off the spirits and show the love in their hearts.'

'A fulsome and loud affair.'

In the gloom a lithe form ran calling towards them. It was Pocahontas. She flung herself into Smith's paternal embrace.

'We shall not harm you, John. You may kill me if we do.'

Smith stroked her head. 'Where is Powhatan, your father?'

'He hunts with his warriors until the dawn. But for our scouts, we are left alone.'

'It is yet a fearsome noise you make.'

She laughed. 'You know well our ways.'

Seated again and with Pocahontas beside him, the president of Jamestown waited. Naked and painted, young women emerged from the woods to move and dance and circle the fire. Some were adorned with leaves and pelts, and others wore buck horns on their heads. All gave themselves to an ecstatic trance. They writhed, the tempo rising, their sweat and fervour captured in the glow of the blaze.

'They are possessed.' An Englishman stared, his mouth agape.

Smith eased himself forward a little. 'I shall not condemn them.'

'Nor I, for my eyes will forever give thanks.'

'To submit to temptation is a sin.'

'While to err is to be human.' The man's attention remained fixed on a swaying pelvis.

'Remember the task we are set.'

But such thoughts could wait a night. The evening was for pleasure, for furthering mutual understanding. Feeling dazed now and protesting only mildly, Smith allowed himself to be led away, vanishing into the sensual embrace of the womenfolk.

By turn, the visitors were selected. They would not fight the natural affections of the savages. Far from England a man could stray; might convince himself to adapt his morality. His fellows would understand. The diplomatic mission would continue in the morning.

Awae stood alone, her skin soft-lit by the fire smoking at the centre of the room. She had summoned Hardy to her quarters. He gazed at her, committing the image to his memory, pausing to savour a beauty few Europeans had encountered. He felt a stab of guilt at his intrusion, a fear that what he brought Awae would irrevocably taint her life.

She spoke. 'You come to me, Christian.' There was ease and acceptance in her voice.

'Am I not chosen by you?'

'It is the gods that decide, that bring us to this place.'

'Then I shall praise each one.'

'You have wives in your land?'

'No one I may call my own. Not anymore.' He let his vision linger. 'None that dance as you do.'

'Are there youngs?'

'I have a son. His name is Adam.'

She repeated the name. 'I see in your eyes you will return to him.'

'A father cannot ignore danger to his own.'

'Nor must he forget hazards to himself.'

'I will be careful, Awae.' He stepped closer. 'What do you know of these perils?'

'Nothing that Powhatan would confide in me. He speaks most often to his elders and priests.'

'So there are rumours? Talk among the tribes and lands of Tsenacomoco?'

'I hear no word.'

'Have you heard talk of a stranger? A pale-skin, as I?'

Puzzled, she shook her head. 'Only those who have wandered from your camp.'

'There is one that is different. He speaks our tongue and yet is not of us.'

'He is your enemy, Christian?'

The intelligencer gave no answer. He could see she told the truth. Had Realm trespassed here, Awae would confess it without guile or calculation.

She reached out and touched his arm. 'We may practise our speech, or we may love.'

'Love is better than discourse.'

They lay in the shadows together, hidden in their burrow of earth and bark and rushes and guarded by the spirits. Hardy breathed in the warm aroma of her skin and the scent of sassafras around them. England could keep its manners and its feather beds, its preaching and its pulpits, its coiffed ladies with their jewels and satin gowns. With Awae he had glimpsed an alternative future.

As Awae slept, Hardy dressed and, taking his hunting bow, headed for open ground once more. Outside the carousing had finished, the welcoming fire slumped to ash. Everyone had found their berth for the night. Hardy stared into the darkness. He didn't know if it was instinct or curiosity that drew him there.

He counted time and steadied his breath, cleansing his mind of distraction. There it was – the hint of a movement. Stay long enough in the murk and even the camouflaged became obvious. His eyes adjusted, and he saw it: a body of men slipping from their hides and making their approach. No attack cry or call of greeting came. It was an unofficial visit.

'Why, if it isn't the sentinel of Jamestown.' A familiar voice carried in the gloom. 'You are far from home.'

'You too, Reino. What brings you here?'

'Both providence and purpose.' The reason in Realm's voice almost masked his hatred. 'Like you, it is the English outpost that draws me to the flame.'

'My task is to guard it.'

'While mine is to destroy.'

Hardy had felt the shadow of Realm's presence too often at his back. Now they met again. For the sake of the colony and himself, for the wrongs inflicted and the memory of his late wife, he would settle scores and finally exorcise the demon.

He kept the hunting bow cocked. 'King Philip is poor served that he should rely on you.'

'His Majesty sees merit in my contribution.'

'A renegade who failed to kill Queen Elizabeth? An embittered rogue who couldn't blow King James to pieces?'

'They were but battles, and we fight a war.'

Hardy brought his bow level.

'Extinguish me and you too will perish,' Realm said. He smiled. 'A pity to end our sport so soon.'

'It was never sport.'

'How well you try to deceive yourself.' The renegade had not shifted. 'I perceive you as you are.'

'I have rarely doubted the nature of your soul.'

'You judge me for my methods?'

'I despise you for your treachery.'

Coldness issued in Realm's laugh. 'We each of us find reason for our acts. We are not so very different, you and I.'

The intelligencer allowed his finger to curl about the trigger. Truth could propel a man to overreact. He would not give Realm the satisfaction.

Realm nodded. 'Thus we endure.'

'A temporary estate.'

The renegade assumed an air of reminiscence. 'You recall how we first met in Lisbon, then those three years gone when you took me prisoner in London?'

'Resolution is at hand.'

'God only knows how it will fall.'

Silence, and Realm was gone.

'We are here gathered to crown a king.'

It was the strangest of ceremonies; an awkward juxtaposition of English pomp and native incomprehension. Yet Admiral Newport persisted in his oration. About him were the gifts to be presented: the bedstead and other furniture, the fine garments, the decorated pitcher and basin. Powhatan viewed the scene with dignified silence. If the pale-skins wished to befriend him and pay tribute, they had not stinted in their efforts.

He stepped forward to examine the objects. His loyal counsellor Namontack had journeyed far across the seas to visit these people in their native land and had spoken of their wealth and power. That they now brought him treasure was either kindness or duplicity. Still his dream of great hordes of whiteskins swarming their land sat heavily in his mind.

Newport swept his arm wide. 'We bring to you our most precious things.'

'Then I and my people give you welcome.'

'Henceforth we are as one.' The admiral paused to search for the requisite words. 'Your enemies are our foes, and we shall stand with you against the Monacan.'

'My warriors need no help.'

'Yet we must explore beyond the falls, go wherever we may.'

'To dig holes in the ground? To cut through forest and fill your casks with earth?'

'Our customs decree it.'

'Peace is more certain should you keep to your fort.'

Powhatan rarely brooked dissent. Around him, his followers saw his face cloud with disapproval. He was a regal presence, an ageing leader whose word yet commanded. No wearer of leg coverings would dictate terms to him.

He stared. 'What is this crowning of which you speak?'

'A token of our respect, an honour bestowed that is rare indeed.'

'I shall accept.'

'On your head we will place a golden diadem and about your shoulders a scarlet cape.' Newport gestured to his lieutenants, who brought the apparel forward. 'Nothing will break the unity between us now.'

'Then I will be generous and permit you your place in Tsenacomoco.'

'Trade and great wealth will be your reward.'

Accord had been reached, and the native chief allowed the crown to be placed upon his head. He would not bow or bend his knee to any.

Somewhere a pistol shot cracked, followed by a skyward volley from the barge that caused Powhatan to shy. He regained his composure and studied his guests.

'I grant you corn for your efforts and safe passage in my lands.'

'You will never regret it.'

'I hear your words and see into your faces. Let not your promises be lies.'

Newport inclined his head. 'We would speak no falsehood to a king.'

At the rear of the delegation, Smith pursed his lips. He had scarcely managed to stifle his mirth at the sight of the admiral struggling to bestow the glittering trinket. He nudged Hardy in the ribs.

'Tell me I do not dream this, Christian.'

'I perceive the same as you.'

'Comedy or tragedy, I am left undecided,' the president muttered.

Hardy nodded. 'Opechancanough seems absent from the masque.'

'So too your night visitor, Realm. You think they are in league?'

'I cannot guess at the machinations of the natives.'

'What if the renegade provides them arms? Suppose he inflames them and directs them to attack?'

'He is not in Virginia to take the air.'

'We are assailed by traitors within and traitors without.'

'A situation Robert Cecil would applaud.'

'Curse his putrid soul.' Smith would not be cowed. 'He will find us harder to erase than expected.'

'I will guard you as I can.'

The festivities ended and the parties went their way, the English shallops heading for the James. Adorned in his new robes, Powhatan watched them go.

CHAPTER 9

'Sweet Lucifer!'

Blistered palms provoked such curses. Downriver from Jamestown another logging expedition was in train, Smith bringing thirty men by shallop to fetch large quantities of timber. The fruits of their labour might persuade the Virginia Company in London to stay awhile the moment of their abandonment. Results so far had been poor. With the departure of Admiral Newport likely soon, there was reason to redouble their efforts.

'For each oath and blasphemy you will have a pail of water tipped on your head,' Smith called to the transgressor. 'You shall be well baptised by the end of the day.'

Axes bit and wood splintered and a further oak was toppled. They were making fair progress. The president buttoned his coat higher at the collar and peered up through the tree canopy. There was a chill to the air: a portent of winter, a sign of the bleakness ahead. Few relished the coming departure of the supply mission.

Hardy approached. 'Do not search for the new season, John. It will find us soon enough.'

'And with insufficient victuals. Peace with the Indians has not boosted our provisions enough.'

'You plan to venture out?'

'I have little choice.' Smith nodded to his work crew. 'When we are done here I will, as usual, go bleating and begging for corn.'

'As good a means as any to test the love and intent of Powhatan.'

'Henceforth to be known as His Majesty.'

Whatever the state of relations with Powhatan, there was yet the Indian's military chief Opechancanough, and Realm's spectral presence. An expedition could gather food and intelligence and flush out the opposition too. Smith rarely shrank from a fight.

'See those oaks, Christian?' The president indicated a pile of felled trunks. 'Each is straight and true for twenty yards and outdoes any in England.'

'You think the nation will be awed by our gift?'

'I trust it will be reminded of our purpose.'

There were shouts and laughter in a nearby clearing as Buckler chased across an obstacle course laid out by Edward Battle. The boy and his companions urged the dog on and were rewarded with an athletic display.

'Your hound earns his keep.' Smith gazed at the scene benignly. 'Like all the Irish, he delights in the smallest things.'

Hardy had returned from a wildfowling sortie with a duck and goose for the spit. They would eat well that evening. Far upriver, beyond the falls, Newport had taken over a hundred men to push into the hinterland, where the fierce and scavenging Monacan and cannibal Pocoughtronack dwelt. Somewhere there must be gold.

The president raised three fingers as a gentleman swung his axe and swore. He turned back to Hardy. 'What of Realm? The renegade who stalks us?'

'He will not rush to the close, for it is the longer game he plays.'

'Are you to be the prize?'

'I would rather be the bait.' Hardy touched the pommel of his Katzbalger. 'His arrogance has upset his plans before, and I daresay it will again.'

The men toured the site, pausing as more oaks toppled in succession. Smith could never be accused of idleness. He bellowed and exhorted and quoted the Psalms and drove his woodsmen on. Every strip of wood was needed.

'They may rail against me, Christian. Yet their sweat and aching backs will be our salvation.'

'Timber will not suffice.' The intelligencer pulled tobacco from a pouch and crumbled it in his fingers. 'Drink in its aroma, John. This is true salvation.'

Smith obliged. 'Spanish?'

'As sweet and mellow as any in the Indies. Break the grip of King Philip on such trade, and we forever embed Jamestown in Virginia.'

'Or it might be its death warrant.' Intensity shone in Smith's eyes. 'Maybe it will sign yours too.'

It was a heartfelt warning. Hardy had walked the narrow edge too many times and enraged and offended the mighty.

Smith continued. 'Hold close the secret, or tobacco may see you killed.'

'Forty shillings a pound in London makes it worth the risk.'

Hardy returned the pouch to his jerkin and headed for the shallop. In spite of his bombastic ways, Smith could be insightful. King James loathed the smoking of tobacco and decried it as a sin; would rage further if informed that a settlement he wished expunged had become a plantation for the crop. Hardy stored the thought.

In the gloaming, as a fire burned and food was cooked, the men paid for their blaspheming. To cheers and laughter, a fifth pail of water was emptied on its victim. The man was stoic. He would not forget the lesson of the day.

'To err is human.' Smith wagged his finger. 'To have a foul mouth is to suck on the teat of Satan. If we are not pious, we dwell solely with the wicked.'

The man shook water from his hair. 'For the present I dwell only with the drenched.'

'Be glad you are not drowned.' The president looked about him. 'Who is next?'

Resigned to his punishment, another stepped forward. 'I, sir.'

Summary justice could entertain. With high spirits and much noise, the evening proceeded and the shadows were chased away. Most of the party would withdraw to the shallop for the night. It was safer there, easier to cast off and make a run for Jamestown were ambush to occur. Whatever the nature of a peace accord with Powhatan, the local Paspahegh had proved an unreliable tribe.

At the edge of the gathering, Hardy and his dog patrolled. The intelligencer preferred solitude to the banter. Behind him he could hear the faint strains of a shanty, its jaunty refrain sounding almost mournful in the fastness. The lyrics spoke of longing and regret and things abandoned.

'You are there, Christian?' It was the voice of Edward Battle.

'I see no other in the forest.'

Hardy angled his musket against his chest and let the youngster join him. Buckler was more effusive in his welcome, prancing about the boy, delighted.

'Why do you prowl here alone, Christian?'

'To escape a surfeit of questions.'

A laugh. 'It is my nature to enquire.'

'As mine is to walk and guard the bounds.'

'You also kill.' Edward did not move. 'Without hesitation you slew a man with your blade.'

'He would have run me through.'

'They say you are more than a soldier; that you are versed in the arts of intrigue.'

'Ignore their ramblings, Edward.' The intelligencer gripped the shoulder of the boy. 'We are loyal friends, and that is all that is important.'

'Is truth not important?'

'It is a much-exaggerated thing. The face of a man often varies from his soul.'

'What then hides within you, Christian?'

'Only God and my enemies know.'

They stood in the darkness, the boy who had survived a great fever and the man who had tended him. Hardy thought again of his son, Adam. Perhaps the intelligencer atoned for his past and his reckless existence through compassion for this youth. He and Edward were exiles in the wilderness.

'I fear one day you will leave us, Christian.'

'My work leads me to many parts.'

'None so threatened as Jamestown.' The words carried feeling. 'John Smith needs you at his side.'

'Is that so?'

'I too prefer that you would stay.'

'There are others you may befriend, fresh diversions to discover.'

'They would be a poor replacement.'

'I have no choice but to depart on occasion. Yet you have my promise: I will return.'

'I shall hold you to such a vow.'

The boy pressed his face against the neck of Buckler now, more trusting of the dog than of any human dealings. Hardy understood. Life could be precarious, and it was wise to stand apart.

They had been watched as they clambered past the falls, an English expedition well-armed and venturing with caution into the interior. Within hours a scout would have borne the news to Powhatan. It was his trusted son Parahunt who guarded the cascades, acting as watchkeeper of the border and defender against the Monacan. Now the pale-skins were heading through.

'Watch every quarter,' Admiral Newport shouted his orders. 'Yet remember we come in peace.'

His pinnace and shallop were moored far behind. It might take a running retreat to reach them, for already they were thirty miles beyond.

A warning came. 'There is movement.'

'Smile as though your life relied on it.' Newport did not break pace. 'We are as friends strolling in a garden.'

On a ridgeline figures appeared, their faces painted and bodies garlanded with leaves. Curiosity rather than hostility had brought them. In their hands were clubs and spears. They stared at the newcomers, their expressions neutral and appraising.

'There seems no threat.' The admiral raised his hand in salutation. 'See how they return our smiles.'

'It is their teeth that I discern,' a young ensign said, wincing.

Those teeth were filed to sharpened points, the better for tearing into flesh. Further details came into view: knotted clumps of human hair dyed and worn at their wrists and ankles, and necklaces of severed ears strung around their throats.

'A land of milk and honey,' the ensign muttered. 'And it is peopled with the diabolic.'

Newport strode on. 'Keep moving and say your prayers.' He shook his head. 'I am glad to have a hundred muskets at my side.'

'We shall winnow them should they charge.'

The admiral turned now to Ratcliffe. 'Are you still pleased I bring you from Jamestown?'

'I would choose any horror above governance by Smith.'

Distance had done little to temper the former president's dislike. Yet there were more pressing concerns. The savages had disappeared from the ridge. Ahead lay the sound of beating drums and ululating chants. Proper welcome was being given.

Armed and in warpaint, Monacan warriors now approached. An elder threw his arms wide in greeting. These were the dreaded foes of Powhatan. It helped that there were captives able to translate.

'We are the Monacan, a tribe of the Sioux.'

Newport doffed his hat. 'Much is spoken of you. We are the English, a people of peace.'

'Yet you bear weapons and have killed warriors of Powhatan.'

'He has come to treat us with respect.'

'Are we to suffer the same?'

Newport shook his head. 'Trust and amity will exist between us.'

'We grow no corn and have little we may give.'

'It is not war we seek, nor theft of what is yours.'

'Why then do you journey?'

'We look for earth and rock, desire samples of anything which may glitter in the sun.'

'Dig where you wish.' The elder waved his hand. 'Our home here is Massinacak, while beyond is Mowhemenchough. We shall not disturb you.'

'Your kindness will go rewarded.'

With picks and shovels and guided by the Indians, the English trooped higher up the valley, searching for hidden minerals and precious metals to placate the investors of the Virginia Company. There was a certain urgency to the mission.

'Mr Percy.'

At the call, George Percy moved to join the admiral. Although not a natural soldier, Percy had an inclination to prove himself and an instinct for avoiding politics.

'Walk with me awhile,' Newport said. He scanned the distant hills. 'Is the air not clearer up here and free from the river fog?'

'It is a wondrous country.'

'With natives that are pliant. Yet I fear their amicable ways may provoke jealousies in Powhatan.'

'We have shown we are a match for any armed with bow and arrow.'

'Yet further battle must be avoided.' The seafarer stumbled briefly on a tussock. 'Jamestown's future rests on the goodwill of the savages.'

'They have proved themselves most unreliable.'

'Thus we should ensure they keep the peace. Nothing must subvert relations.'

'Our president?'

'He weighs heavy on my mind.'

Unrestrained by the council and liberated by the absence of the bulk of the settlers, Smith was likely to be engaged in a frolic of his own. His waywardness and the unpredictability of Powhatan and Opechancanough lent further risks to a situation already hard to calculate.

Percy smoothed the feather in his cap. 'Captain Smith, I would argue, has wisdom and experience.'

'Has he not also the fire and rashness of a baited bull?'

'Manners constrain my full reply.'

'Seniority allows me mine.' Newport raised his arm and brought the column to a halt. 'There are matters of some urgency in Jamestown.'

'Our task seems more pressing here.'

'The Monacan behave and the atmosphere is cordial; I cannot say the same for our settlement.'

'Ninety of our settlers protect the fort.'

'Enough to guard against the impulsiveness of Smith?'

Comprehension registered in the eyes of Percy. He would go where he was sent and do as he was bid. The follies and fate of family members had taught him the value of compliance.

The admiral was decided. 'Take your troop and our shallop and return with haste down the James.'

'My task?'

'To be of assistance to the president. To restrain him in his natural inclinations.'

'An onerous undertaking.'

'One I am certain you shall accomplish with style.'

Percy offered a small bow and Newport nodded. As the column resumed its march, a detachment peeled off in its wake and retreated to the falls.

'Greetings. Are you minded to give us corn?' Smith paused and turned to his companion. 'They hide from us, Christian.'

The village appeared deserted. The presence of armed men and the sight of John Smith leaping ashore to wander brazenly through native land had conveyed a particular message. The president had ventured up the Chickahominy, the main tributary of the James, for a special reason. It was a landscape he had once traversed as captive, terrain controlled by the military chief Opechancanough. Should the peace accord with Powhatan unravel, its fraying edges would be discovered here.

'They do not know what we bring,' Hardy replied.

'The hand of friendship. A simple desire to trade.'

'Gestures may be misread.'

'We are no army.'

'Yet you have the swagger of a general.' The intelligencer peered into the thickets of pine. 'We shall know soon enough if they intend us harm.'

Smith snorted back a laugh. 'Had I desired war, I would have brought more men.'

'Sixteen may unleash havoc.'

'Tell it to Newport.' Smith ran his palm across the butt of the pistol pressed against his chest. 'Our intrepid admiral cannot travel without a bloated contingent of troops.'

'He explores, as is his right.'

'As I fell trees and guard the fort and gather provisions to feed us.'

Hardy nodded. 'Let us see what we may find.'

Spread out in a forage line, the English advanced through the Indian settlement. There was the smell of smoke and cooking and debris from a hasty abandonment.

'They attack!'

It was scarcely a surprise. Yet the ferocity of the assault caused the settlers to fall back and use the shallop as a rampart, the natives pouring down the riverbank before rising to loose their arrows. Smith deflected a projectile with a leather shield he had wrenched from the vessel.

'Regard their swords!' Hardy shouted as he knelt and fired his rifled musket.

The intensity of the battle grew, arrows flickering through the air and spattering the ground. An onrush of Indians collided with a fusillade of shot, the men's war cries lost among the barrel flashes and drifts of smoke. The hunting packs returned. In the haze, Smith parried a blow and then drove home his sword, killing another native with a pistol shot. To his right, a settler rolled in the dirt with an adversary; to his left, another deployed his musket as a club.

'Hold them!' Smith roared his command. 'We shall not yield!'

'Nor will they!' There was terror in the distant voice.

'We did not settle Jamestown to go defeated! We did not journey here to be defied!'

'They swarm like insects!'

Smith had lost both his hat and his patience. Sound relations with the overlord Powhatan plainly had not filtered through to the denizens of Chickahominy.

'Look! It is the second shallop!'

Indeed it was. She hove into view and landed her men, George Percy stepping lightly behind to join the melee.

'I thank you, Mr Percy.' Smith reloaded his pistol. 'Your visit is most welcome.'

Percy drew his own weapon. 'I had a notion you would be at large, running errands. It seems we found you just in time.'

Behind the village a chase occurred, Hardy dodging between trees and then crouching low and leaping to follow the scout. Three arrows had already passed him close. He would not be deterred. Beside a stream he caught the man, the native tripping on a root and then scrambling to recover.

'Put down your blade.' Hardy had the Katzbalger in his hand. 'I am more accustomed to such weapons.'

'I will fight.'

'A brave yet foolish decision.'

It took a few short moves to disarm the Indian. Hardy held him down, his face plunged in the water.

'You do not heed me, savage.'

The native choked. 'I cannot breathe.'

'But you may talk.' Hardy pushed the man's head down again before lifting it. 'Did the pale-skin train you with the sword?'

'He and his demons instruct us.'

'Demons?'

'Their faces are dark as night.' The man choked. 'They are hard and merciless and answer only to their lord.'

'Where dwells this lord?'

'With Opechancanough.'

Hardy rolled the captive on his back. 'What of fire sticks? The weapons we call muskets?'

'I see nothing of such things.'

A message would be sent, courtesy of this redskin scout. Hardy drew his blade across the man's torso, carving a line from chest to hip. The native did not scream. Were their roles reversed, the skin of the intelligencer would be hanging in a tree by now. It was strength that was respected.

'Tell the wearer of leg coverings, the pale-skin once known as Realm, I shall hunt him to his death.'

The communication was received and perfectly understood. Realm wandered through the native village and observed its return to the normal tempo. The excitement had abated and the English were gone. For sure there had been casualties, but they were fewer than expected. The surrender of corn and agreement to barter had served to calm passions and restore a sense of order. Satisfied with his haul, Smith had led his merry band onward.

These colonists helped themselves rather than their cause. The renegade stooped to retrieve a musket ball flattened on impact. He turned it in his fingers. Superior force was how most civilisations gained control. Yet the lead round was merely a seed for a much greater harvest, a harbinger of the horrors to befall Jamestown. The English compounded their mistakes. In requesting grain, they proved they went hungry; in sending a mission beyond the falls, they planted suspicion in the mind of Powhatan. Such things were to be exploited.

Discarding the spent shot, he motioned his pair of Imbangala to follow and moved further through the settlement. He paused to question a brave who was scanning the ground for expended arrows.

'How many were the outsiders?'

'Enough to fill their boats and ward off our aggression.'

'Did they come in peace?'

'They arrived in number and were not welcome at our fire.'

'Powhatan greets them as his brothers.'

'Brothers do not raid or rouse us to anger.' The warrior retrieved an arrow. 'We do as the spirits command.'

Realm continued his tour. It was a pleasure to be trading blows with Christian Hardy once more. His adversary was capable, had outwitted him before, yet lacked the fundamental coldness that aided clarity of vision.

He nodded to a boy. 'Was much corn given to the pale-skins?'

'Their boats were heavy when they left.'

There was often little to distinguish between a diplomatic mission and extortion. The residents of Jamestown had merely reminded their neighbours they could punish at will.

The renegade was pleased that a pile of native corpses could be blamed on the English settlers, that discarded steel blades pointed to their guilt. One could not create uncertainty without first spilling blood.

Realm beckoned the boy. 'Let us walk. Opechancanough grants me freedom to wander where I may.'

The boy fell in alongside him. 'Are we to go far?'

'No further than is needed. I desire to make a sacrifice.'

'For what do you pray?'

'Good hunting and fair chance, and the destruction of our foes.'

'I too will ask this of the spirits.'

Realm placed a hand on the boy's shoulder.

They ventured on, pushing through the cultivated land to the forest beyond. In time, the casualties would be found, something to remind Powhatan of what he faced. No coronation gifts would dispel the undertow of hatred that would follow.

A late November wind tugged at the canvas flaps and caused the light of the oil lamp to flicker. Smith continued to write. He dabbed his quill in the inkwell and scratched out another line of prose, his brow furrowed and concentration fierce. Pride and self-justification could drive a man to fluency.

Hardy ducked into the tent, accompanied by a chill vortex of air. 'I intrude on your pastime?'

'I welcome anything that steers me from penning unpardonable oaths.' The president sat back and reached for a goblet of claret. 'It is to the royal council in London I write.'

'Then your ire is well directed.'

'I map this country, defend this settlement, feed it when it starves—'

'No one would contradict you on that.'

'Yet still they ask for more; still Newport wastes resources on the folly of crowning native kings and leading grand embassies beyond the falls.'

'He may do as he pleases.'

'It is mad and vainglorious.'

'The admiral will soon depart.' Hardy poured himself a drink. 'Ratcliffe, too, is bound for England.'

'May he perish and rot there.' The president gulped and swallowed the toast.

'He will not be the last to seek our destruction from within.'

'Though he is one fewer pressing matter to resolve.'

Hardy nodded. 'Our fort is strong, our numbers swell, our men will cede no inch of ground.'

'And yet.' Smith refilled his glass. 'Our future is as moot as it ever was.'

'It is why I must leave on the ship too, John.'

Smith looked up. 'Reason deserts you.'

'My wits are sound and my course settled.'

'I cannot persuade you?'

'Would you let Cecil continue in his scheming? Permit him to send inexhaustible supplies of those who wish us ill?'

'I know of no person that can counter his machinations.'

Hardy raised his goblet to his lips. 'Should I fail, my effort at least will cause him some discomfort.'

Smith sat back and studied his friend. So much of the intelligencer remained hidden, and still more was rooted deep within his history.

'We shall mourn your absence, Christian.'

'Stay your tears, for I will return.'

'An oath?'

'Upon all that is most sacred.' Hardy gripped Smith's hand. 'Remember, you are become president and Jamestown survives.'

'Each would be happier for your presence.'

'Fear not, John. Our story is far from done.'

There were farewells to make and final preparations to consider before Christian Hardy went aboard. In his absence, Realm would let Jamestown lie, for it was part of their greater sport. Yet others would seek an explanation, and Awae would doubtlessly weep at the news of his departure. He owed it to all, though, to resolve the future of this settlement.

In early December 1608, the *Mary Margaret* and her consort slipped their moorings and headed down the James. From the poop deck, Hardy watched the timbered palisade of the fort recede and the solitary figure of a boy raise his hand in a furtive goodbye before he slunk, melancholic, from view. Buckler scratched and whined. A breeze caught the sails and the ship steadied on its course.

CHAPTER 10

'Is Virginia not the Garden of Eden? Are we not bound by God, as Adam and Eve were, to civilise that garden?'

The crowd answered in unison, mesmerised by the words of the preacher. There were few doubters here. The preacher surveyed his people from the stone pulpit, gauging their swelling numbers and expectant mood. The churchyard of St Paul's was ever the place to sermonise and spread ideas, to imbue the people with a spirit of adventure. London, March 1609. Things were changing.

He leant forward and jabbed his finger. 'Are you to stand idle while other men toil?'

'No!' It was a collective and heartfelt reply.

'Will you drink and whore and dice even as your brothers plough and sow?'

'Never!'

'Then we have work to do.' The preacher glared and clenched his fist. 'Jamestown must be saved, and the natives of those parts delivered from darkness. Will you sail on such a holy mission?'

'We shall!'

'Will you plant and build and colonise the land?'

'We will!'

'Will you reveal to all the glory of the Lord?'

'He commands us! He commands us!'

This was the new beginning. Hidden in the throng, Hardy felt the people's fervour. How different the atmosphere was, and how altered the outlook since he last walked these streets. Somewhere, the agents and informants of Cecil would lurk; somewhere in his mansion on the Strand, the little pygmy would be pacing and plotting his next move.

The intelligencer moved up Cheapside, Buckler at his heel. Every alleyway and tavern possessed its secrets; every step of the cobbles held memories of skirmishes and intrigues. Blood was more easily sluiced away than recollection. For an instant his mind conjured the image of

Awae before it faded again amid the bustle of the street ahead. The girl was an ocean and a lifetime away.

'A penny for a pie!'

'Bottled ale!'

Traders, storekeepers and wandering rogues shouted and peddled their wares. A dispute erupted to his left.

'You thieve from me!'

'I shall take no such insult!'

'Yet you will receive your dues!'

Blades were drawn with a suddenness that carried no surprise here. Londoners were often quick to temper and promiscuous with the sword. Hardy would not interfere. Too many orchestrated murders started with a distraction like this, and too numerous were the corpses produced by a random blow. People had begun to clear a space around the feuding pair. Ever a bad sign. The intelligencer maintained his pace. Sir Walter Raleigh awaited him at the Tower.

To Hardy's rear, loitering unobserved in the shadow of a timbered over-hang, a stranger watched his progress. The deep jetties of the upper floors were perfect cover for such missions. Later, the man intended to close the distance; later, the thrust of a sprung stiletto would punch through flesh and organs and bring a premature end to an infamous career. If Robert Cecil could not be trusted to deliver the coup de grâce, Spain was obliged to sully its hands.

'Watchful and yet so heedless,' a voice whispered in the stranger's ear. 'Resist and you will die.'

'I understand.'

'Depend on it: I demand the truth. How many of you stalk Christian Hardy?'

'On this occasion, I alone.'

'Who sends you?'

'I cannot say.'

'You shall tell me or be ready for your final breath.'

'Zúñiga.' The captive was persuaded. 'The Spanish ambassador.'

'A decision Zúñiga will soon regret.'

The killing would be short and uncomplicated. A hand about the mouth and a blade across the throat. In the hubbub of the day, life went on.

'I am a seer, Christian.' Raleigh puffed on his silver pipe and gazed upriver to London Bridge. 'For in this smoke I spy the future.'

They stood on the narrow stretch atop the walls, the bustle of the river traffic before them and the grey confinement of the Tower behind. No torture was more cruel for a roving privateer and erstwhile darling of the Elizabethan court. Yet Raleigh bore it well, his darker thoughts hidden deep and his yearning for liberty casually described. Hardy knew well how the great man suffered. It was further reason to despise and mistrust his former master Robert Cecil.

Raleigh exhaled and murmured in appreciation. 'It is tobacco as sweet as any from Guyana.'

'Yet grown by an Englishman in the soil of Virginia.'

'Let it make the Spaniards quake and their treasury run dry.' Another draw on the pipe. 'I have lost sufficient wealth and ships trading in such contraband.'

'Doubt not that one day we shall own the market.'

'At forty shillings a pound, I shall rejoice when it is so.'

A man could dream, even when imprisoned. There was excitement in Raleigh's eyes, a sense of possibility.

Raleigh reached inside his woollen coat and withdrew a slender leather-bound volume. 'Everywhere they talk of this, Christian.'

'I am well aware.' Hardy took the book and perused its cover. 'Our friend John Smith pens a pretty tale.'

'*A True Relation*, he dubs it. How closely acquainted is the captain with the truth?'

'It matters little, for the book inspires and enthrals.'

Raleigh nodded. 'It also defends our cause from the malign influence of Cecil.'

'He will not admit defeat.'

Other tomes on Jamestown were also leaving the presses, feeding demand and fuelling debate, extolling the virtues of colonisation. Jamestown had become a cause. In every tavern, men drank and spoke of Virginia; at every opportunity, citizens read of the New World and marvelled at its curiosities. While for some it offered simple escapism, for the ageing Raleigh it provided an opportunity to engineer his release.

He peered at Hardy. 'Prince Henry proves my staunchest supporter. He rails against Cecil for caging me so, and petitions his father to give me freedom.'

'To what effect?'

'Silence both from Cecil and the King.' Raleigh's sigh was stifled. 'Yet I dwell in hope.'

'It escapes neither man that the exchequer is in crisis. Six hundred thousand pounds in debt, they say. To fill it, they need tax, and for taxes they must beg Parliament.'

'How fortunate that I find favour with a few there.'

'So then be encouraged.'

Although now Lord Treasurer, Cecil had found himself weakened by the dire state of the royal purse. Squeezing the Catholics and confiscating land had proved a finite resource and no match for the profligacy of King James. Parliamentarians were speaking out and demanding concessions from above. Perhaps Raleigh might again be destined to sail.

'I write to him, Christian. I flatter the loathsome little turd; tell him of my love and loyalty for that Scottish sodomite of a King.'

'You lose nothing but your dignity.'

'A man must do as his conscience decrees.'

'Or as his preservation directs.'

They shared the laugh.

Raleigh's earnestness intruded. 'What I could do for Virginia, Christian. The glory I could bring to England.'

'You have already done much.'

'Am I to rot here forever? Condemned to watch as others craft our history?'

'We each have our time.'

'And you, Christian?' Inquisitive eyes appraised the intelligencer. 'You do not sail to London merely to provide me with tobacco.'

'There is work left unfinished.'

'I shall hazard to guess. Enemies of Jamestown reside in London and you are tempted to neuter them.'

'I commend your powers of insight.'

'And I applaud your courage.' Raleigh seemed wistful at the thought of danger. 'Cecil and his foul brood will scarce forgive your actions.'

'I am ever on my guard.'

'So too your hound, it seems.' The older man indicated Buckler sitting patiently below. 'I do not jest, Christian. As Jamestown strengthens and puts down its roots, the stakes climb and risks grow.'

At Woolwich, preparations were in train for a small fleet of ships to voyage to Virginia. It was said that Prince Henry himself would visit the docks and give his blessing to the venture. His presence alone would attract the crowds, inspire the public and provide impetus to the project. Meanwhile, King James would fret and Cecil seethe. A deadly combination.

Raleigh raised an eyebrow. 'You plan to return to Jamestown?'

'As fast as I am able.'

'Is it the lure of the wild? The cry of the savage? A game unfettered by restraint or boundary?'

'I have my reasons.'

Raleigh gave a rueful smile. 'I have no doubt John Smith prays each day for your skill at arms and your counsel.'

'Then I hope he shall not be kept waiting long.'

Even as he spoke, Jamestown might be besieged or forced to its knees by starvation. Distance only served to magnify Hardy's fears. Yet he would let matters run and focus on the present; would fill the weeks before he embarked again with battles of his own. The ruling powers of England and Spain might sorely wish him dead, but he had every intention to survive. It was time to bid farewell to the prisoner in the Tower.

He had learnt to be wary and to bolt at the first sign of danger. It was the life he had chosen, the twilight existence of a Catholic priest. Anywhere there might be pursuivants and informants, armed men moving to arrest him. One loose tongue or forced confession, a chance remark, and Newgate or the Gatehouse gaol at Westminster would receive another inmate. Shortening odds decreed his inevitable capture. He knew what this would entail, understood the horrors of torture and the final indignities of hanging and disembowelment. Yet his mission would continue. London was no place for recusants and the faint of heart.

Beside the corner of St Paul's, he murmured a silent prayer for the soul of the late departed Father Henry Garnet. The Superior of the Jesuits had been an extraordinary man, strong until the last. So many had wept on the day when, with such courage, he had met his fate. Indeed, the crowd had surged to cling to his feet to hasten his end as he swung in the hangman's noose. At least that had spared him the agonies of evisceration. Never was a hanger-on so deserving of his title as that day he had speeded Father Henry to his death.

A voice rebuked him. 'Employ your eyes and look where you walk!'

The priest muttered his apologies and quickened his pace. To loiter was to draw attention, and to argue back might incite affray. Neither was welcome. The road to salvation was pitted with incidents.

Sweat sat between his shoulders as he turned into the alleyway. Supportive words at the English seminary in Rome rarely prepared a graduate for the reality of his task, but his flock depended on him. In hidden places they gathered, risking all to receive the sacrament and celebrate Mass, to pledge themselves again to Rome. Robert Cecil, the Earl of Salisbury, was assiduous in his duty to hunt them down.

Climbing the stairs, he entered his chamber with relief. There would be some kind of peace in the privacy of his room. But as he moved towards his bed he was tripped, landing hard and unable to recover before expert hands bound his wrists and wrestled him to the bedstead.

It was Christian Hardy.

'No smile of welcome?' the intelligencer said. 'No greeting for a friend?'

'You are no friend.'

'Yet I am your guardian angel.' Hardy perused the sullen and fearful face. 'I have saved your neck a thousand times.'

'It is never done for charity.'

'Be grateful nonetheless. You still breathe, for I watch your back. You walk free as I forewarn you of the danger.'

'A pact with Satan would be more kind.'

'You would find him less forgiving.' Hardy cocked his head. 'Father Charles Purton, you are the hardest of men to please.'

'How can there be pleasure when my hands are tied and I am propped here as your captive?'

'Perhaps you would prefer the sweet attentions of Cecil, the caresses of the rack.'

The priest glared. 'Ever you hold that over me.'

'I merely tell the truth.'

'Truth is a stranger to an intelligencer.' Purton struggled to sit upright. 'You are no different from the rest, from the bloodhounds that chase our scent and the servants of hell who drag us to the scaffold.'

'Not once have I sought to arrest a priest. Nor do I draw my sword against any who embrace peace and present no threat to the nation.'

The priest scowled. 'Am I not a Catholic, and thus a traitor in the eyes of the King? Would it not ease your predicament to lean from the window and shout that I am captured?'

'For the while, I shall leave you to your merry life.'

'At what price?'

'It is the market which decides.' The eyes of the intelligencer narrowed. 'Tell me what you know of a priest named John Sicklemore.'

Purton looked baffled. 'Why, he is dead.'

'If he is the man I believe him to be, when last I saw him he was much alive.'

'It cannot be.' Purton shook his head. 'Witnesses heard his screams, would swear on oath he succumbed to his tortures.'

'Was there a corpse?'

'Prisoners are kept from the world beyond their cell.'

'What of his nature? He was devout?'

'As committed to the faith as any true believer.'

'Yet deceiving and dissembling. Others have informed me his life was spared in return for selling his soul.'

The priest did not blink. 'Impossible.'

'Unless he was turned and works for Cecil and sailed for Virginia.'

'I cannot believe it. In what guise does Sicklemore dwell?'

'He is no more the priest; he is elevated in rank.' Hardy watched his words have their effect. 'He is now named Ratcliffe.'

'Make for the fort! Run for your lives!'

Something had provoked the natives. In the fields outside Jamestown, the settlers had busied themselves with clearing and tilling and planning for the annual harvest. Members of the Paspahegh had been toiling alongside the pale-skins in return for beads and copper, in a spirit of accord. Until today.

A hatchet buried between the shoulders of an Englishman provided the clearest sign that their agreement with the Indians was forfeit. Then the arrows came. Exposed in the open, the settlers would stand little chance.

His sword drawn, Smith bellowed instructions. 'Fall back, if you value your lives!'

His exhortations drove the stampede. At the edge of the field, a labourer deployed his hoe as a quarterstaff and shattered the face of an opponent. Beside him, hemmed in by the natives as his companions fled, a second man wielded a scythe in desperate defence before he was brought down.

'Kill me!' the settler cried out to a soldier who was levelling his musket. 'I beseech you as a brother!'

'In the name of God, I cannot.'

'You are forgiven! Do it now! You have more mercy than they!'

The soldier's aim was wild and the shot fumbled and a musket ball tore off the arm of a native. It had little effect on the rest, for they already had a prize. Whooping and cheering, they bore their captive away as he screeched in abject terror. Smith strode through the melee to hasten Edward Battle from the scene. 'Do you not hear me, boy?'

'As clear as any in our company.' The youth knelt to discharge a musket. 'I will cover our retreat.'

'You shall heed reason and do as you are bid.'

Defiance gleamed in Edward's eyes. 'The fight is here.'

'Mutiny also.' The president seized the scruff of the boy's canvas jerkin. 'It would be a cruel irony should one Battle be eliminated by another.'

Hauled upright, the youngster finally relented and bolted for the nearby copse and the causeway leading to the fort, Smith keeping pace. Arrows flew close. The president turned and fired his pistol, bundling the boy onward.

A settler took an arrow in the back as they passed him. The man grunted and fell forward onto his face.

'He is dead.' Smith shook the youth, who had paused to stare. 'Our concerns are with the living.'

Pell-mell, they dashed for the fort's open gates as a culverin roared above their heads. The Indians were not dissuaded. They flitted among the trees and scrambled low to the base of the palisade, spreading the targets and confusing the defence.

Bent to recover his breath, Smith watched the stragglers enter and the barrier close behind them.

'We outfoxed them, Mr Smith.' Edward Battle beamed.

'Through miracle and act of God.' The president shook his head. 'A surfeit of folly will see you dead.'

The body tumbling from above and landing at Smith's feet seemed to make the point. He knelt to examine the corpse, his fingers reaching for the wound. He stood.

'They train muskets on our rampart! Take cover!'

Smith clambered fast to a platform. From the treeline, he could see sporadic puffs of smoke. He scarcely noticed the musket ball striking the timber strut beside his head.

'I count five muzzles.' Smith squinted from his vantage. 'Enough to serve as a warning, too insufficient to be the Spanish.'

The guard beside him was not so sanguine. 'What of our truce? What of the crown Admiral Newport placed upon Powhatan's head?'

'One bauble does not make a lasting friendship.' Another musket ball ricocheted near. 'Where the native senses blood or weakness, his instinct is to hunt.'

'It appears he has assistance.'

Smith could scarce deny it. Yet he was certain it would take an army to dislodge them from their redoubt. Smith thought of the man Realm, whom Hardy had warned him of. Perhaps in his machinations against the settlement the renegade would take the longer view, concentrating on wearing down morale and encouraging defection. Walls meant nothing when grain stores lay empty and the human spirit broke.

'To your left!' the president cried.

It was too late for the guard. He moved to grapple with a native emerging above the fortifications, but his adversary was quick and his steel blade keen. Smith responded in kind. The brave fell back, the point of a sword cleaved through his ribs, and toppled from the edge. The president was not done. Another Indian had appeared, his teeth clenched down on a bow and his body ascending behind.

'This is no way for our first meeting.' Smith's boot connected hard and the figure disappeared. 'I choose manners a little more formal.'

Finally the attackers withdrew, and the noise and smoke abated. Jamestown still stood. In the unnerving silence, the bell was sounded for the muster to be taken.

For Hardy, a brazen approach was preferable to an unrecorded death in some rank alleyway of London. As he approached his destination, he chose not to scan the staring faces. They knew him well enough – had once spoken of him in hushed asides and with admiration in their eyes – but might still be plotting his murder. In previous times he had often visited and felt part of their community. Now, as an outsider, he entered enemy terrain. The home of Robert Cecil rarely gave a welcome to those who had fallen from favour.

Their gaze followed him as he mounted the steps and entered the outer vestibule. From the towers and brick facade to the furnishings within, everything reeked of power. Ambition and ruthlessness had built this edifice and kept its owner secure. Each gilded carving and tapestry of precious thread was testament to his cunning. The intelligencer now ignored the petitioners and gentlemen gathered to plead or bribe or pay respects. Fawning was not for him. He was here to confront.

An armed porter appeared. 'Your business?'

'It is my own.' Hardy unbuckled his sword and passed it to the man.

It was possible they had expected him, or were simply shocked into inertia: still they did not halt him. He climbed the stairs and progressed through the guardroom, oblivious to the wave of confusion he created. This was the inner sanctum of authority. Divine right flowed from God to the King, and was then discharged by a malformed pygmy. For a minister with a club foot, Cecil had proved himself adroit. Hardy pressed on. About him, secretaries and clerks looked on in stark amazement.

'Trespass must have its reason.'

Cecil alone seemed unruffled by the intrusion. He sat behind his writing desk, a Lord Treasurer hemmed in by neat towers of paper and documents of state. Government resided here. Nothing happened without his perusal; not a rumour circulated nor was a treasonous word spoken without interception and onward relay to his office. The Earl of Salisbury deserved his formidable reputation.

His focus did not waver. 'Affront me and you offend the King. Offend the King, and it is treason.'

'There is no traitor in this chamber.'

'Yet there is much insolence.' The minister studied Hardy's face. 'You consort with the savage and lose your manners.'

'Perfume and poetry are for the court.'

'You were ever the reluctant gallant. Too bold for your own good.'

'I live.'

Cecil smiled. 'A temporary condition.' He blinked. 'I recall you are no longer in my employ.'

'It makes me no enemy.'

'Men have ended up in the Tower for less.'

'Did I not guard Queen Elizabeth from the aim of an assassin? Preserve King James from Catesby and Guido Fawkes?'

'Gratitude is a most fleeting thing.'

Hardy nodded. 'So too is the loyalty of my former master.'

'I could have you killed where you stand.'

'And risk the wrath of young Prince Henry?' The intelligencer shook his head. 'Your mansion is watched and your movements noted.'

'A perfect setting, then, for discourse.' Cecil gestured to a chair.

Hardy sat. 'What sleepless nights you must endure since Jamestown yet survives.'

'I suspect you have played your part.'

'As you do.' Hardy leant forward. 'Ratcliffe?'

'He serves me, as you serve Prince Henry.'

'Choose better for your kennel.'

The treasurer's smile flared and died. 'You give me counsel? You presume I am a novice at this game?'

'War by proxy is no sport, my lord.'

'You will find it is, in politics.' Cecil rested back in his seat. 'Let me now by turn proffer advice. You have a son, handsome and skilled, a patriot unto death. Ensure that his death is not before his natural end.'

Hardy's eyes narrowed. 'It is unwise to bandy threats, my lord.'

'I point merely to the obvious. Adam is feted as you once were; is matchless in the art of spying. Hence I keep him close.'

In these dangerous times leaders remained fearful. Hardy saw it in Cecil's dead eyes, in the trappings of his office, the papers piled high. Such men accumulated wealth and status and then spent each waking moment fretting their gains would be lost.

Hardy stood. 'I shall not keep you from your affairs.'

'Nor I from yours.' The Earl of Salisbury nodded and then returned his gaze to his papers. 'I trust you learn from our encounter.'

'More than you may tell, my lord.'

The call of the night watch and the intermittent glow of lanterns did little to disturb the evening's peace. In the walled gardens and orchards behind the great houses, there was every reason for guards to doze or fumble with the doxies they had met in nearby taverns. Their lordships would be too busy to care.

Crouched beside an upturned cart, Hardy maintained a patient vigil. His earlier display had been a feint, designed to lull and reconnoitre and throw Cecil from his scent. Now he was returned. It was fortunate the sentries were drunk, their slumber enhanced by potent drops added to their beer; it was fortuitous also that their apparent patrols were conducted by replacements paid by the intelligencer. All was in place. Even the dogs had been silenced with scraps of meat dosed with the same sleeping draught.

He stirred, moving forward, keeping low and tracing the perimeter. Tonight he would avoid the grand entrance, would circumvent formality. This was to be a covert visit.

There they were: the unchanged contours and rough-hewn surface of the shed. Whenever there was need to travel unseen or meet agents in secret, a hidden passageway could prove useful. Hardy had ventured this way on countless occasions. He picked the lock now with practised ease and entered.

It was strange to be moving within the bowels of the house without challenge or incident. Quietly, he climbed the spiral stair, sensing his way, his fingers acting as his guide. Caution was his defence. From the glow of the light upstairs, he could hear voices. The danger was greatest when crossing from one world to the other. He paused to listen.

Now he was back in Cecil's study, a thief at play in the den of another. The hidden door's discreet catch and false panel had presented little difficulty, and Hardy gave thanks to God. Arrogance would always convince powerful men of their invincibility.

Hardy worked methodically now, the gentle illumination from a shuttered lantern leading him to the archives and stacked boxes of dispatches. Everything left a trail, and every spymaster a record of his dealings. Cecil was the most meticulous of men.

Hardy dropped to his knees, alerted to a sound, and snapped the lamp shut. He breathed, calming his pulse and weighing the scenario. He would need to go on the attack to permit his escape. The footsteps retreated on their Turkish silks and a bored steward or inquisitive retainer lived to greet the dawn. Hardy returned to his task.

Revelation often had no fanfare. But as he skimmed the pages, a discovery emerged. This was his evidence, the proof laid bare, the compacts and deceptions on which Cecil had built his empire. The intelligencer made his selection and slipped the papers into a goatskin pouch. Suspicions born in Virginia were now confirmed.

There was a final act. Hardy reached forward and placed the black fragment of obsidian in a dispatch box before lowering the lid. It was important Cecil found it. The Lord Treasurer would comprehend the provenance and know the trespasser. Realm had sent the volcanic glass as a coded greeting to Hardy, and here it was gifted again.

CHAPTER 11

Dinner that evening was an austere affair. Cecil would not waste resources on those he was obliged to reprimand. The opulence of the chamber alone would reinforce his message. It was hung with fine paintings and lit by candles set in gilded holders, the light shimmering off silverware and Venetian glass. He was the power behind the throne, and his guests would bend their knee. Yet all was not tranquil in the Earl of Salisbury's world.

He sipped slowly from his cup and placed it on the table. To either side of him sat John Ratcliffe and Gabriel Archer, late of the Jamestown settlement.

'A vexing thing.' He regarded them both. 'A disappointment.'

Ratcliffe shifted in his seat. 'One that is not of our choosing, my lord.'

'Yet it may be of your making.' Cecil let the silence stretch.

'We laboured hard at your behest, my lord.'

'The result proves your labours were in vain.' He took another sip. 'Smith is president, and Hardy lives to stalk into my London home.'

'My lord—'

Ratcliffe's stammered protest was cut short. 'Everywhere there is talk of Jamestown. Jamestown as a patriotic duty. Jamestown as a sacred cause.'

'I cannot explain it, my lord.'

'In time, you might answer for it.' The Lord Treasurer's words were soft, his eyes glacial. 'It displeases the King to hear the news from Virginia.'

'We are his loyal servants.'

'Where is loyalty in failure? Where is service when the ramparts of the colony still stand?'

'Events overtook us, my lord.'

'Rather, it was your weakness and paltry commitment.' Cecil saw the men flinch. 'I gave you back your life and a purpose, the chance of redemption through striving for our nation.'

'We did all that we could, my lord.'

'Words are no substitute for deeds.'

'At every turn I spread discord and promoted despair, set faction against faction, frustrated the colony with wasteful ventures.'

'So wasteful it seems to thrive.'

'Thrive, my lord?' Ratcliffe rejected the charge. 'Jamestown is diseased and broken and staggers for the grave.'

'How then can you explain the ships gathering at Woolwich? Are they pall-bearers? Mourners come to mock the corpse?'

Unease pervaded the room. An audience with the little pygmy was rarely a comfortable event. He liked it that way. It kept his associates respectful and his underlings in their place. Cecil stabbed at a platter of pork and chewed on a succulent morsel.

'Have you lost your appetite?' he asked his guests. He lifted more meat to his mouth.

Ratcliffe inclined his head. 'Your generosity is too great, my lord.'

'My wrath, too, is noted. It will further rise should my wishes go ignored.' He turned to Archer. 'Why such silence in your corner?'

'My lord, I defer to those better placed to answer.'

'No one is so well placed as one who has lived within the Jamestown palisade.'

'Do not doubt my efforts, my lord.'

'It is your abilities I decry.' Cecil rested his knife and fork. 'From each of you I demanded a result. Instead you greet me with excuses.'

'We seek merely to explain, my lord.'

'I need no explanation. Where there should be doubt, I see the poisonous weed of hope. Whatever my overtures to Parliament, my emollient tone of compromise, I desire Jamestown dead.'

'As you command, my lord.'

'Then we are agreed.' The Lord Treasurer was precise in his delivery. 'You are both to return abroad.'

Sweat glistened on Ratcliffe's brow. 'Return?'

'It is for the best.'

'Smith will hang us there, my lord.'

'I will hang you here should you refuse. You have unfinished work.'

'This is madness, my lord.' Archer stammered his objection.

'You deem me mad?'

'Never, my lord. Yet I beg you choose a different path, one more likely to succeed.'

'I retain a touching faith in you.'

'Always have I sought to repay it. But Virginia?'

'Do not force me to send others.' Cecil selected a slice of pie. 'What I ask for, I shall have.'

Ratcliffe swallowed, then drank deep from his glass. 'Obedience is our way, my lord.'

'There is no other path for you. A second charter for the Virginia Company is currently in draft. It will remove Smith as president of Jamestown and instead create the office of governor.'

'Will that not strengthen the colony?'

'Change brings opportunity, while upheaval begets the chance for further mischief.'

Cecil's was a ruthlessly sophisticated game. Every ploy had its reason and every move by an adversary its matching counterstroke. The Lord Treasurer had not climbed so far only now to upset the King or see his efforts thwarted.

As the men dined and the sound of their conversation rose and fell in the confines of the room, they failed to glance towards the minstrel gallery. Candle flames created many deep shadows and ensured the intruder remained unseen.

Hardy had gleaned enough. He retraced his steps to the study, his pace steady and senses tuned, a servant about his business. He would not lower his guard until he was far away from the place. His former chief had a long reach and an unmatched ability to hold a grudge.

The man he encountered as he fled the house had not expected him; was still less prepared for the single blow that pitched him into unconsciousness. Curiosity could be dangerous. In an instant Hardy had dragged the body inside and closed the door behind it. It would take a while for the alarm to be raised or a search to be mounted. In the ordered world of a private household, irregularities were uncommon and discretion was the key. Soon, though, the injured man would awake uncomprehending to the reality that his mouth was gagged and hands tied, and that he lay in a panelled compartment, his assailant vanished.

Freed from the claustrophobia of the mansion, Hardy loped back to his hiding place. It had been a successful mission. Only later would he revisit in his mind each step and nuance of the evening. Now, distance was needed. He offered a prayer of thanks, cast a final glance back towards the shadowed edifice and slid away.

'Even the best may fall prey to their own confidence.' A voice came from the darkness.

Hardy peered into the alleyway. 'You hold a blade or pistol on me?'

'Would I dare?' The man laughed. 'I know only too well my father.'

'As I my son.' Hardy had not relaxed his guard. 'Do you come as friend or foe, Adam?'

Adam moved closer. 'Merely as your child.'

'That is no reason for your presence.'

'Am I not to be concerned? Should I feel no love or loyalty or duty to protect you?'

'I defend myself.'

'So you do, and with matchless ease. Yet you are mortal and you have your foes. These weeks past I have killed three rogues employed by the Spanish ambassador and intending your murder.'

Hardy nodded. 'Zúñiga and I are no friends.'

'He desires to see you dead. It is by order of his king.'

They grew silent, their caution surrendering to instinct and trust. The wife Hardy had loved was mother to this boy; she had been butchered by Realm in the name of Spain. Forgiveness was for others. The intelligencer should have guessed his own blood would not betray him.

He spoke. 'You imperil yourself by helping me.'

'Is it not my obligation, as your son?'

'There is yet the wrath of Cecil.'

'A burden we must share.' Adam seemed unconcerned. 'He trusts me, as once he trusted you.'

'His affection is fleeting, will in an instant turn to jealousy and hate.'

'I shall be prepared.'

'He holds you as a hostage against me, Adam. If I discover too much, he will feed you to his dogs.'

'Then I am glad to have a guardian angel.' The young man spoke softly. 'I answer not to Cecil, but to my true master, Prince Henry.'

Hardy began to laugh, relief easing the tension of the moment. Little was surprising in the world they inhabited. Like father, like son. Deep within the secret state, Adam was reporting to the heir apparent on the moves and methods of King James and his spy chief.

There was gentle pride in the voice of the father. 'I believed I had a boy. Instead he grows into a magician.'

'Would you have it any other way?'

'For the sake of this nation, I would not.' Hardy was approving. 'Yet be careful, for we stir up many things.' He reached out a hand and touched Adam's arm. 'Go now, and keep safe in how you tread.'

'Where do you journey?'

'Wherever I am sent.'

Father and son embraced, their reunion brief and their parting accompanied by the usual sorrow. Neither would pry too deep. Their chosen trade did not encourage openness. Yet, though separated in age by twenty years, there was more that brought them together than the danger they each faced.

Cantering hooves and the sound of a horn announced the delegation. Twenty miles to the north-east of London, on the beechwood fringes of Epping Forest, a rendezvous was planned by royal command. Here, a monarch and his trusted lieutenant would meet; here, as the April sunlight glanced off the ruins of Waltham Abbey, affairs of state would be decided. Ever fearful of assassination, as well as the plague, the King preferred to keep on the move. It was one way to remain ahead of his enemies.

An answer came, the royal trumpeters giving full vent as the cavalcade hove into view. The sovereign and his minister would now be left alone. Cecil dismounted and bowed. Doubtless there would be the usual cruel jibes and casual put-downs, the obsessive questioning, the fretfulness of a king forever looking over his shoulder. This was a small price to pay for the gift of vested authority.

The Lord Treasurer straightened. It took one malformed freak to know another.

The King's weeping eyes surveyed him. 'My little beagle replies to the whistle.'

'I am ever at your service, Majesty.'

'Though not always to success.' James clambered from his steed. 'News vexes me from every quarter.'

'All shall turn to our favour, Majesty.'

'Will it? Will my son Prince Henry suddenly become less revered than I? Will the parliamentarians be tamed, or that shit-privy of Jamestown slide into the swamp?'

'Arrangements are being made.'

'I see only portents of disaster.' James shook his head. 'Nowhere is safe for me in this kingdom.'

Flattery was required, and Cecil would deliver. 'His Majesty is beloved. His Majesty, by the grace of God and by dint of his own faculty, confounded the Catholic plotters in their foul gunpowder treason.'

'You think they were alone? You trust there are no others?'

'Not once did any in your kingdom rally to their demonic cause.'

'Yet still there is opposition.' A nerve twitched. 'Parliament grows stronger and more defiant, has the base impertinence to challenge me.'

'Coax and charm them, Majesty. They hold the purse strings of the nation.'

The coffers were bare; had been emptied by the profligacy of the King. Only through Parliament and the raising of taxes could they be replenished; only with compromise could a deal be struck. It rankled. A royal debt of six hundred thousand pounds had shifted the balance of power. James might rule by divine right, but politicians and merchants would now have their say. Concession and conciliation were key. Cecil was the most assiduous of fixers.

His master stared. 'Mark my words, my beagle. They will use Virginia as a rod to scourge my back.'

'Your foes shall not prevail, Majesty.'

'How can you be sure?' The King gazed up to the spreading branches of an oak tree. 'So secure do they feel in their purpose, they assemble eight ships at Woolwich.'

'There is many an accident between intention and result.'

'I rely on you, my beagle.'

'Be certain I will not fail you.'

The King's eyes continued to water. 'I cannot countenance it, cannot permit a rotten seed of treachery and misrule to sprout itself abroad.'

'Have faith, Majesty.'

'When there is such ecstatic mood for foreign venture? When my son Henry feeds the hunger? When the Low Countries sign a peace with Spain and will themselves hunt for new territory?'

'Jamestown will perish, Majesty.'

'I shall hold you to your promise.'

The interview had lasted long enough. The King was fidgeting, anxious to climb once more into the saddle and be away. Old neuroses attended him like courtiers. Cecil recognised the signs. He had often profited from such paranoia.

His forehead dipped. 'I shall not delay you further, Majesty.'

'Be ever guided by my wishes.'

A bugle call and jab of spurs, and the royal party disappeared. The Lord Treasurer stood awhile, contemplative in the silence. He was never praised by the little King, only criticised. It mattered not. There were more pressing concerns, which his position depended upon.

Thoughts of Christian Hardy invaded his consciousness. Rarely was the chief minister of state thrown by circumstance or beset by worry. Yet the intelligencer had introduced a new dimension to the game, brazenly setting traps in his path. A novel situation. Cecil reached into his pocket and felt the faceted piece of obsidian. A transgression of such magnitude could not be allowed to go unpunished.

'You suffer.'

It was a simple observation. Pity or concern were extravagances Realm had long ago discarded. He often sought out the dying, for they contained the kernel of truth that man was no more than faeces and dust. The native seemed already to be transported now, his skin pale and eyes uncomprehending, his lips moving soundlessly. No one could outlive a stomach wound like this. In a sense the English renegade was to blame for it; he had provoked Powhatan by his barbarous acts, implicating Jamestown. Sacrifice was necessary. He would not be unduly concerned.

He leant closer. 'Tell me how it feels. Describe the gods or angels that you see.'

The dying warrior was unforthcoming. A disappointment. Things were rarely as colourful as one hoped. Realm reached and pressed a finger hard into the blood-filled wound. At least there was reaction to this.

Realm's finger sank into the man's stomach to the knuckle, tracing the course of the shot. Soon, Opechancanough would lead his people in dance and song and ask the spirits to accept another into their midst.

Realm rose and stepped from the hut, his Imbangala bodyguard falling in beside him. For the moment, they remained welcome in the village and were valued for what they brought. God help them when the reservoir of goodwill dried.

Seated on a cushion of animal skins, Opechancanough studied their approach. By the day, the military chief of the Powhatan empire learnt; by the day, his grip tightened and his influence grew. His gaze missed little.

He gestured for Realm to sit. 'Again we mourn brave men.'

'Are warriors not born to die?'

'Like arrows, they are still precious.' Opechancanough waved his hand. 'We have tried your muskets and they bring us no success.'

'Be patient, Opechancanough.'

'Patience is for those who weave and sew.'

'Such weapons have their uses,' Realm persisted. 'Have muskets not allowed John Smith to travel with impunity? Do they not defend Jamestown from attack?'

'Still we cannot remove the pale-skins.'

'Perhaps they will remove themselves. We know rats infest their grain, that more of the settlers desert, that Smith sends scores of men to scavenge for oysters in Chesapeake Bay.'

'What if further ships should come?'

'Then they will starve the quicker, for having more mouths to feed.' The renegade was confident. 'And you will show Powhatan why he was weak to offer peace and friendship to the English.'

'They will never be our blood.'

'One day you will bind your people together, Opechancanough. One day you will succeed Powhatan and extend the lands of Tsenacomoco.'

'If it is the will of the gods.'

'They reward the bold and not the timid.'

A low howl proclaimed the death of the wounded brave, and the priests now gathered for the rites. Realm would leave them to their superstitions.

He wandered from the scene, preferring to walk the reed banks of the Pamunkey and dwell on other matters. There was every chance Jamestown would disintegrate beneath the weight of its own folly. Yet there was a risk, too, that it might, through fluke or mishap, survive and be saved by resupply. He was certain Christian Hardy was not finished with the project, and that events were now occurring in England that would alter all calculations. The renegade picked up a stone and skimmed it across the water. He would play the game as he found it.

In a wooded glade close to Highgate, a select and extraordinary conference was in session attended only by His Excellency the Spanish ambassador and the misshapen Robert Cecil. Both men wore richly embroidered black doublets, and both had a vested interest in keeping their dealings private.

Cecil held the black fragment of obsidian in his fingers. 'Proof as damning as any seal or signature, Your Excellency.'

'Of what, my lord?'

'Meddling and mendacity.'

'Have our nations not put aside their quarrel?' Don Pedro de Zúñiga was artful in his feigned innocence. 'Are we not as cousins bound by amity and peace?'

'Evidence tells no lie.'

Zúñiga waved a dismissive hand. 'A piece of black crystal?'

'Volcanic glass, Don Pedro. Volcanic glass discovered in Virginia.'

'It is said the savages collect such things.'

'So too the English renegade known as Realm, a man I handed to your care to spare embarrassment in the wake of the great Powder Treason.'

'I cannot vouch for his situation.'

'Nor may you deny he is again loosed, freed by Spain to do mischief upon Jamestown.'

'Is that not what you want, my lord?'

Silence was its own reply. Too much rested on the collapse of the colony to permit chance alone to decide its fate. With events overtaking the Lord Treasurer and a resupply fleet readying to depart, the discreet intervention by the Spaniards was not altogether unwelcome. Prevention of war was the overriding concern.

'I hear of things,' Zúñiga continued. 'Of troubling matters. Of ships gathering and men assembling to support the English colony.'

'The enthusiasm will pass.'

'Will it? Will your Parliament become less vociferous? Will Prince Henry tire of his ambition?'

'He is young and will find fresh distraction.'

'A prediction worth no more than a roll of the dice.' The ambassador shook his head. 'Even the infamous Christian Hardy is protected, walks unchallenged on his business.'

Cecil peered in blank detachment. 'Have you tried to kill him?'

Zúñiga smiled. 'We each pray for what is best, my lord.'

'What is best is hard to judge.'

'We desire continued truce and our monarchs ascendant, and little to disturb the peace.'

'My waking moments are directed to it.' Cecil walked to his horse and extracted from the saddlebag a sheaf of documents. 'These papers contain much of interest, Don Pedro. The new Virginia charter, the details of the ships to sail and the intentions of the latest venture.'

Zúñiga took the documents. 'Which are?'

'Colonisation.'

One word that conveyed everything. A venture that had once appeared contained, condemned to a lingering death, was reborn as a crusade. It would take careful planning to destroy it. Ambassador and Lord Treasurer comprehended. They were gifted men, not given to surrender.

'God save the prince! Long live Prince Henry!'

Adulation swirled about him. He was the chosen one, the heir apparent, the young Hal who embodied the hopes of a nation. So the people flocked. It was 8 May 1609 and, attended by his chaplains and lieutenants, the fifteen-year-old had come to Woolwich. Here, he could inspect the ongoing construction of the magnificent new warship *The Prince Royal*. Moreover he could visit, too, the eight large vessels being rigged and loaded for imminent voyage to Virginia. There was reason for festivity, for the banners to fly and the crowds to cheer. A New Britain was at hand.

An old woman sank to her knees and wept before the prince. 'May the Lord bless Your Highness.'

'Dry your tears, for it is joy we embrace this day.'

Gently he took the old woman's hand and encouraged her to rise up. The rapture grew. The prince was happy to walk among his future subjects, obliging them with smiles and permitting them to touch the hem of his royal cloak. His bodyguards looked on, watching for potential hostility, for any Catholic with murderous intent secreted in the throng. Not everyone favoured a Stuart dynasty.

Henry leapt upon a trestle set between two hogsheads and raised his hand. The hubbub stilled.

'Citizens of England. You know who I am and that I am your servant.' He paused to scan their faces. 'See these ships, the *Sea Venture*, *Blessing* and *Diamond* among them. I bid you remember their names and entreat you too to join their company. A week hence they will sail for Virginia and create for our land a greatness as yet unrealised.'

The crowd responded as expected, their fervour uncontained. The prince spoke with confidence and with conviction in his eye. This was a youth to heed.

He tipped coins from a purse and displayed them in his open palm. 'Twelve pounds and ten shillings, the fee demanded from any worker to embark upon this venture.' He clenched the money tight and raised his fist.

'I will pay the sum for one loyal soul to join such a heroic mission.' The crowd jostled for the honour as Henry stood above them. 'Each man or woman shall have a dwelling, complete with a garden and orchard. Each too will have a share in the profit of all that he harvests or builds.'

The message was infectious. The prince's audience had become his congregation. He preached to the converted. In London, queues formed as volunteers responded; at Woolwich, more were coming forward. The momentum was unstoppable.

Through the glass panes of the day cabin, the dockside clamour of loading and readying pressed on unabated. There were the shouts of sailors and labourers; the bellow of livestock and the whinny of horses; the piercing cry of whistles. Everywhere there was urgency. It was no surprise that Prince Henry had selected a vessel for closer perusal. Few could doubt his commitment. No one need remind him that his father, the King, would scarce approve.

Aboard the *Lion*, he bade his retinue wait and proceeded below deck alone. As he entered a cabin and closed the door, a figure in the worn garb of a shipwright doffed his cap and bowed. Hardy was reporting to his master.

Henry paused, his eyes betraying amusement. 'Is there any disguise you do not adopt?'

'I am less suited to play a wench, sir.'

The prince smiled. 'Then we shall keep you as an artisan.' He nodded his appreciation. 'I am grateful for your effort, Mr Hardy.'

'It is you on whom success or failure hangs.'

'God willing, we will prevail.'

'Eight ships prepare; eight separate reasons to trust we stand a chance.'

'Chance.' Henry repeated the word. 'The King will strive to ensure we have none.'

'I wait with bated breath to see what trickery Cecil unfurls.'

'He is a most tenacious midget.'

'A dangerous one, to be sure.'

They knew already that the Earl of Salisbury had arranged for John Ratcliffe and Gabriel Archer to sail again for Jamestown. There would be other moves, subtle and deadly and hidden from the eye. Cecil did not like to lose.

The prince appraised his intelligencer. 'Am I sending you to your death, Mr Hardy?'

'I accept the risk, and whatever is my due.'

'So speaks a true servant of England.'

'Your father would think otherwise.'

'He owes you his life, Mr Hardy.' Henry spoke with feeling. 'Yet I concede his gratitude is wanting.'

'I seek no praise or plaudit, sir.'

'You earn it a thousand times. I shall not forget your kindness.'

'Nor I the faith you place in me.'

'Providence is with us, Mr Hardy.'

Perhaps it was. The Virginia Company had its second charter, and a fine soldier, Sir Thomas Gates, had been appointed colonial governor. His authority would be absolute and his objective clear. Hostility from the redskin savage would no longer be tolerated; no longer would homage be paid to Powhatan. Insurrection was to be crushed and the natives brought into the light. To this end, a new capital was intended for Virginia and would be sited beyond the falls. Jamestown would lapse to secondary status, receding from pioneering fort and outpost to a mere trading point on the river. Progress ever had its casualties.

Hardy noted the ferocity of the prince's ambition, the belief behind the steady gaze. He too had been young once.

'What of my son?' the intelligencer asked.

There was no hesitation. 'He is like a brother to me – I will not see him harmed.'

'Adam is your spy?'

'I need my wits about me, and sharp eyes and ears in the enemy camp.'

'If he is discovered Cecil will show him no mercy.'

'Then we must make sure he is not.'

The life of an intelligencer rarely ended in old age, yet there were ways to mitigate the risks. Hardy reached for the document pouch hidden at his side and passed it to the prince.

'These papers are precious to our Lord Treasurer.'

'I presume he did not surrender such gifts willingly?'

'Neither he nor the King would welcome their revelation.'

The prince's face lit up with glee. He had suffered enough from the jealousies of his father and the machinations of Robert Cecil. And now he held insight, knowledge and power in his grasp. The youth was learning to be a future king. Prince Henry's overseas project would proceed.

In mid-May 1609, eight ships and some five hundred settlers left Woolwich to make their way along the south coast to Plymouth. Not all of those aboard were driven by dreams of adventure and new beginnings. For some it was an alternative to jail; a means to escape debt or persecution or the noose. There were vagrants and unruly youths and prisoners discharged from Newgate; there were Dutchmen and Schismatics and Protestant firebrands. Everyone had their story and their reasons.

Hardy had his reasons too. On the *Lion*, he felt the swell beneath the keel and watched the pennants stream from the tops of the sister ships as the wind caught their sails. A pretty sight for something so deadly. He could not forget that the *Blessing* carried Archer and the *Diamond* his associate, John Ratcliffe. Two men who did the bidding of Cecil and possessed no goodwill for Jamestown. At his side, Buckler leant against his knee as a reminder of his presence, and he stooped to pat him. Prince Henry had asked Hardy if he was sending him to his death. He would have to wait for the answer.

CHAPTER 12

I give to my wife all my goods and chattels, debts and bills.

Lawyers and clergymen did well in Plymouth, so too the owners of brothels and taverns. Confronted by the sea and their impending departure, and by a sense of their own mortality, travellers were obliged to make their peace in whatever way suited them best. Some prayed or wrote last wishes; others committed themselves to drink and fornication. Sadness and resignation pervaded, but there would be time later for regret.

In the room of a local notary, John Ratcliffe completed the dictation of his last will and testament. There was no going back. The witnesses signed the document, and it was sealed and placed for safekeeping in an iron-framed cabinet. A key was turned in its lock and the meeting concluded.

Donning his cloak and tugging at the brim of his high felt hat, Ratcliffe stepped into the streets and alleyways below the Hoe. Above him, carved white in the escarpment, glowered the twin figures of Gog and Magog, folklore giants, defenders of the nation.

'Well might you write your will.' Ultramarine eyes surveyed him. 'You have not heeded my warning.'

'Christian Hardy.' Ratcliffe's delivery was flat.

'You voyage on the *Diamond*; I journey on the *Lion*.'

'No doubt you have your reasons.'

'I am certain you have yours.' The intelligencer's gaze did not flicker. 'I see you listed as a captain of passengers. A fine title for a villain and a knave.'

'Some would dub me loyal, Hardy.'

'To whom?'

There were many layers to this man; aspects and identities he would never divulge. Ratcliffe, the ousted president of a cesspool in Virginia; or Sicklemore, the former Catholic priest captured and co-opted by Robert Cecil. The politics and religion of the age created strange allegiances.

'Where is your dog, Hardy?'

'He hunts for smaller vermin.'

'You flatter me.'

'It is not too late to retreat, Ratcliffe.' The intelligencer kept his hand close to his Katzbalger. 'Should you and Archer stay behind, you would do greater service to yourselves and to your master.'

'We take no instruction from you.'

'Have it as you wish. Yet remember at your final breath that I gave you the chance of life.'

Ratcliffe scoffed. 'A condemned man offers me a chance?'

'Awaken to the reality. You have lost, Ratcliffe. A fleet sails with five hundred souls to renew and replenish Jamestown.'

Ratcliffe inclined his head. Hardy might enjoy the support of Prince Henry, but in a trial of strength and sheer guile, King James and his Lord Treasurer were the favourites.

'Perchance you have not heard?' Ratcliffe regarded his opponent. 'Gabriel Archer and I have been reappointed to the council in Jamestown.'

'To subvert and spread sedition? I should kill you now.'

'Murder an officer on state business?' Ratcliffe shook his head. 'Expect perilous times, Hardy.'

Hardy shrugged. The ex-president's opportunity to dispose of him had been missed back in his extravagant and half-completed palace in the woods beyond the Jamestown fort.

'Everything is still to play for, Hardy.'

'I never play.'

It was always the eyes that betrayed intent. In an instant Hardy had seized Ratcliffe, holding a knife to his throat even as the ex-president spun to face the threat. Three strangers confronted him then, cloaks draped across their forearms, hiding pistols beneath them.

Hardy pressed in close to Ratcliffe. 'You disturb our friendly discourse.'

'Friendship with a steel blade?' The spokesman did not move.

'There is amity of many kinds.' Hardy watched the faces. 'State your purpose.'

'We bid you come with us.'

'With weapons levelled?' Hardy could smell the sweat on Ratcliffe's neck. 'And if I am not persuaded?'

'All means are granted to us by his lordship Robert Cecil, Earl of Salisbury. Do not keep him waiting. He has travelled from London in some haste and discomfort.'

So the Lord Treasurer was spooked. He was unaccustomed to being outmanoeuvred. Hardy had anticipated a reaction to his recent break-in. Yet the little pygmy would be cautious still. This summons to an audience was simply the opening move.

'Are you so confident now?' Ratcliffe hissed.

'A pig will keep for butchery, Sicklemore.'

Hardy pushed his prisoner aside and stepped towards the waiting escort. They might dispatch him with a sword or a shot in a more secluded place, but he was willing to take the risk.

Cecil stood at the altar and greeted his guest with little more than a stare. The statesman and schemer had chosen his stage with care; the Chapel of St Katherine on Plymouth Hoe was where kings had prayed before going to war and where Drake had knelt as the Armada approached. The message was clear. God and King James favoured the loyal.

Cecil half-shuttered his eyelids. 'You have thieved from me. To steal state secrets is a treasonous act.'

'No, my lord. It is their content that is treasonous.'

'You will hang.'

'Not before the wicker hurdle bears you to the scaffold also.'

'Blackmail?'

'Let us suppose I am moved to pass the documents to the discerning and the good.'

'That would be unwise. Where are my papers?'

'Far beyond your reach, my lord.'

'You dare to bargain with me?'

'All these things and more.' Hardy stared at the spy chief. 'You incite in Jamestown sedition and dissent, and conspire with the Spanish to destroy it.'

'I have my reasons.'

'None will afford you excuse when set before the people and Parliament and the law.'

'What do they know of defending the realm and doing what is needed?'

Hardy shook his head. 'Such base instinct and low cunning from a minister of state.'

'My office demands it.'

'Does it demand you plot against Prince Henry and embezzle from the King? Place traps to snare the nobles you despise?'

'A pity you are trained to read as well as to spy and kill.'

There was almost admiration in the voice, a recognition that the intelligencer had perhaps won the bout. It was not often the spymaster ceded the advantage. Yet there would be repercussions and a sting to this encounter. Hardy had learnt to take little for granted.

The Lord Treasurer rubbed at a flagstone with the sole of his shoe. 'Speak your terms, Mr Hardy.'

'My son Adam is precious to me, and serves in your employ. Should any harm befall him, you have my word that much worse will assail and ruin you.'

'I am sure we shall maintain the peace.'

'It is all I ask.'

'The love of a father is most touching,' Cecil said. 'His death is always felt.'

'I care not for myself.'

'There is no other explanation for your folly. Besides, Jamestown is lost this day or the next, and your effort will go wasted.'

'You forget the hundreds that journey there, and the new governor who will join them.'

A pause and a slow smile. 'Sir Thomas Gates is detained.'

'Detained?'

'His demotion to the rank of vice-governor is immediate, and supreme command is granted to Lord Delaware.'

A further act of sabotage. It was the natural reaction of Robert Cecil when cornered or confronted. A coup had been mounted before the fleet had even sailed. In place of Gates, the hardened and respected soldier, Delaware, the peer and privy councillor, was appointed. There could be no mistaking where the loyalties of the nobleman resided or to whom he would report. A wood stockade offered scant defence for a colony so beset with foes.

Cecil raised his hand in a gesture of farewell. 'May fortune smile on you, Mr Hardy.'

Their meeting over, his lordship would return to London and Hardy to his vessel. Each to his own project, one aiming to erase and the other to protect. Cecil did not care to view the fleet. He was confident it represented nothing but a costly suicide pact. Moreover, he would strive to ensure it.

On 1 June 1609, the ships weighed anchor and headed in line astern for the open sea. Their route would carry them to the Canaries, and then onward westerly through a perilous ocean the several thousand miles to Virginia.

How quickly hope could fade and the memory of cheering crowds be lost to howling storms! The journey had seen treacherous waves and pitching ships, and men and rigging vanishing overboard in a raging vortex of wind and rain. Prayer was wasted and seamanship worthless. Then came the sickness and disease, the blackened corpses of humans and bloated carcasses of livestock thrown unceremoniously into the deep. Even newborn babies were among the dead and joined the funeral drop. Yet the mission endured. By mid-August 1609, battered, listing and stripped of much of their rigging, six transports finally tied up at Jamestown. It had taken two months to make the crossing, and their flagship the *Sea Venture* was yet to arrive.

'Look at them, Christian. You bring me a consignment of the dying and the lame.'

Smith was in no mood to hide his opinion. Each side had met the other in shock and grim dismay, established settlers staring aghast at what appeared from the ships, and newcomers scanning their surroundings with dumb incomprehension. There must have been some mistake. This was not a place of fruitfulness and possibility, an orchard garden scattered with homes fit to occupy. For certain there were storerooms and hovel dwellings and a small church at the centre. Yet there was also a pervading sense of desperation. Jamestown was ill-suited to optimists and dreamers.

'We last another year, and must be grateful for it.'

The president rubbed his beard and observed the scene before him. 'I cannot claim it is perfection.'

Hardy sat on a barrel and crimped a fuse. 'A week in London, and you would race to be here.'

'Yet the cancer returns aboard the *Diamond* and the *Blessing*.'

'We shall find a cure for both Ratcliffe and Archer.'

Hardy held in his palm a ceramic grenade and bent now to seal its mouth with wax, a precise and laborious task. About him were the tools and debris of one of his favourite pastimes: the powder horns and flasks of naphtha, the firkins of pitch and tar. He was fortunate to have Jan at his side, a large and silent Dutchman good with his hands and an expert in explosives. Care was needed in the production of wildfire.

Laughter interrupted their dialogue. Edward Battle was retrieving a dead rat from a prancing Buckler. Boy and dog were reunited. They ran, the youngster wiggling the rodent beyond the canine's reach. It was a furious and gleeful chase.

Smith watched. 'I am glad at last to witness mirth.'

Hardy nodded, then inspected his completed munition. 'What is left when all else is woe?'

'Perhaps not everything is darkness. Here at the fort a new well is dug and fifty homes are constructed. Our ramparts are strong and the causeway secure, and in every quarter there is industry.'

Hardy glanced up. 'And yet?'

The president gestured to the game playing out before him. 'Rats of every kind, gnawing at our being.' He shook his head. 'I tell you, Christian, it is not the Spaniards or savages I fear so much as the Englishmen among us.'

'Traps may be set and a barrel arranged to shoo them off.'

'Will it suffice? Counter such infestation?'

Circumstance would reveal. Hardy thought of Realm and how the renegade would be awaiting his return. Hostilities could resume. Neither party had been idle.

The men heard shouts, the gathering dissonance that foretold of riot or a lynching. Smith wearily backhanded the summer sweat from his brow and touched the butt of his pistol.

'There he is!'

'A president in name alone! See how brash and bold he stands!'

'Well fed too, you will observe!'

A well-armed group advanced with swords already drawn, led by Ratcliffe and Archer. It had not taken long for those answering to Cecil to form an uprising. Buckler ran to sit beside his master.

'What have we now?' Smith too had unsheathed his blade. 'Mutiny?'

'We answer to the second charter,' Ratcliffe replied. 'To rules that replace you with a governor.'

'I see no written document. I spy no *Sea Venture* with Sir Thomas Gates aboard tying up at Jamestown.'

'You no longer have authority.'

Smith jutted out his chin. 'Have you? You traitor; you seditious knave. I vowed you would hang should you return.'

'A tyrant is soon deposed.'

'I am president of Jamestown.'

'You imagine much. Your councillors are dead, killed by fever and the flux. In every corner there is disquiet and discontent.'

'Discontent promoted by you.' Smith jabbed an accusing finger.

It provoked a hurt expression. 'I am innocent of such a charge.'

'Who forced Powhatan and his natives into peace? Who brought this place through hunger and despair until our isolation ended?'

'Your time is spent.'

'There is neither court nor just cause that decrees it.'

'Surrender to us, Smith.'

'I will not.' The president swept his sword in a slow arc to encompass the assembled. 'Submit instead to my governance.'

'What a pity it should come to this. A creature at bay, brought low by its own dim wit and pride.'

'My steel is still keen.'

'Prepare to have it blunted.'

The spearhead of men had flattened for the attack, spreading into a wider front. A fighting force could soon become a rabble. Hardy stayed seated. He studied the individuals, noting the hotheads and the doubters, the gallants and the strays. Ratcliffe and his henchman Archer might have inspired a revolt, but they were no leaders of men. Few here had an appetite to die without reason.

Resolution arrived, an earthen projectile relayed from Jan to Hardy and then lit and launched spinning into flight. The smokepot exploded on impact. As sulphurous fumes engulfed them, the opposition scattered. Men choked and screamed and clutched at their burning eyes, desperate to escape. Their collapse had been instantaneous.

Smith applauded the spectacle. 'What theatre, Christian! What a fine diversion for our jaded tastes.'

'It will hold them awhile.'

'More than that; it will teach them a lesson they shall not forget.'

'Let us hope it is so.'

'Justice is done and the enemy routed.' The president returned his sword to its scabbard. 'I declare this session closed.'

'I trust faction and tumult prevail?'

Realm greeted his informant without so much as a cursory nod. Niceties were not required. Each understood both risk and reward and the long-term goal for which they planned. They were two Englishmen alone in secret rendezvous, answering to different masters and yet committed to the same purpose. Others had defected from Jamestown, had been driven by hunger or disaffection to wander from the settlement. This source stayed on, burrowing deep, listening and watching and letting all collapse about him. He was either brave or foolhardy. Certainly he was dangerous. It deserved a cautious respect.

'Faction and tumult?' The visitor smiled. 'It is ever thus at Jamestown.'

'Yet its numbers swell.'

'More mouths to feed; more grievance and complaint; more seeds with which to sow its ruin.'

Realm studied the man. 'A confident assertion.'

'It is born of observation.' The informant returned his gaze. 'Debate is heated and division is everywhere.'

'They will not see your hand?'

'I play it close. Revelation would not assist my cause.'

'Or be conducive to your health.'

'Indeed so.' The man was unperturbed. 'Better that Ratcliffe and Archer are viewed as the obvious villains of the piece.'

'They have their uses. What of John Smith?'

'He is a bellicose ruffian and a fool.'

'Nevertheless he is the president. He is sly and persistent and forever on his guard.'

'You will find a boil may be lanced there.' The man's gloved hand hovered near his rapier pommel.

'He has plans?'

'To quell disorder, to propel onward his colonial ambitions.'

'Such an onerous task.'

'One destined for a miserable ending.' The visitor gazed into the distance. 'Jamestown founders; its vice-governor Sir Thomas Gates is not arrived, and its governor Lord Delaware sits comfortable in London.'

'Amen to chaos.'

'We must each murmur the prayer.'

But faith was not enough. 'Still there is Christian Hardy. Beware of him.'

'I know him to be skilled with the sword.'

'His eye too is piercing and his instinct sharp.' Realm's tone was almost wistful. 'Get too near, and he will smell your guilt.'

'You admire him?'

'I am aware of what he may do.' Experience had taught the renegade to take little for granted. He had lost to Hardy before, had seen victory snatched in the final seconds of the melee. He would not allow that to happen again. Nor would he allow others the privilege of carrying out the execution. A lifetime of mutual enmity gave him alone the right to the intelligencer's scalp.

His guest readied himself to leave. 'I will report back again.'

'Be certain of my gratitude.' On occasion Realm could affect the manners of the civilised.

The informant bowed and strode away. It was no challenge for him to rejoin his companions and enter the fort with the rest. That was the pernicious charm of an agent placed deep. It was only now that he had become activated. Cecil had chosen well.

By day the ships were patched and their rigging repaired, while at night they became dens of drunkenness and vice. Every town had its seamier quarter; every man or woman consigned to the margins of existence felt compelled to find release. Jamestown and its denizens were no different. Offshore was out of sight. There drums beat, the horns and fiddles played and singing and stupor pervaded. In one corner, men laughed and quarrelled over dice and cards, and in another a youth paid a penny to mount a doxy bent forward over a capstan. Trade everywhere was brisk.

The oppressive heat and the swamp stench of high summer kept people to the upper decks. To go below was to be returned to the nightmare of the recent past; to memories of churning seas and shrieking gales and the piteous death of comrades. It suited Hardy, though. He lay there on a blanket with Awae, stowaways naked and hidden, listening to the sounds around them. The ceaseless murmur evoked the bawdy houses and pleasure gardens on the south bank of the Thames, although England and its capital were only a distant echo. At the locked door of the cabin, Buckler stood guard.

'Why did you come back?' Awae ran a hand across his torso. 'Was it for me?'

'Need you ask such a question?' He leant to kiss and reassure her.

'Tell me again of the storms.'

'They were so loud no man could hear his own voice; so great no one believed they would outlive the night.'

'Yet you are here.'

'For so many reasons, I am glad.'

He pressed himself close, feeling her warmth and give and her sinuous line. Her limbs wrapped around his and her mouth caressed. His fellow countrymen would give their lives for such an experience.

She whispered in his ear, 'I will tell Pocahontas I have been on a ship and that it is made from a forest of oak.'

'She may wonder where you are.'

'Is it not fitting that I am aboard? Do I not show the friendship of our people?'

'I cannot fault your efforts.'

She nipped lightly at his neck. 'Powhatan desires peace and intends you no harm.'

'His tribes will often differ.'

'They fear you, watch ships arrive, hear of forage parties that attack and burn and choose never to parley.'

'Some among us prefer war.'

She entwined her fingers with his. 'They are bad men.'

'Yet often their evil is disguised.' He chose his words with care. 'I know of some among them who would kill both Powhatan and me.'

He sensed the girl's anxiety, felt the response of her body to news of this threat. It helped to have the love of a native girl. Gently he held her face and put his lips to hers. Then he reached over and snuffed out the lamp.

When she slept, and the noise and tempo of the night had ebbed to silence, Hardy rose and dressed and made his way to an unshrouded cannon port. Nimbly he exited, dropping on a knotted rope down to the small lighter stationed at the waterline. Taking the oars, he cast off, his muffled strokes carrying him among the gathered and shadowed vessels. There were no sentries to shout a challenge to him, or crewmen left sober enough even to notice. He proceeded on. Tonight he would focus on the *Falcon*, would explore her as he did her sister ships, trawling for evidence of intrigue and sedition. Anything might betray a plot. It was his role to prowl and pry, to seek out what others had hidden. Jamestown depended on it.

'Bring them down! Strike them hard!'

Football had turned into affray. It was not unknown for the game to include death or serious injury, to descend into bloody cry and battle. Sportsmanship was for others; the unruly youths that had disgorged from the moored ships were intent on a win, and their rivals would suffer for it.

'Hold them!' Edward Battle shouted to his comrades. 'I have the ball!'

His possession of it did not last. He was tackled in a welter of flailing arms and legs, the encounter drawing others into the fight. Blows rained, teeth were spat out and more blood flowed. Some were come armed with cudgels or with their knuckles bound in studded leather; others chose to bite or claw, or stamp with their nailed boots. Few would escape unscathed. Half-conscious, another victim was now dragged unceremoniously from the pitch.

A spectator turned to his friend. 'What do you wager?'

'A shilling there will be a death.'

'I declare the odds too short.'

The man laughed. 'If only their vigour could be harnessed.'

On an oppressively hot day, there was little else to amuse or distract. The scum from London held no other value. Yet the local boys were holding their own and inflicting punishment on the newcomers. Again the ball rolled free and the pack went in pursuit.

'Stop this now!' A pistol shot cracked and John Smith bellowed an order. 'Whoever ignores me will suffer a beating!'

The response was instantaneous. The warfare ceased, and in the midst of the strewn and limping figures, the president stood implacable.

He glared. 'Is this how our colony is to be? Are we no better than the savages?'

The youths affected contrition, left sullen and wordless at his rebuke. No matter, for there would be a future opportunity to settle scores. They began to drift away.

Smith spied his young charge hunched on the ground and nursing his injuries. At least he was not prone. The president approached.

'What ails you, Edward?' He crouched and turned the boy's head towards him, confronted with blackened eyes and deepening bruises. 'It hurts?'

'Their injuries are worse.'

'Spoken like a veteran. Yet you must clean your wounds and tend your cuts with salve before they are become infected.'

Edward fingered his ribs and jaw. 'I promise to visit the physician.'

'Go instead to Jan.' Smith helped the boy to his feet. 'He is not lacking in wood spirit of every kind.'

Obediently the youth hobbled on his way. It was a short walk across the compound to the Dutchman's hovel dwelling. The pitch manufacturer was rarely talkative, yet had become a stalwart of the settlement and an ally of its leader. Religious commitment and a residual hatred of the Spanish were as sound a motive as any. Besides, he had hurled a smokepot at Ratcliffe and his coterie, and that deserved respect.

'Jan?' The boy pounded on the rough-hewn door. 'Mr Smith bids me seek you out.' Hearing no answer, he raised the latch and entered, his eyes adjusting to the sudden gloom. There was reason for the lack of invitation. Already flies had discovered the hanging corpse and the smell of voided bowels and early putrefaction permeated the air. 'Come quick! In the name of God, come quick!' Edward Battle was running, the reason for his visit forgotten.

CHAPTER 13

'Papist!'

'Brownist dog!'

'Tow rag!'

'Reserve such terms for yourself!'

Insults were traded and daggers drawn as two gentlemen prepared to fight. Their dispute was one of many that flared within the fort, a product of the malaise that afflicted all. A man could die for giving offence, for comparing another to the dangled length of tow rope on which defecating sailors wiped their arses. Reason and goodwill had evaporated in the heat.

A new voice interjected. 'Put up your blades, sirs. Or a third will join the fray.'

Christian Hardy did not bother to unsheathe his sword. Implied menace would suffice. Of late, he had become de facto constable, patrolling the bounds and keeping watch on the colony's febrile antics. It had not saved the Dutchman. Pressure was building. Jamestown was becoming ungovernable.

Their attention swung at the sound of a whistle and the ears of Buckler pricked up. President Smith was calling. The intelligencer responded, taking his leave of the feuding pair with a nodded warning.

He approached his friend. 'More disturbance?'

The adventurer levelled his gaze on the far side of the fort. 'There is no calm in Jamestown. I need you and your Buckler at my side, Christian.'

'You expect trouble?'

'None we cannot defeat. But an audience is arranged.'

A delegation appeared, Ratcliffe and an accomplice walking unhurried to meet them. There was insolence in their manner and disrespect in their eye. Since their last confrontation, Ratcliffe had refined his tactics. They halted some feet away.

Smith observed them. 'What is it you want?'

Ratcliffe proffered a weak smile. 'You are aware of Francis West?'

Smith gave a cursory glance to the other man. 'We have had the honour of meeting.'

'Then you will know him to be the younger brother of Lord Delaware.'

'Delaware is in London.'

'Yet he is our governor by dint of the second charter.'

'A charter I have not seen.' Smith stayed calm. 'A charter that has no power until it is delivered to this shore.'

'Your tenure is soon over.'

'Soon is not today.'

Francis West cleared his throat to interject. His emergence in the Ratcliffe camp was scarcely a surprise. Family connections lent him influence, and his natural superciliousness ensured instant enmity with Smith. He was a Cecil asset about to be deployed.

He peered at the president. 'Our fort is scarce large enough to house us all, Mr Smith.'

'It suffices.'

'We languish. We squabble. We decline.'

'Decline?' Smith bridled. 'You, a newcomer, know little of our progress.'

'I see there is no purpose or direction, not food enough even for the men you sent to Chesapeake Bay to forage for oysters.'

Smith trembled as his anger rose. 'You would speak to me of purpose? What is yours, Francis West?'

'To perform my duty.'

'You deceive.' Smith spat his contempt, forsaking his self-control. 'For all your airs, you are but a grub, a worm in Cecil's employ.'

'Give insult and you shall regret it.'

'More than I regret you sailing to Virginia?'

'At least you will applaud what I do next.' West paused, enjoying the moment. 'I will be taking some one hundred and twenty men upriver to found a settlement.'

Confused, Smith shook his head. 'I will not hear it.'

'So listen well.' It was Ratcliffe who responded. 'A new colony will be built in accordance with the second charter.'

'This is mutiny and desertion.'

'It is what it is. It is what is needed.'

'By those that scheme and wish us ill, that would divide and destroy us for their sport.'

'Not sport, Smith.' Ratcliffe had a glint of triumph in his gaze. 'Rather it is the exercise of a right, the provision of an answer.'

'What I discern is treachery and sedition.'

'You ever were a fool.'

'And you?' Smith trained his ire on West. 'What do you know of this place? How will you and your merry band fare in a land you have never explored?'

'I have time to hand.'

'At the expense of us all.'

Muttering oaths and expletives, Smith stormed away. Had he remained, he might have been tempted to draw his sword, or been lured into a political trap. Hardy did not move. He stood and contemplated the scene, calm in the face of such ploy and calculation.

Ratcliffe smiled. 'He seems angered by the news.'

Smith threw another meal sack onto the deck of the shallop. There was no lessening of his fury or slackening of his pace. This was a contest, and pride was at stake. More bags landed. Already Francis West had commandeered a vessel and headed up the James; would by now be scoping for locations or fighting the natives. Smith had no time for such imbeciles. He had risked all to cut a passage through the wilderness and forge relations with the savage, and West was simply a novice bent on a purposeless task. It demanded reply.

A loaded sack thudded to join the rest, and the voice of Hardy intruded. 'You give chase?'

Smith did not pause in his labours. 'What choice is there?'

'Reflection?'

'I cannot let my enemies win; must not cede an inch.'

'You would abandon this fort to Ratcliffe and Archer?'

'Better than to see my authority slide.'

'Think on what they may do, John. Consider their rejoicing while you are away.'

Smith turned. 'It is why you will stay as my eyes and ears.'

Hardy nodded his acceptance and the two men toiled, stowing provisions and rolling kegs of fresh water aboard. Fury and not thought was the driver of this mission.

Smith hefted a cask of gunpowder inside and then leapt into the boat himself. 'We shall discover how they fare when cornered by steel and shot.'

'Over one hundred of them?'

'Mewling and snivelling knaves to a man.' Smith stepped back to inspect his ordnance store. 'They are no match for my soldiers.'

'Should you catch them, what then?'

'Mood and moment will decide.'

'Be careful, John. Your rivals need no reason to kill you.'

Caution was a concept poorly grasped by the adventurer. Forward momentum was his creed. He believed he had right and Providence on his side and would easily swat away his rivals. A latecomer from England, however well connected, hardly posed a challenge.

Hardy crouched on the riverbank. 'Who will you take?'

'A mere handful will suffice.'

'You were never wanting in fearlessness.'

'Nor do I lack in faith.'

He would require both. Perhaps Francis West had foreseen this response; maybe John Ratcliffe intended such an event. A showdown was inevitable. Smith seemed eager at the prospect.

Within the palisaded confines of the fort, men and women stretched limp in the heat and waited for rain. Many already regretted their migration to Virginia. They offered up their plaintive prayers and complained among themselves, whiling away the hours and hoping for salvation. It was an environment that encouraged neither loyalty nor calm. Rich pickings for those minded to exploit it.

Glancing about him, Ratcliffe moved among the tents and timbered hovels. The place had scarce improved since his earlier sojourn, yet he was fortunate to have made friends, to have recruited volunteers and hirelings to his cause. On board the *Diamond*, he had encountered criminals and rogues easily persuaded and clearly without scruple. They were a gift.

He entered a storehouse and closed its door. There was still some illumination, the sunlight piercing and fragmenting through the skeleton beams of the uncompleted roof. A solitary carpenter worked inside.

The man lowered his mallet and chisel. 'Why, if it is not the Lord of Misrule.'

'Know your place.'

'I know it too well.' An insolent grin flickered. 'You are no better than I, Ratcliffe.'

'Yet I have not been crapped from the bowels of Newgate.'

'Here all men are equal.'

Ratcliffe would not argue, nor dwell long on the matter of their backgrounds. They were each refugees of a kind. His life had once been one of faith and devotion to the Catholic Church. It had brought him to the attention of Cecil. Torture could be the most effective of things.

The carpenter studied him. 'Why do you come?'

'A man may visit an acquaintance.'

'To interrupt his honest toil?' There was scepticism. 'Tell me truly.'

A leather purse landed at his feet. 'I provide you with silver and, in return, you will give me loyalty.'

'Much depends on the task.'

'Francis West is gone upstream and Smith prepares to follow.'

A shrug. 'Such rivalry is no concern of mine.'

'Yet my payment ensures it will be.' Ratcliffe watched the man stoop and collect the purse. 'There is more, should you succeed.'

'Succeed?'

'I want Smith dead. A stray blade or misplaced round; a fire in his quarters. Whatever it takes.'

The carpenter examined the coins. 'You do not jest.'

'Laughter can wait.' Ratcliffe raised his mutilated hand, a reminder of deep-rooted enmity.

The recruit peered at his visitor. 'As you command, master. But why now? Why slay Smith when his presidency soon ends?'

'He will forever be a curse on this settlement so long as he still breathes.'

The artisan thrust his fee in a pocket and reached again for his tools.

Ratcliffe nodded. 'You will join the crew of the president's shallop and prove yourself a willing hand.'

'And then?'

'Do as you are contracted.'

Smith had caught up, had come to remonstrate and reason and if necessary to threaten. Already the party loyal to West had measured and pegged out the ground, were labouring to clear and level and set the foundations of their camp. It lay on the south bank of the James, some sixty miles upriver from Jamestown itself, a symbol of division and a declaration of intent. As heir presumptive to the presidency, Francis West was reinforcing his position. Smith gazed about him, a handful of crew armed and ready at his side. 'You believed I would applaud your efforts? That I would bring felicitations and goodwill?'

The reply from an officer was curt and defensive. 'We answer to Mr West.'

'What does he know of this territory and the dangers you will face?'

'Enough that we place our confidence in him.'

'I am your president.'

'You alone embrace it.' Men had stopped their work and began to gather round. 'Here you are nothing, Smith.'

'Mutiny will see you killed.'

'So too your misjudgement.'

'I give you advice and fair warning.' Smith was calm in the face of the massing danger. 'This place is a product of a rash decision, a thing that will not last.'

'Not unlike yourself.' The man said. There were jeers and hostile laughter.

Smith persisted. 'Heed what I say. The woods will allow the savages near and the low ground will let in floodwater.'

'Your jealousies do not persuade us.'

'Then sense and reason should. I know Francis West has returned to Jamestown to arrange for the transport of supplies. I have found another site upstream, a place ready-fortified and fit for planting, a tower we may lease from the redskins.'

'We are happy here.' A voice shouted out.

'Happiness will not outlast your coming woes.' The adventurer pointed to a labourer. 'You give this home a name?'

'It is Fort West.'

'Naturally so. A testament to pride and folly.'

Someone drew a sword. 'What of your folly, Smith?'

'I have the wisdom of experience.'

'Learn then to retreat. Learn that we take no orders from a man whose office ends in days.'

'My task is not yet over.'

'Our discourse is.' The officer levelled a pistol at Smith's forehead.

The president's natural pugnacity and instinct to fight were outweighed by force of numbers. He bowed to the inevitable. Anyway, on 10 September 1609 his presidency was due to expire. He could not expect his authority to outlast his presidency, to escape unchallenged from the plots and subterfuge about. Yet he would never surrender to any wishing ill on his settlement. Jamestown was all.

As he took the tiller and his men bent to the oars, he spied a lighter ferrying materials to the shore. It deserved an interception. Outnumbered on land they may be, but there were plenty of other tricks to play.

'What do you find, Captain?' one of his men asked.

'Perhaps an answer to everything.' Smith adjusted his course. 'Pull hard on the oars and leave all speech to me.'

They met the smaller craft, Smith raising his hand in salutation and command. The vessel would not be making land on that side of the river. Its coxswain tried to protest, but was obliged to comply. Shadowing close, the shallop escorted her prize back to the mother ship.

The master stared confused as Smith and his companions clambered aboard. He had not anticipated so unorthodox a situation.

'Fear not, brother.' Smith thrust a bottle of brandy wine in his hand. 'We come in peace and friendship.'

'Yet in the manner of pirates.'

Smith clapped him on the shoulder. 'You say it of your president?'

'I have my orders, Captain.'

'Consider them revoked.' The adventurer was jovial. 'Francis West is downriver, and I am here.'

'He gave me strict instruction to deliver the supplies ashore.'

'So you shall. Yet to a different location.'

'I cannot.'

Smith clenched the man's shoulder tighter. 'Adapt to local conditions, to the circumstances you find.'

'You ask me to disobey command?'

'I merely proffer you counsel.' Smith glanced to his men. 'Some might deem it foolish to spurn the request of your president.'

'Where is this other place?'

'Closer to the falls, and better suited to our purpose. I have named it Nonesuch.'

The argument was won and the ship commandeered. Smith's rivals might posture and strut, yet without the necessities for construction, their vaunted fort would never rise. How West and Ratcliffe would rail against him. In the meantime, he would create something magnificent and lasting: a second colony on the James.

He doffed his hat in farewell to the stranded settlement. Its denizens would rue the day they expelled him from their nascent fort and would come begging for his help. Too bad. The wind was set fair behind him.

'I like it not when the pale-skins move.'

Opechancanough observed events from the far bank. The sudden flurry of activity among the colonists had drawn him to the river. It was a disconcerting sight, and one the military chief could scarce ignore. First the English had landed to establish a new fort, and next their president followed with a strategy of his own. Indeed, Parahunt, the son of Powhatan and chief of the territory about the falls, had permitted Smith the use of an existing camp. It was best to encourage the enemy to split their force. Whatever the intentions of these wearers of leg coverings, the tribes surrounding them would keep their distance and await command.

Beside him, Realm and his black Imbangala bodyguards watched with the same dispassionate air. The Englishman had heard from his informant of the internecine clashes at Jamestown, of Francis West deploying men to create a further settlement and of an enraged John Smith giving chase. There was reason to enjoy this comedy of errors and failure.

He indicated the departing vessel with a restrained nod. 'It is a sign of their weakness that they roam about the river.'

'While they roam, they spread.'

'To what effect, Opechancanough?' The renegade glanced at the native. 'They seek more living space, for they starve and fight among themselves. They send out soldiers and slowly bleed their own defences.'

'Still we cannot pierce their walls.'

'Give it time.' Realm was confident in his counsel. 'Perhaps they think they have you in awe, have cowed you into acceptance.'

'I will never accept them.'

'Yet be patient. Let the weight of numbers, the bellies they must feed, gnaw at their existence.'

'My warriors wish to fight.'

'You will choose the moment. It is easier to bring down a bear that sickens than one that prowls, ferocious.'

'When Jamestown is gone, all the tribes will pay us tribute.'

'So we have much to plan.'

Realm saw once more the flash of ambition, the quickness in Opechancanough's eye. The savage was learning, and it made him dangerous. Until he and his kind were forced from their lands and became subject to a new order, peace and coexistence would remain mere illusion. The military commander understood. Perhaps he grasped less well that Realm represented the King of Spain, and that he too was the spearhead of a colonial claim.

Realm gazed across the river. 'There stands a camp as yet unprotected and without a palisade.'

'It is no Jamestown.'

'Until more ships arrive, more freight and men are landed, more stakes are driven in.'

Opechancanough was willing to be persuaded. 'Their presence is unwelcome.'

'A challenge, Opechancanough,' Realm pressed him. 'They insult your dignity, have not paid in goods or copper, sought no permission from Parahunt.'

'So we should attack?'

'For sport alone, to throw them from their balance and cause them havoc and fear.'

'At what cost for us?'

'Advantage far outweighs any cost. Lie passive and they will trample you.'

The god Okeus would approve.

There was ever a pause between violent act and realisation, before voice was given and the alarm raised. So it proved at Fort West. It was in this moment that the Indians swarmed forward, their battle cries piercing and their arrows unleashed. Settlers ran. In an instant their situation was changed and their hopes punctured, the promise of untrammelled riches rudely arrested. They were inexperienced in the ways of the savage.

'May God preserve us!'

'Fire your musket or He will not!'

Soldiers and settlers tumbled over each other in blind and direction-less panic. Their commander, Francis West, was in Jamestown, sixty miles distant. The ambush had started with a pair of settlers leaning on their shovels and a third urinating into the undergrowth. The scene had altered as all three fell to a flight of arrows. The Indians had crawled near and picked their targets well. One victim staggered for a few seconds, amazed by his own fate and the shaft of a projectile jutting from his mouth. Then, chaos.

'Direct your fire! Do not waste shot!'

'I am hit!'

'Have mercy on us, Lord!'

Prayers and curses mingled. They should never have left England or obeyed the man West, never ventured so far up the James with such confidence. The place would be their grave. A labourer employed a mattock to fend off attack before his skull was split; a soldier discharged his musket in error and propelled a ramrod direct into the chest of an oncoming native.

A different sound arrived, eddying through with a volley of shot. A counter-attack was under way. At its head was Smith, striding with his sword drawn and pistol raised, leading by example.

'We have put them to flight!' The adventurer roared his satisfaction when the fierce fighting finally began to subside. 'It seems, after all, that we are needed!'

Smith had won both the battle and the day, and Fort West would be the casualty. The combative veteran was vindicated. He could afford a certain triumphalism, to stroll as victor among a band of men from which he was so recently expelled. But the insult was not forgotten.

He stopped and pointed. 'Bind him.'

Others too were chosen; the officers and sergeants who had shown discourtesy when last they had met. Justice and punishment would be meted out, and a message conveyed to West and his ilk.

The prisoners were tied and the instruction given. 'Flog them.'

Inflicting sentence was a grisly thing, the impact of the lash heavy, the screams muted by a leather strap tied between the teeth.

Smith turned back to his silent audience. 'See where mutiny ends, where folly and ignorance lead? It is not a pretty sight. Yet it is better than being skinned alive by savages, than falling prey to the deceit of false leaders.'

'We are with you!' a voice shouted from the company. 'Each man here owes to you his life.'

'Show me more than words. Show me loyalty and a sense of duty.'

'Demand and we will give.'

Smith regarded the gathering. 'Am I your president?'

'Aye,' they replied in unison.

'So who is it to be?' In reality he offered no choice. 'Francis West or John Smith?'

Their answer was as he thought. It was Providence that had ensured West was ensconced elsewhere during the Indians' attack, and pure coincidence that he was at hand. Fortune favoured the persistent. How cowed and pliant his recruits now seemed.

'Pick up your weapons and your tools and assemble on your ship. We head upstream for Powhatan Tower, the redoubt I have named Nonesuch.'

Victory was sweet, and he could savour another win in the contest with his rivals. As the men bent to their tasks, he walked among the scratchings and debris of their stay. No one would remember this place.

He paused beside a body, unmoved by the sight of a native sprawled face down with his spine blown out. In the heat, the corpse would soon blacken and bloom and lose all its human features. Wild animals would see to the rest.

Smith turned the cadaver with his foot, nudging it onto its back. Even a perfunctory examination could be useful, but he had seen patterns of warpaint about the eyes indicating rank and fighting prowess that he recognised from Opechancanough's entourage. This had not been a random incident. Powhatan's military chief had sent one of his chosen into battle. Things were stirring again within the tribe.

'Better the devil we know.' Smith did little to hide his rage. 'We sail in the morning for Jamestown.'

So that was that. The president slumped disconsolately in the deck well of the boat, a man thwarted by the manoeuvres of his enemies. He had not reckoned on the sudden arrival of West, nor on the residual obedience of his men. In an instant, authority had shifted and the game changed and the entire contingent returned to Fort West. To remain at Nonesuch with a skeleton crew would make Smith little more than a vainglorious fool, a laughing stock and a target. He would need to salvage something, somehow.

A crewman proffered a flask. 'Brandy wine, Captain?'

'Drink will not dull my fury.' Yet he took the flask and gulped a mouthful.

'There is much to do at the settlement.'

'And so many foes against me.' The president again tipped the bottle to his lips. 'They spread and grow like weed.'

'We have proved their match before.'

'Have we? Do we prevent West and his fort? Are Ratcliffe and the lawyer beaten?'

'They will trip themselves.'

'At the expense of our lives and the future of our colony.'

Smith would not be persuaded otherwise. Damn the satanic lot of them! Easing himself against the mast step, he settled down to ruminate. Virginia was the most unforgiving of places, and its settlers the most ungrateful of souls. He would tame and civilise all, if it killed him.

The evening darkened to night, and the murmur of voices drifted away as sleep came. At least it was cooler out on the river. When dawn arrived they would resume their journey, and late the following day they should reach the familiar, weathered frontage of Jamestown. The snores of the men and the gentle slap of water against the boat's hull added to the somnolent rhythm.

A disturbance erupted upon the scene with shock and fury and the staccato blast of gunpowder. Shouts echoed as the crew were startled from their slumber. Confusion abounded. Figures stumbled about. Someone was on fire and had leapt screaming overboard.

'It is the captain?'

'In the name of Christ, what occurs?'

'He drowns!'

'Bring him aboard! He dies if we leave him!'

Perhaps he might have thanked them if they had, for Smith was in an altered state. His mouth was agape and his arms thrashed, his torment obvious and his agonies screamed loud for all to hear. Men jumped into the water to save him. What they hauled back was not the captain they had known.

A terrible event, mused the carpenter. One moment his captain slept with a bag of gunpowder resting on his abdomen and the next there was an explosion. Accidents could happen, of course. He congratulated himself on a task near completed, on the deftness with which he had flicked that smouldering slow match onto the dozing form. Conditions had hardly favoured John Smith. With luck, a corpse would be delivered to Jamestown and further payment received.

CHAPTER 14

'I will live.'

His eyes tight shut and his teeth clenched, Smith repeated the mantra. It reflected stoic resolve rather than conviction. His wounds were grievous, and the surgeon himself was doubtful of his recovery. The patient was in torment, lurching from delirium to agonised cries, no opiate or salve bringing relief. In that hideous instant on the James, all had been changed. Smith had lost skin and flesh from his thighs and midriff and seen his genitals blown apart. Grim decline and eventual death were the outcome most expected.

'You think me not a man?' Smith reached and gripped the surgeon by his throat. 'You think I already take my leave?'

'You are still much with us, Captain.'

'That I am, and let no one forget it. Though some conspire against me, I am far from done.'

'God and time will decide.'

'Do they pray for me?'

'The chaplain held a service, and several of our company keep vigil in the church.'

'Not Ratcliffe or the lawyer Archer, I'd wager.'

'I cannot speak for them.'

'They seek my murder.' Smith groaned as he spasmed. 'Mark me, they will pay.'

The surgeon bent to apply a wet compress to his forehead. 'Rest now, Captain.'

'Rest? While rabid dogs are loose? When I must strive as president to govern?'

'Let others concern themselves.'

Weak now, Smith fell back against his pillow. He could not fight alone, could not take upon himself the responsibility of command. His presidency was all but ended. How his enemies would gloat. They had succeeded; had by plot and sleight of hand condemned him to this twilight state. Every one of his achievements was void now; each step he had taken to colonise the land would be replaced by ignominious retreat. His suffering at least distracted him from the magnitude of the loss.

The surgeon proffered a beaker of water and he drank a little. 'I must endure. I must.'

'We are each in the hands of the Almighty.'

'I more so than you.' Smith gazed at the ceiling deliriously. 'Is a man so maimed and disfigured worthy of life?'

'We are all His creatures.'

'Creature I am become.'

'Save your spirit and your spleen, Captain.' The surgeon busied himself with his instruments. 'I have done what may be done.'

'A verdict far from heartening.'

'Yet it is the truth.'

'So leave me with brandy and get you to your quarters.'

Grateful, the surgeon departed. Perhaps he would find Smith a corpse in the morning. In the meantime, in a chamber lit by a single lamp, Smith whimpered and recited a Psalm. He took a gulp of liquor. Beside him, he felt the smooth hardness of his pistol, its chamber ready loaded. He lifted the weapon, resting it on his chest and letting his finger curl about its trigger. Agony was his greatest foe now. There would be no emotion involved in taking this final decision. Death came eventually to everyone, and whoever had intended his had only part-completed the mission. He would do them and himself a favour.

With a grunt, he slid the gun aside and panted at his folly. Suicide was no answer. His mortal remains could serve neither God nor England, nor keep at bay the servants of the Antichrist. He fumbled for the lamp and extinguished its light.

Shadows could hide many things. In the darkness, two figures slunk between the clusters of storehouses and cottages and made for the ailing president's dwelling. Silently they approached, pressing against the clay-daubed walls and inching towards the open shutters.

Buckler attacked. Furious growls and human screams filled the air as the two men pitched through the windows. Hardy and his dog had lain in wait, hidden.

The intelligencer spoke. 'Most guests employ the door.'

He felled one man with a single punch and followed through with a booted foot driven into the ribs. It allowed a pause to uncloak a lamp. In the soft glow, a pair of men writhed, disarmed, on the floor. Buckler stood above one, his teeth bared and his body poised to leap for the throat.

Hardy hissed at the assailants. 'Stay down.'

'You are as dead as Smith.' The man he had struck spat out a tooth.

'Such boldness in adversity.'

'It is a mercy to put the captain from his misery.'

'A decision that is not for you to make.' Hardy tossed a discarded pistol out of reach. 'Your kind have no manners.'

'Things change in Jamestown, Hardy.'

'Your rank impertinence does not alter.'

'Would you not rather follow those that win? Those who will soon take command?'

'My loyalty is clear.'

'It will see you killed.'

A knife had appeared, plucked from a leather sheath strapped against the man's forearm. It was a reckless move by the visitor.

Hardy peered at the weapon, amused. 'A true combatant knows when to give in. Is it money that moves you?'

The man shook his head and spat again.

It would be too easy to finish the assailant, to stamp on his fingers and then crush his throat. Hardy decided to let matters run. The man rose unsteadily to his feet, his eyes darting and the dagger weaving dangerously.

The intelligencer studied him. 'You would still disturb Captain Smith?'

'I will silence you.'

'So let us begin our lesson.'

It was brutal work, done both to punish and to warn off. The knife fell, its owner taking longer to drop, his knees buckling and torso jerking beneath the welter of blows. Hardy turned and felled the second trespasser.

He dragged the men's bound and bloodied forms and pitched them through the window. Their condition was somewhat changed. Should they recover consciousness, they might relate what they had encountered. It would perhaps delay awhile any further attempts at murder. Summoning Buckler, the intelligencer shuttered the lantern and left the president's room.

Ratcliffe still scented blood. He was not unduly dismayed by the setback. Smith yet ailed, and there were plenty of tricks left to play. September 1609 should prove a fateful and eventful month.

'I will recognise no summary trial, no vexatious act, no verminous den of traitors!' Borne on a litter and protesting loudly, Smith was carried to the church. Whether this was a hearing or a trial, there could be no doubt he would be judged. Seated near the altar were his peers, the hierarchs of the colony and their henchman; the lawyer Gabriel Archer was already on his feet.

Wincing as he was helped to sit up on his stretcher, the president now glared. 'What is this foolery?'

'You are summoned to our presence.' Archer revealed little in his tone.

'Summoned? By you? By frauds and mutineers?'

'Yet you are here.'

'I had no choice, since I was carried.' Smith sat in a bitter rage and cast an accusatory glance to the audience surrounding him. 'There is no law or constitution which permits this.'

'We shall be the judge.'

'Doubtless, too, my executioner. But remember, I have served this settlement, have striven with every breath to promote the cause of England.'

'You serve yourself.'

'I do?' Smith scowled. 'What of you, Archer? And you, Ratcliffe? Or your entire devil's brood?'

'Be careful in your statements.'

'Why so? I may be caught by another explosion?'

There was a frisson of laughter, then a shiver of anticipation. Smith would be brought down. His injuries had already cost him dear. Now, buoyed by his misfortune, his enemies were arrayed. Their moment had arrived.

Grimacing defiantly through his pain, Smith eyed his jury. 'Calumny and lies will fail to destroy me.'

'Your own misdeeds condemn you.'

'Misdeeds?' Smith gave a snort of derision. 'My sole misdeed was not to have you hanged for mutiny.'

Archer inclined his head in mock respect and turned to his brief. 'It is a sorry tale which brings us here, a litany of woes.'

'I shall give you woe.'

'It is alleged you gathered power to yourself and sought to become a king.'

'I am not guilty of the charge.'

'What of the claim that you forced settlers from this place? Sent them out to fend for themselves? Gorged, without remorse, on private stores while those about you starved?'

Smith shook his head. 'All that I do is for my fellows and for this fort.'

'Then where is the benefit?' Archer did not wait for a reply. 'Some say you are driven by self-aggrandisement. That you seek to steal these lands for yourself.'

'They are wrong.'

Smith was losing ground. He could not rely on his allies. Hardy prowled outside. The courtroom was not his arena. No weapon was drawn, and yet Smith's assassination was this contest's aim.

Archer sneered. 'Did you not plot to seize the crown and cape bestowed on Powhatan for yourself? Do you not lust after Pocahontas and plan congress and union with her?'

'This is madness.' His breath labouring and his speech ebbing now, Smith slumped enfeebled on his stretcher. His foes desired the conveyance transformed into a bier. He needed to rest, to think, to escape from the asylum.

Ratcliffe had entered the pulpit and leant down to point an accusatory finger. 'Jamestown is not yours, Smith.'

The president was broken. Let them have what they wanted. He would provide them with the chalice and then watch them drink its poison. He fumbled beneath the thin mattress. Would that he had his pistol to hand! With an effort he withdrew the official papers, the letters patent and seal of office, and flung them to the ground.

'Will these suffice? Or is it my head on a platter that you crave?'

Archer retrieved the items and delivered them to Ratcliffe. Feigning cool aloofness, Ratcliffe flicked through the pages. He had won. The humiliation of his rival was complete. His maimed hand throbbed. One freak gunpowder blast had deserved another, he supposed.

He squinted down at Smith, now prone. 'I did not expect your capitulation to come so easily.'

'Enjoy it while you may.'

Ratcliffe nodded to the stretcher bearers. 'Return him to his quarters.'

Defeated, the former president was carried off in silence. In his absence, a new council would be formed and his successor chosen, to guide Jamestown to the future.

Palaces rarely preserved secrets. There were too many watchful eyes and wagging tongues; too many courtiers with agendas and ambitions. The agents of Robert Cecil might be anywhere. It explained why a lone figure in dark clothing had waited until nightfall to climb from an upper window of St James's Palace and, by way of a rope ladder, land softly on the ground. The royal guards were a shield against external threat. They would not be looking for a shadow flitting from within.

Out in the walled deer park, a small pavilion sat beside a pond. It was a place to which none but royalty was permitted entry. Yet the visitor was assured. He had trodden these pathways many times and outstripped all pursuit. There would be no interruption.

'You came, Your Grace,' he whispered.

'A prince cannot fail his intelligencer, Adam.'

They embraced as brothers, the young man and his even younger patron bound by friendship and common cause.

Adam Hardy closed the door and unshuttered his lantern. 'This is not a scene Cecil would welcome.'

Henry nodded. 'Let us pray he never links the two of us.'

'First my father steals his secrets, and then I pass them to you.' Humour flared in Adam's eyes. 'I would not blame him were he piqued.'

'Nor the Spanish ambassador.' The prince seated himself on a bench. 'I would hate to have you as my adversary.'

Adam smiled. 'As I once safeguarded your sister, I would give my life for you.'

He spoke with meaning. In a previous guise, during the dangerous and febrile days of 1605, when Catholic malcontents plotted mass murder with their gunpowder, it was he who had penetrated the Warwickshire home of Princess Elizabeth to prevent the kidnap of the nine-year-old girl. It had proved the riskiest of assignments. Those traitors might be dead and their bodies decomposed, yet treason persisted.

The prince stared into the lamplight. 'Will Jamestown endure?'

'I cannot say, Your Grace.'

'Though I can speak of my regret at consigning your father to such peril there.'

'He went with gladness and good cheer.'

'Let us pray it is rewarded.'

'The reward is in spiting Cecil, in thwarting Spain, in breathing life into a new colony.'

'I would pay a ransom for such bravery, and more for such a father.' There was sadness in the prince's voice. It was born of being heir to a sybaritic king, to a father he despised for his grotesque and lavish ways. A chasm existed between monarch and prince, polluted by mistrust. At least Christian and Adam Hardy kept watch.

Concern creased the boy's royal brow. 'Still our endeavours are haunted by Realm.'

'Despite all he is but a mortal, Your Grace.'

'One who means us ill, who creates great hazard and harm wherever he goes.'

'Be comforted: my father will finish him.'

'Think of it, Adam.' The youth reached out and gripped the arm of his friend and protector. 'What we discuss here will shape events and nations a hundred or even five hundred years hence.'

'Then our meeting is not wasted.'

It would be a tired prince who, in the early hours, rose to attend matins. Yet he would not show it. Piety and self-discipline informed every action of his day. Now, with a whispered farewell, he slipped away to retrace his steps and return to his private quarters. No alarm had been raised or patrol alerted. Little could challenge the spirit and self-possession of he who was next in line to the throne.

'What a curious hour to meet a prince.' There was obvious threat in the voice.

Adam had leapt down from the wall and was climbing to his feet when the challenge came. It emanated from a few yards distant and was accompanied by the directed glow of a lantern. He had been observed and cornered, and malicious intent was in the tone.

Adam peered towards the man. 'Sykes?'

'You are nothing if not perceptive.' Sarcasm dripped from the words. 'It is why our master employs you.'

Adam strained to detect other figures. It was more likely Sykes worked alone, driven by resentment and ambition and the overween-ing suspicion of the motives of another. Imagine the reward should he deliver evidence of treasonous duplicity into the hands of Robert Cecil.

'So, your petty instincts bring you here, Sykes.'

'Rather it is a feeling in my belly for your black practices and perfidy.'

'I do the business of his lordship.'

'Of our master?' There was derision and incredulity in the man's voice. 'Your lie does not persuade.'

'Perhaps the papers I carry will.'

'Papers?'

'Would you report to Cecil what he already knows? Will you undermine his secret dealings with Prince Henry?'

'There are no such secret dealings.' But Sykes sounded uncertain. 'You do not come on errand for Cecil.'

'You would stake your reputation and position on it?'

'Show me proof.'

'It lies within this letter.'

Adam reached inside his loosened jacket and withdrew a paper scroll, proffering it. Tentatively, the lantern in one hand, his rival stepped forward to inspect it.

The man's death was immediate. With sudden speed, Adam moved to deliver a blow to his throat. It took a fraction of a second to crush the windpipe and send the body convulsing to the ground. The corpse still shivered as the intelligencer completed his rapid search. Sykes should never have attempted such a venture on his own. Tomorrow he would be found, another inexplicable casualty of a rough and random encounter. London forever chewed up people.

Adam snuffed the lantern and went on his way.

'May the Lord make us thankful.'

Few were in the mood for grace, and fewer had an appetite for the meagre fare before them. Yet at the table of the new president there were standards to maintain.

George Percy surveyed his guests. Garbed in a satin frock coat and jaunty hat, he was a reluctant and unlikely incumbent. A sense of duty had informed him; a desire to bring together the warring factions in a common quest and purpose. To this end he would dress in fine clothes and break bread with the other gentlemen, would guide his fellow settlers and lead by example. Good manners would prevail.

Carving meat from a haunch of venison, he beckoned his steward forward. 'Take what remains and deliver it among the camp.'

'Who is most deserving, sir?'

'Those that are most famished.'

Resentful stares followed the progress of the dish. Its contents had been a gift from Powhatan, a goodwill gesture from the native king in the wake of recent misunderstanding.

Hardy sat back to view the men around him. They would eat together and yet just as soon put a blade to their neighbour's throat. At the far end of the table, Ratcliffe and Archer returned his gaze. It was an awkward and sour-tasting gathering.

Percy forked a small morsel of meat into his mouth and reached for his glass of claret. 'We are yet unvanquished, gentlemen.'

'All may change when the ships depart.' A diner said before returning to chew on his food morosely.

'Then we must bear the burden.' Percy sipped his wine. 'It is no secret our stores are low and need to be replenished.'

'Replenished how?'

'I cannot lie. At reduced rations, there is meal enough to feed us for just three months.'

A fist hit the table. 'Three months? What of the coming winter? How shall we live?'

'It is nothing we have not faced before.'

'We tire of it.'

'I also, sir.' Percy dabbed at his lips with a napkin. 'Faith and purpose will sustain us and carry us through.'

'To what?'

'Spring, and the seasons beyond. Each month is one more we have survived.'

'Or a further step towards our damnation.'

Their new president waved an elegant hand. He would not permit hot tempers or disputes to spoil the social gathering. Above their heads, rain began to patter down onto the canvas awning. Soon the downpours would come, the great autumnal fogs and then the harshness of the winter. The smell of famine already hung in the air.

He cast a patrician glance around his company. 'I will send out forage parties, establish a fishing camp on Point Comfort at the mouth of the James, will despatch an envoy to Powhatan.'

'Powhatan?' A senior captain frowned. 'Will he not judge us as weak?'

'We have no choice but to trust him.'

Another responded, 'Trust counts for little where savages appear.'

'As may be.' Percy adjusted the lace at his cuff. 'We shall not lower our guard. Yet he has provisions and we have need. He already delivers proof of his regard. We feast upon it.'

There could be no denying the munificence of the gift. Hardy stared across the compound, glad Awae was among the delegation from the mighty chief of chiefs. But Powhatan, the mighty Mamanatowick and ruler of Tsenaco-moco, wanted something. It might be to parley or, eventually, to war.

Ratcliffe stood to address the president, secure in his position, sur-rounded as he was by his acolytes.

'It seems Captain Smith is indisposed.' There was caustic mirth at the remark. 'An ambassador is needed to speak with Powhatan.'

Percy nodded. 'There will be dangers, Captain.'

'They are outweighed by opportunity.'

'You take the commission?'

'With heart and soul.' Ratcliffe basked in the moment. 'With my wits and soldiers about me.'

'Cometh then the man.'

Cometh the conspirator and devious servant of Robert Cecil, Hardy thought. He noted the flicker of ambition and pleasure that came into Ratcliffe's eye. Matters were falling into place. In stepping forward, Ratcliffe would be hailed as dealmaker and hero; as saviour of the set-tlement. It was far from the reality. Smith was removed. Next would be the colony itself.

Shouts rang out, excitement and alarm drifting from the direction of the gate. Lunch was interrupted. In his chair, Percy remained the master-ful host, sanguine and unruffled. Explanation would come.

'Why, it is Captain Martin.'

Dishevelled and exhausted, the officer approached. He was trembling, his face distorted with fear and confusion. Days before he had been dropped downriver with seventeen men to scour the area for supplies. Now unaccompanied, he was returned.

Percy arched an enquiring eyebrow. 'You are scarce dressed for the table, Captain.'

'Forgive my rude intrusion.'

'It seems you forget both your manners and your men.' The president surveyed the shaking form. 'One is an oversight and the other a dereliction.'

'Events overwhelmed us.'

'How so?'

'Afraid of what they faced, my men threatened me and mutinied; they have deserted for the natives.'

'Yet you are unbloodied.'

'What recourse did I have?' There was pleading in the captain's voice. 'What sanction could I wield to persuade them to remain?'

'You have a sword and pistol.'

'Still, I was outnumbered.'

'Your lieutenant?'

Excuses failed in the man's throat. Around the table, there was silence. Captain Martin had plainly abandoned his command, shedding dignity and pride in a bid to save himself. Cowardice was a subject requiring little debate.

Turning to Hardy, the president gave his orders with the mere flicker of an eyelid. Already on his feet, Hardy strode for his quarters, shouting to stable hands and whistling a call for volunteers. Preparations would be brief. Within moments he had reappeared, dressed in his plated leather brigantine. He was ready for hostilities.

'You will both come,' he said, indicating two Poles, dependable types untainted by politics, horsemen who were undaunted by any threat and accomplished with blades. They would relish the venture. 'Each will carry a boar spear.' Hardy distributed the weapons. 'All else will rest on skill and luck.'

The gates swung wide and settlers watched as the small cavalcade began to depart. Perhaps it too would vanish. A pity, for the complement of horses was sparse and their flesh much prized in a depleted larder.

Riding by, Hardy acknowledged Edward Battle with a smile and a nod. He noted the worry in the boy's eye. 'I shall not be long. Guard my dog; keep him close.'

The boy cleared his throat. 'We will defend each other.'

At the luncheon table, the president and his guests had completed their repast. Still standing, abandoned by his fellows, the disgraced captain stood alone. His reputation was unlikely to recover.

The deserters themselves were now tiring of their lieutenant. He appeared to think he could persuade them or return them to a righteous path. Yet they had made their decision. Captain Martin had already fled, recognising the futility of his task. His junior was different; he was adamant, insisting their loyalty was to Jamestown and their immediate duty to him. The fool clearly did not comprehend.

'Sergeant, you will obey.' The lieutenant tried again, stumbling after his troop.

It prompted a snort of derision. 'Is that so?'

'I will not accept your insolence.'

'Nor I your rebuke.'

The face of the officer coloured. 'Take care how you speak to me.'

'Or what?' The burly sergeant sneered. 'You will mewl and cry, and pout like a distressed maid?'

'Be warned.'

'Such warning means little when our captain has deserted.'

'All the more reason for discipline,' the lieutenant insisted. 'The more need we have to be true to our task.'

'Tell it to those that will heed you.'

'I command you to halt!'

The men ignored him. Accustomed to the near anarchy of Jamestown and now loosed into the wild, the soldiers would pursue their own agenda. Hunger drove them. They would head for the village of Kecoughtan and barter with the natives; would strike a deal and elude any reprisal action from the fort. This was freedom. No whining lieutenant would ruin their chances.

'Catastrophe awaits you.' Still the junior officer attempted to persuade them. 'You will pay for such insubordination.'

'As you will lose your tongue should you not control it.'

'Stand and do your duty.'

There was the rasp of steel being drawn from the lieutenant's scabbard, a pause as the implications were weighed. The officer had committed. Almost with a shrug, the sergeant turned, his musket readied. His accomplices too had stopped.

'Let us be, Lieutenant.'

'I will not suffer your insolence.'

'Receive, then, my apology.'

The musket was discharged and the face of the officer exploded in a blizzard of bone and smoke. He'd had it coming. The sergeant rammed home more powder and shot, and reslung his weapon. With barely a backward glance, the men continued their march.

'Welcome, all.'

The man sat on a branch, his voice unmistakably English, a master of ceremonies at home in the woods. The men gazed, perplexed. Certainly the stranger was unthreatening. Perhaps he would offer shelter and food.

Realm stared down at the men. These soldiers were unversed in his ways, would cling forlornly to the belief that he intended them no harm. It was touching, in a way.

'Is it provisions you seek?' He would distract them for the moment. 'Venison? Bread? Maize?'

'Whatever you may offer.'

'Anything is possible, my friends.'

The sergeant cocked his head. 'I do not recall you being at Jamestown.'

'I have dwelt for some time away.'

Had he felt empathy, he might have pitied them now. They were so vulnerable in their enclosure, unknowing of what would come, blind to the presence of his two black Imbangala lying watchful nearby, and of the natives that surrounded them. He would play awhile.

'How fare you all at the fort?'

'We are here, and that speaks enough.'

'Some would condemn you as traitors.'

'They may call us any name.' The sergeant grinned. 'We do as is required.'

'Is desertion not punishable by death?'

'It has done you little harm, it seems.'

'For I am fortunate.' Realm sat calmly in his ringside seat. 'You less so.'

The sergeant might have seen something, or sensed a darkening in the man's tone. He looked about him. Nothing was quite as it seemed. Yet he would humour the stranger; he had no wish to provoke him.

'You bid us welcome.' He peered up at his fellow countryman. 'Your kindnesses will be rewarded.'

'Your trespass also has its due.'

Arrows struck the three men closest to the sergeant. He blinked, paralysed by shock, unable to respond. There was ever that instant before realisation dawned. Realm breathed deep. Thirteen creatures remained, confused and helpless in their pen.

The sergeant shook now, his words thick with fear. 'What is the meaning of this?'

'War.'

Realm gave the signal. The general slaughter could begin.

An Indian scout had been flushed from cover. He ran, feinting and dodging and fording a stream, yet he could not outpace a horse and rider. At Hardy's command, a Pole galloped in pursuit, clutching his boar spear and chasing down his quarry. The scout strung an arrow and turned to loose it, the projectile travelling wide. Still the horseman gained. A deadly sport was reaching its conclusion.

The Indian halted. He must have heard the horse's hooves pounding close and the snort of the beast as it strained in the final stages of their race. Winner and loser were decided. He would not offer his back to the enemy.

There was acceptance in the native's eye, accommodation of the fact that oblivion approached. He braced himself. From an early age he had been taught to face his demise; even when tortured to hurl curses and insults at his foes. No pale-skin would see him quake. He watched the horseman's spear as it was lowered and the distance vanish. Then he was struck. A cross-spar prevented the corpse travelling too far up the weapon's shaft.

Hardy arrived. 'A Paspahegh.'

They would ride on, slipping through the woods and hoping their direction and speed provided some advantage. The local tribe would not expect such madness. After all, the pale-skin wearers of leg coverings preferred to travel by water and in strength. A land sortie was something different.

The intelligencer gave his instruction. 'We take the scalp and head onward. Look both to the trail and trees, for plentiful danger lurks.'

It would include muskets provided by Realm or plundered from dead Englishmen. The renegade had visited these woods. Hardy sensed it. He understood his enemy; expected to glimpse his figure moving between the trees. Nothing was ever done without thought or calculation. His adversary would present himself when it suited him.

It would not be long before they passed into Kecoughtan territory.

With a hand signal, Hardy brought his small troop to a halt. 'Stay and keep watch.'

Surrendering his spear, he dismounted, unslinging his crossbow and loading a bolt for the forward reconnoitre. He was confident if challenged of wreaking severe damage. Maybe he had seen something; perhaps a broken twig or a glancing light jarred deep within his consciousness. He felt the presence of death even before he smelt it. The body of an Englishman lay decomposing on the path.

Already wild animals had gnawed at it and dragged it a short distance. A hand was missing and the skin was colonised; maggots and beetles crawled. It could happen fast in this hot and humid air. Yet there was no mistaking the cause of death. The entry wound was catastrophic and the exit of a musket ball marked by the shattered absence of the rear section of the skull.

The intelligencer returned to his companions. 'One corpse. A single wound, and a close kill at that.'

'His own men?'

'Without a doubt.' Hardy mounted up. 'I suspect he is the lieutenant, abandoned as his captain fled.'

'We proceed?'

Hardy recovered his spear and walked his horse on. 'It is our task to discover the truth.'

Such a discovery was swift. Soon the party came across a clearing, the bodies of sixteen mutilated Englishmen displayed throughout. Some hung in the trees and others were posed, stripped and grotesque and with their genitals removed. All had bread stuffed into their gaping mouths. It was a vivid tableau, a taunting gesture, a message of intent.

It felt good to play Smith's role, to have usurped the belligerent rogue as negotiator and chief contact with the native emperor. Ratcliffe sat content. He was confident of his ascendancy and certain he would return to Jamestown on a vessel laden with grain. The savages could not resist the lure of copper and beads. This was simply another waypoint in the consolidation of his influence, a mean trick by which he would convince all of his benign intent. His fellow settlers were naive, and their refined president a political novice. Conditions could scarcely be more favourable.

He scanned the length of the low-built hut. Thirty soldiers had accompanied him and a further twenty waited on the barge. It should be sufficient to counter any unpleasantness. Yet he did not anticipate trouble. Powhatan himself had extended the invitation, professing friendship and offering trade. It would have been churlish to refuse, to avoid sailing up the James to the Chickahominy and push onward to the royal outpost of Orapaks. Such an effort was worthwhile. Each side understood the rules.

'He approaches,' a guard warned.

Ratcliffe climbed to his feet and stepped outside. He would not be hurried. Protocol had its uses, but the ageing Mamanatowick and his redskin people needed the occasional reminder of the natural order.

Attended by a retinue of priests and braves, Powhatan studied his guest. 'I am told your Weroance is injured to the point of death.'

'Captain Smith is strong.' Ratcliffe laboured with the Algonquian tongue. 'A new chief is appointed, and I come as proof of our eternal friendship and the bond of brotherhood between us.'

'I shall not betray it.'

'Nor we, Powhatan.'

'You are fed?'

'Our bellies are full and we thank you for your kindness.'

The Mamanatowick gazed towards the detritus of the feast. 'All men must eat.'

'Should you have corn to spare, we are willing to pay.'

'You shall have what you need in the morning.'

The evening's discourse was over and Powhatan retired for the night. Gifts were exchanged, and a clutch of European boys left in goodwill with the natives as hostages and former surrogate sons were reunited with the English party. Ratcliffe and his company returned inside, secure that preparations were in train and that tomorrow would provide.

CHAPTER 15

Powhatan had kept his word. In a storehouse thatched with bark and sassafras, baskets piled high with grain awaited the English visitors. Their relief was obvious and heartfelt. They could return to Jamestown triumphant. Ratcliffe looked on. The agonies of John Smith would be compounded by such an event.

Ratcliffe motioned to his men. 'Our business is concluded. A fair trade is done, and we carry home our spoils.'

Their pride would add strength to their shoulders. There was much to carry, and half a mile to cover before they could load the barge. It was fortunate the ruler had been so gracious, so eager to strike a deal. All could celebrate.

'Each man will bear a basket and then return for what is left.'

Eagerly they stepped forward. There was no reason to delay. Within the hour they would have the provisions stowed and would bid farewell to their hosts. Happy to act as pack animals, the men braced themselves to lift the loads and swing them onto their backs.

Perplexed, a voice spoke out. 'Something is wrong.'

'Do as you are ordered,' a lieutenant rebuked.

'I tell you.' The man was insistent. 'My basket is too light.'

Another soldier tested a basket in his hand. 'Mine also.'

'Make trouble and you will receive it.'

The warning was ignored. 'It is a trick.'

'We are cheated.'

Perturbation swept the gathering. A basket was upended and its contents tipped out, the false bottom and small heap of corn revealing the woeful truth. Powhatan had preyed on their hope and ignorance. Now it was fear that prevailed.

'Back to the boat! Take what you may!'

'Do not tarry!'

'Run for your lives!'

Panic ensued and soon the arrows flew, raking the soldiers as they struggled with their meagre bounty. They should have suspected. From the surrounding woods and fields came the chilling war chants of the enemy, a strange ethereal sound pursuing their retreat. Order was lost and the grain abandoned as the English contingent fled.

Several men went down in quick succession, their bodies leaking blood and spotted with feathered flights. One man screamed and fell, an arrow projecting from his thigh, another pausing to grasp and heave him onward. The next arrow struck, hitting the would-be saviour in his side, dropping him beside his companion. Painfully they began to crawl, desperation forcing the pace. Further arrows found their mark as still they proceeded, muttering prayers and exhorting each other, defying the inevitable. Eventually they halted, more dead than alive, bristling with the quills that destroyed them. Even as native braves sat astride them to take their scalps, they offered no resistance.

For the survivors fleeing for the barge, salvation was in sight. It propelled them forward, some turning to loose a ragged volley while others clambered to be the first aboard. The Indians were disinclined to let them go. From either side arrows converged, spewing from cover and speeding fast. The natives charged.

Ratcliffe shrieked a command. 'Form about me! You must protect your captain!'

'Defend yourself!' The rebuff was shouted, concise.

English steel met native club along with blade of bone and sharpened reed. It should have been enough to stem the onslaught. Yet the numbers weighed and the casualties mounted and the ferocity of the attack never slowed. Where once twenty reinforcements stationed on a boat might have altered the outcome, here they made little difference. Confronted by ranks of painted savages and the horror of a howling frenzy, the defence faltered and guttered out.

The final executions were under way. Ratcliffe did not care to glance down as a skull was smashed with a stone and brain matter spilled across his boots. They began to lead him away, ecstatic in their victory.

'Where do you take me?' he cried. 'I will speak with your king.'

There was no answer. Ratcliffe stared ahead, attempting to banish the terrible scene around him, reaching for dignity in the depths of his terror. The situation demanded stoic resolve.

'Unhand me!'

His entreaties went ignored. They had brought him to the royal enclosure now, and were tying him to a tree. They had set a fire close by. Ratcliffe strained in his bindings, shouting his demands. This was not how he had imagined the culmination of his plans. Cecil would never forgive him.

A lone figure ventured forward, a young native woman come as messenger and envoy. The Englishman recognised her as chaperone to the girl princess Pocahontas. She would understand, would convey his felicitations and regret to the great ruler of her people. Awae stopped before him.

For a while she did not speak, but simply looked at him with her warm and knowing gaze. In gentler times he would have lusted for her strong and graceful form and dreamt of her embrace. Savages had a singular beauty.

Her voice was calm and her eyes pitying. 'You are become our prisoner.'

'A matter we may discuss.' He found reason to hope in her choice of the English tongue. 'Are we not bound by language and experience?'

'Many of our warriors die.'

'It is through accident alone. We come to trade and renew our friendship.'

'Too much blood is shed.'

'Was it not Powhatan who called us here? Was it not we who placed a crown upon his head and a robe about his shoulders?'

'His power is his own.'

'Thus we pay tribute and seek good relations.'

'Here is where it ends.' She spoke plainly. 'I know of what you do.'

Ratcliffe frowned. 'Then you will know too of my regard for your people.'

'I am told you plan to murder Powhatan.'

'Murder?' He shook his head.

'I was sent to watch your camp, to be the senses of the Mamanatowick.'

'You are mistaken in what you find.'

'Christian Hardy would not lie.'

Ratcliffe felt rage wash over him as realisation dawned. He shook his restraints, protesting his innocence and pleading for his life.

Awae turned to leave.

'All may be explained,' Ratcliffe cried.

He would scarce be given the chance. In place of Awae came other maidens, dancing and singing in sinuous approach. Struck with horror and hypnotised by the rhythm, Ratcliffe stood as target.

'Tell Powhatan I will talk.' No one seemed to listen. 'I shall give him anything!'

Diplomacy was ended. The Englishman gagged on his own terror now, vomit and drool looping from his chin. A native girl stepped close to stroke his face. It was a gesture both sensual and menacing.

He jabbered. 'It is not the end. It is not the end.'

For him, it was just the beginning. The edge of the mussel shell cut into his skin. He heard his own scream lift high and far from his body; from somewhere he watched as the native girls crowded to flay him alive and tease apart their victim. Shock was a natural anaesthetic. Soon there was the smell of burning, as flesh and organs were deposited in the flames.

Long before he had become John Ratcliffe and an agent of the state, he had been a Catholic priest named Sicklemore. In return for his life, he had agreed to sell his soul; to avoid the barbarity of being hanged, drawn and quartered, he had opted to serve his former enemies. Yet here, as his past overtook him, he suffered a similar fate. Lord have mercy.

Smith would not mourn his adversary. He lay on his sickbed, savouring the news, a glimmer of pleasure bringing life back into his pallid, sunken features. Should he die, he would at least depart in the knowledge that Ratcliffe had predeceased him. It was victory of a kind. In his diminished state there were few other things to celebrate. The settlers were famished and the Indians encroached, Jamestown teetering ever at the brink. That a fleeing soldier had witnessed and relayed the final moments of John Ratcliffe was the best curative of all.

The adventurer glanced towards his visitor. 'Your doing, Christian?'

'He fell prey to himself.' Hardy sipped claret from a goblet. 'But it is a triumph for the forces of Prince Henry.'

'And a blow against the forces of darkness.'

'They are not yet vanquished.'

'It will hold them for a while.' Smith winced at a spasm of pain. 'Such blessings help restore me.'

'Men would be wrong to claim you are finished.'

'Some pray for it.'

A wounded creature was an endangered one, inviting further attack. Hardy could not protect the former president every moment of each day. There were too many other priorities. The survival of the settlement was imperative.

It was Smith who finally declared what both men were thinking. 'I must return to England. I have no choice.'

Hardy nodded. 'You will die if you do not.'

'That is the truth, Christian. Yet I make a vow I shall be back.'

'Dwell first on your recovery.'

Smith peered intently at his friend. 'What of you?'

'My task remains.'

'Have you not fulfilled your duty? Have you not put life and limb in jeopardy to save Jamestown from itself?'

'Dangers remain.'

'Ratcliffe is dead, and Percy a good and honest president.'

'More reason I cannot walk away.'

Hardy rose. He wondered at how Smith endured, marvelling at his strength. Lesser men would have slipped gratefully to their grave. Perhaps the adventurer had invested too much here now to relinquish his interest.

'What is your plan, Christian?' Smith asked. 'Where do you go next?'

'Fort West.' The intelligencer nodded. 'I will leave Buckler with you for company.'

Smith lifted a little from his pillow. 'You would risk yourself for the worthless hide of Francis West?'

'There are many with him who deserve to live.'

'None of them listened to my counsel.'

Circumstances had changed. Everything would be forfeited if the Indians descended in huge numbers on the outpost and an ordered retreat imploded into chaos. Hardy had no fondness for the irascible latecomer who traded on his name. Yet he could not stand idle while those deployed upriver were abandoned in their hour of peril.

'Will this land ever be at peace, Christian?'

'You may ask our descendants that.'

'Let us hope they never know the war and starvation that face Jamestown.'

It was a destiny orchestrated by others; by Powhatan and Opechancanough, by Realm and by the factions manoeuvring within the settlement. Everything conspired against its survival. Hardy hurried away, content to meet the threat.

The retreat was inevitable. With no reinforcements forthcoming, and hostile natives arrayed against them, Francis West and his small garrison floundered between panic and terrified flight. The savages had worked their way round to the riverbank and intended to harry any exodus; they had already picked off the sentries around the flimsy stockade. This venture upstream had been catastrophic. Though few dared share such a view with its architect and commander.

Francis West was in no position to listen. Closeted with his lieutenants, he paced and fretted, cursing his misfortune. The wreckage of his ambition lay in the dead they buried, in the faces of his coterie and the urgency of their departure. Jamestown was as distant as the chance for recovering some dignity and pride from the endeavour.

'Do not stare at me so,' he snapped at an officer. 'I will not have you judge me.'

'I serve you loyally, sir.'

'How many others may say the same? How many others keep their nerve and do not hold me in contempt?'

'Sufficient to keep control until we abandon this place.'

'Abandon.' West repeated the word. 'It is a term forever to haunt me.'

'Be that as it may, sir. We have no choice.'

West struck him a petulant and backhanded blow. 'Who are you to tell me of choice?'

The man spat blood from his mouth. 'I beg forgiveness, sir.'

'Am I not the brother of Lord Delaware? Am I not entitled to be here?'

Weak and preening characters were most dangerous when they sought to counteract their flaws. West was no different. He should have listened to Smith; to those with greater knowledge of Virginia and its natives. Yet like any politician he would soon extricate himself and turn matters to his advantage.

He addressed his subordinates. 'I have been betrayed, let down, conspired against and wronged.'

A captain protested. 'We are with you, sir.'

'With daggers drawn and ready at my back.'

'We would see you as president, sir.'

There was a movement, the rustle of canvas and the flicker of candlelight, and Hardy stepped into the tent. He had evaded the natives and the English alike to gain entry to the compound, and carried himself with the ease of one acclimatised to all extremes.

West observed him. 'This is a surprise.'

'Circumstance demands that politics are set aside.'

'That decision will be mine.'

'So make it.' Hardy was in no mood for debate. 'My men and I will cover your withdrawal.'

Irritation flickered in West's eyes. 'You will?'

'Ratcliffe is dead. Skinned and disembowelled by order of Powhatan. Stay here, and you will be next.'

The colour drained from West's arrogant features. There was ignominious failure, and there was evisceration and dismemberment. He shuddered. The choice was easy. He would rebuild his authority in Jamestown; would portray his reappearance there as nothing less than a strategic masterstroke.

He nodded. 'Very well.'

Hardy turned and left, striding to instruct the troops hunkered sleepless at their stations. As the retreat began, the odd flicker of a lantern or the glow of a slow match, the occasional murmur or shuffle of a boot, should convince the encircling Indians the pale-skins remained. Long may they believe it. Focused on his task, the intelligencer had put from his thoughts the look of resentment and rank hatred he'd seen in Francis West's face.

The operation began and, for a while, the illusion held. On the periphery a mock skirmish occurred, a volley of shot loosed into the undergrowth. Then silence again; the slithering of men back to their waiting vessel. Then arrows began to hit.

'We are discovered!' a soldier cried.

'Hold your nerve! Hold your ground!' another shouted.

'In the name of Christ, move!'

They tumbled for the boat, firing wildly into the shadows. West would be one of the first back on board.

He screamed at his crew. 'Cast off!'

'We must wait, sir.'

'Tarry and you will get my blade. We must away!'

'When all are come aboard, sir.'

Anti-personnel cannon swung on their pintles and discharged cartridge shot to clear the flanks of the enemy. It was a withering and violent display, the flame briefly lighting a scene of scrambling figures and chaos. From the darkness, the shriek of war cries echoed. Out there, Christian Hardy fought a rearguard action.

Neither welcome nor recrimination greeted the survivors of Fort West. Theirs was simply another escapade collapsed into the wider cauldron of futility and defeat. Celebration was scarcely in order. They were more mouths to feed, more malcontents to add to the simmering mix. At the heart of his private army, removed from the general throng, West brooded and nursed his wounded sensibilities. One day, at some future moment, he would have satisfaction.

Cheerless and a little drunk, he surveyed the scene. 'Regard this pestilential shithole.'

An officer drained his tumbler. 'We see it.' He smiled. 'It is best viewed through the eye of a bottle.'

'Or through the skull sockets of a dead savage.'

'Amen.' Those gathered thumped their drinking vessels in accord.

'It is true I am not liked, that portions of this camp despise me,' West said.

'We stay true.'

'For sound reason.' He belched. 'Remain with me and I will make you gods.'

West rose unsteadily to his feet. Even the well-connected needed to piss on occasion. He would review his plans and then work to further project his influence. When his brother Lord Delaware arrived as governor, he would surely reward his commitment. A deputy role would suit him well.

Away from his men, he loosened his britches and prepared to relieve himself against the palisade. Suddenly he found himself lifted from his feet and his face pressed against the dirt. A voice hissed into his ear.

'I fear our discourse went unfinished.'

'Hardy?' West spluttered.

'One move and I will slit your throat.'

'What do you seek?'

'Your absence.' Hardy knelt heavily on the man's back. 'Like Ratcliffe, you are malign. Like Ratcliffe, you will die should you foolishly remain.'

'Your threat is an affront.'

'Whether to God or man, I do not care. I have stuck a blade into many of your kind.' Hardy ground West's face deeper into the earth. 'You are better far from Jamestown.'

'For whom do you speak?' West choked and snivelled. 'That dog Smith, without his balls?'

Hardy laid his knife flat against West's cheek. 'Enough of words. Your flight to Jamestown from Fort West was merely the first part of your journey.'

An agreement was sealed. When Francis West returned to sit among his company, his demeanour had somewhat altered.

Oil lamps were set around, illumination for a temporary stage erected for a performance. Sermons and demonstrations of fencing skills would entertain the settlers for a while. It allowed them to forget their ills. Trepidation could breed instability.

'Have at him, sir! Now is your chance!'

Even the president took to the boards, his elegant presence and exquisite swordsmanship delighting all. George Percy acknowledged the cheers with a gracious bow as he foiled another contender. The Italian technique had won out again.

It was time for English and Spanish duelling to be tested in a mock skirmish. As Percy exited, Hardy stepped up to take his place. He surveyed the expectant faces. Perhaps they would learn something, would wonder at the artistry and brutal ruses of Destreza. The platform was reminiscent of so many things: of displays he'd once conducted on the Southwark side of the Thames; of the moment he had trounced the hothead Earl of Essex. Beyond the glare of the lanterns, his friend John Smith would be watching.

'A challenger is needed.'

Two men answered his call, the Poles already well-rehearsed and entering the fray from both right and left in the spirit of the occasion. Showmanship was demanded. To applause and rowdy laughter, the rolling fight ensued. Blades worked and figures tumbled in acrobatic display, the participants lunging and retreating with parody and skill. White spots appeared on the Poles' leather cuirasses, chalk marks signalling each body blow. Hardy remained unscathed.

The melee was evolving, further combatants joining the fray now to cries of derision and delight. The action was paused as a gentleman stumbled onto the stage clutching a bottle and a rapier and demanding satisfaction.

'What has he that I have not?' The man swayed, unsteady in his finery. 'What defence has he to breeding and high birth?'

Hardy smiled and leant on the pommel of his sword. 'An instinct to survive.'

'Theatre will not save you.'

'It provides a little mirth.'

'I find more in this bottle.'

'So take your seat where you may enjoy it more.'

The newcomer glared. 'You dare counsel me?'

'I will deem you an ass should you not retire.' Hardy's rapier twitched. 'Stay with the revels you know.'

'Here is where I choose.'

'Then I am sorry for your loss.'

Hardy gave no warning. With economy and fluent ease his rapier point darted, unstopping the man's bottle and then removing his hat and severing the ribbons that tied his britches.

The intelligencer laughed. 'You are nothing if not undone.'

Shorn of his dignity and accompanied by a baying tumult, the man staggered from the scene. Behind him, Hardy nodded to the crowd. They were warm in their appreciation.

'Come quick!' a voice cried, severing the mood.

Tensions rose, the murmurings of the throng ebbing as the news was brought. A panting figure had leapt into the light.

'He is gone!' The messenger gulped for breath. 'Francis West is gone!'

George Percy moved forward. 'Gone?'

'Aboard the pinnace! With some forty men attending!'

From the gathering came curses and shouts and the reflex of dismay. West was a coward and a traitor. May he sink, may he perish, may he burn in hell.

The president raised his hand, his thin face unvexed. 'Calm your rage and still your consternation. We have fewer mouths to feed now. We shall endure where others quake and flee.'

The evening's performance was ended. On stage, Hardy collected the tools of his trade and thanked his fellow swordsmen.

'Farewell is bittersweet.'

With a sigh, Smith tossed a bundle of papers into his trunk, bound for England. He had not intended things to end this way. His diaries and letters were all that remained of a dream turned sour. The future of Jamestown lay now in the hands of others.

Hardy viewed with quiet empathy the labours of his friend. The shuffling figure before him was not the rumbustious and indefatigable Captain Smith who had explored, fought and traded and pushed on into the interior. He was a shadow, a cipher shorn of his office and his manhood. He pitied him for what was lost.

Hardy sighed. 'I failed you, John.' He spoke low. 'I blame myself for what has occurred.'

'We cannot challenge fate. You guarded me as would a brother.'

'To little discernible effect.'

'My enemies are scattered, and that suffices.' Smith threw more possessions into the chest. 'Ratcliffe is butchered and West is heading fast out to sea.'

'Measured success is better than none.'

'Indeed, Christian.' If there were nuances or questions, Smith kept them hidden. 'Our stable is now cleansed.'

'I will do as I can to preserve it.'

Smith nodded. Yet something weighed heavily on him. He paused to stare at the intelligencer. 'Come back to England, Christian.'

'For what purpose?'

'To improve your longevity.'

'Has that ever been a condition of our employ? A reason to shy from duty?'

'That duty is complete. Prince Henry himself would laud your endeavours.'

Hardy shook his head. 'I will finish here.'

'Why, Christian?' Smith exhaled. 'For the love of this infernal place? For rogues and ingrates who would smile and then slip a dagger in your back?'

'Such charms are part of the lure.'

And such things were the stuff of their existence. Hardy felt no need to explain that to the man before him. Yet Smith spoke a certain truth. Few obvious foes remained in Jamestown – famine and the savages posed the greater threat. The lawyer Gabriel Archer was nothing without his master Ratcliffe; George Percy was a solid president and should hold the fort. But there was still Awae and the call of the wilderness. None in England would comprehend.

Hardy drew a sealed envelope from his buckskin jacket and freed the lanyard and silver cross from his neck.

He passed them to Smith. 'You know well the story of this crucifix, how my father wore it at his throat as he fought on the ramparts of Malta.'

'Your own tale is not ended.'

'Neither you nor I may say for sure.' The intelligencer gazed at him intently. 'Give the letter and cross to Adam, my son. If he hears no more from me, he is to relay them to William Shakespeare.'

'On what grounds, Christian?'

'A promise I once made.'

The adventurer slammed the lid of the trunk shut. 'You have instructions or messages for others?'

Hardy nodded. 'Tell the hunchback Cecil his sabotage fails.'

Outside, the youth Edward Battle was seated, waiting. Life was hard and kindness fleeting, and kindred spirits rare. He had come to depend on Hardy.

'What happens, Christian?' He jumped up to enquire.

The intelligencer clamped a reassuring hand on his shoulder. 'A trade in memories of past mischief.'

'Will you leave?'

'A question I should ask of you. Our former president will be in need of company.'

'I will never go.' The boy was adamant. 'Answer me, Christian.'

'Am I so spent that I should be banished to England? Am I so weak and feeble that I am required no more?'

Edward brightened. 'You will remain?'

'I would shirk responsibility to let you to your own design, to leave you wild and untutored.'

'I will make no trouble.'

'As my apprentice, you will not.' Hardy smiled at his charge. 'Captain Smith cedes possession.'

The news was met with a shout of approval. A likely sentence of death rarely elicited such a response, the intelligencer mused. Like the rest, the boy must take his chances; like the feral youths soon to be dispatched homeward, he might otherwise die a vagrant in the squalid misery of a London street. Buckler would be pleased.

Edward extended his hand. 'I thank you, Christian.'

'Reserve your verdict for the future.'

Man and boy crossed the compound, the Irish dog trailing behind. There were defences to inspect and preparations to make; final words to exchange. Fear and anticipation sat heavy in the settlement, and already a distance existed between those voyaging and those still stranded. A stowaway was dragged weeping from a ship and thrown unceremoniously ashore. The violent spite of the ocean held fewer terrors than Jamestown.

In late October 1609, the small fleet began to leave. Several of the vessels would never reach England.

CHAPTER 16

'Again they come!'

The Indians wanted the blockhouse, the squat structure topped by a low tower that straddled the causeway to the Jamestown fort. If the natives took it, they would tighten their grip; if the defenders held it they might keep their assailants at bay a while longer.

December was a cruel month for fighting. The snow lay deep and the chill was glacial, breath and limbs freezing on contact with the air. It did not hinder the redskins. Directed by Opechancanough and armed this time with muskets and steel blades, they went on the attack. Tenacity, good fortune and the blessings of the warrior god Okeus would surely grant them victory. But Hardy and his small band of volunteers sat directly in their path.

'I cannot see them, Christian,' a Dutchman called from the flat roof.

The intelligencer climbed the ladder to join him. 'Listen,' he said.

The chants were rising in pitch and intensity as the warriors readied themselves once more for combat. Powhatan would hear of their triumph. No matter the element of surprise was gone. Scalps would be taken this night.

'Hold your fire until they close,' Hardy shouted. 'If you are wounded, tend yourself.'

Lead shot whined overhead and the ragged crackle of musketry rippled among the trees. All around them was the soft somnolence of winter, yet nothing slumbered here.

'Are they shadows or savages?' asked one of the Poles.

'Shadows do not sing.'

An English soldier stood. 'So let us greet them as brothers.'

The musket ball took him in the chest, dropping him to a lifeless sprawl, a sad end to a popular man. His comrades ignored the loss. In front of them, the ground was alive with moving figures chasing forward in attack. Momentum alone might carry them over.

'We must withdraw into the fort.' A doubter discharged his musket and rolled hurriedly to reload.

Hardy did not shift his gaze. 'Retreat is for the weak.'

Crawling back to a group lying prone in reserve, the intelligencer whispered his instructions. This was his inheritance, the bloodline of his father: siege warfare at its most ferocious. Wildfire could put a stop to armies, and now it would find fresh employ. The slow matches were already lit.

'Launch the grenades!'

In unison the ordnance flew, earthen pots with spluttering fuses arcing high to fall among the vanguard. It was a biblical scene, an inferno bursting into flame with an oily detonation, holding the screams and writhing forms within its deadly radius.

'Shoot now! Shoot true!'

Few could survive such punishment. Yet still the natives pressed in, crawling to outflank and confuse the defence and to capture their objective. A warrior gained purchase on a timber and heaved himself upward towards the roof. He was met with a sword through the throat. Another had leapt up the walls to engage and was brought down as he swung a machete.

'Watch your back!'

The warning came too late. An Englishman staggered and fell, a brace of arrows piercing his shoulder and spine. Around him the battle surged, polluted by smoke and the stench of charred bodies. A painted face swung into view, disappearing again as Hardy levelled and fired a musket. Then another. The intelligencer swung the butt of the weapon and stove in the front of a skull. It was methodical and dispassionate work.

A new warrior confronted him, his body lean, muscled and painted and his head adorned with feathers and dyed and knotted deer hair. An experienced combatant. In one hand was a sword and in the other a shield of hide; at his throat were amulets and beads. There was a certain regret in snatching the life of so magnificent a being.

Hardy stayed his weapons. 'Leave this slaughter,' he said. 'Tell your Weroance that all were bold and brave.'

His invitation was refused. Hardy expected no less. Until Realm visited these shores, this native would never have possessed steel. It could provide a man with a false sense of security. The savage shifted now, preparing to do harm, his chest heaving as he filled his lungs. Just ahead of the lunge, moving fast, Hardy slid the Katzbalger deep beneath the warrior's armpit.

'Still they fight, Christian!' a voice cried.

He admired the Indians' resolve. It was the fault of the English renegade who had employed them as his surrogates and directed them in frontal onslaught. But courage was no substitute for military preparedness. Such considerations mattered little to a traitor for whom the sport was all.

Arrows flicked about him as he climbed for greater height. Noise from the upper platform had now curiously abated. As he mounted the lip, the reason was apparent. Slumped haphazardly were the lookout and gunners, their bodies raked by musket shot. None below had noticed the blood dripping through the boards. Hardy crouched down. He would not offer his outline too as an instant target. The platform was rent with shrieks and groans and the undulating din of murder at close quarters.

Quickly he reloaded the saker, his fingers nimble. In the breech sat a charge and cartridge primed and ready to let fly. Hardy swung the barrel. He had performed the act so many times, had cut down swathes of enemy in countless engagements. This was just another night. A blow on the match, a last view of the aim point, a light touch of lit sulphur to gunpowder. His vision blurred.

'You are no stranger to such a scene.'

Taunt or observation, the words filtered thin on the frigid air. Realm was paying a visit. He would converse from a distance, gauging his enemy and testing the mood. Hardy scanned the darkness and the deeper shadows along the treeline.

'Wherever you tread there is blackened earth and carnage, Hardy,' Realm called out. 'Whatever you do leads to chaos and collapse.'

'I defend, and that is all.'

'All? Do you recall your house off Fetter Lane? How you guarded that with incendiaries too?'

'Similar threat begets similar answer. Tonight you are defeated.'

'And tomorrow?' The voice would not be silenced. 'Jamestown is stripped of time and hope; it will not outlast the future.'

Hardy looked down at the scattered corpses and blistered debris, stark against the icy landscape. 'Once more you herd men to their fruitless end,' he said. 'Once more you hide behind others as senseless killing prevails.'

'What are a few savages to me? What is a pen of exiles and vagrants to you?'

'I am tasked with their protection.'

'While I am ordered to destroy them.'

There was never room for compromise. One day a reckoning would come. That it could occur in the wild lands of Virginia was mere chance. The bullet or the blade could have taken either man at any time over twenty violent years. Hardy planned to bring a conclusion to events.

'What are you thinking, Hardy?'

'How a fusillade may finish you now, how a cannon shot from the fort behind might pulp you in an instant.'

'Would it not spoil our game?'

'I tire of the contest.'

Realm laughed. 'You do not enquire why I come.'

'It does not matter why. I shall kill you.'

'Such things may wait.' Realm paused and silence pervaded. 'Your female savage is my captive.'

Hardy swallowed, then spoke again. 'What concern have I?'

'That of a weak man. That of a gallant who risks losing all.'

'I lose nothing.'

'She is precious to you, Hardy.' The renegade would not parley. 'Such sweet eyes and softness of skin. Such loyalty to you.'

'Base trickery will not help you.'

'Nor will your stubborn ways save Awae.'

Hardy paused. 'I listen.'

'Find her and fight for her, and redeem your soul and conscience. Make amends for failing in your duty to Emma, your late wife.'

'Where is Awae?'

'At the place the English call Powhatan Tower, dubbed Nonesuch by your lamented Smith.'

'You think I would stray into such a trap?'

'All challenge is meat to you.'

'There is meat and there is bait.' Quietly Hardy applied a fresh cartridge to the saker. 'I am no novice to your actions.'

'So Awae will die.'

'You bring scant proof that she lives.'

'Trust I shall soon bear proof she expires.' Realm had delivered his message. 'You have a week to save your savage.'

The renegade was gone. In the blockhouse, the remaining defenders hunkered down against the cold and waited for the morning. They had won the skirmish and inflicted heavy casualties; had once more reminded the natives of the folly of frontal attack. Yet it did not alter the outlook and could not prevent starvation. Their isolation was complete.

'Where is he?'

There was a clamour at the door, the sound of protest swept aside. In this modest Lambeth street on the south bank of the Thames, occasionally a constable might call to search for a wanted miscreant; a bawdy house might be raided or a Catholic fugitive dragged off by a crew of pursuivants. Permitted to thrive beyond the City bounds, the area had been allowed to become a haven for alchemists and soothsayers. This December day was different. Robert Cecil would go where he pleased.

'I will ask once more.' The Lord Treasurer gazed coldly at the maid. 'Where is he?'

She trembled. 'Who, my lord?'

'Whichever patient is cared for in this place.'

'Captain Smith?'

'You learn well for a dullard and a servant.'

Cecil pushed past the terrified woman. He would not be kept waiting. In the dark confines of the house, there was the smell of camphor and alcohol spirit and the mustiness of books. A noted physician owned the premises.

A manservant stepped forward. 'Our master is away.'

'It is Smith, not your master, I seek.' Cecil hobbled onward, his club foot landing ungainly on the flagstones.

Shadowed by his two guards, he entered the room. In seconds he had appraised the situation, noting every detail. It was a small chamber, sparsely furnished. Wrapped against the chill and propped up with a pillow bolster, John Smith was reading his Bible.

He looked up. 'An assassin or a well-wisher? Rarely are my visitors of such high standing.'

'Be flattered, then, by my presence.'

Smith gave Cecil a sceptical look. He would not be cowed by the hunchback. 'Have you come to gloat?'

'I will save that for your funeral.'

'Through the grace of God, it is delayed.' Smith closed the text. 'As you see, I live and breathe, although . . .' The adventurer perused his adversary. 'It seems we are both disfigured.'

'Alas, your maladies are more grievous.'

'They will not keep me from my task.'

It was a threat as much as a promise. Smith had already learnt something from Cecil's visit. The little hunchback was losing control, desperate to ensure his plans remained ascendant. The monarch relied on him. Yet all around London there were rumours of another mission to rescue Jamestown, of preparations for Lord Delaware to sail for Virginia as governor to bring order to the rotten state.

The adventurer yawned. 'You must have matters elsewhere to address, my lord.'

'None that would prevent a visit to a friend.'

'A friend?' Smith snorted in derision. 'You come to put your mind at ease, to mine for information.'

'I was passing.'

'So, pass by. There is little I can tell you, except that Jamestown clings to life.'

'Through the winter? Without provisions or supplies? When starvation and savages press in from every quarter?'

'You have long proclaimed its end.'

Taking shallow breaths against the pain, Smith swung his legs over the edge of the bed and rose. He didn't need a pygmy to lecture him on Jamestown: too much had been invested and too much lost. For all his finery and fur-trimmed robes, Cecil was a speck against the immutability of fate.

'Heed me, my lord.' Smith swayed, sweat beading his face. 'Your Ratcliffe is cut to pieces as Christian Hardy endures.'

Cecil turned, aware that he could not win this bout, but Smith was not done.

'My lord, a final thought.'

'Make it quick.'

'Christian bids me tell you that your sabotage will fail.'

When Cecil had left, Smith sank exhausted to his couch. Even a soldier who had outlived every danger could feel trepidation in proximity to the Antichrist. He stared at the ceiling.

There was a knock at the door and the gentle voice of the maid. 'Another visitor craves your pardon, Captain.'

Prince Henry appeared in the doorway, his face concerned and his eyes kind. He drew up a wooden stool beside Smith.

Smith mumbled a greeting. 'An honour, Your Grace.'

'All honour is mine. It is you who have suffered in our service.'

'A mere scratch, Your Grace.'

'One that renders you back to London.'

'I am healing well, Your Grace.'

'I pray it is so, Captain.' The youth smiled. 'My father the King would scarcely favour this fraternisation.'

'Nor his pygmy Cecil, who has just departed.'

'They are caught on the wrong side of history.'

'It may yet make them more threatening, Your Grace.'

'I fear you state the truth.' There was a near-imperceptible sigh. 'But I am not ready to surrender or submit.'

Smith nodded. 'How to proceed, Your Grace?'

'Your prince will never quit.' Henry leant closer to the patient. 'I have read your works and studied your map; have ensured supplies and new settlers will again be sent.'

'Then you shall hear my cheers from the gallery.'

The adventurer and his prince had a bond forged by mutual respect as well as by the prince's desire to challenge Spain, civilise the pagans and spread the glory of the realm. Smith had laboured hard for the project.

Henry lowered his voice. 'Speak to me of Mr Hardy.'

Slipping again, Hardy clutched at a rock and hauled himself upward. The falls were no place for a man in such conditions. Ice covered the surfaces and snow lay deep on every ledge. At least the local chief Parahunt would be away hunting, his scouts taking shelter from the cold. Raiding was for warmer weather.

The intelligencer paused, waiting for the Pole to clamber up beside him. If Realm expected a frontal assault on Powhatan Tower, he would be disappointed. There were other ways to rescue Awae; different means to cover the approach.

Hardy listened. There was no warning cry, nor yet an arrow in the back. He trusted such luck would hold.

'I slow you, Christian.' The Pole muttered his apology.

'Caution is better than haste.' Hardy blew to warm his hands. 'Our task is to reach the summit.'

'Beyond it?'

'We use our wits and the goodwill of earlier meetings.'

'Should that fail?'

'Then we surely die.'

Acceptance and improvisation were suited to the circumstances. There were a multitude of variations to this threat. Somehow Realm had struck a deal. Parahunt was the son of Powhatan; he must have fallen prey to the persuasiveness of Opechancanough and colluded in the snatching of the native king's concubine. As in Jamestown, loyalty was a transient and fickle thing.

The Pole stifled the chattering of his teeth. 'Why do they set such a trap?'

'To taunt us and to take more scalps.'

They had slipped away by stealth and without the president's permission. Hardy had no wish to burden Percy with the details of his plan.

Recklessness was a private affair. Close by the base of the falls, he had left the second Pole to guard the skiff with musket and shot and a plentiful supply of firepots and stink grenades.

They resumed their climb. Had any traitor in the settlement already guessed their plan, it would be wise to abort it and launch themselves to their deaths. Captivity was no option. Hardy put such matters from his thoughts. His concern was for Awae. The English renegade would not treat her with kindness.

'We are there, Christian.' Relief sounded in the panting voice. The two men were soaked in sweat despite the freezing conditions. Urgency would spur them on.

Hardy unwrapped his rifled musket from its oiled canvas. 'Let us hope we may be persuasive.'

'We shall know soon enough.'

'Should I be wounded, you have your orders.'

'Your execution will be quick.'

He could depend on the Pole. There was no need for gratitude or sentiment. It was the way of things.

Hardy peered ahead. 'We move.'

Clambering to their feet and hunched against the cold, the men proceeded through the silent thickets. The intelligencer stopped. His companion tensed, tightening his grip on his cradled gun.

'What do you see, Christian?'

'Either our salvation or destruction.'

Figures emerged from among the trees, natives holding their clubs aloft, picked out by the random glow of a flaming torch. They came closer.

'Those are not weapons they carry.' It was the Pole who spoke.

Positioned on the tip of each stick, a human skull grinned. It was the Pocoughtronack. One of their members smiled in greeting, his teeth filed sharp. Cannibals were by their nature curious.

'You English are wedded to the past.'

Don Pedro de Zúñiga offered the comment as observation, not insult. The Spanish ambassador was content to stroll with Cecil now, to take the air and trade diplomatic pleasantries, to watch archery at the butts in the frost-rimed pleasure grounds of Highgate. Beside him, the little hunchback seemed almost comic in his sable-trimmed cloak. But neither man would be so foolish as to underestimate the other.

The minister awaited the next arrow strike before responding. 'Rather we prepare for every eventuality.'

'Jamestown?' The Spaniard followed his gaze. 'Did you expect it to cling to life with such tenacity?'

'It surprises me.'

'Worse, my lord. It vexes and tests the patience of my king.'

'Mine also. But I have no doubt it will fail.'

'Hope and prayer scarce suffice. Even now fresh ships prepare to sail there, and Lord Delaware is tasked by the royal council to save the colony.'

'He will find only a grave, Don Pedro.'

The ambassador shook his head. 'A pledge you have too often made. A promise ever overtaken by events.'

'You question my word?'

'I speak it as it is.'

Cecil considered the statement. 'They have no food in Jamestown, and are divided and diseased. What lifeblood they possess leaks daily into the earth.'

The Spaniard looked doubtful. 'Perhaps I should find comfort in the fact that Captain Smith is since removed.'

'No better outcome could be wished upon so vile a man.'

They walked on, their guards trailing at a distance, powerful hierarchs plotting for the future.

Cecil looked about him. 'Be certain of our love for King Philip and his people.'

'His Majesty is grateful.'

'You have studied my reports, Don Pedro. Where once Jamestown strove to build outposts, today it retreats within itself. When once it sowed and planted crops, it now plants nothing but the dead.'

'Long may we hear such news.'

'One day there shall be none.' There was a cheer as an arrow hit its target.

Zúñiga glanced towards the proceedings, then frowned. 'There is yet Christian Hardy.'

'As there is your agent Realm.'

'So let carnage and chaos prevail.'

Old enemies fraternised here as, in Virginia, other state servants fought. May the most vicious win, the Lord Treasurer mused. Peace between England and Spain had thrown up rich irony and an unholy alliance. People could be crushed by the consequences.

Awae had not wept or struggled, had not fought to save her honour. But then, she was only a primitive. Her passivity had irked Realm. It diminished his victory and took something from his conquest. Maybe she intended to insult him. No matter, for the result was the same: her violation was complete.

He stood and regarded her. 'You know you will die.'

Once more, the blank acceptance. He resented her dull courage, but savages had their own way. Perhaps Awae waited for Hardy; perhaps she possessed a touching faith that the impossible might happen. Realm's pair of Imbangala and a hidden formation of native warriors would ensure the outcome went his way.

The naked girl hugged a blanket close.

'To the victor the spoils,' he said. He let his gaze travel. 'I wonder at your thoughts.'

He would need to, for she refused to give reply. It must have been a shock to be lifted from her lodgings, stolen without trace from the royal camp of Powhatan himself. As military chief, Opechancanough could arrange such a disappearance. It was for the greater good and the purpose of an ambush.

The renegade stepped from the hut. Outside, the air was crisp. Congratulation was in order. He had plundered what Hardy had so assiduously cultivated; had again despoiled what the intelligencer believed was safe. Nothing in their twinned existence was beyond his reach.

Still there was no movement, no report of an expedition launched in haste from Jamestown. He had plainly overestimated Hardy. In earlier days, his rival would have jettisoned caution to effect a rescue, answering with ruthless impulse to avenge or save a loved one. A man could grow timid with age.

He wandered to the bluff, feeling the breeze on his face, noting the prowling figures of warriors armed with bows and swords. An elite few had muskets. 'The Monacan!'

A cry sounded the alarm, but it was already too late. Smokepots exploded, blinding and disorientating, their contents drifting in a sulphurous haze. From every quarter, the enemy attacked. They had the advantage of surprise, their ferocity loosed upon their foe for whom their hatred was instinctive. The sounds of battle climbed.

Pocoughtronack too scurried in the melee. Theirs was a more specialist undertaking. They came for meat, to scavenge off the dead and replenish their supplies. High mortality meant produce for the winter larder.

His Katzbalger drawn, Hardy roared his command. 'Search for a pale-skin and capture him alive!'

Arrows peppered the murk, marking the advance. Within the noxious cloud, figures engaged and disengaged, warriors weaving through to bludgeon and cut and kill. Powhatan Tower had become more slaughterhouse than sanctuary.

About the hut, battle was in full cry. Hardy pushed towards it. He felt the heat of a musket ball close to his forehead and then the grunt of a Monacan downed by an arrow. The brave floundered helpless in a pool of blood. His destiny was his own.

'Awae?'

She already stood, serene amid the clamour and remote from the corpse of the Imbangala spreadeagled at her feet. The African had not anticipated the blade through his throat.

Her voice was quiet. 'I had to kill him, Christian.'

'He hurt you?'

'Others have.' She stared, the knife still in her hand. 'The man you call Realm.'

'We will hunt him.'

'You have found me, and it is enough.'

There was no reproach, no accusation in her words. Her ordeal was over. He went to her and gently prised her fingers from the dagger's hilt, letting the weapon fall away. Then he held her. It was a simple act, heartfelt and fleeting, bringing her back to him.

In a night rent by the whoop and holler of combat, the Monacan put their enemy to flight. They would savour the moment and then be gone before their presence invited a counter-attack. Out on the hard ground, a Pocoughtronack squatted beside the body of the second Imbangala and reached into the open chest to remove the steaming heart. Prey with dark skin was something of a novelty.

In London, bills were posted on boards throughout the city urging skilled artisans and committed patriots to volunteer for service in Virginia. Nothing less than national pride and the survival of Jamestown were at stake. The supporters of the colony and its princely patron were not yet ready to capitulate. Time and circumstance stood opposed.

CHAPTER 17

Starvation arrived with the new year, bleak and cheerless as the cold, hollowing faces and ending all hope. Beneath their shroud of snow, the inhabitants of Jamestown endured and suffered and waited for oblivion. Some sat mute and accepting, some went mad, some vanished beyond the palisade and never reappeared. From horses and chickens to snakes and rats, all animals were eaten and supplies finished. It was January 1610. A merciless time.

'You are awake, Awae?'

Hardy stirred the pot, mixing the foul stew of fungus and roots. The ingredients had been hard-won. Perhaps Edward and Buckler might return from their evening hunt and offer their master fresh rodent kill. It would be gratefully received. Here in the blockhouse, set apart from the rest, they were a self-contained crew alert to the dangers about. Behind them were famished settlers; before them the lurking presence of the Indians. This was no man's land, the frontier, the causeway between fort and hostile territory. The safest place to be.

She stared at him from their makeshift bed, her eyes accepting and her nakedness cocooned beneath a blanket. The snow might lie deep outside, but in here they were warm enough. He felt a pang that he must desert her and climb to replace the sentry on his watch. Even in deep winter, observation was required.

He went to her, stooping to kiss her lips and then committing himself to a more intimate embrace. Their passion was easily ignited.

'I put you in peril, Awae.' He caressed her face. 'Forgive me.'

She brushed his fingers with her lips. 'I will blame you for nothing.'

'Without me, you would not have fallen prey to Realm.'

'And without you, I would never have been saved.'

'Now I bring you here. To a place of famine, to a life that is no life.'

'It is one I choose.'

She had a tone of quiet assertiveness, a look that suggested her decision was made. He was thankful for her love and loyalty. Yet he worried too. Someone had betrayed them, had discovered his weakness and ensured she became the bait in a trap set for him. Ratcliffe might be gone, but clearly other minions of Cecil still plotted.

Awae sat upright and reached to hold his hands, the cover falling from her shoulders. 'I must speak, Christian.'

'I listen.'

Her eyes dipped. 'I am ashamed.'

'What is shame when we each stand at the edge of a void?'

'You do not understand, Christian.'

'I will try.'

'Do you know who I am?' Tears pricked, and emotion caught in her throat. 'Do you know I was sent by Powhatan to spy on your encampment?'

'I would think less of your ruler had he not relied upon such a ruse.'

'It was wrong.'

'No, Awae.' He leant to kiss her again. 'It brought you to me, and it is all for the good.'

Reassured, she let him hold her and pressed her face into his neck. Everyone had their secrets. But he could not protect her at Jamestown. The lack of food and the pervasive threat would take their toll on all. He preferred to see her live.

'You cannot stay with me, Awae.'

'You ask me to go?' She clung tighter. 'You rescue me, then send me from you?'

'It is for your safety.'

'I am safe with you.'

'I cannot guard you every moment.' He spoke in an earnest whisper. 'You and the boy Edward will journey to the mouth of the James and the place we call Point Comfort. Its stockade lies close to your village of Kecoughtan.'

She protested. 'I belong with you.'

'And I with you, to the end. Yet I have unfinished work here.'

'Come with me to Kecoughtan.'

He put his fingers to her lips. 'Our parting will be brief.'

'Swear it.' Her demand earned another kiss.

He rose and returned to his kitchen duty, his nose wrinkling at the aroma. The Lord could not force a man to be grateful. Yet it was what kept them alive, what passed for victuals in this grim season. Soon his foragers would return.

Garbed in his buckskin and fur hat, he climbed the ladder to take the watch. It was easier to confront the cold than Awae's restrained anguish. She was too proud to plead, too understanding to condemn him. The decision had been made.

'You are early, Christian.' The Pole greeted him with a muffled salutation.

'Your food is ready and awaits.'

'Food?' Woollen layers failed to mask the harshness of his laugh. 'This ice and wind are a less bitter foe.'

'Summon, then, your courage.' The intelligencer smiled. He unslung the rifled musket from his back and squinted into the darkness. He would not release the weapon from its protective shroud until he was sure the enemy approached. Numbness already crept into his fingers. In the fort, a bell clanged the hour dolefully.

'Hear it, Christian?' the Pole said, hovering still. 'Is it to mark time or the passing of our lives?'

'I shall not hazard to guess.'

'Yet I will hazard no savage is so foolish as to stand in the open at this hour.'

'Our strength lies in our lack of reason.'

'Content yourself with such thoughts.'

It was uttered as a farewell. The Pole descended and Hardy was alone. He began his evening rounds, stamping the circulation back into his feet, inspecting the ordnance and scanning the woods.

'Seek it, Buckler.'

The boy and dog hunted, foraging at the base of the Jamestown palisade. Pickings might be meagre, but instinct and a canine nose provided some advantage. They were committed in their task. As Edward Battle beat and prodded with a stick, his companion prowled and sniffed the air. A kill was close.

'We have them.'

Excitement erupted as two rats dashed from their cover. Buckler was waiting. He pounced, snarling and efficient, addressing one with a single bite and then turning to dispatch the other. A quick and easy kill.

'Christian will be proud.' The youth retrieved a rodent and slipped it into a canvas bag. 'You may keep your prize.'

They moved on, methodical and slow, a pair of friends focused in their labours. Soon they would return to the blockhouse. The fort was no place to loiter.

Another nest was disturbed and more rats taken. There was lichen, too, giving a chance to supplement the diet. The youngster clapped his arms about his body to warm it. He trusted his effort tonight would make a difference.

'What is it, Buckler?' The dog had growled and edged forward to protect him. 'You see something?'

Figures appeared, wrapped against the cold and distorted in the gloom. They had clambered to the ground by rope and clearly did not come with kind intent.

'Be on your way,' Edward shouted out, fumbling for his blade.

'Who are you to give command?' The words carried malice.

'I am armed.'

'We too, youngling.'

'Retreat or you will pay.'

'A higher price than you?' The enemy had spread out to encircle them. 'We each hunt here this evening.'

'Go then to your task.'

'It seems we find our prey.'

'What I find is mine.' The boy held the knife low, tracing the direction of the threat. 'I take rats, and that is all.'

'It is the dog we want.'

Edward pressed himself against the timbers, his breath high and his limbs trembling. He should not have ventured so close to the camp.

This was his punishment. Yet he would rather die than give what they demanded. Buckler crouched low and snarled.

'We starve, boy,' the man said. 'Would you deny us provision?'

'With my life I shall deny you the dog.'

'Put down your blade.' The space between them lessened. 'Or we shall feast on you too, as on a suckling pig.'

There was no jest here, no accompanying laughter. Hunger directed everything. It infected the settlers' thoughts and mired their instincts, hardened their hearts and diseased their souls. The boy could not blame them. But he must fight.

'Verdict is given.' Finality was in the words. 'You will feed us well, boy.'

In a flurry of action and hard, committed blows, Hardy announced his arrival. Within seconds he dominated the skirmish, the butt of his musket slammed into foreheads and jaws.

'Mercy.' The man's mouth dribbled with blood and spit as he pleaded.

'You would have shown none.' Hardy stood poised. 'Crawl back while you are able.'

'We meant no harm.'

'Yet you would kill what is precious to me.' The intelligencer pushed the barrel of his gun into the crotch of the ringleader. 'Go.'

He collected the boy, wrapping his arm about his shoulders and walking him away. Buckler fell in beside them. Behind, the victims of their recent encounter would limp back into the fort.

'An eventful night.' Hardy felt the youth shivering beside him. 'I am glad I came in search.'

'I too, Christian.'

'Your haul?'

'Rats and moss and a handful of berries.'

'A mean exchange for your life.' The intelligencer drew him closer. 'You have created enemies, Edward.'

'I would say the same of you.'

'It is my vocation. You should be set on a different path.'

'I choose to be with you.'

'To vex me? To distract? To deflect me from my duties?'

The boy halted. 'You dismiss me?'

'I promote you.' Hardy patted him on the shoulder and marched him on. 'You are of more use alive than dead.'

'What is in this promotion?' Hope and doubt wrestled in Edward's voice.

'A skiff is readied with one of my men. Escort Awae to the mouth of the James and seek shelter in our fort there.'

'For what purpose?'

'That one of us survives.'

It provided at least the smallest of chances. At the tiny stockade downriver there were still a few pigs and chickens and a winter catch of shellfish, luxuries remote to those at Jamestown. There would be no argument. Man and boy trudged up the snowbound causeway.

The roll call served only to reinforce despair and remind the settlers of their plight. Men and women hobbled out, gathering in a marketplace emptied of all trade. It was simply a ritual, an attempt to bring order and meaning to an existence devoid of both. There were no provisions, so people chewed on leather; surrounded as they were, there were few chances to gather firewood, so inhabitants broke up their furniture and homes. Jamestown had turned inward, was feeding on itself.

'How long?' Percy spoke almost to himself. 'For how long may we stand?'

Attired in his rich clothing and warmed by a fur-trimmed cloak, he stood with his officers and viewed the dismal scene. Desertion and death had again winnowed their number. Yet there were standards to maintain and the office of a president to uphold. He could do it. He owed it to the ghosts and ciphers before him.

He gestured to a lieutenant. 'Call the roll.'

The names were read and then met with silence or a muttered answer. Few wished to confront the reality, and fewer still would shed a tear. No matter that a child perished or a wife went missing, or another ravenous soul stumbled into the forest, never to return. Each meant one less mouth to feed. Even the distant screams of those caught by the savages had ceased to move or bother.

'Adams?'

'Here.'

'Beck?'

'Sick.'

'Harries?'

'Dead.'

'Waud?'

'Here.'

It was a list that provided its own epitaph. Percy bowed his head at news of every death. None envied him his role. At his side, Hardy looked on. He had helped drag more corpses from the fort earlier that morning.

The president sighed. 'Another bleak hour of another bleak day, Mr Hardy.'

'It is one we live to see.'

'Too many of our brothers and sisters do not.' Percy motioned towards the assembled. 'I fear it is more funeral wake than roll call.'

'With courage and luck we shall prevail.'

'Luck?' There was the hint of a melancholic smile. 'A bizarre and foreign notion.'

'Yet our walls stand and the natives are held back.'

'Would that starvation also was banished.' It was a restrained and heartfelt plea.

Hardy cast him a supportive glance. 'All here look to you, and you will lead us through.'

'Trusting words, Mr Hardy.'

'Not one of them is wasted.'

'As for you, I sometimes think that you and your Irish dog are the sole defenders of these ramparts.'

'I will not lower my guard.'

A speech to the crowd was demanded; an attempt to shore up morale or at least stave off its complete collapse. Dying colonies were fragile affairs. The president yet had faith.

He stepped forward, scrutinising the bowed forms and haggard faces. His audience was unlikely to be fooled by lies and rhetoric.

'My brothers and sisters.' Percy cleared his throat. 'We are hard put to it and tested by misfortune. Each hour we pray, each day we weaken and sicken and starve.'

A settler called out. 'Yet we live.'

'I give thanks that it is so. We must endure, must strive, must bring succour to whoever is in need. Increase your endeavours and embrace your fate. God is with us now.'

George Percy was no orator. But a few words were better than none; might coax a little warmth back into their spirits. Then they could disperse once more to huddle in their wrecked and cheerless hovels.

A mad chattering intruded, a man staggering ragged through their midst and giving vent to his insanity. Foam clung to his chin as he howled and cursed.

'We are sinners! We are lost! We are damned!'

Percy was calm. 'The Lord is with us.'

'You deceive! For you are a servant of Beelzebub, and it is he that guides us to the slaughter!'

Sergeants attempted to restrain the settler, yet he broke free to continue with his ranting. Clearly his mind was gone; the strain had corroded his humours and senses. His situation was worthy of pity.

'I will not condemn you.' Percy was gentle in his address. 'We each share the same terrors and trials.'

'God abandons us! Satan alone stalks this ground!'

Without further word, the unfortunate ran. His objective was the gate, the guard throwing it wide to release the jabbering idiot out into the wild. A couple of stragglers followed. They would be neither missed nor invited back.

Peace descended once again, the inhabitants returning to their homes. During the disturbance, it was the presence of Gabriel Archer that had caught Hardy's eye. Despite the commotion, the lawyer's stare had never flickered from his own. A curious triumphalism sat obvious in his eye.

'Winter brings its harvest.'

Realm turned the corpse with his foot, noting the stench, the mauling by animals and the feathered stubs of arrow flights. Only the cold had slowed the decay. He should congratulate the Paspahegh spotters for their swift response and their true aim, for tightening the noose on the settlement ever further. It must be hell inside. Daily the starving sought to escape and were inevitably brought down. This example and the other slain beside him were fortunate to have avoided capture.

The renegade switched his gaze to Opechancanough standing near. 'See how they bleed.'

'We too have bled.' The military commander was impassive. 'My warriors have been wasted on your adventures.'

'None is lost in vain. We force the settlers to retreat, to ensure they starve within their fort.'

'How often have you promised their end?'

'It is a pledge I shall not break.'

'Yet your Christian Hardy lives.'

Realm could scarce deny such a truth. Results had been disappointing of late; had involved carefully laid plans going terribly awry. Opechancanough was right to be concerned. Yet there was ever tomorrow and the days beyond, the possibility of bringing matters to a conclusion.

He gestured to the corpses. 'Like Jamestown they have no future, are rotten and decayed.'

'I seek victory, and that is all.'

'Time and patience will deliver what you wish.'

'Did you not say the same of ambush and attack?'

'As hunters, we adapt.'

There was tension between the men now, a recognition that the renegade might have overplayed his hand. He had promised much to his hosts. The Monacan had inflicted grievous hurt in their assault. Even his African bodyguards were dead. Goodwill could be a transient thing.

The Englishman peered at Opechancanough, would claw back some respect. 'One day soon, the gates of the fort will hang wide and you will stride through as conqueror.'

'Our people await it.'

'Do they not hail you as their protector? Does Powhatan not regard you as the shield of his nation?'

'I would choose to be their king.'

Realm nodded. 'When Jamestown is finished and the pale-skins crushed, all of Tsenacomoco will bow down.'

Flattery would hold him for a while. The pair had other sites to visit and more cadavers to review. Of those fleeing the English camp, women and children alone were permitted to survive. In exchange for food and shelter they would abandon the past and embrace the native life. They would become the spoils of war. Siege was a numbers game.

Realm paused to study an English female in the company of savages. 'Your name?'

'Elizabeth.'

'You seem frightened.'

'I am not.' Her face betrayed the lie.

'Then as one outcast to another, I give you welcome.'

'Who are you to offer welcome?'

'A friend of sorts; a deserter from the English way.'

'I wish only to eat.'

'You shall, I have no doubt.' He reached and stroked her hair.

'You are a traitor? A Catholic?'

Realm pinched the woman's face and saw her wince. 'Be careful how you speak.'

She was taken away, a prisoner and future breeding stock. Already her circumstances were improved. Realm walked on. He did not envy the famished remnants left behind in their palisade.

Conditions had worsened. In a corner of the fort, a man was on his hands and knees eating bloodied snow in the wake of a passing corpse. Close by the church, another scratched for grubs that might be hiding in the timber. Again the roll had been called, and once more the responses dwindled. Afterwards the settlers lay entombed in their ice-clad dwellings. There was little to say and hunger alone to fill their thoughts.

'Give entry!' There was a furious hammering at a door. 'We are sent by command of the council!'

The order did not elicit an answer. People were disinclined to care these days. Yet the squad persisted, prepared if necessary to force its way through. The sergeant had orders to search, to maintain the peace, to use whatever means needed in policing and enforcement. His was a challenging task.

He bellowed through the shutters. 'Do as we say or suffer the penalty.'

Refusal would lead to a beating or the stocks. Worse, the dwelling would be confiscated and its present occupant expelled.

A key was finally turned in the lock and the door was opened hesitantly. A middle-aged man with dead eyes and a nervous twitch stood before the visitors. He appeared somewhat dazed at the attention.

'Henry Collins?' The sergeant was a stickler for formalities. 'We are charged to search this dwelling.'

'You are?'

'Prevent us in our labours and we shall seize and bind you.'

The man blinked. 'What brings you here?'

'You have a wife heavy with child.' The sergeant thrust his chin forward. 'She is reported absent.'

'She rests, and that is all.'

'We will be the judge of that.'

'Does a baby in the womb not tire a woman? Is she not permitted to shut herself away?'

'Stand aside.'

Protest would be futile. Obedient and meek, Collins stepped back and allowed the team to enter. A shout. 'She is not here.'

'Find her.' The sergeant kept watch on the occupant. 'Leave nothing unearthed.'

There was sound from every quarter, the noise and clatter of plaster being ripped and boards being torn away. Dismantling the most humble home required a certain effort. Then came retching and blasphemies.

'Christ in heaven!'

'We are damned! Lost to Satan!'

A soldier stumbled from a room, his face contorted and bile staining his front. In his hand was a human foot still attached to its ankle and defleshed shin bone.

The sergeant stared. 'Where?'

'In a cauldron.' The man's trembling fingers dropped the article. 'Set beside the stove.'

Further discoveries and yelled oaths filtered to the chamber. There was no need for explanation. The suspect had murdered and jointed his wife, salting her remains.

The sergeant advanced on his prisoner and knocked him to the ground. Others might favour due process, but for a snatched few minutes he would vent his opinion.

'You monster.' He punched. 'You demon and angel of death.'

'We do as we must.' The man cowered.

'In that we may agree.'

They dragged the bleeding man from the premises and took him to the church. Already the bell tolled, summoning the president and council. Back in the abandoned dwelling, a soldier snatched at a roving mouse and crammed it in his mouth. None would deny him such a savoury. Filling his pockets were cuts of flesh discovered in his search. He was no fool. Every man for himself, and every morsel an opportunity.

'Bring forward the prisoner.'

Percy did little to hide his disgust. Daily the horrors in the settlement grew and the squalor and baseness of human existence laid bare. But this! He peered at the man. That anyone could butcher and eat their own wife and destroy their unborn child was beyond comprehension and the worst of sin. No plea would mitigate the crime.

'In my darkest hour, I did not imagine such a diabolic happening.' He frowned. 'In my blackest nightmare, I did not think I would preside over what occurs this day.'

The captive was in no rush to offer apology. He stood before his audience, remote from their opprobrium, occasionally muttering to himself but otherwise silent.

'Do you confess to your heinous crime? To barbarism beyond compare?'

The prisoner fidgeted. 'A man must eat.'

'Consume his wife?'

'I will be judged by God alone.'

'Here you are judged by your fellows.' Percy struggled to control his ire. 'Here you stand as a man before other men.'

'If it contents Your Honour.'

'You have no remorse?'

'What is done is done.'

A councillor erupted in rage. 'How dare you speak such things in the house of God!'

'He fled us long ago.'

Shock and melancholy greeted the exchanges. The settlers wanted vengeance, for they recognised the darkness in themselves. None was beyond reproach. They would atone by punishing another.

The president stroked his immaculate moustache. 'Is there not one part of you that cries out in self-loathing?'

'Why so?' Collins was perplexed.

'Confess your guilt or receive full retribution.'

The threat gained nothing in reply. Percy sighed. His tenure had been one of woe, a haphazard descent into despair. However distasteful, an example must be made. Prove too lenient and the settlers would soon devour each other.

'You will confess by volition or through pain.' Percy rose. 'Take the prisoner to the tree.'

He had hung by his thumbs for an hour, the weights on his feet pulling him down and his hands and wrists dislocating. The man had proved stubborn. Yet eventually he was convinced, broken until he wept and screamed in a piteous display. The questioning continued, the lawyer Archer acting as inquisitor.

'Did you kill your wife?'

'I did.'

'By what means?'

'An axe.' Words seeped out through the man's pain. 'I struck her with an axe.'

'What happened to your unborn child?'

'I tore it from her womb.'

'Tore it from her womb?' Archer glanced to his audience. 'You felt no remorse or disgust? No horror at such depravity?'

The man's body strained and his face contorted. 'I did not think.'

'Thus you hang before us.'

'I confess to you all, before the Almighty God. Please speed me to my grave.'

'We shall play awhile.' The lawyer would not be rushed. 'What happened to the baby ripped from within your wife?'

'I flung it in the river.'

Archer allowed a dramatic pause. 'You did not see fit to eat it?'

'I could not.'

'A discerning palate for one who eats his spouse.'

'Pass sentence and let me from this world.'

Appalled by the truth confronting them, the settlers stared mute, ready for the verdict. Before them was the very disintegration of their dream. Virginia had plunged into darkness.

Percy muttered to Hardy. 'We come here to civilise and find it is we instead who are the savage.'

'Clothing does not change the soul of men.'

'Nor it seems does our Christian breeding.'

'This place tests any faith.' The intelligencer observed the ongoing torture. 'Timber and sassafras are scant reward for all that we must face.'

'Yet face it we shall.' In spite of his fragility and poor health, the president was determined.

'I do not envy you your office.'

'We each accept the fate that is bestowed upon us.'

Percy would now bring proceedings to an end. A confession had been made and the conclusion was foregone. Fastidiousness would not aid the cause of justice. The president stepped forward, his voice betraying his disdain.

'We have what we need, and there is no doubt of the crime's gravity and the perpetrator's guilt. By the powers and law vested in me, I sentence this man to death. Henry Collins will be burned at the stake for his misdeeds. Let it serve as a warning.'

The proclamation was complete, and a brutish act would be met with a brutish reply. The settlers might starve and be shorn of hope, yet there were rules and standards to which the English clung.

Beyond the palisade, the winter snows still settled. Within the fort, a funeral blaze was planned.

CHAPTER 18

The execution day dawned and, to the mournful beat of a drum, the prisoner was brought from the guardhouse. It was a short parade, shorn of the customary ceremony and pageant. Spectators had gathered. They watched as the man shuffled by, his hands bound and body trembling, his long cotton shift already stained with the product of his fear. Silence pervaded.

The cortège reached the pyre, the wood faggots piled high and the scent of pine pitch strong. That Jamestown had offered up such a precious supply of its winter fuel was a declaration of intent. None could ignore a burning at the stake.

'Make ready the prisoner.'

There was some resistance, the reflexive urge to flee. The man was quickly pacified and lifted into position.

'Have you any last words?'

It appeared the man did not. He sagged. Courage was for those who had never faced such an end. Perhaps he had already retreated deep within himself; perhaps he scarcely recognised the unfolding scene. About him, a hushed reverence settled.

The chaplain stepped forward to bring religiosity to the event. Formality was needed.

'Do you make your peace and go to your death a Christian?' He paused and took the man's silence as affirmative. 'Are you ready to accept cleansing by fire and to be punished for your wickedness?'

There was little choice. Collins clenched his eyes shut tight, murmuring profanities or prayer. Neither would change the outcome. Soon the flames would be scorching his feet and the smoke invading his lungs. There was no concession to mercy; no small casks of gunpowder strung beneath his armpits to speed him to oblivion. Every blistered and agonised second would move at its natural pace.

The chaplain raised his hand. 'From dust you are born and to ashes you are consigned. May God have mercy on your eternal soul, and may you repent at the hour of judgement.'

There was a strange lowing noise, the subdued bellow of a beast await-ing slaughter. Some in the gathering whispered it must be demons fleeing the murderer's body.

He finally opened his eyes to speak. 'What I have done is beyond all sin, and I shall first burn here and then forever in hell. I ask the forgive-ness of the Almighty, of my fellows in Jamestown, of my late wife and unborn child. Release me now from this world.'

His oration was complete and he lapsed once more into his own thoughts. There was no further reason for delay. A soldier advanced upon the brushwood, a slow match in his hand. Blowing on the tip, the under-ling navigated his way to set the fire. Sparks blossomed and caught, and the conflagration could begin.

Hardy would not stay. A prisoner of the Inquisition and victim of an auto-da-fé, his mother had died at the stake in a public square in Lisbon. She had been a good, strong woman, full of joy, humanity and Christian duty, a beautiful thing soon reduced to screaming torment and then to charred remains. Realm had once described the scene to him. Immola-tion was for others to enjoy.

He reached the gate to the waterfront and took his leave of the fort. Behind him, the tension of the crowd had grown as the flames rose fast. He pushed the sounds from his thoughts.

'You do not watch the theatre?'

A carpenter planed the keel of a fishing boat, pausing to view his handiwork. He nodded to the intelligencer.

Hardy seated himself on the rotten carcass of a longboat. 'You too avoid the festival.'

'One horror is not banished by another.' The carpenter resumed his toil. 'Besides, I can think of better ways to use our precious timber.'

'So speaks an artisan.'

'I say it as it is. Without this boat, I would go mad.'

'At least she will not eat or burn you.'

They shared the joke, briefly removed from the cares and brutality within the bounds of the palisade. Hardy was glad Awae was gone and Edward Battle removed downriver. This fort was no place for them.

The carpenter eyed him. 'Do you regret your voyage here?'

'It is too late for sentiment.'

'Each waking minute I think of food. Each sleeping moment, I dream of it.'

'You are no different from the rest.'

'I build this craft, and already I see an oyster or fat sturgeon in my grasp.' He shook his head. 'I should give thanks I am not the president, with all his cares.'

Such cares would not diminish. The intelligencer gazed to the *Discovery* moored silent and empty offshore. In kinder circumstances he and a crew could have mounted raids or sailed across Chesapeake Bay to seek alliance with the fearsome Massawomeck. The enemies of Powhatan were always potential friends.

'I know what you think.' The carpenter nodded to the vessel. 'No one would let you go, through fear you would escape for England.'

'Suspicion grows faster than any weed in these parts.'

'As it strangles amity and trust.'

'Not every inch of our nature is lost.'

Reaching into a pouch at his belt, Hardy withdrew a package of cooked meat and threw it to the man. The sustenance was devoured without question.

'Why your generosity?' The carpenter had finished his meal.

'To prove that we yet live.'

Bidding a wordless farewell, Hardy left the carpenter to his toil. For most of the ravenous, the taste of real food was merely a memory. He stared downriver, watching the chill mist lie sullen on the James. Soon the rain would come and another season with it. Only a fool would predict if by then a single individual survived within the fort. Above the ramparts, a plume of smoke rose thick and grey and spread acrid in the air. The punishment was complete.

Nights passed slowly in the blockhouse, marked by constant vigil and the occasional Indian attack. The local tribe would not permit the wearers of leg coverings to go to their deaths in peace. Armed foray still mattered, and musket rounds and arrow shot yet peppered the exterior.

Buckler growled, aware of the presence outside. His master calmed him and called up to the sentry.

'We have company?'

Reply came. 'Our own, out on a forage.'

He would not ask more. By darkness, the starving of Jamestown emerged like truffle hounds in search of human pickings. There were always freshly killed natives to unearth and carry back as staples for a meat broth. Hardy would not condemn the ravenous or judge any in such plight. Insanity created the insane.

He sat on a mattress and stropped his Katzbalger blade on a whetstone. This was home enough. About him were the tools of his trade, reflection of a talent well-honed: his crossbow, musket, pistol and brigantine. Everything was readied for action. He held up the stabbing sword and turned it in the light. Butchery required a sharp edge.

There were voices, the arrival of unexpected guests. The president was making his rounds. As he entered, Hardy observed Percy's pallid features and elegant form rendered more gaunt by circumstance. An unenviable task had not lessened the man's dutiful commitment.

A smile ghosted weary on his lips. 'I wish you a pleasant evening, Mr Hardy.'

'Little so far interrupts it.' Hardy gestured to a bench. 'You are welcome to our quarters.'

'I shall not stay long, or hinder your endeavours.'

'We are honoured by such a visit.'

'It is we who should be honoured.' Percy seated himself and scanned the interior. 'Day and night you guard our position and fend off all attack.'

'A more rewarding labour than dwelling within the fort.'

Fatigue was etched into the president's face. 'Who in England may imagine how we suffer? Who could guess what we sacrifice here?'

Perhaps he thought of the recent burning, or simply of the impossibility of his task. Managing extinction was the imperative of his role. The president was allowed a hint of melancholy.

'Will we endure, Mr Hardy?'

'I shall do my utmost.'

'I fear we ask too much of you.'

'Fear not.' The intelligencer wiped the oiled blade. 'I find comfort in the harshest climes.'

'Then you are most singular.' Percy's appreciation showed.

For a while, the president watched the intelligencer in his combat preparation. There was an order and discipline in the blockhouse that was lacking elsewhere in the settlement. The president stirred from his ruminations.

'I should continue with my rounds and then return to my brood in the fort.'

'They will not survive without you.'

'I strive, and can do no more.' His fingers played with a satin cuff. 'Whatever is said, I have tried to lead by example.'

'One that shall be remembered.'

Percy rose and offered a gracious bow. 'I am glad to have had your ear, Mr Hardy.'

Accompanied by his lieutenants, the president departed into the night. There remained gun positions to inspect and sentries to interrogate. Maintaining a routine kept forlorn chance alive. Despite the ice and cold, the leader of Jamestown persevered.

Left with his companion, Hardy reapplied himself to his own evening routine. It would be too easy to lower his guard or retreat to the despair of others. In the corner, Buckler whined and scratched at a supporting timber. He alone was immune to darker reflections on the precariousness of life.

'She is gone!' The cry went up. 'The *Discovery* is set adrift!'

It was another blow to a settlement decaying to oblivion. Sick and emaciated forms stumbled out to see, some weeping and others cursing at the latest revelation. There, several miles downstream and resting on a sandbank, the vessel lay stranded and unmanned. A lookout had sighted her masts pricking the horizon.

'Even our ship deserts us.'

'Do you blame her?'

'How could it happen?' Another desperate voice. 'Now our isolation is complete.'

'There is no escape from here.'

The event appeared to signal finality and the abandonment of hope. Few had the strength or the willingness to venture out and fetch her back. Starvation made for timid souls.

Percy leant from a gun platform. 'We must return her to her mooring.'

'Why so?' The response of the soldier beside him was sullen and unyielding. 'We cannot waste resources.'

'Ignore her, and all is lost.'

The laugh was harsh. 'Most believe it is already.'

'Some are inclined to disagree.' Percy drew his sword. 'Your president among them.'

From his vantage point, Percy watched as doubt and mutinous comments circulated below. A rabble was not easy to control. Yet he was fortunate to have allies at hand.

It was Hardy who served as marshal now, and he would brook no disobedience. With quiet ferocity in his eyes and a keen blade in his hand, he stepped in to quell the dissent.

'I am first to volunteer.' He gazed on the assembled. 'I shall choose who joins me.'

'And should we refuse?' a man said.

'I will put you to the sword.'

The crowd absorbed his words; understood it was no idle threat. Their hesitation vanished. He moved among them now, selecting with a nod or gesture, unhurried in his process.

One man blinked. 'I am not for this.'

'Each accepts his share,' Hardy said.

'What would I know of sails and seamanship? I am of more use here.'

'Fate and I have decided otherwise.' The intelligencer placed his hand on the man's bony shoulder.

The crew was now complete. To the sound of a whistle they collected supplies and headed for a pair of longboats. Any sortie might be hazardous; an encounter with a redskin could prove to be their last. The unwilling recruits had a right to be nervous.

Their commander was sanguine. 'You are ready?'

'We are.'

'Then we proceed. Row well and follow my lead.'

'If savages lurk?' one of them asked.

'Bring down as many as you may.'

The instruction was of a basic kind by necessity. They either succeeded or failed, lived or died, and needed little briefing. Hardy saw the resignation in the men's faces. He could not rekindle dead spirits.

'Let none fail me or the settlement.'

They launched, ragged in their strokes and halting in their progress. It helped that they were borne onward by the current. Weakened men, huddled low against the elements, were scarcely a formidable boarding party, but Hardy would deploy what he had. In the prow, his dog crouched and stared forward. Experience had trained him well.

The *Discovery* was lightly aground, a trading vessel abandoned and finally cornered. It should not take long to recover her. With hand signals alone, Hardy ordered the approach. Oars dipped and men peered, apprehensive. A ship with battened hatches and no apparent movement was ever a forbidding target. Caution was advisable.

'Seek.'

To a whispered order and passed upward from one crewman to the shoulders of the next, Buckler scrambled into the open heads and vanished through the prow. He was an expert scout. At the waterline, the humans chose a different route. Grapnels flew, their steel hooks catching and holding, the knotted lines tautening behind as the men swarmed aloft.

Then, chaos. The ambush had been well prepared, the natives prone and waiting. They emerged, war clubs brandished and bows drawn, intent on giving battle.

'Greet them, men!' Hardy levelled his crossbow and delivered its quarrel at close range. 'Give no quarter!'

They needed scant encouragement, for their lives depended on victory. Even the malnourished could tear open an enemy heart. So they yelled and closed and hacked their way through, discharging their muskets and pistols. In the background, wild and ferocious, Buckler flushed out more for the kill.

'Man the wheel! Put your shoulder to the capstan! We walk her from this bank!' Hardy sauntered through the melee, a commander ever at ease amid confusion and pressing home the fight. There had been too many armed encounters now to warrant terror or panic. Only novices were fearful. He headed for the ladder and with Buckler went below.

The pistol shot cracked, its report loud and muzzle flashing bright in the darkened confines of the lower deck. Reloading would take time. In a few strides Hardy was upon the native, eviscerating him with a practised twist of the Katzbalger. Buckler would enjoy the entrails. Hardy continued, methodical and deadly, leaping empty gun cradles and searching behind bulwarks. A noise, a response, a kill. Above, the sound of battle diminished. The clearance was complete.

Emerging once more, Hardy surveyed the bloody scene.

'Put a line to the boats. Our toil yet begins.'

There was truth in his words. Corpses were plundered and ditched, and the sails on their yards unfurled and dropped. Urgency was everything. The Indians would have reserves, would be mustering to make good their loss. Fury could add fervour to a pursuit.

Another command. 'Row with all your might!'

Returned to his longboat now and manning an oar, Hardy strained at the forefront to pull the *Discovery* from her fastness. Other exhortations came.

'Bend to it! We shall succeed!'

'Savages are no match for us!'

Belief had replaced despair. Slowly the ship turned, swinging in a faltering manner and protesting as she edged to point upriver. Men swore and redoubled their efforts. At last she was free.

'Now make haste,' Hardy called out to the companion boat. 'We steal back what is ours.'

In an ungainly parade the men drifted for Jamestown, the ship towing her escorts. The endeavour had been worth it.

A crewman shouted. 'Canoes to stern! The savages give chase!'

His warning was muffled by the duel of muskets and the whine of passing lead shot. The redskins would not cede their prize happily. From the banks of the river and the pursuits behind, puffs of smoke blossomed from guns. Aboard the longboats, the haze was thick as men hurried to ward off the attack.

'They gain on us!'

'Please God that the wind blows stronger!'

'Cease your words and fight!'

They had no choice, for the distance closed. Slowed by her lack of canvas and the drag of the craft she towed, the *Discovery* lumbered homeward. The hunting pack was tenacious. Hardy loosed his musket and seized another, blinking away the residue. He noticed the heavy blood spill on his shoes and the dead weight of a corpse resting at his side. The recruit earlier so reluctant to join the mission had taken a clean round through his forehead and the back of his skull was gone.

The intelligencer glanced to the larger vessel and the frantic actions of her crew. They could at least repel an attempt to board, and would reach the settlement unscathed. Those journeying closer to the water were nearer to the threat. Hardy aimed and fired again. He thought of Realm and the agents of Cecil who most likely still resided at Jamestown. It was clear that someone had set out in darkness and deliberately cut the mooring of the ship.

'Cast off the line!' he yelled above the din. 'We engage, and shall do so unshackled.'

A bold move, thought Realm. Most would choose safety in numbers and the comfort of pressing close to the host. Not Hardy. He was a singular man and a worthy rival, dauntless in adversity. He would not have wished to burden the ship or compromise her escape. Jamestown was blessed for his presence. Yet he was but flesh, and his longevity was finite.

'Do not slacken,' the renegade pressed.

The natives obeyed, the arrowhead of canoes spreading into a wider formation. They were overhauling the labouring English. The renegade imagined the final stages of the battle, the encirclement, the slaughter. It would teach the settlers the futility of their daring.

In an adjacent canoe a warrior stood and trained his musket, his legs braced and balance perfect. A melding of the old world and the new. The savages had absorbed his teaching and would help bring him results. Realm sensed his eternal game with Christian Hardy would soon reach the end of its cycle.

There would be setbacks before that moment. His quiet reflection was interrupted as the warrior catapulted backward, his chest erupting. His canoe rocked and steadied and then the advance resumed. Progress had its price. From his vantage point he peered ahead, hearing the grunt of the natives and the dip of their paddles. There were few more pleasant ways to be conveyed to battle. Briefly, the fog of skirmish lifted. He spied Hardy and felt the sharp jab of anticipation go deep.

'They slow! We shall take them.'

He allowed himself a rare semblance of emotion. The situation demanded it. The pace quickened and the Indians fitted arrows to their bows. At close quarters, ancient methods prevailed. Their strength bleeding and their oarsmanship now awry, the English quarry limped to follow the mother ship.

Then came the whir of a cannonball and a distant blast, followed by an erupting column of water. They had come within range of Jamestown. A second shot. The projectile scudded on the river's surface and ricocheted wide, screaming as it went. Chaotic retreat ensued. Canoes capsized and natives floundered as the attack flotilla dispersed and the predators became prey. A third shot landed, shattering wood and carrying off bodies. On the settlement ramparts, the gunners busied themselves, labouring to ram home more ordnance.

Realm sat proud and aloof from the fray. He was accustomed to incurring the wrath of others, would not cower in the face of threat. A pity indeed that Hardy had outpaced them and turned a trap to his advantage. It was the nature of the beast. Yet fortunes could change, of that he was certain. He heard the celebratory volleys of the longboats and swore the delight of their crews would be a temporary affair.

Realm's instincts were proved right. Still no relief came to Jamestown, and its slide to eventual collapse was inexorable and cruel. At the centre of the fort, three men stood bound in the pillory, nailed by their ears. They had been found guilty of pilfering in a world where there was little remaining to steal. Few took any notice. The settlers had their own concerns, their own kith and kin to bury. Spring, and the first nourishing blades of grass were uppermost in many minds.

'Good day, Mr Hardy.' With a grave and considered nod, Percy greeted the intelligencer. Afflicted by sickness as he was and now racked by a consumptive cough, the president yet retained his decorum and manners. Here in the church, where the council met, they were representatives of England and standards would prevail. Percy turned to the mortician. 'How many more dead are we?'

'Seven since last sundown.'

'Too many.' Percy bowed his head. 'Would that we could save each one.'

Another councillor interjected. 'Three soldiers have vanished to the enemy.'

'They will find the savages most unwelcoming.'

All were in accord. With suicide a mortal sin, some instead volunteered to wander out and meet an arrow. The options were not kind in Jamestown.

Percy cleared his throat. 'Amid our suffering, it must be said that we have our triumphs. The Paspahegh keep from our gates and we snatch back our ship from beneath their noses.'

'To what avail?' Vehemence and bitterness sounded from one councillor.

'Our pride, our spirit, our story.'

'Our story?' The man's shallow laughter reflected his incredulity. 'It is but a tale of misery and woe and abandonment by God.'

'We sit here in His church.'

'A monument to false dreams and fading hope; to the folly of our venture.'

'I would be nowhere else.'

'Then you are mad or blind, thus suited to be our president.'

The insult went ignored. Life and death could fray tempers and corrode all common purpose. Percy was bred to ease doubt and smooth anxiety.

He looked to Hardy. 'Does quiet prevail at the blockhouse?'

'The natives learnt their lesson.'

'Well they may, for we yet best them in a fight. I doubt the savages will again venture so close.'

'They have no need, for it is the end here.'

The president sighed. 'Despair is a malady we each must cure.'

There were no further matters to discuss, and even last rites were more useful than debate. Yet Percy insisted on procedure and the illusion of normality. Once the councillors had departed, he and Hardy walked the bounds.

'Where is your dog hiding, Mr Hardy?'

'I keep him from the fort to prevent him from being eaten.'

'A wise decision.' Percy moved at a slow gait. 'Perhaps in time we shall all be devoured.'

'Some may cheer my ending in a bowl of potage.'

'Not I, Mr Hardy. You are too precious to our fortunes.'

'My orders are to serve.'

'I am glad we yet have matters to address.' The president halted. 'The ground will warm and the seasons change, and I wish you to travel to our new emplacement at Fort Algernon.'

'For what purpose?'

'To build our defences at the mouth of the James and to ensure life clings on there. To parley with the natives and bring food from their village of Kecoughtan.'

The intelligencer could not refuse. He thought of Awae and the boy Edward who had preceded him there, of the chance to put some distance between himself and the ordeal of Jamestown. Replacing one palisade with another would scarcely be such a curse.

Nearby, a brawl had erupted between the settlers. Shouts rippled out and the alarm was raised. Percy and Hardy strode to intervene. Food was likely the culprit.

'Come quick!' a man cried. 'There will be a death! They fight as animals for scraps!'

Tension had shattered into violence, and the waterfront was now full of fury. A skiff had landed with a paltry catch of oysters and a riot had ensued. Men, women and children fought and scratched and tore at each other. Most were beyond reason or caring. One man seized the back of a head and rammed it against a log; another, with frenzied blows, plunged a knife into a rival. There would be more dire statistics to raise at the next council meeting.

'Make ready to land.'

March had drifted in, and at last the spring intruded upon the winter. Hardy did not miss Jamestown. He stepped ashore below the timber fortifications, hailing the soldiers who approached. They were probably more scared by an influx of their own starved countrymen than by the possibility of Spanish attack. Point Comfort seemed far from the travails of the settlement. Dominating the approaches to the James and looking out across Chesapeake Bay, Fort Algernon was an outpost that continued to survive.

'Lieutenant Davies?' Hardy extended his hand. 'I am glad to see you well.'

'We are better than our brothers in Jamestown. You come to live among us?'

'Perhaps even to die.' Hardy slung his pack onto his shoulders. 'Yet I prefer to endure awhile.'

They headed for the gate, the expert eye of the intelligencer gauging the mood and mettle of the garrison. He had spied so often on the Spanish, wandering unchallenged through enemy positions, the habit was difficult to shed. Buckler paced at his side.

He noted the gunners standing ready. 'I commend you on your discipline.'

'We function as a ship, and one prepared for war.'

'You have provisions?'

'Sufficient to sustain us.' There was pride in the lieutenant's voice. 'A few pigs and chickens, and whatever fish and wildfowl we catch.'

'Contact with the natives?'

'They still trade on occasion.'

A tight and well-kept vessel. Hardy admired the young officer. There was something in the man's eye, a haunted quality brought by the burden of responsibility and paucity of good news. Yet he was a dutiful man who inspired respect and loyalty. Hardy suspected the politicking of others did not concern him.

'Christian!' Edward Battle had spied them. 'Buckler!'

Reunion arrived with outstretched arms and tight embraces and a dog whirling in delight. The old friends were together once more.

'You grow stronger, Edward.' Hardy clapped him on the shoulder. 'Starvation did not suit you.'

'Nor a diet of rats and worms.'

'A man may grow accustomed. His dog also.'

'I thank God for the miracle that you are here.' A sob was stifled in the boy's throat.

Hardy smiled, and then turned to view his new surroundings. There were but fifty men in total, a group blessed by kinder circumstances than their brethren upstream. Should salvation ever come, maybe they would prove to be the last ones standing.

The youth wiped his nose on his sleeve. 'What news of Jamestown?'

'It worsens by the day. Yet we will carve our own existence and prosper as we may.'

'We shall.'

Escorted by his young apprentice, Hardy made his rounds. It took stern words to summon Buckler from stalking the nearby poultry. Neither intelligencer nor canine were accustomed to such plenitude. They reached the observation tower and scanned the panorama, the crew working on the deck of the moored *Virginia*, the distant glimmer of headlands about the bay. Purposefulness and not catastrophe existed in one corner of the colony.

Hardy stared out to sea. 'Where now is Awae?'

'She returns to her village and her people, yet brings us food and goods on occasion.'

'Relations with her tribe are good?'

'She has calmed and persuaded them.'

Should conditions permit, he would venture to Kecoughtan and offer his thanks in person. Awae's absence created a hollowness he would first fill with toil. There was yet Jamestown to consider, and the dangers lurking there. He could not idly watch its extinction from afar.

'Mr Hardy?' It was the lieutenant who called for his attention.

Hardy turned to catch a twig broom thrown in his direction. He laughed. 'I am more skilled with the sword.'

'Then you will master with ease several other arts.'

He was glad for such employment, to merge with the rest of the settlers and put housekeeping before his other trades of espionage and killing. All men required diversion. In this fort perched above the water, soldiers and settlers waited. Tomorrow could bring anything.

CHAPTER 19

It was April 1610, and still Hardy and the denizens of Fort Algernon lived. He accepted the fact as he would his demise, with cool objectivity and a rational mind. Reality informed him that his odds of continued survival were poor. Yet he would do what he could for his fellows and give thanks the winter was over. Jamestown would not have fared so well.

'I am no threat,' he said now. His pace was slow and deliberate and his words in the Algonquian tongue.

From among the groves of sassafras, native eyes watched. Within seconds, the Kecoughtan warriors could send a dozen arrows direct into his body. Unless they spared him for prolonged and less charitable treatment. He would not provoke or grant them an excuse.

He spoke again. 'I come in peace.'

They did not respond. Perhaps they liked to test the nerve of a pale-skin or reassure themselves it was no trick. He could not run now.

Several braves fell in beside him, an escort with painted faces and feathers in their knotted hair. Their bows and clubs stayed ready in their hands. He walked onward, a commanding and untroubled figure brought in by a silent troop.

The headman surveyed him. 'You have set foot before on our territory.'

'I was hunted by the Paspahegh.'

'We were glad to give you shelter.' The Weroance maintained his shrewd and knowing stare. 'Yet conditions change.'

'Friendship may endure.'

'Powhatan decrees that all treaty is dead and the place you call Jamestown is doomed.'

'He does not control your hand.'

'Still he is our master.'

There was a glimmer in the chief's eye, the glint of calculation. Politics was not the preserve of the settlers. The native could benefit from sound relations with the fort and trade with passing ships; could pique the neighbouring Paspahegh through his different approach to the pale-skins. Tsenacomoco was a land containing many tribes and a thousand different agendas.

'We owe to you our thanks,' the Weroance said now. He opened his palms wide. 'Was it not you who rescued Awae?'

'She is precious to me.'

'Also to us.'

'Then I am glad to have returned her safe to you.'

'Though you are a pale-skin, a wearer of leg coverings and a stranger from beyond, we are in your debt.'

'I ask for nothing but harmony between us.'

'A power within my gift.' The headman remained grave. 'Awae will see you.'

'She has not departed to join Powhatan?'

'We forget to tell him she is here.'

Hardy found Awae in the low-built dwelling of saplings and fronded thatch, the home of a princess once more among her own. Her warm eyes regarded him.

'You do not come with fire and fury?' Her tone was gently teasing. 'With sword drawn and warriors at your side?'

'The occasion has no need.'

'These are yet threatening days, a time of fear and dread.'

'Better then that we are not parted.'

He met no disagreement. He crossed to her as he had before, a man impatient and hypnotised breaching the divide. This was the life he chose. Her taste, her feel, her breath, her warmth. Feast so often followed famine.

They watched the shallop manoeuvre to its berth and the president step painfully ashore. George Percy had become a spectral figure, aided by lieutenants and hobbling on a stick, his body wasted and his face ravaged by the sickness afflicting all. In this one man alone the desperate plight of Jamestown could be seen.

Without warning or ceremony he had arrived, a visitor to Fort Algernon. There could be no comparison to the scenes he had left behind, and no telling the reason for his journey. He was unlikely to serve as a bearer of good tidings.

At the centre of the fort he paused, greeting its commander with a courteous nod and acknowledging Hardy beside him.

'I cannot fault your endeavour, Lieutenant.' Percy glanced about him. 'Would that we all dwelt in such order and contentment.'

'Fate has been merciful.'

'Alas, in Jamestown it proves most unkind.'

'I pray that there is remedy, sir.'

'Our prayers too often go unanswered.'

Drawn by the sound of hogs, Percy let his attention wander to their pen. To the starving, the porcine grunts were akin to the sweet harmony of angels. It took some time for the president to gather his thoughts.

'Your countenance betrays you, Lieutenant,' he said.

'It does, sir?'

'You view my coming with trepidation; perceive me as some kind of executioner.'

'We seldom host parties from upriver.'

'A rare event indeed.' Percy turned to the intelligencer. 'You would not miss Jamestown, Mr Hardy.'

'I have no doubt it is ably defended.'

'Less so since you left us.' A wistful look crossed the president's face. 'But we strive as we always must.'

'There are more deaths?'

'Disease and famine take many. Yet you have my solemn vow that I shall not submit to failure.'

The intelligencer could believe it. In spite of all the challenge and tribulation, Percy stayed calm and immaculate. He would not permit disaster to throw him from his task. Death alone would sever him from his duties.

Percy brushed imagined dust from his cuff. 'What are we to do, Mr Hardy?'

'Wait and hope and watch.'

'Wise counsel from a man well versed in all manner of strange horror and practice.'

Hardy smiled. 'I have found such experience useful.'

'Useful enough to save us?'

'I can make no promises.'

Percy had seen all he needed. Fort Algernon survived and stood aloof from its ailing parent. It was sufficient.

He addressed the lieutenant. 'Am I not president of Jamestown?'

'You are, sir.'

'With the authority of the royal council and Virginia Company vested in me?'

'It is undisputed.'

'Was I not elected and charged to promote our great venture? To guard it to its conclusion?'

'We are in accord.'

Percy had decided. 'It is no accident this fort adopts the title Algernon, name of my beloved nephew.'

'An honour reflecting its importance.'

'Now it must show how important it is.'

Silence greeted his words. The garrison was wary, nervous of any intervention that might alter its existence and bring misfortune on its head. Glumly, the inhabitants listened.

'I will neither lie nor demand of you what I do not ask of others.' Percy swept the gathering with an understanding stare. 'We each of us suffer, and all of us make sacrifices. Yet Jamestown is on its knees and will soon be in the grave.'

'We cannot help,' a voice shouted from the back.

'Fail, and we shall all perish. Stand aloof and your idyll here will eventually succumb too.'

'At least we have a chance,' the voice said.

'You also have an obligation.' The president focused on the most vocal dissenter. 'Are you to bring succour to your brothers and sisters, or walk by as Pharisees?'

The lieutenant spoke. 'What would you have us do?'

'Give shelter to one hundred or more of our starving and needy and sick.'

'You place on us a sentence of death.'

'We already stand at the scaffold.'

His pronouncement made, George Percy bade farewell, and with his entourage in attendance, issued from the fort. Alarm and consternation travelled in their wake, but the orders had been given and they could not ignore them. On the James, the shallop caught the tidal surge and disappeared again upriver.

'By God, a sail!' Both fear and excitement were echoed in the shout. 'To your stations, every man!'

Tumult erupted, men snatching weapons and racing for the walkways atop the palisade. Invasion or salvation, no one could hazard to guess. A gunner loosed a warning shot, the round splashing short in challenge and greeting. It was 21 May 1610, and visitors to Fort Algernon were unexpected.

'They put out a boat!'

The debate was ceaseless as the longboat made its approach. There seemed no aggressive intent. Men watched and waited. It had been weeks since their president had delivered his edict, and nothing had occurred. Now this: two ships were anchored in Chesapeake Bay.

Hardy walked with the lieutenant to meet the longboat, his musket primed and held loose in his hands. The craft had paused offshore, maintaining its distance, its occupants keeping low and studying the threat.

'They are English.' The intelligencer shouldered his gun. 'Tell your men to put down their arms and give welcome to their fellows.'

'How may you be sure?'

'The manner of their approach and lack of any cannon.'

'Pray Jesus you are right.'

Raising his hand in a friendly gesture, the lieutenant hailed the strangers. Each side remained as cautious as the other. Measures to build confidence were required.

'Declare yourselves and your intent,' he called.

'Englishmen,' the response eddied back. 'And you?'

'You will find that we too are English.'

Delight carried. 'We feared you were the Spaniard.'

'They are not welcome here.' The lieutenant pointed to the ships. 'What vessels do you bring?'

'All that is left of the *Sea Venture*.'

'She is lost?'

'Wrecked on the island of Bermuda, where we have spent these ten months since. We built anew and now complete our journey.'

The news was met with astonishment and glee. For seven hundred miles through treacherous, vortex-swirled seas the pairing of little ships had journeyed. It was a sign, proof that the impossible could be conquered.

'We shall fetch the Lieutenant-Governor and the Admiral of the Fleet,' the man said.

They were duly brought, the august personages of Sir Thomas Gates and Sir George Somers finally reaching the Americas, somewhat ragged in their sun-bleached clothes.

Gates stood awhile in silence, a military veteran appraising the situation. He had recognised the intelligencer.

'I should have known you would thrive where others faltered, Mr Hardy,' he said.

'Fortune has smiled upon me.'

Gates gave a laugh. 'You are most content when the world falls apart.'

Hardy nodded. 'Idleness ill serves me, sir.'

Motioning Hardy to his side now, the lieutenant-governor walked a distance from those gathered on the shore. There was trust between the two men, a respect born from careers spent fighting the enemies of England. Both men had once answered to Queen Elizabeth. Glory and common cause forged an enduring bond.

The soldier glanced to his companion. 'Tell me what I encounter.'

'These weeks past we have had no word from Jamestown.'

'Percy remains president?'

'Of what, I cannot say.' Hardy would not lie. 'Many die or desert, and more are soon to follow.'

'We shall travel there tomorrow and see it for ourselves.'

'I wager the scene is piteous.'

'Yet perhaps it may be saved.'

A reply was unnecessary. So much had been invested and so much lost, a retreat from Jamestown would be the cruellest of surrenders. The opponents of England would have won, and Virginia and the lands of North America left open for the taking. A dread and awful prospect.

Gates peered over his shoulder. 'Wherever man sets foot, it seems discord and destruction abound.'

'Bermuda was no happy sojourn?'

'At first we believed it paradise and an answer to our prayers, a shelter from the tempests that near drowned our ship and held us naked for days as slaves at the pump.'

'You survived.'

'For that I have no explanation.' There was a grim set to the man's jaw. 'When oakum spewed from the seams of the ship, we even caulked her with slabs of meat.'

'A novel means for any shipwright.'

'Then finally our island appeared. A place of plenty, of fish and turtle and wild hog. And a site of division and mutiny.'

'It was ever thus.'

Gates snorted. 'How true your words are. Somers and I had rival camps with rival views and rival parties of men.'

'Welcome to Virginia.' Gates might come to regret his posting even further.

On the beach they were offloading provisions and relaying them to the fort. A feast was in prospect. For a garrison sustained on the strictest of rations, pilchards in brine and stacked heaps of turtle were the stuff of dreams. Men stared in dumb amazement.

The lieutenant snatched them from their reverie. 'Earn your bread and your keep. There is yet work to do.'

They obeyed, moving to assist and to make new acquaintances. Whoever volunteered to sail for these parts was surely mad or misguided. Yet their food would be gratefully received.

Gates watched. 'I have seldom witnessed such rapture.'

'Enjoy it, Sir Thomas.' Hardy too observed the spectacle. 'Our harvest in Virginia is more often bodies and despair.'

Others had spied the arrival of the ships. Running fast, the scout headed from the James for a camp set within a glade several miles distant. It was a forward base, a temporary location from which matters might be coordinated and future attacks launched. The military commander

Opechancanough and the renegade Realm were in residence for the season. Events demanded they keep close to the strategic routes and strongholds of their enemy.

The native's breathless news was met without emotion. Opechancanough pondered the tidings. Around him, his warriors rehearsed their battle skills and practised bowmanship against the trees. Preparation was all.

He glanced to Realm. 'You promise me much, and still we are thwarted.'

'The result will be as I told it.'

'My priests see only blood.'

'It will be that of the settlers, Opechancanough.'

'Or perhaps it shall be yours.'

Relations had cooled between them. Certainly there had been disappointment; Hardy had seen to that. Yet still there was the prize, the slow death of Jamestown and all who inhabited it. This ornate savage could not comprehend the beauty of his plan, the simplicity of using others to clear the ground for the Spaniards who would later come. Soon the Spanish king would elevate him to the status of a hero.

Opechancanough fingered the beads about his throat. 'What thoughts have you?'

'Visions of the future and the triumph that awaits you.'

'Though more pale-skins arrive? Though two of their great ships sit at the river mouth?'

Realm shook his head. 'They are small vessels, insignificant and of no value. There is little they may do to raise Jamestown from the dust.'

'You speak as a man who was proved wrong before.'

'Time alone will reveal the truth.'

With a triumphant shout, a brave sent an arrow through a sliver of bark tossed high into the air. The warrior's skill and marksmanship were impressive. Opechancanough let his gaze linger, making his point, reinforcing his threat. His guest felt no discomfort. The loss of his African bodyguards might have stripped him of armed protection, but he was secure in his own certitude. Providence would tilt matters in his favour. Christian Hardy should enjoy the few remaining days of his existence. His source in Jamestown confirmed it.

The military chief rose now, an imposing figure attended by his retinue. As the enforcer for Powhatan, his power was unmatched. It was unsurprising that at his approach, recalcitrant tribes paid tribute and opposing warriors laid down their bows. Muskets ensured he would now conquer all, even his ageing emperor.

'We move.'

His command would not be questioned. Instantly the mood altered and fires were quickly doused. Every possession would be carried. Shelters were collapsed and pouches filled, quivers of arrows shouldered. There was the glint of steel too: the machetes and swords and other blades that had filtered into this kingdom. Realm could pride himself on the changes he had wrought. Further transformation was close.

He regarded the military chief. 'Where do we go?'

'To wherever the god Okeus sends us.' Opechancanough raised his hand to signal the start of the exodus. 'We shall study these strangers new to our lands.'

'Do the spirits of people inhabit this place?'

Leaning from the poop of his ship, his voice betraying emotion, Sir Thomas Gates surveyed the whole. Jamestown did not present a reassuring sight. Its palisades were collapsed and its waterfront lay wrecked, the debris of abandonment everywhere. Life seemed to have been sucked from the place. There was no sound, no challenge from a sentry, no cannon shot to greet them. Just the stench of decay. The crews of the two vessels stared.

'I named my ship *Deliverance*.' Gates scanned the rotten frontage. 'It seems now a cruel and monstrous jest. This is a blighted and dismal place, Mr Hardy.'

Hardy would not disagree. He stood beside his new commander, appraising the crumbling scene, curious at what confronted them. The familiar had become alien. Even the gates hung derelict and agape, and the small boats lay holed and scattered like carcasses. Everything had been cannibalised.

'I have looked upon better.'

'To think we voyaged from England for this.' The lieutenant-governor spoke almost to himself. 'To think I am commissioned to rule, and instead must make land to bury.'

'Perhaps we should proceed,' Hardy said.

They progressed ashore, an advance party supported by soldiers, a leadership silenced by the moment. Mausoleums deserved respect. Within the group was Admiral Newport, stalwart of the supply missions returning once again. His efforts and feats of seamanship appeared to have been in vain.

Gates halted. 'What soulless ruination.'

About them spread the fort's interior, the tumbledown shacks and emptied storerooms, the guardhouse devoid of sound. Lifelessness prevailed. Hardy tried to remember how it had been, summoning images from the past, superimposing event and incident on what now lay dead before him. There were the market and the muster ground; there the dwelling in which a Dutchman was hanged; there the homes where settlers lived and once trusted they had a future. A dread and sorrowful conclusion.

Newport wandered to his side. 'You did not expect it?'

'I have learnt to curb both hope and fear.'

'I also.' The vice-admiral grimaced. 'A pity our enterprise is wasted.'

'Should we read the future, none would ever strive.'

'Then we must delight in embracing futility.'

In solemn assembly, the visitors entered the church. At the centre of the camp it dominated all, a symbol of early optimism, representing the fragility of man. Care and workmanship had been lavished on it. From the carved font to the painted altar, Englishmen had prayed and laboured and believed. There could be no greater monument to the tragedy. Outside, Buckler lifted his leg on a headstone.

'It is time to wake the quick or the dead.'

Striding to the bell rope, Gates issued his summons with a forceful tug. Someone must notice. He listened to the sound, working harder, letting the bells peel on.

'They come, Sir Thomas,' a soldier called out. 'There is yet life in Jamestown.'

The party moved out of the church. It was life of a diminished kind. Some crawling and others on their feet, creeping uncertainly; shadow people who shuffled dull-eyed in their direction. Each side was disbelieving. The newcomers shied from the settlers' approach.

Skeletal hands reached out. 'Feed us, for we starve.'

'Have mercy.'

'We must eat. We must eat.'

Pity and grief enveloped the scene, the horror growing as more people emerged from their hovels, men and women who had been waiting to die abruptly roused from their stupor.

'My wife!' A crew member ran to cradle a young woman, toothless and ragged and weeping on the ground. 'It is my wife!'

As upright and correct as he could manage in his diminished state, George Percy threaded his way through the emaciated cluster to present himself to Gates. His presidency was ended. There was a bittersweet note to the occasion; a trembling emotion behind the reserve. A resignation had never come easier. With a shaky bow, Percy surrendered his commission.

'I bring you the letters patent and the seal, Sir Thomas.'

'You have guided this place through terrible times.'

'It was a task thrust upon me.' Percy glanced about him. 'It is now a burden passed on.'

'Your duty will be rewarded.'

'That some survive is reward enough.'

He sagged, a man depleted by his efforts. Others rushed to aid him. It was the moment for the restoration of order and the distribution of food. An officer stepped forward and unfurled a scroll.

'By the authority of Almighty God and King James, this colony and its territory are forthwith subject to the commands and laws of Sir Thomas Gates as Lieutenant-Governor, guided by his Council.'

Attended by a bosun and physician, Hardy moved now from house to house, distributing salt fish and counting the dead. How forlorn and foolhardy the Jamestown venture seemed now; how accusatory the gaunt faces. John Smith had once paraded here, had drilled and marched and mounted expeditions. Should he ever return, he would not recognise his former haunt. A decision approached, on whether to maintain a pretence or abandon this folly. Wreckage was all that remained.

'What is left but despair? What is lost but a wood fort in the midst of a foul wilderness?'

The verdict was expected. Flanked by Admirals Somers and Newport, Sir Thomas Gates presided. He took no pleasure in his conclusion; had endured storm and shipwreck to reach these shores. Yet Jamestown was beyond all rescue. There was no peace with the natives or prospect for planting; there were few provisions and insufficient military force to mount punitive or foraging raids. Wisdom and courage were required here, and each suggested one conclusion.

From his seat before the altar, Gates viewed those assembled in the church. Much history had played out in this hallowed space, and now he brought matters to an abrupt finale. The chaplain had read the names of the dead and the missing and committed their souls to God. It had proved a lengthy recitation.

The lieutenant-governor gazed towards the ceiling, as though seeking strength or inspiration. 'Near five hundred lost since Jamestown was founded: struck down, deserted or missing.' He paused. 'Some two hundred or so remain.'

'Yet they still breathe.' It was an old soldier who spoke.

'To what end? To suffer more? To fall prey to faction and pestilence, hunger and native arrows?'

Another spoke. 'Are we to abandon our gains? Do we set our backs to all the sweat and blood and sacrifice?'

'Retreat is no surrender.'

'Yet it is the greatest betrayal to those we have lost.'

An argument erupted, some shouting at those who presided and others quarrelling between themselves. Everyone had an opinion.

Gates stood and spoke loudly and calmly. 'I shall have silence.'

'So you may preach? Deliver to us your blasphemy?'

'I am a soldier and no cleric. I am, too, your commander.'

The cry came back. 'So command us to stay!'

'Let the scales fall from your eyes.' Gates spoke patiently. 'Look around and see that there is no future here.'

'Spain will seize that future, will seize our fort.'

'Should providence favour us, she will not.'

'Favour us?' the voice scoffed.

'We shall not burn or ruin what remains. Good Englishmen have built Jamestown, and we leave it as their monument.'

'It is a monument only to our cowardice.'

The lieutenant-governor stared the man down. 'Cowardice would be to evade decision, to ignore circumstance, to forget that our provisions run low and starve within two weeks.'

Hardy left them to their discourse, exiting the chapel and heading for the gates. The blockhouse was his destination. He could not alter the outcome; perhaps he never could. Yet he had tried, had with ruthlessness and persistence and the skills of a Destreza master executed his responsibilities as well as the enemies of England. Many bodies lay scattered or hidden. But at Jamestown he had failed. True, Ratcliffe was killed and others had fled; true, Gabriel Archer had succumbed in recent weeks to the great starvation and now lay buried beneath the chancel of the church. Those who had plotted against the settlement were in turn consumed by it. It changed nothing.

Climbing to the watchtower, he found the Pole seated cross-legged, devouring a helping of biscuit and gruel. Through heat and ice and varied fortunes, the man had kept faith and vigil. Few would pause to thank him.

He continued to eat. 'What brings you, Christian?'

'Memories of time spent, of friend and foe alike.'

'We fought some battles here.'

'All is in the past now.'

'Maybe it is where we belong.' The Pole took another mouthful.

Simple men spoke simple truths. Hardy looked about him, absorbing the views from the fort to the woods and the causeway he had once defended. Robert Cecil had won. The little pygmy would enjoy scurrying to the King and imparting with glee his tidings; would further enrich and advance himself on the back of his success. It was the nature of power. Realm too would celebrate.

He watched a pair of soldiers, new arrivals, ambling unconcerned. They were plainly unused to the rigours of life under siege, and were intent on exploring the environs. It was unwise to wander so far.

The Pole's spoon clattered in the bowl. 'Your guard never lowers, Christian.'

'Does a dog forget its tricks?'

'We soon leave this hateful place.' The Pole belched with satisfaction. 'I will not visit it again in my lifetime, even in my thoughts.'

Instinct had alerted Hardy, his animal sensitivity to an intruding presence or danger. In the distance, the two soldiers strolled on. They paused at the sound of a gunshot, peering towards the blockhouse, momentarily drawn by the sight a figure gesticulating with his musket.

'Savages,' Hardy hissed to the Pole.

His warning shot was lost on the soldiers. They replied with a wave and continued their idling. Yet behind them there was movement, the flitting of shadows and a shiver of undergrowth. Native warriors had come hunting.

'Run for your lives!' Hardy loosed a second shot. 'In the name of God, run!'

Realisation finally jolted the quarry to flee. They did their best, spurred on by war cries, desperately scrambling towards the camp in a haphazard escape. Little ground was covered. In quick succession the Englishmen fell, brought down by well-aimed arrows.

From his eyrie, Hardy continued to observe. He could hear the whoops of the killers and saw them crowd to take their spoils. There was a grim inevitability to the outcome and the ritual, the death and mutilation that resulted from trespass in a wilderness. Virginia was offering its last bloody farewell.

CHAPTER 20

'Heed my count and hark my word.' The sergeant stood over his men. 'Now strain, you curs.'

Shoulders heaved and ropes tautened, and the great culverin guns that had once defended Jamestown shifted and toppled on their cradles. Their descent was abrupt and dramatic. No ordnance would be left for the benefit of an enemy to redeploy against future English missions. That was the order of Sir Thomas Gates. It was the beginning of June 1610, and the end of this colonial venture.

Across the settlement the inhabitants gathered their meagre possessions or stood dazed in groups to confer. Events had outpaced their reasoning. They had voyaged to Jamestown for so many reasons, and now escaped it driven by one imperative alone. Survival. Yet what faced them was the lesser evil: the bleak prospect of the ocean, the uncertainty of boarding small ships to head for Newfoundland and thread a passage to England. There might at least be vessels fishing in distant waters that could relieve the overcrowding. Hope sprang eternal for the desperate.

'Leave no item for the Spaniards or the savage.' Sir Thomas Gates strode among his flock, energetic and encouraging. He would not permit disorder and collapse in these final stages. The English still had their pride, their achievements, their memories of a struggle that might yet enter folklore. What a bold enterprise it had been.

At the waterfront, the Admirals Somers and Newport checked the stores and rigging and supervised the loading of their paltry fleet. Three ships, the weathered *Discovery* and the fragile newborns *Deliverance* and *Patience*, constructed in Bermuda, waited at the jetties. Small wonder the men and women prayed.

'You, boy,' Gates called to Edward Battle as the youngster walked by. 'Where is Mr Hardy?'

'He often sorties out alone, Sir Thomas.'

The lieutenant-governor nodded. 'He is the man I remember.'

'He has done much for Jamestown, Sir Thomas.'

'I do not doubt it.' The military man peered closer at the youth. 'Why did you come aboard my ship from Fort Algernon? Why visit again this infernal place?'

'An infernal place may be a home.'

Gates inclined his head. 'I bow to your tenacity and pluck.'

Every musket and sword and item of food would be stowed in the transports. There was no predicting what lay ahead; no telling the hazards or hostile natives they might encounter. In these climes, one peril was too easily swapped for another.

Some of the settlers had wandered from the confines of the palisade, were foraging in the woods beneath the watchful gaze of soldiers. Should the Paspahegh force a contact, they would suffer casualties. Beyond the trees was the field, lying fallow and full of weeds, an epitaph to the colony and a grave for all their hopes and dreams. The survivors of the time of starvation would be allowed a chance to reflect.

'A celebration is deserved.'

Realm addressed the informant with satisfaction in his voice. This meeting would be their last. It had been a long and arduous campaign, a project marked by challenge. Yet they had prevailed. Let the losers limp away and the victors seize the spoils. It would be strange to walk among the ghost homes of the departed, to tread on ground once defended by his countrymen. Such defence had proved inadequate.

He studied his visitor. Together they had succeeded, had confounded the designs and foreign ventures of the enemy. Spain would applaud him and its King bestow honours. A fitting end to the story.

'What we achieve is no mean feat.'

His guest concurred. 'I pinch myself now this day is come.'

'Come it has, friend.' Realm savoured the moment. 'How is the mood among your fellows?'

'Sorrow and delight, resignation and despair.'

'I am amazed so many survive the flux and ague and starving.'

'We English are resilient.'

'And persistent as the pox. Yet for the moment they are thwarted and will think awhile before any future escapade.'

'What of those who deserted to the natives?'

'It matters little how they died.'

The visitor narrowed his eyes. 'You are a cold and bloodless man.'

'Are we so different?' Realm searched his visitor's face. 'We each seek the same.'

'Our motives are at odds.'

'Yet we combine to grasp the prize.'

'Will you stay?'

'For a while. The power of Opechancanough grows and that of Powhatan recedes. I shall serve as kingmaker.'

'It appears you already do.'

'Armourer and counsellor, perhaps.' Realm opted for false modesty. 'They will thank me and be distracted even as I prepare the way for an eventual Spanish conquest.'

'We leave Jamestown intact to aid you in your purpose.'

'My gratitude is boundless.'

As King Philip would reward the renegade, so Robert Cecil and his monarch would heap riches and praise on their own hidden servant. The informant had done well. War between two nations would be averted and a source of irritation addressed. No longer would Englishmen sit poised above the Spanish Main; no longer would a base for piracy and privateers exist in the locale. Harmony was restored.

A shot cracked loud through the forest glade and Realm was hurled to the ground. High on his chest blossomed a crimson entry wound.

'Draw your sword and you are next.' It was Hardy who emerged with his rifled musket to drag and prop his victim against the trunk of a black walnut.

George Percy trembled in the aftershock, his hand hovering close to the hilt of his rapier. Horror and confusion played out on his thin, pallid features.

'His lungs fill with blood. He will drown in a while.' Hardy turned to the former president. 'How will you choose to die?'

'Is there a choice?' Percy stammered weakly.

'Humour me and I will decide.'

'Would you listen to my reasons?'

'I already know them.'

The intelligencer had seen the evidence of Percy's betrayal, had read the letters in Cecil's study. Nothing condemned a man so convincingly as his own quill and seal. Percy had signed a compact with the devil.

'So gentlemanly, so mannered, so reluctant to be the president.' Hardy viewed his captive. 'You convinced almost all.'

'Yet not you.'

'How deft and assured and hidden in full sight. And all the while a snake.'

'You would never understand.'

'Betrayal is the easiest of things to comprehend.'

'I did what I believed was true.'

'What is truth in a place like this?' Hardy glanced from Realm to Percy. 'What is truth when Cecil holds the Earl of Northumberland, your brother, in the Tower and would do him harm should you resist?'

'I could not defy him.'

'So instead you undermined on his behalf. Subversion and sabotage, a ship cut from its mooring to float downstream.'

'Crime upon crime for which I cannot atone.' Percy's voice cracked to a sob.

'There is redemption of a sort. I watched and waited and then you led me here.'

Hardy switched his attention to the dying Realm. Strange noises emanated from the renegade's mouth, a bubbling exhalation of air and blood. Hardy crouched to study the man, to feel his breath and hear his words. To reach into his soul. This was the monster who had slaughtered his wife and left a trail of destruction; who had come so close to killing a great monarch. On this warm day in a land the natives called Tsenacomoco, the planets had realigned and fortunes changed. The eternal game was finite after all.

'You hear me?' Hardy gazed into Realm's dimming eyes. 'I would not have let you win.'

'Yet the English leave.' The words were hissed out on a breath.

'You depart before them.'

'None of us is immune to fate.'

'Nor to the vengeance of others.' The intelligencer saw the renegade's life force pulsing weak now. 'So much wrong you caused, so much evil.'

Realm gagged and vomited blood. 'Each to his cause.'

'And each to his end.'

Hardy rose. He had seen enough, would not wait in vain for a confession or remorse. Their breed was disinclined to such indulgence. Realm was just another agent on a foreign mission; a further corpse to rot into the earth. He trusted his final seconds would be racked with pain and horror.

'You will leave him here?' It was Percy who spoke.

'It is a fitting tribute.'

'And I?' The thin lips twitched. 'Am I to be taken back in chains?'

'Your secrets and deceit lie buried here. Rebirth is yet possible.'

They left, participants in events and subterfuge that had their genesis in the halls of Europe and were now concluded on a foreign shore. The intelligencer did not look back. Reino, his rival, already was the past.

Later, a native warrior appeared and stole what he could from the pale-skin. Perhaps there was still life there; a gossamer breath that floated undetected. It made no difference. The Indian went on his way and would report to Opechancanough.

There was ever the summer stench and threat of plague to keep King James from the capital. Present too were the imagined or real threats posed by malcontents turned assassins. The possibilities were grim and endless. It was but five years since Catholic saboteurs had plotted to use gunpowder to blow him to oblivion. Yet James could display courage; would return to London when duty called and the situation demanded. He would certainly show his son who was sovereign.

'Henry, Prince of Wales.'

Formality and chill deference were in order. The young prince bowed and genuflected, aware that his father was sensitive to nuance and quick to take offence. Hampton Court was hostile territory.

The King's weeping eyes appraised him. 'You come when you are called.'

'It is the duty of a son.'

'Would that others obliged me so.' The King scowled. 'I have had the Spanish ambassador pay a visit to my court.'

'He is a knave and a schemer.'

'His nation is our friend.'

'Our friend?' Henry frowned. 'A treaty between us brings no amity or trust.'

'Yet it rewards us with a peace I am anxious to maintain.'

'Peace at any cost?'

Irritation creased the features of the monarch. He knew the motives of his son, his popularity, his religious devotion and his overweening colonial ambition. Each could be dangerous, viewed with suspicion and contempt. The upstart would be tamed.

He stared at his son. 'More ships and a lord governor will not preserve your Jamestown.'

'God and fate will decide.'

'You wish to antagonise? To provoke a war?'

'I desire only to advance the prospect of England.'

'Instead you do us hurt.'

'Your pride alone, I think, father.'

'What vile and quarrelsome notion pierces your head?' James cried.

'One of glory and Christendom and bringing light to the darkness.'

A sneer. 'It seems you imbibe too much the thoughts of the prisoner Raleigh.'

The son regarded his father and the father glared at his son. The sixteen-year-old had plainly forgotten his place and his manners. Eventually he would be whipped in and brought to heel, married off in a strategic union to the daughter of the King of Spain. Cecil was working on it.

Motioning to the prince to follow, James retreated along the gallery, pausing before a portrait of himself. There he was, a drop pearl hanging from his ear, an expression of grace and wisdom writ clear upon his face. A fine likeness. His country needed him.

He purred with a soft malevolence. 'Remember I am King.'

'Earthly and not divine,' Henry retorted.

'Appointed, however, by God.' He glanced at the youth to reinforce his message. 'Venerated by the people.'

Henry was too astute to pour scorn or protest on the King's words. 'Our nation is scarce worthy of your interest and endeavour.'

'I am but its humble servant.'

'We all may learn from such humility.'

Were there coded sarcasm, James chose to ignore it. He could not trust his son; would not rest until his machinations were undone and his zeal for foreign venture quashed. His own flesh and blood had allies among the merchants and parliamentarians and through dint of popularity caused him sleepless nights. Unfettered offspring were the ruin of a king.

'Listen well.' The King stroked the state ring on his finger. 'No good will come of your pursuits.'

'Good intent brings good reward.'

'Rather it blinds and sets a trap, leads the unwary to damnation.'

A warning had been given. Without farewell or pleasantry, the King exited the chamber. Alone now in its panelled length, Henry stared after him. He would not hazard how events might end, or guess at outcomes far away. Yet he would pray that somewhere in a distant wilderness a glimmer of hope remained.

'Let it be said that we tried.'

The eulogy would be brief. It was a little over two weeks since Sir Thomas Gates and his party had arrived, and the survivors of Jamestown were mustered for the roll call. They would answer for the last time, and with conflicting emotions of relief and dread would step aboard their transports.

Gates studied the settlers' faces. 'We do not so much abandon this place as leave it to the future. We do not so much desert as accept what is our lot.'

Perhaps they believed him. It mattered little, for the tide would not wait and sentiment was a luxury few could afford. As a soldier and lieutenant-governor, Gates did only what he knew was right.

'I desire no commotion or complaint. In ordered manner and to the beat of the drum, you will proceed to take your berths.'

Command and regimentation provided the solution to most problems. At last the people of Jamestown were silent; at last dissent and factionalism were ended. It had taken the demise of their settlement to achieve a certain peace.

'Sound the drum.'

To a funereal beat the settlers paraded through, a shuffling line of the defeated. For some there was a backward glance; for others, a set jaw and determined forward stare. Circumstances indeed had trounced them.

Attended for the moment by his officers and gentlemen, Gates would be the last to leave. It was his task to pay his respects and to lay the ghosts to rest, to ensure no fool or hothead stayed behind to set the whole ablaze.

He spied Hardy and strode towards him. 'You stand apart.'

'Observing is my creed.'

'Today it is obedience.' Gates scanned his face. 'I know you well, Mr Hardy.'

The azure eyes stared back. 'Does such knowledge inform you?'

'I detect mutiny and resistance.'

'Call it what you may, Sir Thomas.' The intelligencer's gaze had not wavered. 'My nature is constant and my loyalties true.'

'That is what concerns me.'

They watched the crowd awhile, acknowledging the occasional nod or pleading eye. A woman passed by, weeping. No one could know if they were condemned; if they might ever disembark.

'Starvation, or a watery grave.' Gates glanced to the dwindling band. 'It is the meanest of choices.'

'One we all have made.'

'You will join them?'

'I shall not.'

The lieutenant-governor paused. 'You would defy me?'

'I simply answer to another.'

Hardy would give no reason; would not explain that he had resigned his commission and no longer served the secret interests of the state. Neither King James nor Prince Henry could summon him to do their bidding; never again would the hunchback Cecil conspire to ensnare him. His journey from intelligencer to free agent was complete.

Gates sighed. 'A man tires of things, does he not?'

'Sometimes he embraces the new.'

'I envy you your resolution.' Gates proffered his hand. 'Farewell until next we meet.'

The lifeblood of Jamestown was draining, and only the hierarchs now remained. As the group progressed, George Percy slowed at its tail to peruse the man who had unmasked him. There was no accusation in his eye, no baleful instinct lurking. Hardy had released him from his compact and given him a fresh chance. The two exchanged a cool stare, and then the former president was gone.

Newport strode across. The veteran admiral could not leave without comment; would award himself the final word. It had been a while since he had first brought Hardy to this savage shore.

His verdict was perfunctory. 'Did I not predict you would bring little but trouble?'

It required no riposte. The drum continued to beat its morose tattoo and Sir Thomas Gates saluted. Then he turned and left the scene. Before the fort, a squad of soldiers raised their muskets high and loosed a fusillade in martial valediction. A hot summer's day in 1610 and a nascent empire was buried.

Whistles called and crewmen moved about the spars and rigging, readying for departure. From atop the palisade, Hardy and his dog bore witness. Soon the three vessels would sail, carried on the ebbing tide, silence and emptiness closing in behind them. Perhaps the native Paspahegh would send their scouts to loot or kill, or perhaps they would keep their distance until they were sure no ambush had been set. The intelligencer would greet whatever came.

'Christian!'

A figure scrambled from a ship and ran towards the fort. It was Edward Battle. Men attempted to block him, but he dodged their efforts and raced to join his friend.

Breathless, he arrived. 'You cannot stay, Christian.'

'I have heard more convincing argument.'

'I beg you.' The youth fended off a delighted Buckler. 'Consider what you do.'

'I have thought of little else.'

'Yet you act as though you were a madman.'

'I blame it on these climes.' The intelligencer smiled. 'You will not drag me from here.'

'Then I will stay too.'

'So you too lose your reason?'

'Do not jest, Christian.'

Hardy gripped his arms, noting the moisture pricking his eyes. 'Your future is not mine, and your place is on the ship.'

'I wish to be with you.'

'To suffer? Starve? Expend your life on some false venture?'

'Better than to die in failure and retreat.'

'In Jamestown you grew from boy to man.' Hardy did not release his grip. 'You owe yourself a chance.'

He embraced the boy and sent him on his way. A prince of similar age waited to ascend the throne of England, and in Virginia another courageous soul was drawn to his colours and his cause. Time would decree when Edward Battle met his Maker.

The sails dropped and their canvas filled, and the ships edged from their moorings. In stately parade they floated away and headed down the river. Hardy kept them in his vision as long as he could, would let the details merge and fade until only the landscape remained. Command was ceded to him. Somewhere in this wilderness a native girl named Awae waited.

Aboard the *Discovery*, a human shape clambered for the masthead. It reached the zenith and then stood perched and motionless, an arm lifted in distant recognition and goodbye. Hardy turned to view the deserted township at his feet. Okeus, warrior god of the savages, would laugh, for what had been intended as the cradle of a nation had since become its grave. The intelligencer rested his palm on the pommel of his Katzbalger. Certainties were for the weak.

ENDING

Two days had passed. Anchored near a small island at the mouth of the James, the tiny flotilla waited on the winds and tide that would bear them across Chesapeake Bay and then northwards. Tension and trepidation prevailed. Lieutenant Davies had abandoned Fort Algernon, too, and brought his garrison across on the ketch *Virginia*. More mouths to feed and worries to absorb. His men were like the rest: fretting and pacing, playing dice cards, at once eager to be gone and anxious at the consequences. In confined spaces, rumours and sly words could inflame fears and in turn encourage feuds and fighting. There were four vessels and several hundred unhappy crewmen.

Gates paced, occasionally conferring with the admirals. When the moment came, they would disperse among their fleet and travel in convoy until storm and fate intruded. One of them at least might reach the shores of England and place on record for their countrymen the tale of their venture. What a dismal escapade it had been.

'Sir Thomas! A longboat!'

Gates swung himself onto the rigging and scrambled higher to see. Indeed, it was true. A boat was approaching, its oars rising and dipping, an officer upright at its prow, waving a note. Hope and horror mingled in Gates's mind as he watched, baffled. The Lord or the Devil were playing tricks.

'Have I permission to come aboard?'

'Identify yourself.'

'Captain Edward Brewster, sent by Lord Delaware, who as I speak sits with three ships at the entrance to the bay.'

The settlers' astonishment silenced them and then turned to wild cheering. Rapture was upon them, and yet many still disbelieved. It could not be. Against the odds and contrary to all imagining, salvation was at hand. Men and women shrieked and danced and cried out their hallelujahs. It was Saturday 9 June, 1610. Divine intervention had spared a colony and given blessing to an empire.

Gates met Brewster on the poop. 'I commend your timing, sir.'

'Providence rewards us.' The captain surrendered the letter in his hand. 'I bring instructions from his lordship.'

'Victuals too, I trust.'

'Sufficient for a year.'

'Then you are most welcome.'

The soldier read the letter.

'There are with us three hundred souls, and soldiers and munitions aplenty,' Brewster added.

'So we build anew?'

'His lordship bids you turn about and retrace your passage up the James. With iron and fire, Jamestown is reborn.'

It was a simple promise, and a command. Gates breathed deep. He should not have been surprised. Fate was strange and the gods capricious. Once more, circumstances had shifted. He relayed the order. The empire could begin.

At that same moment, in London, a carriage departed from the fine brick mansion of Robert Cecil on the Strand. Seated within and shuttered from view, the diminutive Lord Treasurer pondered his imminent meeting. It was becoming increasingly hard to convince the Spanish ambassador, to reassure His Excellency that all was well and Jamestown continued its slide into the abyss. Matters were yet in hand. The little hunchback closed his eyes and relaxed to the sway and movement of his transport. There was ever hope, and always opportunity to exploit and control. Tomorrow, and tomorrow, and tomorrow. He was deformed by nature, and by nature not one to quit. Outside the coach, Adam Hardy rode escort.

HISTORICAL NOTES

In the period following the providential arrival of Lord Delaware in June 1610, the colony began to spread. Additional fortifications were constructed at the mouth of the James, a new settlement named Henrico established upriver near the falls (south-east of present-day Richmond), and plantations created on both sides of the James. Relations with the local tribes fluctuated, agreement and trade often being interspersed with savage bouts of violence. It was a harsh and unforgiving environment beset with starvation and disease. Yet the colonial impulse continued and the momentum did not cease. Jamestown planted the seed, and from it grew America.

Opechancanough gained control from Powhatan and became chief of the Tsenacomoco region. He tried both peace and war to stem the advance of the settlers. In March 1622, on his orders, the Indians launched a coordinated assault upon the colony. The attack caused 347 recorded deaths, forced retreat once more to the Jamestown fort and almost extinguished the project. Despite these reverses, and the continued politicking and infighting in both England and Virginia, the colony endured. It was the beginning of the long decline of the Indian nation.

John Smith recovered sufficiently from his injuries to return across the Atlantic in 1614. This time he reached the coast of Maine and Massachusetts Bay, naming the region New England. Two further expeditions followed, but after his capture and subsequent escape from French pirates off the Azores, the adventurer and explorer finally retired. He died in England in June 1631, aged fifty-one.

George Percy was appointed Esquire by Lord Delaware and was for a time in charge of the military element at Jamestown. He led several reprisal attacks on the Indians and was unstinting in his brutality. Returning to England, he attempted unsuccessfully to raise funds for an expedition to Guiana and returned once more to military service. In the late 1620s, he participated in renewed fighting against the Spanish in the Low Countries and died aged forty-seven in 1627.

Robert Cecil, Lord Treasurer and 1st Earl of Salisbury, found his ability to influence events at Jamestown weakening as the royal finances dwindled and the pressure exerted by leading parliamentarians grew. His health too was suffering. A loyal and Machiavellian servant of the Crown, he died aged forty-eight from cancer in May 1612.

Prince Henry, seen by many as the great hope for the Stuart dynasty, never succeeded his father James to the throne. He died aged eighteen in November 1612 from an illness historians believe was typhoid fever. His younger brother Charles inherited, an event that would lead eventually to the catastrophic English Civil War.

William Shakespeare and his company of players, the King's Men, presented his new play *The Tempest* to King James at the Banqueting House in Whitehall on 1 November 1611. With descriptions of an enchanted isle that matched those of a recently colonised Bermuda, and with musings on a land without laws or hierarchy, there were coded references to democratic notions flowering in Virginia. Savagery was to be tamed; the playwright had joined the conversation.

Realm is a composite of many Catholic renegades and 'hispaniolated' Englishmen operating at the time. He also incorporates elements of Francis Limbrecke, the Spanish agent who once served as pilot to the 1588 Armada and was later captured while spying on Jamestown. He was hanged from the yardarm aboard the ship *Treasurer*, the same vessel that carried to England the native princess Pocahontas.

Turn the page to read the opening
from the first book to feature
Christian Hardy

TREASON

Available in paperback and ebook now

PROLOGUE

New Place, Stratford-upon-Avon, April 1616

Commotion at this hour was unexpected. He would ignore it, the barking of dogs and the whinny and stamp of a horse, and focus on the book before him. Let his servants deal with the matter. He hoped his Anne would not be roused from her slumber, for all their sakes.

He turned another page, adjusted the light cast by an oil lamp and leant to fill again his claret glass. Some fifty years on and a few hundred paces from where he had been born and now he was moneyed and revered and content. What fortune and acclaim his life had brought him, and with what skill he had navigated the treacherous waters of his age. He had served monarchs and yet never lost his head, had played alike to the gallery and groundlings and retained to this day their love. Tonight, William Shakespeare was in a reflective mood.

'Master?'

At the intrusion, the playwright peered towards the doorway. He had given strict instructions that he was not to be disturbed. Yet affection for his staff and the frown of apology on the face of his manservant were sufficient to permit a lapse.

'Why such consternation, George?' Shakespeare smiled at his old retainer. 'You enter the room of a studious man and not the lair of an ogre.'

'I had no wish to trouble you, master.'

'It seems you are the more disturbed.'

'A horseman came, master. A stranger bid me deliver you a package.'

'He would not stay? Gave no name? Offered not a single word of explanation?'

'No, master.'

'Then let us unravel the mystery of the saddlebag.' Shakespeare held out his hand and took the proffered bundle. 'Now get to bed and leave me to the night before our mistress wakes to scold us both.'

Alone once more, he examined the item wrapped in its linen windings. Perhaps it was a manuscript or the letters of an admirer or part of some prank dreamt up by his friend and brother-writer Ben Jonson. He sighed.

Across the years they had caroused and drunk, indulged in trick and escapade of every kind. The ageing should be allowed to reminisce. How he hankered on occasion for the sounds of London, for the urgent energy of its streets and taverns and the excitement of his youth. His past was but a whisper and his present bound by predictability and aching bones.

The small silver crucifix fell onto the open page and his world tilted. With a trembling touch he held the object to the light and turned it in his fingers. In this one tarnished artefact was history, a memory of the old religion and those who in its name would do murder to a king. There was a thick sheaf of papers too, a confession or dossier he freed carefully from its binding. Sleep could wait. As the hearth embers glowed and died and a predawn chill drew in, Shakespeare read. Before him was laid out an intrigue in which many had been ensnared and that had set a deadly trail from the manor houses of Warwickshire to the great Gunpowder Treason Plot of 1605. By the grace of God he was on the side of the victor and through dint of providence once knew the horseman who had ridden here tonight. Faith and passion drove men to heroism or folly. Remember, remember, the fifth of November. He would leave others to judge.

BEGINNING

The Azores, late summer 1591

'Sail ho! Enemy to windward!'

Spanish masts crowded the horizon. They had the weather gauge and advantage, a vast formation of swollen sail inbound for the fray. These were not the laden nau and caravel transports the English had expected, the annual migration of the treasure convoy from the Americas they lay in wait for. Instead a battle fleet encroached from the east. Almost sixty Spanish galleons bore down on a squadron of six English ships. It was the afternoon of 31 August 1591, and the ambushers had been ambushed.

In the crosstrees of the waiting vessels, the lookouts strained to see and hollered their reports, their calls echoing and forcing the pace. Everywhere was action. The English had believed themselves safe, anchoring in a small bay on the northern tip of this small volcanic island of Flores. Here the sick could be taken ashore and parties sent to forage among the waterfalls and meadows; here decks could be swabbed clean with vinegar, ballast replaced, and the hulls caulked with tow and pitch. Everything had changed, for hell was visiting paradise. As whistles blew and crews scrambled to make ready, skiffs splashed a frantic path back to their mother ships and figures swarmed to man the braces. All were preparing for flight.

On the poop deck of the warship *Revenge*, its captain leant on the rail and surveyed the scene. A veteran of close encounters with the enemy, of tight odds and chances seized and of wresting possession from the King of Spain, Sir Richard Grenville, privateer and vice-admiral, was not inclined to panic. At this spot aboard his ship had once stood Drake, the legend who had chased the Armada to its destruction. Three years on and the Spanish had rebuilt and ventured out with vengeance on their minds. Now it was Grenville's turn to find glory.

He straightened to acknowledge a young gallant approaching from the main deck to join him at his station. Ceremony was unnecessary.

There was a bond between them, a trust and familiarity born of combat and strengthened by shared loathing for the adversary and love for the melee. At twenty-four, Christian Hardy was no ordinary seafarer. As a soldier and spy he had lived and taken more lives than most, and killed ruthlessly anyone who threatened his Queen. It had cost him much. Yet there remained the steady confidence of ultramarine eyes, and the swagger and latent ferocity of a natural fighter contained within the armour plates of a faded blue velvet brigandine jacket. With sword and pistols to hand, Hardy felt most alive when in proximity to death.

Grenville gestured seaward. 'It seems we set a trap and are ourselves ensnared.'

'Howard signals we should run to sea.'

'Run?' The captain frowned. 'Our Lord Admiral knows us not.'

'You would fight?'

'I will do as my conscience and nature command.'

'It will be some trial, Richard.'

Grenville smiled. 'Are they not the ones we embrace and our people cheer?'

His companion nodded. The breath of wind on his cheek carried his thoughts back to Drake and the Armada and the fire ships he had led into Calais Roads. Ghosts still wandered here, the images of past friends and flying splinters. Another place and a different commander but Hardy was here again.

Grenville regarded him. 'They complain the *Revenge* is an unlucky ship. What do you say?'

'Ill-fortune may be turned.'

'We have some forty cannon and four hundred tons of leaking oak beneath our feet.' Grenville scanned the tops. 'Perhaps it will not.'

'Then we pray and brawl the harder.'

Grenville laughed and clapped him on the shoulder. 'I am a corsair and you are a gentleman adventurer. Well, we shall have adventure enough this day.'

An enemy admiral named Don Alonso de Bazan would ensure it. He had brought his great fleet from the northern Spanish port of El Perro intent on redressing past ignominy and restoring dignity to his homeland.

He carried seven thousand infantry and was accompanied by giant Apostle galleons with which he would close with and crush the pirates of Albion. Pausing off Terceira, two hundred miles to the east, to gather intelligence and arrange his formation, he was ready for quick victory.

But he had been sighted. Christian Hardy had been gathering information of his own, meeting agents, leading raids across the islands and spying on this Spanish hub. He had watched and tracked the fleet and, guessing at its true purpose, had sped aboard the pinnace *Moonshine* yesterday to deliver his report. A fragment of his soul believed the Spaniards hunted him.

'We aim for the heart of the beast.' Grenville pointed and called out to his officers and men. 'Weigh anchor and make all sail and ready the guns for action. For England!'

The *Revenge* groaned as her tethers loosened and canvas dropped, and cheering eddied from the gun deck to the yards. *For England.* Perhaps they did not yet comprehend their fate, or they did not care.

Hardy glanced back to the slumbering volcanic peak of the Morro Alto, tracing the verdant slopes and black lines of basalt down to the grey sands of the shore. Ponta Delgada they called this protective spur of Flores. It had given only temporary reprieve.

Grenville had followed his gaze. 'No volcano will match the fury we encounter.'

'So let us seize the fire.'

Sails tautened, the helm swung, and the little ship turned into the maw of the approaching host. At least she had distracted the foe; at least the rest of her squadron were clawing to sea. As the sun began its evening plunge and puffs of cannon smoke marked the defiant exodus of Lord Howard, the *Revenge* continued alone. Hardy nodded to Grenville and returned to the main deck. At the step of the centre mast and with his schiavona blade drawn, he would make his stand.

Jostling for the kill, the enemy swept close, the *Revenge* becalmed in their midst as her sails bled wind and her decks bucked to raking broadsides. Smoke rolled in and the world diminished to keening noise and glimpsed morion helmets and falling spars and bodies. Roaring soundless in the din, Grenville directed and stood firm.

Hardy stood at the centre of the fray. He felt the impact of the *San Felipe* as she grappled on the starboard side, her masts blocking the light and her infantry rushing to board. To the flash of muskets and with pike and sword they flowed in and were met with a fury that stalled them. The ache of anticipation was over.

'To me! We have them!' Hardy swung an arquebus and discharged a round, the steel ball designed to bring down rigging and instead removing a face. He was among the enemy now, at ease with their ragged oaths and cries, hewing with his sword and selecting from his brace of matchlock pistols. Fire belched from the pan and muzzle and another Spaniard fell away.

A second galleon, the *San Bernabé*, collided and took hold, her troops racing to seize the prize. Next it was the turn of the *San Cristobal* to ram the English ship, shattering the aftcastle and disgorging a fresh wave of boarders. Hardy moved with murderous fluency through a flickering landscape of bloodspill and wraiths. He was killing as profession and in revenge, for his mother burnt at the stake in a Lisbon square and his wife butchered by an assassin sent to kill the Queen, for his mentors and patrons Sir Francis Drake and the late spymaster Sir Francis Walsingham. In their name he slashed off a head and prised wide a ribcage and thrust through a groin with the point of his sword. The tactics of the alley were not for the squeamish or refined.

Yet they could not stem the onrush. Where one Spaniard vanished to the firefly strike of musketry, others took his place; where resistance ebbed, the enemy pressed in and forced retreat.

Grenville emerged, scrambling low beneath the whine of lead, his face scorched and his doublet torn. 'They bait us as dogs put to a bull.' The words faded in the storm.

'We hold them yet.'

'Though our stern is lost.' Grenville crouched and peered aft. 'I vouch they do not like us, Christian.'

Hardy grinned. 'We hate them more.'

Again the enemy surged and was repelled across the tangled wreckage of men and timber and rigging.

Rudderless and dismasted and with her upper works shot away, the *Revenge* had ceased to be a warship. Yet as daylight leached to dusk, the contest was far from over.

'Now, Christian!' commanded Grenville.

In a clearing framed by debris, Hardy loosed the contents of a fowler cannon into the encroaching ranks of Spaniards. Grey mist turned pink as the cartridge shot plumed wide. The enemy might have seized the colours, but the English counter-attack had begun. Yelling their rage, the crew chased over lost ground, their momentum for a while reversing the flow. Grenville led the pursuit.

More ships clustered around the dying hulk, the *Asuncion* and a flyboat gripping fast to accelerate its demise. It was near midnight when Grenville took a shot to the chest and was ferried to a dressing station beside a toppled gun. Hardy knelt close, his own face lacerated and etched with red.

'What a pretty sight we are, Christian.' Grenville panted shallowly while the surgeon applied a linen compress. 'God is merciful: this is only a scratch.'

'Be still and let the surgeon tend you,' Hardy urged his commander.

'How goes the battle?'

'We endure and shall fight on.'

Satisfaction ghosted through the pain. 'Then we will kill any in our reach.'

'An English victualler probes near to draw their fire, and others seek to aid us.'

'Keep them distant, Christian. I would not have them squander men or effort on our plight.'

With a sigh the surgeon slumped, an entry wound to his temple. Grenville grabbed a rapier and rolled away beneath the cover of the culverin. There were new enemies to greet.

The early hours brightened to the salvoes played into the hull. A relay of Spanish galleons paraded by, brushing point-blank or drifting to leeward, inflicting constant punishment. Below her shroud of smoke, *Revenge* wallowed and replied.

Daylight brought a terrible scene. Ringed by blackened and stricken vessels, the *Revenge* continued to fight. Her firing was desultory, her crew largely dead or injured, her commander now mortally wounded. Propped against a wood block and attended by his diminished band, Grenville lingered between consciousness and death, the old tenacity burnt strong.

'What news?' He stared up at his men.

A lieutenant answered. 'Two of their galleons are sinking and the sea around us is littered with their dead.'

'So there is merit in what we do.'

'They wait on us, sir.'

'Then they must wait longer.' Grenville closed his eyes. 'What are their demands?'

'Their admiral asks that we yield.'

Anger flamed in the captain's face and his voice strengthened. 'We submit to none but God. We throw ourselves on His mercy and not at the feet of a Catholic dog.'

'Our powder is almost gone.'

'You have your teeth and fists. You have your pride. You have the honour of England to defend.' Exhausted, he lapsed to silence. Occasionally a cannon discharged, marking time and magnifying futility, the ball travelling to splash harmlessly in the water.

Grenville roused himself. 'Where is my master gunner?'

'I am here, sir.'

'Gather what powder you can and put a match to it. We have fought too long to go meekly into bondage.'

The men exchanged glances and another officer spoke. 'Have we not been true and steadfast and earned our right to live?'

'And you, Christian? Will you join this mutiny?' Grenville turned his head slowly, his eyes seeking out his friend.

Hardy knelt beside him. 'They have been brave and done more than Queen or country might expect.'

'To surrender the *Revenge* is to commit treason.'

'And to waste these gallant men would be a greater crime.' Hardy took his captain's hand. 'Our ship is spent and no real prize. She will sink and we shall live to tell the valour of this action.'

'Perhaps you speak the truth.'

'I always do.'

'Then pray for me, for it is all I have left.'

In the dismal aftermath of battle and surrender, Spanish longboats shuttled to transport the living and dispose of the dead. The defeated English were worthy of respect. Their *Revenge*, so unequal in size and so ruined, remained afloat only by a miracle. Spaniards gazed in wonder.

Removing his scarred brigandine and abandoning his sword, Hardy sat on the deck among his fellows. Fatigue and desolation weighed on them all. He had survived when others had not; there was little point in questioning the mystery. Instinctively he felt for the silver crucifix at his throat, a talisman from his past once worn by his warrior father. Its contours were as familiar as the grip of his sword.

'What fates we enemies weave.'

The measured words were delivered with a sword tip pressed against Hardy's chest, a hand reaching to snatch away the cross. Hardy stayed motionless, gazing at the face he loathed above all others, recalling the wounds inflicted on the body of his slain wife. He had learnt to understand the darkness in this man's heart. Realm, the Englishman turned traitor, the agent codenamed Reino by his Spanish masters, had returned.

Hardy stared into the pale eyes. 'I believed you dead.'

'I am alive and the Inquisition kind.'

'So again you venture out on a lost cause.'

'But I have a rapier and you are my prisoner.' Realm picked at a thread on Hardy's coat with the blade point. 'Like the *Revenge* itself you are driftwood and flotsam.'

'You failed to kill our Queen.'

'Our religion is patient and all may change.'

'What here is changed? What is altered when it takes a fleet to crush a single English vessel?'

'You alone are consolation.' Steel stroked Hardy's cheek. 'An eternal game is made of many steps.'

'And I will shadow your every one.'

The sword pricked his flesh and Hardy got to his feet. He might be destined for execution or imprisonment, for whatever torture or inhumanity his captors had prepared, but acceptance was part of his calling. There were plantations to work and the rowing benches of oared galleys to fill; there were transports on the Spanish Main to crew and the deep mines of the Americas to dig. Escorted by guards, he was taken to a skiff and transferred to a galleon. Realm was right. An eternal game was formed of many stages.

Want to read
NEW BOOKS
before anyone else?

Like getting
FREE BOOKS?

Enjoy sharing your
OPINIONS?

Discover

READERS
FIRST

Read. Love. Share.

Get your first free book just by signing up at
readersfirst.co.uk